Praise for *Things We Didn't Say*

"*Things We Didn't Say* is a standout novel as brilliant and brave as its heroine. I was moved to both laughter and tears while tagging along with Johanna Berglund on her emotional and spiritual journey. When I wasn't pausing to savor a particularly profound passage, I was turning the pages as fast as I could to see what Jo and Peter would say next. An utterly satisfying read you'll want to share as soon as you reach its conclusion."

—Jocelyn Green, Christy Award–winning
author of *Veiled in Smoke*

"This compelling novel of life on the US home front during World War II fascinated me from beginning to end. *Things We Didn't Say*, told entirely through letters, newspaper accounts, and other documents, kept me turning pages as it shed light on our prejudices and the way our fear can prompt hatred. Amy Lynn Green's characters wrestle with obeying Jesus' command to love their enemies at a time when showing kindness to Americans of Japanese descent or to German prisoners of war might be interpreted as treason. And tucked between the pages is a gentle love story that provides the icing on this gem of a literary cake."

—Lynn Austin, author of *If I Were You*

"An outstanding debut novel! Much will be said about the unique format of *Things We Didn't Say*, but what truly shines in this novel are the characters. Outspoken and delightfully antisocial, Johanna sparkles with wit, but she also comes to see the heart and depth of the people around her—and the flaws within her own soul. With impeccable research, Amy Lynn Green casts a light on the POW camps in America during World War II and on the dangers of prejudice. Make space on your bookshelf, because this book is a keeper!"

—Sarah Sundin, bestselling and award-winning author of
When Twilight Breaks and the Sunrise at Normandy series

"Amy Lynn Green's debut novel kept me guessing to the very end—twist upon twist upon twist. She is a master plotter, so read every single word! You'll be thinking about Jo and her companions long after you finish reading *Things We Didn't Say*."

—Beverly Lewis, *New York Times* bestselling author

"Amy Lynn Green pens a fascinating story of intrigue and love in her book *Things We Didn't Say*. Set against the backdrop of World War II, Amy takes care to bring history alive as she moves her characters through situations that force them to take a deeper look at who they are and what they really want out of life. I thoroughly enjoyed this book and believe my readers will as well."

—Tracie Peterson, bestselling author

"*Things We Didn't Say* is the best sort of book: where the characters feel like friends, the story feels like home, and the pages beckon you to turn them ceaselessly, immersing you in an absorbing world. Amy Lynn Green expertly wields wit, heart, history, and enveloping storytelling in this glorious debut!"

—Amanda Dykes, author of *Set the Stars Alight*
and *Whose Waves These Are*

"Told in a series of letters, *Things We Didn't Say* is the story of a reluctant female translator working in a German POW camp in the American Midwest. Based on actual World War II experiences, and sparkling with humor and touches of romance, this is an impressive debut from a multitalented writer."

—Julie Klassen, author of *The Bridge to Belle Island*

"A fascinating excavation of a little-known moment in US history executed with an inimitable voice and extremely clever style. Excessively readable, this winsome epistolary is underscored by a deep look at patriotism, prejudice, unwavering faith, duty, and love. I guarantee you will not have a similar reading experience this year. Green's compassionate exploration of the many facets of forgiveness and humanity involves a Japanese American military intelligence instructor, German POWs, and an intelligent woman who must learn the depth of loss beyond the words she so easily finds solace behind. A dazzlingly smart and confident debut, *Things We Didn't Say* is as moving as it is memorable."

—Rachel McMillan, author of *The London Restoration*

THINGS WE DIDN'T SAY

Amy Lynn Green

BETHANYHOUSE
a division of Baker Publishing Group
Minneapolis, Minnesota

Published by Bethany House Publishers
11400 Hampshire Avenue South
Bloomington, Minnesota 55438
www.bethanyhouse.com

Bethany House Publishers is a division of
Baker Publishing Group, Grand Rapids, Michigan

Printed in the United States of America

Library of Congress Cataloging-in-Publication Data
Names: Green, Amy Lynn, author.
Title: Things we didn't say / Amy Lynn Green.
Other titles: Things we did not say
Description: Minneapolis, Minnesota : Bethany House Publishers, [2020] |
Identifiers: LCCN 2020023530 | ISBN 9780764237164 (trade paperback) | ISBN
    9780764237874 (casebound) | ISBN 9781493428199 (ebook)
Subjects: GSAFD: Epistolary fiction.
Classification: LCC PS3607.R4299 T48 2020 | DDC 813/.6—dc23
LC record available at https://lccn.loc.gov/2020023530

Scripture quotations are from the King James Version of the Bible.

This is a work of historical reconstruction; the appearances of certain historical figures are therefore inevitable. All other characters, however, are products of the authors' imagination, and any resemblance to actual persons, living or dead, is coincidental.

Cover design by Jennifer Parker
Cover photography by Mike Habermann Photography, LLC
Minnesota landscape photography by Drew Geraets / Unsplash

20 21 22 23 24 25 26   7 6 5 4 3 2 1

To my parents,
for your faithful and unconditional love

Prologue

From Johanna Berglund to Charles Donohue, attorney-at-law

January 26, 1945

Dear Mr. Donohue,

 If I were an expert in criminal law, I'd be sick to death of outraged clients claiming to be falsely accused, and especially of weepy female clients wringing their hands and saying things like, "How could it have come to this?" Which is why I deliberately avoided any of that in our initial meeting, though it occurred to me later that I might have come across as cold or detached.

 So allow me to say thank you for agreeing to take my case. I'm aware that representing a civilian charged with involvement in prisoner-of-war–related crimes is a complicated affair.

 The following file contains all of the documents I've gathered related to the incidents at Camp Ironside this past year, arranged by date received. I wasn't sure what would be of use, so I've sent everything, including some information that might, at first glance, seem incriminating.

Many of the letters I translated for censoring and for the camp records had carbon copies, and the *Ironside Broadside* archives have been helpful as well. Quite a few of the people I wrote to had other reasons for keeping my letters to them—Brady McHenry saves all correspondence to the newspaper office because he's paranoid about being sued for libel; Pastor Sorenson hasn't thrown away anything larger than a Doublemint gum wrapper since the start of the Great Depression; and Peter . . . well, his reasons should be obvious as you read on.

In assembling this collection, I've found that every letter has two messages: the one written on the lines and the one written between them. Both are necessary to give a full picture of what really happened during my employment at the camp.

This morning I was seized by a sudden, crazed instinct to burn every last page instead of giving them to you. I even opened my nearly brand-new Acme Tires matchbook—only one match missing; you'll get to the significance of that later—and pictured these papers curling into shriveled black ashes. Not because I'm afraid their contents will condemn me, but because they will reveal me, every detail of my personal life made public.

Since I gathered up enough common sense to present you this paper trail undestroyed and complete, I hope you'll agree that it provides evidence to clear me of any wrongdoing. I am innocent, no matter what the outcry surrounding this case has led people to believe.

No, I should clarify. Years of reciting "If we say that we have no sin, we deceive ourselves, and the truth is not in us" with the rest of the congregation every Sunday has trained me. I am guilty. I know that with certainty after reading these letters again. Guilty of selfishness and bitterness and foolish, reckless pride. Guilty of hurting the people I love the most.

But not guilty of treason.

I want others to know the truth. Not the newspapers and their readers across the country, eager for a spy scandal. Just the people closest to me: Dad and Mother. The Sorensons. Peter. I hope, whatever the judge decides, that they can forgive me for all of the hurt I've caused, starting years before the first piece of evidence.

Now I just need to forgive myself.

In any case, thank you for the book of legal terms and procedures. I read it cover to cover and now consider myself fluent in seven languages, including jurisprudence. Memorizing vocabulary is at least one thing I'm unfailingly good at.

Please let me know if you have any questions about the enclosed as I prepare my testimony.

Johanna Berglund

CHAPTER ONE

From Major J. E. Davies to the citizens of Ironside Lake, Minnesota
To be read at the January 1944 town hall meeting

My fellow Americans,

Yes, it is as Americans that I appeal to you, not Minnesotans or residents of Ironside Lake. This call to sacrifice goes far beyond the tenuous ties of state or even community!

After careful consideration and planning, within two months, Ironside Lake will be home to a camp of German prisoners of war, who will work at several farms requesting day laborers with the Trade Center Committee.

The army considered several factors in making this decision. First, the people of rural Minnesota have been exceedingly generous in lending us the use of your strongest and bravest sons, with thousands fighting Axis forces far from home. However, because of this sacrifice, last year's harvest from your county was minimal.

Second, if you would, imagine your community on a map of the United States, far from oceans and government buildings, without any mountains that might provide security challenges. You are, quite plainly, the ideal location for such a camp!

Construction has already begun on the other side of the lake to repurpose the abandoned Civilian Conservation Corps facilities built there in '35. All is proceeding according to plan!

I myself was called up from the Army Reserve to serve as camp commander, overseeing twenty of our finest soldiers, who will be assuming guard duty. In addition, we will be posting open positions for a cook, secretary, and other support staff. We have a special need for a translator, as it is necessary to keep fluent German-speakers on duty at all times.

To address a possible concern, I will reassure you that most of the Germans in the prison camp will be enlisted men captured in the North Africa campaign and certainly not dangerous, as all prominent Nazi officers and SS agents are kept in a high-security camp in Oklahoma. We are confident that through the hard work of tilling the fertile American soil, our enemies will become our allies!

I will come myself in person to a special meeting at your town hall in one week's time to answer any questions you may have. Thank you in advance for your enthusiastic support of your country's efforts!

> With Great Respect,
> Major J. E. Davies
> US Army, Fort Snelling

Editorial in the Ironside Broadside *on January 20, 1944*

Dear Editor,

This paper's coverage of Tuesday night's town hall meeting made me sick. Sticking in one timid quote from that backwoods politician Carl Berglund doesn't show the town's real reaction to news of a prison camp on our doorstep. "I invite you all to think carefully about the situation and raise any appropriate questions" hardly begins to cover it!

Why not mention the cry of outrage that erupted before the letter was even halfway through, I ask you? Or talk about the mothers who wanted to know why, after kissing their older sons good-bye, they have to stand by and see their young ones endangered too? Or quote from Mr. Dahl's speech about how we don't owe the German prisoners any care or courtesy?

And another thing: We may have been behind in our quotas last year, but who says putting prisoners to work will help and not hurt? We've all seen the *Sabotage Can Outweigh Production* posters. It's a warning we'd best heed, if you ask me.

As for the translators, the camp planners are crazy as loons if they think we'll stand for bringing a truckload of those foreigners from New Weimar into our town to watch over their own countrymen. We might as well tear down the fence and hand the POWs a ticket back to Germany.

We've all heard the reports on the radio and gotten letters from our boys. We know plenty about the brutality of German soldiers. None of us will be safe with them as our neighbors, mark my words.

A Soldier's Mother

January 23, 1944

Dear Mother (and Dad),

Your last letter certainly set me back on my heels. Something actually happening back in Ironside Lake? It makes a person wonder, What next? Will John Wayne star in an operatic ballet? Hitler send roses and an apology note to Versailles with his unconditional surrender? Roosevelt resign and join the tightrope act of the Ringling Bros. Circus?

That's not very sensitive of me, is it? I'm sure it's very upsetting and that Dad has to deal with complainers calling the mayor's office at all hours. Still, that's what he signed up for when he sold the chickens and took up politics, trading one sort of squawking for another.

I'm sure the army will be vigilant about security, and in my view, everyone should thank God for the additional help, no matter who offers it. Only a few months ago, all Dad could talk about was how low our agricultural production numbers had dropped, with so many men enlisting. It must have come up five times during my Christmas visit.

What on earth did Pastor Sorenson say about the camp? I can only assume he addressed it in his sermon, the family connection and all. Poor man. Caught between Jesus' command to love your enemies and the entire roaring collective of Ironside Lake saying they shouldn't have to. I don't envy him.

I'm hard at work, as usual, writing papers and pretending to study for exams while I actually work ahead for my planned summer courses. Besides that, Peter managed to find a used copy of *Notre-Dame de Paris* in

16

the original French for my birthday present, which will provide me with a week's worth of light evening reading. I used your gift money to buy a stockade of Earl Grey to accompany my reading of Victor Hugo, since coffee is hard to come by these days. When you're approaching a tragic ending, fortification with a hot beverage is essential.

Don't worry too much, Mother; I do venture from my apartment when forced to, mostly by Olive. Why I thought it was a good idea to room with the most social co-ed on campus, I have no idea.

While I'm obviously justifying my introversion, I do get along tolerably with everyone in the program. But I wish Peter were here instead of down at Camp Savage. He gets leave sometimes on weekends and comes up to help me with my Japanese—I pay him in eternal gratitude and chop suey. (Apparently Chinese food is safer to sell than Japanese these days; there's a shop next to the USO servicemen's club where we met.)

I don't report these extracurricular studies to Dr. Smythe. The university is convinced that students must remain within the borders of their assigned classes, and they hold the line like there's a minefield beyond it that would blow us to bits. I'm attempting to persuade Dr. Smythe to approve an independent study in Japanese this summer, but I assume the answer will be no. It's not that he hates women in general—he shows remarkable equity in his treatment of female students. He just hates me in particular. Every now and then I think maybe I should stop correcting him in front of the class, but I only do so when he's blatantly wrong. He shouldn't take it personally.

In other news, I'm proud to say most of my meals these days are meatless and wheatless—although admittedly it's motivated not by patriotism but by the fact that rice, beans, and the occasional vegetable are cheap and easy to prepare. Even I can't burn boiling water, at least not yet. The one variation was last week, when Olive attempted Chelsea buns for my birthday. Evidently our American ingredients are "all wrong," and they turned out as hard as the sidewalk. I managed a few bites to be polite but nearly chipped a tooth.

Of course I miss you, and I'll try to visit sometime this summer, but train fare is expensive, and you know I haven't got a car or the gas rations to fill it. But do write back and let me know how the prison camp fracas resolves. I'm eager to hear all about it.

Love,
Jo

From Dr. Smythe to Johanna Berglund

January 27, 1944

Dear Miss Berglund,

I was told the best place to leave this note for you was with the campus head librarian. He assures me you're in at intervals as regular as the chiming of a clock and has promised to pass this along, as it contains time-sensitive information that could not wait until our next class.

Please make an appointment at your convenience to meet with me, but make sure that you find today or tomorrow convenient. I have an exciting opportunity to discuss with you.

Attached as well are my notes on your proposed study of the structural similarities between Japanese idioms and the epic poetry of ancient Greece. I'll summarize my position briefly here: I can't see how your proposed research has any practical application and would advise you to apply yourself to a more worthy pursuit.

> Dr. Sheridan Smythe
> Chair of the Modern
> Languages Department,
> University of Minnesota

From Major J. E. Davies to Johanna Berglund

January 24, 1944

Dear Miss Berglund,

A pleasure to meet you, even if that meeting is only by means of a stamp instead of a hearty handshake. Why, I feel as if I know you already from all of the impressive things I've heard about you—child prodigy, top of your class, entire translation of Dante's *Inferno* submitted with your application to the university! It downright boggles me. Keep this up and someday you'll be secretary of state, and I'll be saluting you!

By the time you receive this letter, my old friend Dr. Smythe should have presented you with the basics of our offer of employment as camp translator, but I wanted to write you myself to convey how essential you would be to our new camp's function. Vital, in fact!

We believe you to be not only an ideal candidate, but *the* ideal candidate. Why, you ask? We are running into a bit of—how should I phrase this?—an unanticipated public relations difficulty with Ironside Lake. The other camps in Iowa and Minnesota faced scrutiny upon their founding, but not the outright hostility we're experiencing from the citizens of your hometown. It's quite unprecedented! We are hoping that having you on our staff

19

as a local girl made good—and the mayor's daughter, no less—will bring them reassurance.

While discussing this issue at the fort, one of our language-school instructors (from a military intelligence initiative—highly secretive, you understand) giving a report to my superior said he knew the very person for the job, qualified for the work in both skills and temperament. Namely, you! You must realize how this struck me. Two recommendations of the very same person for this translation position. An amazing godsend! Truly, it felt like the decision had been made for me. I trust you'll come to the same conclusion.

I must confess, when your parents and our language-school instructor alike assured me that "Jo Berglund" would be perfect for the job, I assumed that "Joe Berglund" was a man. It was only upon speaking with Smythe that I was informed of my mistake. Other camps are reluctant to bring female staff members into the post, even attempting to limit contact when POWs work at canneries alongside civilian women. However, I have heard nothing but praise of your character and abilities, and being a bit of a progressive, if I do say so myself, I do not anticipate any problems.

Thank you once again for considering this position, and I look forward to hearing from you shortly!

> With Great Respect,
> Major J. E. Davies
> US Army, Fort Snelling

January 27, 1944

Dear Major Davies,

I have a friend who says it's best to start out communications with a compliment when possible. So let me say that the Fort Snelling letterhead is appropriately impressive without being gaudy.

On to the bad news. I regret that I must decline your offer of a translator position in Ironside Lake. Must emphatically decline.

My program of study here at the University of Minnesota is much too demanding to allow for any break. I had intended to take summer courses as well, so it would be impossible for me to spend nine months in a prison camp. Besides that, the scholarship donor allowing me to be here would not look kindly on a long leave of absence.

Peter Ito is quite right that I am qualified for the position. (I'm assuming he was the one who spoke to you.) Probably overqualified, since I am also fluent in French, Danish, Greek, and Latin and have begun studying Japanese. But I'm afraid you'll need to find someone else. Might I recommend asking in New Weimar? It's a forestry town, and most of their population emigrated from Germany only a generation or two back. I used to pick up phrases when my family stopped at a filling station on our annual trip to Duluth, which is what prompted my interest in the language.

As for my being a godsend, I hope this won't shake your faith, but God already sent me here. To Minneapolis. And here I will stay until I've gotten my degree and can start the work I've dreamed of all my life, hopefully in Oxford, England, and certainly not in Ironside Lake.

Again, I appreciate being considered, and the stationery really is striking. I wish you all the best in finding a better-suited candidate.

Sincerely,
Johanna Berglund

From Johanna Berglund to Peter Ito

January 27, 1944

Dear Peter,

You've really done it this time. I can't decide whether to upbraid you for your treachery or to thank you for the misplaced compliment. So I'll do both, and you can decide which one I mean more.

Why in heaven's name did you make Major What's-His-Name think I'm the perfect candidate for the translator position? Skills, I'll grant you, though you're taking my word on my fluency in German since you don't speak anything beyond *gesundheit* and *Sauerkraut*. But temperament? Were you joking? You're too kind to say it, but we both know I'm a disaster when it comes to relating to people, nothing at all like Olive or Mother or even my sister, Irene.

It's difficult even visiting Ironside Lake. Dad and Mother are happy to see me, of course, but I always time my visits so they fall over as few Sundays as possible. Church in a small town is more to see and be seen than it is to actually worship, and I'm no longer a precocious ten-year-old in a sailor dress, singing "Jesus Loves the Little Children."

Why were you even at Fort Snelling? I thought you've

been so busy at the language school that you barely have time for sleep.

Regardless, if the major contacts you again, tell him to go away. Or, since you probably wouldn't be that blunt, change the subject. Or better yet, recommend someone else for the translator position. Anyone, in fact, who isn't me.

This was my parents' idea; I'm sure of it. Mother is always writing me teary, guilt-inducing letters about how empty the house seems now that Irene's married and I'm off at school, when they probably barely noticed me when I was there. Even Dad never fully approved of the linguistics program, although I do think he admired the way I gathered the money for it. I know he and Mother would be perfectly happy if I came back to Ironside Lake, got swept off my feet by an industrious banker's son like Irene did, and gave up this nonsense of Oxford altogether.

I've spent all evening working on a tactful reply to the major, and now writing to you. Consequently, my poor volume of Ovid is entirely neglected in the corner. Real life is dreadfully tedious, the way it interrupts reading.

But enough about me and my woes. Are you finding teaching these new recruits any easier?

Your friend,
Jo

Appendix: Would you like to make a bet on when the last snow will be? I'm not as much of a weakling as you when it comes to winter, but even I might sing for joy and toss my gloves in a bonfire once it gets to fifty degrees for the first time.

From Peter to Johanna

January 31, 1944

Dear Jo,

You're a regular prophet. Major Davies did seek me out again, asking about you. I had to interrupt my class to run to the office to take his call, and the first words of it were, "Mr. Ito, why didn't you tell me that Berglund girl was so blasted difficult?" Only he didn't use *blasted*.

Honestly, Jo, what did you say to him?

What's so bad about taking a semester off, two at most, to use the skills you're learning? I know you dream of a life in England translating *Beowulf* and the tragedies of Euripides, but in case you haven't tuned in to the radio lately, the Germans are trying to bomb it into oblivion. Even if you finish your bachelor's, you won't be able to get over there just now.

But I shouldn't be too hard on you. Probably everyone else is saying the same sort of thing, and I know you love your cozy apartment and teakettle and study desk in the Modern Language section of the library. I want you to be happy, Jo. But at least think about it.

On how I came to be speaking with Major Davies: Great news, there's so much interest from *Nisei* around the country in joining our training school that they're considering moving the program to Fort Snelling. Now that some of our graduates have gone into the field and proven themselves, it's starting to dawn on the military brass that our true loyalty is to America, not Japan. (Which is exactly what we've been telling them all along.) It would mean a lot to get official recognition instead of being segregated away at the slipshod facilities here. We're at full enrollment—over a thousand now—and bursting at the seams. Since all the bunks are taken, some of the boys are sleeping on mattresses on the floor.

The latest new arrivals are a younger crowd, averaging around twenty. All of them are eager to learn, though it's interesting interacting with the Hawaiian students, who speak a different dialect of English. The government finally allowed them to apply, and we've got the cream of the crop from the hundreds who did.

Most of the mainland students signed up primarily to get out of the internment camps, but they work hard, knowing time is short and there's a huge demand for translators in the Pacific. We've even caught a few studying in the privy after ten o'clock, since it's the only building with a lit bulb after lights-out.

The trouble is, we had to lower our requirements to fill our quota, from high-school equivalency to third grade, so our Beginning level is much more crowded than Middle and Advanced. At least total immersion seems to be helping them. (Did I tell you I dream in Japanese now? I sometimes have to struggle for the right English word when writing to you.)

There still aren't quite enough instructors for the number of students we have, so the hours are long. Most of us aren't Ivy League faculty, for sure—there was a reason I was studying accounting at the University of California—but we have good motivation to learn quickly so we can teach the students army jargon, cryptology, basic military tactics and maneuvers, and, hardest of all, cursive. (I'm not joking. Most of them have never seen writing in *sousho* before, much less tried to read it. Very difficult to master. That's why I haven't showed it to you yet.)

I'll take a last-snow bet of March 8 and hope I'm wrong and all the snow melts tomorrow, never to return. For most of the boys, the novelty of snow has worn off—there are few of the joyful frolics we saw in our first several inches. But some of them still like the excuse for a prank. I caught one student slipping an icicle down another's shirt during class one morning. The poor fellow tried not to react, but his squirming couldn't be contained, and when he untucked his shirt and the melting shard fell to the floor, the classroom dissolved into laughter. It was all I could do to keep a straight face.

Have I mentioned I'm still mad the training school moved from San Francisco to Minneapolis? I don't know what they were thinking, bringing a bunch of Californians and Hawaiians to this frozen meat locker. Even under three layers of sweaters, I feel like a sirloin packed in ice. How do you stand it?

Your friend,
Peter

P.S. Only you would have an appendix instead of a usual P.S. Are you going to start footnoting your letters too?

P.P.S. Terry Tanabe, the icicle culprit above, went to the Nisei USO club last weekend and reported that the senior hostess asked about you, wondering why her favorite summertime junior hostess suddenly disappeared. She still doesn't realize you only crashed the USO club because you wanted to learn Japanese, does she? I figured it out right away, for the record. All I wanted was a game of Ping-Pong, and instead, the girl on the other side of the net kept missing the ball, firing linguistic questions at me between serves. How did you get away with that for three full months without being found out?

26

From Johanna to Peter

February 3, 1944

Dear Peter,

I promise I'll think about the position.

There. I thought about it. For a good ten seconds. And then put it right back in my mental files where it belongs, alphabetized somewhere between *Never* and *Not a chance.*

Well, it's about time the army deigns to adequately equip you for your work. You'd think they'd prefer we lose the war in the Pacific, the way they've dallied on training your linguists. I'm glad to hear the new students will live up to your expectations, particularly since you've only got six months to turn them out as experts. See, that's an example of the stress that accompanies the more "practical" applications of language study. I could never do what you do, and I don't intend to, no matter how many exclamation marks Major J. E. Davies fires at me.

As for the USO, now that I'm sure you won't turn me in, I'll confess: I forged a badge with a stencil patterned off a brochure requesting I apply as a junior hostess. I didn't have time for letters of recommendation and interviews when there were only three summer months before the start of the term. So I pinned that false badge to my blouse, then marched up to the club and distracted Mrs. Murray by responding in Japanese the first few times she greeted me (the only phrases I knew, and badly pronounced, I found out later). She was delighted to have a fluent speaker at the club, thinking it would make her Senior Hostess of the Year, I suppose.[1]

It was good of you to give me lessons, though, when you were surrounded by books and study the rest of the week. I still have those first *kanji* you penciled in on a napkin pressed in my *Naganuma Reader*. Duplicitous means or no, what would I have done if I'd never met you? One chance glance at a newspaper article to see that a Nisei USO was starting up in the Cities, and I found the luckiest choice of Ping-Pong partner I could have made.[2]

March 8? You're a hopeless optimist. I'm calling April 2, and not a day earlier. Loser has to buy malts once it's warm enough to ingest something frozen, which will be at least June.

Jo

[1] She was under the impression that my parents were missionaries for a decade in Nagasaki, though I swear I never said so. Not directly, anyway.

[2] Before you criticize me for faking my hostess role, remember, you were patronizing the USO as a civilian instructor, completely nonmilitary, which is against USO rules.

From Major Davies to Johanna

February 1, 1944

Dear Miss Berglund,

Thank you for taking the time to write back so promptly. The fort's stationery also appreciates the compliment, I'm sure.

I'm sorry you felt you should decline our offer, but allow me to present you a few details that might change your mind.

We have already investigated the option of hiring a

translator from New Weimar but have encountered two obstacles: First, we can obtain B-level gas rations for a translator, but most residents of New Weimar don't have access to a car or the desire to make a daily forty-five-minute round trip, which would make transportation difficult.

Second, the citizens of Ironside Lake are not—how should I put this?—especially in favor of bringing outsiders, particular those of recent German extraction, into their fair town. This point was emphasized to me quite clearly at my visit there only a few days ago, and we promised to honor those concerns, baseless as we believe them to be.

As one of Ironside Lake's own people, you will be trusted, and your assistance will help us to build goodwill with the community. Think of all the good you can do! Why, if my own daughter were presented with such a chance to serve her country, she would be packing her bags immediately!

This is the sort of opportunity any language student should be deeply grateful for, particularly a woman who seeks independence and respect in her field.

Take a few days to think about it. I can't emphasize enough how important this is.

> With Great Respect,
> Major J. E. Davies
> US Army, Fort Snelling

From Johanna to Major Davies

February 4, 1944

Dear Major Davies,

I'm sorry if my last letter gave the impression that there might be room to persuade me, because it was not my intent. I won't be any help at all for good relations with Ironside Lake. Persuasion, you might have guessed by now, is not my gift. I do love words. I memorize them and enjoy finding the exact way to translate them to accurately communicate the author's meaning . . . but I am not good at putting words together on my own, especially when speaking to people.

I can assure you that I'd be no help with your public relations efforts. No doubt the people of Ironside Lake are as glad to be rid of me as I am to be gone.

Keep up the good work. I'm sure you'll find just the person you need for the job, but I'm sorry to say that it isn't me.

Johanna Berglund

From Mrs. Berglund to Johanna

February 2, 1944

Dearest Jo,

Now, dear, you know how I feel about your sarcasm. People around here are very upset by all this talk of prisoners of war, and the weight of it is falling on your father. Of course, it's our duty to make the best of it, but it's much easier for you to laugh from the safe distance of the city when it doesn't affect your life—at least not yet.

Construction on the prison camp is almost finished, as the men will be arriving at the beginning of next month. I'll admit to driving by it once so I could take a peek. Most of it looked rather ordinary—same old paint-peeling CCC buildings and wide stretches of tramped-down dirt—but that hideous barbed-wire fence! It made me shudder. I'm glad they have it, of course, but Ironside Lake has always been a safe place, and now it seems less so. Politics aside, that's how I feel, and I can't help but say it.

As to Anders's sermon, he didn't mention a word about it. Now, I know what you're thinking, but please don't demean his faithful service to our community by implying that was cowardly of him. I've always said the church doesn't need to interfere in every civil squabble. A pastor must concern himself with heavenly things, and I'm sure I wasn't the only member of Immanuel Lutheran Church who found last Sunday's message on the Babylonian captivity very uplifting.

After the service, Annika asked about you. She does sometimes, you know, and it sounds to me that she doesn't hear from you often. That's such a shame, dear, your best friend for all those years.

Which brings me to the translation job. I'm surprised you didn't write or even call after you received the offer, but Major Davies told us all about it on his latest visit, and about your refusal. Half the town knows by now, I'm afraid, although I'm sure you know they didn't hear it from me. I would guess the leak was Major Davies's wife, who accompanied him. She seems to be the chatty sort, though very elegant. Used to New York City as she is, she probably doesn't realize that in a small town, if you speak someone else's business in a whisper, it will be shouted from the rooftops by noon the next day.

I hope you weren't rude to the major, dear. Your father is in a delicate place coming up on November's election, trying to keep the town agitators mollified and still maintain good relationships with the army and Farm Help Coordinating Committee. Your cooperation in this would certainly be appreciated. I think it would comfort people a great deal to have someone they know translating at the camp. And your father and I would be delighted to have you back home.

Of course the decision is yours to make. After the dance-hall incident, heaven knows I've given up trying to force your hand on anything. But it's something to consider.

At the very least, you'd get some decent food here. Dear old Cornelia Knutson is quite handy with stretching ration coupons, and I've been borrowing some recipes from her to get by until the farmers market opens. I'm making potato soup now, and your mouth would water just to smell it. Rice and vegetables seven days a week—how can you stand it? Remember, if you're undernourished, you'll be susceptible to pneumonia, especially in this cold. There's nothing worse than being sick away from home, so please do take care of yourself.

Much love,
Mother

From Dr. Smythe to Johanna

February 7, 1944

Dear Miss Berglund,

It has come to my attention that the anonymous administrator of the trust from which your scholarship is drawn has decided that, for future semesters, the funds will be granted to a student using his or her language degree for patriotic purposes—diplomacy, foreign-aid efforts, government service, etc.

If you would like to reapply for the scholarship, you may do so. An essay will be required to demonstrate fulfilment of this new requirement.

Before you storm to my office to accuse me of interfering, I assure you I have done no such thing, although I agree that the timing is rather suspicious. Even though I do not know the donor's identity, I suspect Major Davies considers him (and half the city) an "old friend." Need I say more?

I have heard from Fort Snelling about your difficulties with accepting the offered position at the new POW camp. Should you change your mind, I am willing to administer your spring examinations early. Judging by your consistently flawless assignments and your frequent glazed looks in my class, I think you'll be more than ready. And I hope it's not too indiscreet to point out that the generous proposed salary will go considerably further than your wages from your current part-time employment at the campus library.

You have great potential, Miss Berglund. I'd caution you not to waste it out of stubbornness and to direct your considerable talents toward a more realistic goal.

Dr. Sheridan Smythe
Chair of the Modern
Languages Department,
University of Minnesota

From Johanna to Major Davies

February 9, 1944

Dear Major Davies,

No compliments this time. If you feel comfortable asking my scholarship donor to withdraw funds for my schooling, then I don't need to keep to rules of etiquette anymore. I've always thought of etiquette as institutionalized insincerity anyway. Much better to say things straight out.

I find myself in the unenviable position of being blackmailed into serving my country. You army gentlemen are all about conscription, aren't you? It doesn't seem like I have any alternative other than to take a leave of absence from my studies and come to your POW camp.

I hope that's left you feeling guilty enough to make you more amenable to the compromise I would like to propose:

If I come back to Ironside Lake to serve as your translator, censor, girl-of-all-work, etc., I want you to agree to reevaluate the position on August 1 of this year. If morale in the camp is high and relations between the town and the camp are running smoothly, as I'm sure they will be, then having me around won't be necessary, will it?

I'm offering to surrender six months of my life to serve my country in a role no one else wants. I hope you'll agree that this is a reasonable compromise.

Make no mistake: I am qualified, and I will do my work with excellence. There's no need to worry on that front.

I hope you will consider these terms and respond as soon as possible.

Johanna Berglund

From Major Davies to Johanna Berglund

February 12, 1944

Dear Miss Berglund,

I can't tell you how delighted I was to receive your response in today's mail! Chatted with Smythe this morning as well, and he said he's happy to have you going too. Very accommodating fellow. I thought he'd slap my knuckles for taking away his star pupil, but he seemed relieved that we'd found someone for the position. He also advised me that you have a slightly abrupt manner, so I interpreted your letter in that light.

My wife, Evelyn, will appreciate having another woman about the camp in addition to my secretary and some of the soldiers' wives. She's been distressed all month at the thought of leaving her friends in Manhattan, even though I assured her that we'll certainly be home for Christmas, as the camp will close for the season in November.

To that point, your recommendation of reevaluating your employment come the end of summer seems reasonable to me. Just save this letter and remind me of it in a few months, and we'll see what's what. With any luck, all will be calm as a graveyard, and off you'll go to your studies again!

I will say, though, that I had nothing to do with taking your scholarship away from you! Perhaps you might hold back on your accusations and simply consider if Providence has guided your path to the very place where you belong.

Further instructions regarding transportation, arrival, etc., will follow from my secretary, Miss Harrigan. Again, we look forward to your assistance with this essential wartime effort! America is grateful for you!

With Great Respect,
Major J. E. Davies

Telegram from Johanna to her parents on February 16, 1944

```
COMING HOME THIS MON TO BEGIN TRANSLATION JOB.
ARMY TO PICK ME UP FROM DULUTH STATION. WILL
ARRIVE AROUND NOON. PLEASE AIR OUT BEDSPREAD.
```

From Peter to Johanna, left with her and found while on the train to Duluth

February 21, 1944

Dear Jo,

If you're reading this, it's because our last conversation was just what I expected: full of forced smiles and things we didn't get a chance to say. I guess that's the way good-byes usually are.

You've never said exactly why you hate the thought of going home, and I don't need to know, but I remember how hard it was when you went back for your friend's funeral last year. It was six weeks before you even smiled again. (Yes, I counted.) I'd rather you not spend the next six months stewing in misery.

So make a new friend or two. Do your work as well as I know you can. Keep praying and ask for help every now and then. And write me if you have the time. I'll even tolerate a little complaining, but only if you also report any interesting baseball stories, since I haven't got time to listen to games on the radio. (Don't even think about telling me you don't know the terms—you taught yourself Latin from books you smuggled out of your pastor's library before you were fifteen. You can learn what a pop fly is.)

One more thing. I've mentioned my grandmother

Baba Yone before, but I don't think I ever told you what she said when the news came that our family would be sent to the internment camp in Arizona. The first part wasn't a surprise, it's what all of the older generation say in response to adversity: "*Shikata ga nai.*" *It can't be helped.* But then she added (in Japanese; she doesn't speak English), "We can do anything we must. How we do it, though, is up to us."

Then again, she also didn't want me to leave the internment camp and teach here at the language school. So maybe it's harder advice to follow than either of us thought.

Anyway, you've got a right to be angry about being forced somewhere against your will. So do I. But I keep thinking about what John Aiso (the head of the language school) said in one of his motivational speeches: "We must live like the cherry trees in our nation's capital: of Japanese origin and symbol of their knightly lore, but taking root in the richness of American soil, enhancing with beauty in their season the Washington, Lincoln, and Jefferson Memorials."

It's not a perfect metaphor, but you can be Ironside Lake's cherry tree. You don't really belong, but you've been planted there for now, and this is your chance to bloom.

You can, and you will. I know it.

All that said . . . come back soon, if you can. I'm going to miss you.

> Your friend,
> Peter

EVIDENCE FOR THE PROSECUTION

FROM LIEUTENANT WALTER ROSS, COMMANDER OF POW CAMP OWATONNA, TO MAJOR J. E. DAVIES

February 11, 1944

Major Davies,

I was pleased to receive your letter, having heard of you through your work in this war and the last. I share your interest in radio, though I never advanced past tinkering with a Philmore Crystal Radio set in my youth to actual cryptography. I hope the following information proves useful.

This post has been an unusual one, but for the most part, the prisoners are well behaved, expressing their requests through their spokesman and working hard enough to please their employers. Many even attend church services on Sundays.

There has only been one incident of note. Last September, three of our prisoners dug under the fence after the Saturday night bed check, knowing there would be no such check on Sunday. Two were captured nearly immediately. The third returned on his own the next day, in civilian clothes . . . after having attended the county fair, of all things. His list of "criminal activities" was as follows: buying a sandwich, playing a carnival game, and riding the Ferris wheel. Clearly no significant espionage or sabotage occurred.

However, this incident proved how simple it would be for prisoners, if inclined, to evade confinement. The trouble, as I'm sure you're aware, is that, under the Geneva Convention, it isn't technically a crime for prisoners to escape. It's a mad world we live in. A guard can shoot a

POW on sight if he's seen crawling under the fence and refuses to halt . . . but if that same POW escapes and is returned days later, the maximum legal penalty is a few weeks of solitary confinement.

We simply don't have the manpower or the resources to turn the camp into a true prison. The New Ulm camp has also reported incidents of German-sympathizing individuals assisting the POWs in breaking camp regulations and even conspiring to let them outside of the camp at night for meals or entertainment.

Among this group, young women are most likely to bring you trouble. The prisoners will work alongside these women, whose natural compassion, and perhaps also the need for adventure and a lack of available American young men, will cause them to begin secret assignations with the prisoners. There have been a number of reports of such women helping the men steal away from the fields and even, on occasion, the camp itself. All of this to further their romances.

We are used to treating men as the enemies, Major. But I cannot overemphasize that, in this case, your greatest foes may be the most unlikely among you.

I wish you all the best in your new position. Please don't hesitate to write again if you need any further advice.

Lieutenant Walter Ross

CHAPTER TWO

Editorial in the Ironside Broadside *on February 18, 1944*

Dear Editor,

With all the tomfoolery going on in the world these days, nothing should surprise me. But I can't guess what those stooges in Fort Snelling were thinking, coming up with this scheme of hiring the mayor's daughter. I asked ten different men at Nelson's Bar and Grill what they thought of some doll sauntering into a POW camp to "translate," and each of them said the same thing: "It'll be nothing but trouble."

They've got guards for the towers, sure, but who's going to guard her? She oughtn't trouble her pretty head about it, just resign and let the men do the work with the blasted prisoners.

They're tossing us something they think we want, but they don't know us. City slickers, the lot of them. Looks to me like we're being bribed to let this dirty scheme through.

That's right, dirty. That's what I think of foreigners being hauled in to do our work.

And another thing: What happens when our boys come back and they've got migrants and Krauts doing their work? What'll they think of us when they can't even get a working wage in their own hometown and have to go off to the city? I bet then you'll be ashamed you stood by and let it happen.

Well, not me. If you're smart, you'll start asking the same questions I've been asking and realize we haven't gotten a single answer.

A Concerned Citizen

From Major Davies to Johanna, left at her home

February 20, 1944

Dear Miss Berglund,

I've taken the liberty to write so this letter of instructions will await you upon arrival, as I will not be coming from Fort Snelling until tomorrow. First of all, deepest congratulations on your new position! I hope your travel was pleasant.

I'm sure you'll want to take a day or two to unpack and greet hometown friends. Please report to Camp Ironside (that's our new facility; we're not very creative at naming in the army!) on Thursday at 0700 hours to begin your training and some initial translations for camp signage. You are then welcome to join my wife and me for lunch in our new quarters—Evelyn will be delighted to meet you!

Welcome home, and to the place I'll soon consider my temporary home as well. I'm sure we will find it as utterly charming as it appears!

With Great Respect and
Deep Gratitude,
Major J. E. Davies

Note in Johanna's top drawer, with her handkerchiefs

February 21, 1944

Jo,

your mother spent an hour pressing these yesterday, fretting that it was cold and flu season and you might not have a decent handkerchief with you. I wanted you to know that.

I know these aren't the circumstances you'd have chosen. But we're happy to have you home anyway.

Dad

From the Lutheran Daughters of the Reformation to Johanna, left at her home upon her arrival

February 21, 1944

To Miss Johanna Berglund,

The Lutheran Daughters of the Reformation would like to extend our welcome back to Ironside Lake, as well as to invite you to attend our next meeting, next Thursday evening at 7:00 p.m. in the church basement. Should you, at that time, decide to join as a full-time member, we would be happy to have you without the recommended trial period, since we all know your family. Your interest in languages would be very helpful for our support of and correspondence with foreign missionaries, and we could always use another hand at our monthly potlucks.

If you have any questions, please don't hesitate to reach out after church on Sunday to any one of us.

> Mrs. Roberta Wyatt, president
> Miss Hattie Knutson, vice
> president
> Mrs. Dorothy Lewis, treasurer
> Miss Annika Sorenson,
> secretary

From Annika Sorenson to Johanna

February 22, 1944

Dear Johanna,

I wanted to say that you should feel no obligation to join the Lutheran Daughters of the Reformation. Mrs. Wyatt and the rest of the ladies believed we ought to invite you as a way of welcoming you back to town, but I remember the jokes you made about the LDR when we were girls. (They really were awful, especially the one about the Communion wine.)

I'm sure you think I'm silly for joining, but once I came of age, I was drafted into Mother's former role as official minute taker. It's nearly Scripture that someone from the pastor's family has to be involved, and if you want to survive in Ironside Lake, you have to find a social group to join. Not all of us can just leave like you did.

But what matters is that you'd hate our monthly meetings. At our last one, after praying for the unreached in Burma, we spent a full half hour debating whether we would include all recipes submitted to our annual cookbook fundraiser or only those selected by a committee. Someone indirectly referenced Mrs. Wyatt's tomato and olive aspic rings, and it quickly went downhill from there.

I'm sure the other ladies will understand that you'll be quite busy with your new job at the camp, and I've heard you aren't sure how long you'll be staying, which would make membership difficult. I expect you'll want to get back to your program at the university as soon as possible.

I'm sure I'll see you at church for the Ash Wednesday service. Until then, I hope the adjustment back is an easy one.

Annika Sorenson

P.S. Please enjoy the shortbread cookies, although they're not even close to the same when made with margarine. Don't even ask me about the pathetic excuse for a pound cake I attempted without butter. I suppose we all have to make sacrifices these days.

A draft of a letter from Johanna to the Lutheran Daughters of the Reformation, never sent

February 22, 1944

Dear Mrs. Wyatt et al.,

I was surprised to find your letter greeting me ~~the moment I collapsed on my bed from a tedious train ride~~ so promptly. Of course I remember your ~~ridiculous~~ active group from growing up at Immanuel Lutheran. I regret that I ~~loathe committees with a fierce passion, exceeded only by my hatred for making small talk at potlucks~~ must decline your kind invitation.

Annika has informed me that you'd understand if I'm too busy to accept, which I'm sure was ~~influenced in~~

~~no way by the fact that she only wants to see me when absolutely necessary~~ very thoughtful of her.

Mission work is noble, ~~though I admit, prayer for the unreached has always confused me. Hasn't God known since the beginning of time who will come to faith? If so, what good do our prayers do?~~ and I will be first in line to purchase one of your cookbooks ~~Mrs. Wyatt's suspect aspics included or no,~~ as a token of my support.

From Johanna to the Lutheran Daughters of the Reformation

February 22, 1944

Dear Mrs. Wyatt, Miss Knutson, Mrs. Lewis, and Miss Sorenson,

Thank you for your gracious welcome in inviting me to join the Lutheran Daughters of the Reformation. I'm grateful for the way you serve missionaries and local charities, but I'm afraid that my irregular hours at the camp make it impossible for me to accept your kind offer.

I hope you will consider the prisoners of war in our own backyard as among "the least of these" whom Christ asked us to serve: "I was a stranger, and ye took me in; I was in prison, and ye came unto me." I've heard there has been some resistance to the camp among the people of the town, but I'm sure the LDR women, as Christlike pillars of the community, are fully in support.

Again, I appreciate the honor of the invitation.

Yours truly,
Johanna Berglund

Left on the Berglund kitchen table

February 23, 1944

Went for a walk down by the lake. I know you wanted me to go to the Ash Wednesday service, but I thought it would be better to give the congregation time to adjust to my being here.

As I walk, I'll smudge some dirt on my forehead in the shape of a cross and think of some sins to confess. "Remember you are dust, and to dust you will return." There. I've covered the important parts of the service.

And don't worry, Mother I'm wearing my wool coat, boots, and two layers of socks. I won't catch a cold or my death or anything else.

Jo

Left on the Berglund kitchen table

February 23, 1944

Jo,

Your father refused to let me go out after you, even when I found your scarf draped over your bedpost. You don't have to catch your death; it's chasing after you, and the point is to prevent, not encourage it. As for your wilderness Lenten service . . . I can't imagine confessing to the squirrels contains any actual spiritual benefit.

yes, people will talk about your return, but only because they're glad to see you again—and perhaps they're honestly curious about the POW camp. Don't let one silly anonymous writer in that McHenry boy's poor excuse for a newspaper let you think otherwise. (Your father told me you saw it. If I find out who sent in that letter, I will have words for him.)

When you finally come back, I've left some chicken broth on the stove. It's good for what I'm sure will soon be ailing you.

Much love,
Mother

Editorial in the Ironside Broadside *on February 24, 1944*

Dear Editor,

Imagine my surprise to find an antipatriotic screed in our very own newspaper about Miss Berglund coming to the camp as a translator.

For shame. Shame on "Concerned Citizen," whoever you are, and shame on each and every one of you who agreed with him. That editorial was a personal attack, not to mention an insult to women everywhere. I didn't campaign for twenty straight Novembers for the right to vote just to keep hearing lines about women being "delicate" and "pretty." We aren't china dolls.

The letter writer wants us to think he cares about propriety, though I doubt he even knows the word. Well, I say the army has had a good deal of practice at that, so we needn't concern ourselves. There are Women's Army Corps members at Fort Snelling just like any other base in the nation, and a pool of female secretaries serving their country with the artillery clatter of their typewriters besides. Were I a few decades younger, you can bet your bloomers I'd be there with them. How is this any different?

Besides, I served as a chaperone at those dances Miss Berglund organized at the high-school gymnasium to gather money for her studies—what was it, two years ago now? She asked me personally to do so, and let me tell you, I have never seen a more thoughtful and respectable young woman in all my days. And I've had a lot of days. Never even took to the dance floor, she was so busy keeping everyone on task and everything to standard. Johanna Berglund isn't some loose, rouged Liberty Girl. She's one of us, city education or no. And if the army has decided she's the best-qualified translator for the job, we ought to be proud of her.

As a politician's daughter, she knows the whole town is watching her; I'd put my last dollar into shares of stock on that. What's more, she's probably reading this right now. So, Miss Berglund, I'll write this directly to you: You won't let us down. You can't. The stakes are too high. Thank you in advance for keeping your chin up and proving everyone wrong.

Mrs. Cornelia Knutson,
an Unconcerned Citizen

From Johanna to Peter

February 27, 1944

Dear Peter,

Well, here I am. Nothing has changed in Ironside Lake in two years except me, although no one seems to realize that yet. In their minds, I'm frozen as my nineteen-year-old self, like a piece of olive quivering in aspic. And who can blame them? I'm sleeping in my childhood bedroom, buying stamps at the same old post office, and occupying the same pew while hearing the same sorts of sermons from Pastor Sorenson, consistent and bland as Meatless Monday's mushroom gravy.

Sorry for the barrage of food analogies. I pretended I was feeling unwell to avoid going over for Sunday lunch at the Sorensons', and now I'm regretting that choice. But I could tell that Annika was only offering because she felt obligated. It would have been excruciatingly awkward.

Several of the Lutheran Daughters of the Reformation have asked Mother if she and Dad think it's "suitable" for a woman to work in "a man's role," and whispers follow me down the streets wherever I go. The only thing that's saved me from a torch-and-pitchfork protest is Cornelia Knutson's vociferous defense in the local paper.

(What can I say to give you a picture of our town matriarch? Last year she planned a Crosby Medley Event to lure young people into the church—but they soon found the Crosby in question was Fanny, not Bing, and the greatest hits were "Blessed Assurance" and "Take the World, But Give Me Jesus" rather than "Pistol Packin' Mama.")

Thursday was my first glimpse of the camp. Picture a Gene Autry–movie ghost town with rows of faded wooden buildings, their windows clouded with cobwebs and a decade's worth of accumulated dirt. As I arrived, carpenters hammered away despite the cold and snow, reshingling the roofs to prepare for the arrival of the POWs.

The guard towers and wire-tipped fences surprised me. I knew they would be there, of course, but seeing the stark platforms mounted with searchlights and the twisting steel barbs . . . well, it wasn't my first choice of a workplace aesthetic. The least they could do is add a reinforced steel welcome mat to give the place a homey feel.

Major Davies was "delighted" to see me, and according to him, we are already "old friends." I thought he'd shake my arm clean off. After he introduced me to his executive officer, Lieutenant Charles Bates—a man so stiff he reminds me a of a department-store mannequin—it was time for a grand tour. The major narrated the purpose of the rough structures as if I were a debutante strolling the streets of Rome and admiring various Michelangelo sculptures.

While he rattled off statistics about the mess hall and how the guards' quarters are, per the Geneva Convention, exactly the same quality as the prisoners', I counted spiders. Twenty-nine distinct sightings! I subsequently declared war on them. Even though I've inflicted heavy casualties, they are winning; I am in frantic retreat. Reinforcements may be needed. I will keep you apprised of further developments.

After this, I was finally left to my office, an alcove in the post headquarters. Lined up on my desk in proper regimented order were a Royal typewriter, miscellaneous office supplies, an ashtray, and an Acme Tires matchbook (even though I explained to Major Davies that I don't smoke). A German-English dictionary was placed prominently in the center. Which made me wonder if it's true: They don't really trust me to do this job; they hired me only to placate the town and buy my father's support.

Since there wasn't anything to be gained by accusing anyone of this, I started by translating a booklet of prisoner regulations and several signs—short ones like *First Aid*—and more involved placards like one insisting that all flyers posted to the camp bulletin board must be approved by the camp commander. All very simple and dull, though I'll admit to looking up the German for two military terms.

Around noon, the major's wife, Evelyn, fretted around her half-unpacked dining room and served us chicken and dumplings (which she apologized for twice because their housekeeper only started yesterday and "good help is simply impossible to find around here"). The meal's side dishes were so many stories about her life in New York that I feel no need now to visit the city myself. I already know almost everything about it: the best department stores and concert halls, as well as the superiority of its roads, fresh fruit, electrical output, and selection of perfumes.

Mrs. Davies also gave me instructions about my clothing, something the major apparently found too delicate to discuss. Since I'm a civilian, I won't have a uniform, but I'm expected to wear practical, modest clothing in neutral tones. Except for the pale blue dress Mother made me for Easter several years ago, this is a fair description of my entire wardrobe. I'm not exactly Jantzen-bathing-suit-ad material with my limp blond hair and flat figure, so I assured her it wouldn't be a problem.

Still, Mrs. Davies felt the need to illustrate her instructions with cut-out catalog pictures with bright red slashes through them to indicate their inappropriateness for work. They can't have anyone looking too pretty at the prison camp, you understand—very dangerous around all those men. "Of course. Loose slips sink ships," I said very gravely, and Major Davies looked like he'd explode for trying to bottle in his laughter.

I dreamt that night of army trucks filled with swastikas

that turned into a swarm of thick-legged spiders. That's a fair picture of how well I've been sleeping lately. The best nights are the ones where I dream I'm back at the university, with its familiar bookshelves and clear expectations and beautiful dead languages to translate.

I'm sorry. I set out to write an update the length of a postcard, and it's turned into a novel. That's the occupational hazard of making a friend whose favorite books are *The Iliad* and *Beowulf*. Everything becomes an epic. At least fewer people died in the making of this letter; that's something.

I hope things in Camp Savage are better than here and that you aren't facing people who question both your integrity and your ability to do your job. Are you beginning to thaw yet? Any news from your family these days?

Jo

From Johanna to Brady McHenry, editor in chief of the Ironside Broadside

February 28, 1944

Dear Mr. McHenry,

Everyone knows that "letters to the editor" are very rarely meant for the editor personally. However, this one is and is thus not intended for print.

Your father had a policy of never publishing anonymous letters, and I would suggest reinstating that policy before things get out of hand. As I see it, no one should be able to sling mud from a dark and shadowed corner, and I'm not only saying that because I was the one criticized.

I'd hate to see any trouble when the men arrive at Camp Ironside in seven days, and I'm sure you feel the same based on your sense of civic duty, no matter how smashing a headline about riots and violence would be for you.

Thank you for your time.

Cordially,

Miss Johanna Berglund

From Brady McHenry to Johanna

February 29, 1944

Dear Miss Berglund,

I thought it wouldn't be long before I heard from Camp Ironside's translator, though I didn't think it would be a typewritten query about policy. I'd have imagined you'd be over the moon with my paper after I printed old Cornelia's rebuttal this week. Jiminy, that letter of hers! I posted half of it, the bottom torn off, in Nelson's Bar and Grill, and didn't I get a dozen men without subscriptions storming into the office later, demanding a copy to read the rest. Signed them all right up.

I don't suppose you'd ever want to submit something? A dramatic exclusive from the woman behind the barbed wire, that sort of thing. My mailbox is always open if you ever do. The POW camp is the best thing to happen to this newspaper since my father's passing.

As for anonymous letters, far be it from me to deny freedom of expression to some poor pseudonymous fellow who hasn't got the guts to jot down his name. It's my journalistic duty to include everyone . . . and to keep up circulation. I'm trying to bring this paper out of its dusty legacy and into the future using all the tricks I learned as an ad man in Duluth.

Best of luck with those Krauts. You're going to need it.

Brady McHenry
Owner and Editor in Chief,
Ironside Broadside

From Peter to Johanna

March 2, 1944

Dear Johanna,

It was good to hear from you. I'm sorry for the delay in writing. My excuse is a pathetic one. Two days ago, we had a three-hour training hike in full gear. It's supposed to be for just the enlisted men, not the civilian teachers, but John Aiso made up some line about instructors setting an example, so away I went, pack and all.

How hard could it be? I asked myself, strapping on my pack.

Answer: miserably hard. We trooped through all kinds of terrain covered in spring slush, carrying supplies for a battle we'll never face here in small-town Minnesota. In between trying to breathe, I kept thinking: I wanted to be an accountant. Lots of numbers, absolutely no sweat involved. How did I get here?

When I woke yesterday, I was so sore I'd have sworn someone ran me over with a Jeep. Now at least I've recovered enough range of motion in my shoulders to lift a pen.

As long as I'm focusing on the positive, have you ever considered the possibility you might be imagining that everyone has a grudge against you? Maybe your friend

Annika invited you to lunch because she's actually your friend. Anyway, even if the company was awkward, you'd have gotten a free meal out of it.

Your camp sounds like it's in the same state Camp Savage was when we arrived. The buildings could have been knocked down with a hearty sneeze, the walls so full of cracks that if you slept too far away from the potbelly stove in the center of each barracks, you'd freeze, but too close and you'd roast. They've made improvements, but of course no one joined the language school for the posh luxuries.

Then again, given the stuffy tar-paper accommodations back at the relocation centers most of them came from, maybe it was an upgrade.

Speaking of which, I know all about having my ability and integrity questioned. Did you forget how long it took for the American government to allow Nisei to serve in the military? Add that to the fact my family and hundreds of other Japanese Americans from the West Coast are still stuck in internment camp lean-tos, waiting for someone to let them go home, and I guess you could say I relate to your frustration. It's bad enough Roosevelt sent them there in the first place, but even now that he's overturned his own order, the bureaucrats are still dragging their feet about shutting down the camps.

My parents write pretty often from Gila River, which is about the same as here in terms of being overcrowded and flimsy but with warmer weather. Marion is enrolled in an after-school calligraphy class taught by one of the older women. She's taken to embellishing the flaps of envelopes with little butterflies and flourishes and is getting quite good, unless it's just my brotherly pride speaking. Between her letters and yours, I get ribbed pretty often during our daily mail call. I've recently gotten rumors that she's mooning over a young man by the name of Harvey Seki, so she's just fine with staying in Arizona a while longer. (I distrust him with the suspicion of a thousand hard-boiled gumshoes, if you're wondering.)

Everyone else, cramped and dusty and idle, would like to be home yesterday, if possible. Thanks for asking after them. I'm sure they'd like to meet you if they could, though Baba would be merciless about your Japanese pronunciation, same as she was with mine.

It's none of my business, but are you lonely there? Baba tells me that's how she feels in the relocation center, partly, I think, because the younger generation all speaks English, even at home. It's a strange kind of isolation, feeling alone even when surrounded by people.

One last thing before I start working on tomorrow's lesson: Keep a rolled-up newspaper around to kill the spiders. You can sometimes dispatch two or more that way. Besides, think of the satisfaction you'll get whacking around those anonymous editorials.

Your friend,
Peter

From Johanna to Peter

March 5, 1944

Dear Peter,

You, Peter Ito, are exactly right. As always.[1] You've gone through precisely the same prejudice I'm experiencing, only much worse, and I'm sorry I was so wrapped up in my own troubles that I couldn't see it.

So tell me: What do you do? How do you prove yourself

successful when you're not even sure you want to? As I see it, I have two possible paths before me: I can do my work with excellence, receiving very little but my town's scorn and an (admittedly generous) paycheck. Or I can prove myself so incompetent or disruptive that Major Davies will be forced to admit this was a terrible idea and hire someone from New Weimer to take my place, leaving me free to escape to my classical tomes.

It wouldn't be so hard, would it, to fake ineptitude? People do it all the time accidentally.

Here are a few of my best ideas on the subject.

Ways I Could Be Semi-Honorably Discharged:

- Create a number of noticeable errors in my clerical work or translation. This is not a serious suggestion. I don't think I could stand it.
- Make myself personally odious to Major Davies. The trouble is, he seems to be absurdly easygoing. He even gets along with his wife, who might be the most irritating person I've ever met. Maybe if I didn't shower for a week?
- Have a sudden injury that would make my work impractical. I could break an arm, fake partial blindness, or contract a lingering case of whooping cough. Too risky?
- Violate minor regulations, such as hemming my light blue Easter dress above my knees to wear to work, or bicycling between the barracks, or loudly singing "*Bei Mir Bist Du Schön*" by the Andrews Sisters at morning roll call.[2] Or all three at the same time.

Did you ever want to do that when you were asked to teach Japanese to your peers who would go back to spy on your family's homeland? Find some plausible reason to get out of it? I'm sure it would have been simple for you to fail a language test and disqualify yourself.

Tomorrow is a momentous day: The POWs will be arriving in Ironside Lake by guarded motorcade. It will be a reverse parade, with everyone gathering to gawk and glare and mutter slurs involving sauerkraut and sabotage as the defeated soldiers march past. Who knows? There might be a protest, even a riot.

I hope the POWs will look so human and harmless that everyone realizes German boys aren't so very different from our own. That, at least, makes sense to me; I don't understand why everyone is so upset.

And as for that last question: lonely, ha! Peter, you should know me better than that. I'm a true Northwoods pioneer, capable of spending long winters with nothing but the howling of the wind and a stack of books to keep me company. Ironside Lake is good for that much at least.

Jo

[1] One day you will be wrong about something, and on that day, I will shamelessly rejoice at your confirmed humanity.

[2] Cornelia Knutson asked me to translate that song for her last week. Apparently she was convinced it was German propaganda until I assured her it meant, "To Me, You're Beautiful," and also that the Andrews Sisters are probably not high up on the list of suspected American traitors.

Evidence for the Prosecution

LEFT IN THE OFFICERS' BARRACKS IN THE REGIONAL
DETAINEE CAMP IN ALGONA, IOWA, AND TRANSLATED
FROM THE ORIGINAL GERMAN

March 5, 1944

Tomorrow, more than two hundred of us, including myself, will be transferred to a town called Ironside Lake (46.7° N, 93.7° W), near the northern boundary of the Mississippi River. They haven't announced this location to the men, so take care not to reveal this information. It is a rural farming community of little interest. With one notable exception: The camp commander has a background I would like to learn more about.

If I discover any information that might be of use, I will return it to you to deliver to our mutual friends, as previously discussed.

They plan for us to return to Algona at the end of November. If I'm unable to contact you before then, we will meet again in eight months.

Heil Hitler.

CHAPTER THREE

Article in the Ironside Broadside *on March 7, 1944*

POWS ARRIVE AT IRONSIDE LAKE

Yesterday afternoon, the sidewalks of Market Street were crowded with an estimated six hundred onlookers as armed guards marched two hundred forty German prisoners of war to the newly opened Camp Ironside.

The procession was orderly, with the only incident of note being a rotten egg hurled from the watching crowd and hitting one of the prisoners in the shoulder. The culprit was never discovered, though the sheriff questioned a group of high-school students stationed on the corner.

Twenty-two of the guards returned by train to Fort Snelling, but the other twenty army men will remain to be sent out with prison work details, as well as to secure the perimeter of the camp. Major Jeffrey E. Davies, the camp commander, led the procession. A veteran of the Great War and a native of New York City, he was also a pioneer in the field of radio cryptography.

Some of the prisoners were Panzer men in German tank lines, parachuters captured behind lines, or submariners brought to the surface by a depth charge, but now they all look alike. Faded shirts with *PW* written in dark letters across the back and on the sleeves form their new uniform. Staff from the Algona base camp estimate that only a third of them speak rudimentary English, with a mere dozen considered fluent.

The latter group includes Captain Stefan Werner, the POWs' spokesman and one of the few commissioned officers at the camp. "Many of these men lived on farms in Germany," Werner stated. "They are familiar with hard work. Their only desire is to be treated fairly by the community."

He acknowledged that his own upbringing was as the heir to the largest meat-packing factory in Frankfurt and that he has never grown a potato. This presents no trouble, however, because according to the Geneva Convention, commissioned officers cannot be forced into labor but may remain at the camp during the day while the enlisted men are picked up and trucked to participating sugar beet and potato farms, beginning midspring.

Depending on rank, officers will be paid a salary between twenty and forty dollars per month for doing no work at all, while laboring POWs will be paid the market rate for farm labor, around thirty-five cents per day. All payment is made in coupons to be used at the camp canteen. POWs are not permitted to have actual US currency, as it might be useful in an escape attempt.

Following the procession, Mayor Carl Berglund gave a brief speech of welcome, addressing the service and patriotism of the army guards transferred here from Fort Snelling. He says he hopes that 1944 "will be remembered as a partnership beneficial to everyone involved."

No reference was made to how the results of the experiment might impact the upcoming fall election, when Berglund will presumably run for a fifth term.

From Peter to Johanna

March 9, 1944

Dear Jo,

By the time you get this, you'll have a full camp. When you get a chance, let me know how the arrival went, but for goodness' sake, stop talking about getting kicked out of your job. You might actually like it if you aren't determined to be miserable.

As for me, I've never wanted to give up teaching here, at least once I started. Where would I go? My childhood home in San Francisco is boarded up, probably vandalized, and my family is locked in Arizona till who knows when. I took this job willingly, and I'm keeping it willingly.

Just so you don't call me perfect or barely human again, here's something I never told you: I didn't take this position out of patriotic duty or a love of teaching. No, I signed up to escape an arranged marriage.

Intrigued? Well, I can't leave all the dramatic revelations to you and fill my letters with nothing but talk of grading and physical training runs.

Don't think all Japanese Americans still honor the practice of arranged marriages—most don't—but the Matsuos are very traditional, and they'd been close to my parents since their arrival in America, so it made sense to everyone to pair me off with their only daughter. Aya was younger than me, a sweet, shy girl, and pretty. She always wore two silver heart hair clips and avoided puddles on the sidewalks.

Those are fine things to know, but most important is this: Since she was fourteen years old, she'd had her heart set on a neighbor of ours, Sunao, and we both knew it. It was as obvious as those musicals where the orchestra swells when the hero and heroine meet for the first time. She walked home from school with him every day, smiling like he scattered the stars in the sky just for her.

After I came back from high school in Japan, I'd ring up Aya's groceries at our family store, and she'd barely even look at me. Not in a blushing, demure sort of way, either. She was afraid of me. Or maybe she feared getting shoved into a life she didn't choose.

The match might have happened regardless—breaking it would have destroyed her relationship with her family. I couldn't do that to her, so when I got a call from a former neighbor serving in the army, telling me about the language school, I realized it was the perfect way out for both Aya and me.

Like I said, Aya's father is a firm believer in the old ways, and my offer to serve with the Military Intelligence Service infuriated him. "A traitor's move," he called it, even though, as a civilian, I won't be sent into active combat. (You've probably guessed, but the reaction of *Issei* to their children's involvement in the war is mixed, especially after Roosevelt ordered us away from the coast and into internment camps.) Not only did Mr. Matsuo call off the engagement, but he hasn't spoken to anyone in my family since then.

So that's how it came about. I'm not teaching for America, but for Aya. She's now married to Sunao, with a baby on the way, at the same relocation center where my parents, sister, and grandmother are being held. I hope she's happy.

In the end, I've found a purpose in this work that I never would have guessed. After the war, I might help with the Red Cross's war-relief efforts in Japan. If you study hard enough, you could join me. (I know you'd never do it, but think of this: Suggesting the idea to your parents might make them feel more comfortable with Oxford by comparison.) It's a beautiful country, and sometimes I miss it.

But here I am, making the best of things. Hope you're doing the same.

Your friend,
Peter

P.S. Where is my baseball news? I demand a full report.

From Olive Bradshaw to Johanna

March 10, 1944

Dear Johanna,

Every time I shelve books in the Modern Languages section and pass your favourite study table, I'm tempted to sob into my hanky. It doesn't seem fair that I've been dying to go back to London for years, and then you're sent back to your hometown against your will.

All that to say, I miss you.

I've done some digging, like you asked me to, with Smythe (stuffy old fellow, isn't he?). He wasn't quite so easy to get information from as the chair of the natural sciences department, but I worked him around to it. I'm afraid he's not lying; he doesn't have the foggiest idea who was funding your scholarship, so that's a dead end. I'll keep an ear open to the university rumour mill as best I can, though.

Another few weeks before the term ends and I'm exiled to Uncle James's home again. Did I tell you Charlie's got it in his head that he wants to stay here after the war and be a farmer, of all things? I very nearly fainted when he told me. Before the Blitz, this was supposed to be a few months' holiday to give Mum time to focus on her work at the hospital. And yet, here I am.

I comfort myself with daydreams of the two of us in jolly old England as soon as that rotter Adolf signs the surrender documents. Though of course I'll have to be the one to make the drive to Oxford for visits, since you'll be so immersed in your books that it will fall to me to pull you away for trivialities like a social life.

Did I mention my older brother is quite dashing? And that I want to introduce the two of you once the Royal Navy finally lets him go? Except do try not to start off with talk of dead languages or dead Greek poets or books in which everyone dies. Morbid is only charming in select circles.

But I'm getting ahead of myself. For an update on the here and now, here's the latest from campus. It takes much longer to write it all out than to say it, so I'll abbreviate, and I'm sure you'll know who I'm talking about: KL jilted BR and asked some fresher to the movies a week later; FS quit the basketball team and no one knows why; HR took first-chair violin from RD, and now they're not speaking to one another.

There, that should satisfy you for a while; I need to read for chemistry. I don't think I've ever written so many words in a row. Three full pages! You ought to frame them.

All the best,
Olive

From Johanna to Peter

March 11, 1944

> German Idiom of the Day: *Ich verstehe nur Bahnhof*.
> Literally, "I only understand *train station*," meaning
> barely anything the person said is comprehensible.

> Context: I translated as the camp doctor—sorry, the
> "post surgeon." Really, the jargon they insist on around
> here—described the scientific details of frostbite to
> shame a POW into wearing gloves while working
> outside. He nodded along the whole time, then, once
> the doctor had gone, grinned and said this.

Dear Peter,

Camp Ironside has gone from ghost town to boomtown
overnight. You were right—the men wasted no time
on making the camp livable. Based on their prewar
occupations, they were assigned to crews, each led by
an expert: a construction foreman, a welder, several
carpenters, and so on. Those who had no relevant skills
hauled supplies and cleared rocks from the road.

In another several weeks, all will be quiet during
daylight hours once most of the men begin work on
the farms, but today it was all hands on deck. It's been
difficult to focus on the paperwork Major Davies gives me,
but almost every day he runs short of administrative tasks
and sends me out to walk among the men, asking for any
needs or concerns. Don't worry—I'm always accompanied
by one of the guards. Even Mother was satisfied when I
assured her of that, although I may have minimized to her
the contact I'll have with the prisoners.

It's comforting, actually. Walking toward the gate
each evening, I'll hear two of them arguing about trivial

matters, such as what sort of meat was in that night's stew and others exchanging outrageous stories of feats from back home, or a strong tenor singing a folk song while scrubbing at the pump. When you can understand them, you realize how ordinary they are.

I wish I could convince the anonymous letter writers and general mutterers of this, but alas, it's not to be. I continue to weather my share of snide comments around town. You'd be proud of me, Peter. Not once have I raised my voice or stormed away in a huff or accused anyone of being a hypocritical misanthrope. The better part of social adeptness, I think, is keeping one's mouth firmly closed.[1]

My German is holding up, for the most part. Regional vocabulary and differences in pronunciation abound, and the rough German of the average soldier—I'll admit, I've made a secret list of profanities so I'll know when I'm being sworn at—differs enormously from the speech of the more educated officers.

Hauptmann (Captain) Stefan Werner, the camp's spokesman, manages to find the balance between them. He watches me as I listen to the men, and if he can tell I'm struggling to understand, he finds a way to rephrase the statement to give me the definition in context so that I don't have to admit my ignorance. It's very kind.

I met him quite by accident earlier this week in a rather humiliating manner. As I walked from the gate to post headquarters early in the morning, I came upon a group of men sitting on a bare patch of grass near the walkway, stretching their arms toward their toes—shirtless, I'm afraid, so a point to the citizens concerned with the impropriety of my employment.

Their leader noticed my confused staring and asked if I liked what I saw, laughing at me, as I'm sure my face was ablaze. It's a trial having coloring like mine, so pale that it gives away every single emotion.

I started to explain myself before I realized we were both speaking English, and his had barely a trace of an accent.

As the men continued to drill, dropping into an uncomfortable-looking stretch where their forearms bore their entire weight, he explained that he was continuing a calisthenics program started in Algona. "I've never heard of our soldiers doing calisthenics like this," I said.

And Peter, didn't he smirk and say, "Maybe if they had, you wouldn't be losing the war."

I informed him that America was not, in fact, losing the war and then asked him how he had learned English. "In 1936, I ran with the Olympic relay team in Berlin. What I saw there inspired me, and I determined that I would do all I could to dedicate my strength to my country again."

I started to say I didn't understand what that had to do with anything, when he smiled and added, "The 1944 Olympics were to take place in London."

Isn't that fascinating? Stefan learned English just for that, and some Japanese too, since the 1940 Olympics were to be in Tokyo. He never suspected the war would cancel both of them. It's easy to see why the men chose him to be their spokesman; he has a natural air of authority. That will serve us well when interacting through him with the POWs, I hope.

Now back to you, Peter. I had no idea you were such a tragic hero, sacrificing yourself for the sake of true love. You've got all the makings of a Greek myth, except without interfering gods disguised as humans. Probably for the best. The arrival of a god or goddess in the mortal realms only seems to make things worse.

Do your parents let you know how Aya's doing? And do I detect the faint traces of a broken heart for the girl who got away?

Either way, you can be glad everything worked out as it did. I learned more from you in three months than I've learned from some professors in two years, so you're clearly a brilliant teacher. America is lucky to have you, even if you didn't take the job for America's sake.

Remind me, when is this latest class set to graduate? I've heard our boys island-hopping through the Marshall Islands are facing resistance even when they outnumber the Japanese 10–1. It seems like the Japanese would rather be destroyed than surrender. What a terrible thought.

You don't think Stefan is right about the Axis powers inching ahead, do you? All of the radio reports imply we're winning the war. They say the Allied forces in Italy are just a few battles away from breaking through into Rome, although casualties have been numerous. It's terrible to say, I know, but it all feels very far away to me.

Tomorrow I begin censorship duties. It seems to be a heavy responsibility . . . and I'm not entirely sure I agree with all of the regulations. I certainly wouldn't want anyone reading my private letters.

Too late now. Like Faust to Mephistopheles, I've sold my soul to the devil—sorry, army—and that means blindly taking orders. Onward, then!

Salutes,
Jo

[1] In one instance where I desperately wanted to quote the Geneva Convention to snobbish Dorothy Lewis, I pictured my mouth cemented shut with Peter Pan

peanut butter, causing me to laugh and Mrs. Lewis to become offended anyway.

P.S./Appendix: Baseball news: No major league teams are allowed to go south for spring training this year, since the military needs use of the railroads and the baseball commissioner is unswervingly patriotic. I got this from Mother, of all people. Turns out she decided to fill the silence of my absence by listening to baseball games. Her team is the St. Louis Cardinals, purely because she read a book called *Meet Me in St. Louis* last November. I tried to tell her this was not a logical way to develop an association, but she's remained steadfast.

Given to Johanna by Major Davies on March 13, 1944

SUGGESTIONS PERTAINING TO THE CENSORSHIP OF POW COMMUNICATION

FROM THE OFFICE OF CENSORSHIP

The only explicit requirements of the Geneva Convention regarding postal regulations are that prisoners must be able to send and receive letters and postcards in their native language, and that any censorship of this mail must be carried out "by the shortest route," without objectionable delay in delivery.

The following guidelines should be followed by all local camp censors:

- For Algona-based camps, the outgoing mail limit is two letters and four postcards per month without cost. No packages.

- Prisoners must be permitted to receive unlimited incoming letters and packages.
- Letters in English may be examined by any trained censor; those in foreign languages must be examined by those who have passed a university-level fluency test. We ask that as much mail as possible be handled on the local level, as the Chicago office is currently overwhelmed with correspondence.
- Mention of any war news, real or fabricated, must be censored. Repeated inclusion of such information, or any information connected with possible sabotage, collusion, or espionage must be reported immediately to the Office of Censorship.
- Personal and familial news is permitted; however, prisoner letters that praise the Nazi regime or encourage resentment of America must be censored in whole or in part. All nationalist content must be removed.
- All prisoners must use the approved letterform stationery. In an effort to prevent any secret messages, its sensitized surface prohibits hidden writing, requires no stamp, and is marked on the addressed side with *INTERNEE OF WAR*.
- Small, incidental infractions need not be reported to camp authorities, merely cut out with a razor. Larger violations (i.e., anything of concern to national security) can result in a letter being Returned to Sender and reported to the Office of Censorship.

Silentium Victoriam Accelerat
The Office of Censorship

From Private First Class Fritz Arnold to his mother
Translated from German and censored by Johanna Berglund

March 11, 1944

Dear Mama,

I am well, but in [CENSORED] now, a place that is colder, but with more trees. At the last camp, in [CENSORED], you could see for miles in any direction. It was like God took a trowel and scraped clean a level foundation, then gave up before building anything on it.

They tell us that in late April, we will begin work at a farm, but until then I am filling potholes and replacing the dining hall roof out in the cold. I don't mind growing American food. Their treaty keeps them from making us build weapons, and beets and potatoes are good crops.

The chocolate here is terrible, though. Not worth the scrip I paid for it at the canteen. We are allowed to spend our coupon wages there on cigarettes, soap, razors, soda, and other small items. I took a bar with the label *Hershey*, and, Mama, it tasted like a tablet of brown wax. I do not exaggerate. Last night I dreamt of *Marzipankartoffeln* powdered with cocoa dust. Even in the lean years, you gave them to us each Christmas season, remember? I wish you could send them now. From now on, I will spend my scrip on model wooden ships to assemble. They have some very nice ones.

I think often of the field where I would play football with Karl, of the way you would gather the chamomile flowers for tea, of Uncle Arnold's exaggerated hunting tales. You must write and tell me every detail you would think is dull or ordinary.

All for now. I am out of space, and if we write more lines, they tell us they will return our letters.

Your dutiful son,
Fritz

From Dieter Bormann to his girlfriend
Translated from German and censored by Johanna Berglund

March 12, 1944

My dear Rose,

Your last letter, written at Christmas, arrived two days ago. What bliss to read your words, dearest!

I'm glad to hear of your father's improved health and that you've perfected a chicory coffee. I'd give anything to see you in that "new" dress you described, made-over or not. You always light up any room you enter.

Only one part made me frown. Please, Rose, don't let your mother keep inviting stuffy old Arland von Bethmann over for dinner—you know just what she's trying to do, and you deserve better than a middle-aged bureaucrat. I'll be back soon, I know it. It's agony hearing you describe your talks with him . . . does he still chew with his mouth open? I'll bet he does. Listen to me: Arland von Bethmann is nothing but trouble.

I've heard a rumor that one of my comrades is planning to start an orchestra here in the camp. Ha! What instruments do you suppose he'll find, darling? I'll play the tin cans with a spoon. Maybe they'll give me a solo part.

Today I asked a guard if he'd ever seen an Indian, and he said dozens of them. They still roam the woods. He said that's one reason there's a fence around our camp, besides the packs of wolves they say live there. Many of the cities here are named in the natives' language to appease their gods, and he warned me never to be seen close to the fence at night—it's within arrow's range of the trees. I won't survive Rommel's campaigns only to die at the hand of an American native.

Are you keeping spirits up? The other day, I heard that [CENSORED]. I wish I could count down the days till I'll be with you again. No matter the number, it would be far too long.

Yours as long as the stars endure,
Dieter

From Captain Stefan Werner to his father
Translated from German and censored by Johanna Berglund

March 12, 1944

Dear Father,

I have waited several weeks to write again, hoping I would hear from you first, but no replies have reached me since I've come to America. Is all well at the factory? Are you in good health? I know letters can take many months to arrive with both Germany and America censoring mail.

We were recently transferred to a new camp. The men are being sent to plant at local farms once the soil is thawed, and they seem relatively content, though this doesn't mean they have no complaints. Recently, they have been, in this order: quality of food, demands for a Catholic priest to hold Sunday Mass, a supply of thicker blankets, and a showing of a Western film starring Marlene Dietrich as a saloon girl.

They come to me because I've been elected camp

spokesman. I can't change everything, but the American commander will usually at least listen, although his executive officer doesn't care for me at all. I often find myself reporting to him at post headquarters these days. Not the circumstances I would have chosen for a command, but one can't always choose.

Tell me all you can of the family. Does Amalie still express an interest in medicine? I'm sorry she is too young yet to serve as a field nurse, but perhaps she might gain training when she is older. I know Aunt Karin is strongly against it, but you must reason with her. One of our female translators at the camp has gone to college, and it doesn't seem to have spoiled her womanhood at all—though she does have a temper, particularly when confronted with inconvenient facts that do not fit with her American ideals.

I've kept up with my calisthenics, but I haven't been able to improve my sprinting time since arriving here. Maybe the next Olympics will be in Berlin again, after all of this is over and [CENSORED].

They say that a representative from the YMCA War Prisoners' Aid will be coming next week, and I will be leading him around the camp. His organization provides recreation and educational opportunities to prisoners. We've heard rumors of what he will bring with him. An easy way to sort one type of man from another is to ask whether he's more excited about the possibility of a library of German books or a Ping-Pong table. I, of course, am with the readers. Finally, a way to pass the long, cold days! If we are lucky, perhaps we will be allowed a movie projector. I haven't seen a film in over a year and greatly miss it.

I'm sure you can guess I haven't heard anything recently about German athletics beyond our own football teams here at the camp. Please write when you can and give me news of how the Wolves are doing, especially any victories.

This is not, I know, what you wanted for me when you sent me off in uniform, proud and brave and foolish. None but God can know where we end up and why. My thoughts and prayers are with you and the rest of the family, and I hope yours are with me.

Stefan

From Johanna to Pastor Sorenson

March 13, 1944

Pastor Sorenson,

I stopped by while you were out visiting the shut-ins, and Mr. Watson interrupted his cleaning of the sanctuary to explain that all of your books are organized by subject matter, era, and theological affiliation, with a special section for books you personally enjoy more than the rest—meaning I couldn't possibly find what I was looking for in your absence.

I have to admit, I'm appalled at this system. Couldn't you sort by last name? Why do we bother having an alphabet if no one's going to arrange anything by it?

Anyway, if you wouldn't mind setting aside a few volumes of Luther for me, I'm trying to find his views regarding the Jewish people. I can't say whether that would be found in a collection of sermons or a commentary, but give me whatever seems useful, and don't worry about the size. I'm a fast reader. I can pick them up on Sunday.

Thank you for taking the trouble.

Johanna (Berglund)

From Pastor Sorenson to Johanna
Left in the front cover of On the Jews and Their Lies *by Martin Luther*

March 14, 1944

Dear Johanna,

Ah. You've stumbled upon a much-discussed controversy. Had you wandered the halls of my seminary when Erik and Annika were just toddlers, you might have caught more than a few heated discussions on the subject, particularly after news of the Kiev pogroms in 1919. Terrible things, and I'm ashamed to say we cloaked academics reduced it to a debate over the division of covenants.

I've placed a marker in the section of the book where you'll want to start. If you want to start. I can't say it's reading I would recommend for a young woman, but then, I imagine you have your reasons for wanting to know. You always do.

It wouldn't have anything to do with your new employment, would it?

I give you this caution: Luther was old when he wrote these thoughts, and deeply pained from numerous chronic illnesses. His frustration was compounded by years of unsuccessful attempts to convert Jewish audiences. That's not to excuse his harsh views, you understand.

Or perhaps it is. Perhaps I worry that in my later years, I will begin to calcify into bitterness, looking at the failed aspects of my ministry and spewing ill-considered words that will become part of my legacy.

Should that happen, I hope someone would reason with me, or even gently guide me away from the pulpit, dearly as I love it. That would be better than leading my flock astray at the end. Will you remember that, please?

Ah, but I forgot. You won't be here long enough for that. It seems so natural to see your face in the congregation beside your parents that it slipped my mind that this is a temporary visit.

As to my organizational system, when one is preparing a sermon on the twenty-third psalm, in haste for a funeral perhaps, one doesn't have time to look up each and every passage to see who might have written commentary on it. Besides, what of Irenaeus and Augustine and their like, who have no surnames by which I could alphabetize?

Peace be with you,
Pastor A. Sorenson

From Johanna to Olive

March 15, 1944

Dear Olive,

Your letter made me smile; it's so good to hear from you. Thanks for trying your best at the detective work. No one seems to know anything about the suspiciously coincidental timing of my scholarship's termination, so I'm doing my best to—as you Brits say—"keep calm and carry on."

Work at Camp Ironside is going as well as can be expected. Nothing particularly exciting, just translating written and verbal communication with the German prisoners. We have an American staff in place to cook and someone to clean the guards' quarters and the post headquarters, where my office and, more important, the commander's and executive officer's offices are located.

The worry, apparently, is letting Germans inside who might overhear or confiscate sensitive information, though I am to serve as chief censor of incoming and outgoing mail, so I'd catch it before it could be transmitted. (Official permission to be nosy—how you would love it, Olive!)

The POWs themselves are assigned to crews to pick up trash, clean the barracks for inspection, wash dishes, and keep the recreation hall and other common areas neat and tidy. This is all supposed to take place after six o'clock supper (I refuse to call it "mess" or "chow line"—really, the military managed to assign the least appetizing words possible to food), or on Sunday afternoons and evenings. We have a good list of farmers in need of help, and I'm sure they won't be disappointed with their new workers. Given enough time, I'm sure the town will calm down, realize they don't need my position, and release me to return to Minneapolis. I'll be back in our cozy flat before you know it.

Thank you for mentioning Oxford. It's easy to get so mired in day-to-day life that I forget what I'm working toward. I know the dons there won't take just any Yank who wanders through their gates, but maybe this translation work will set me apart from those with a similar academic record. I can only hope.

As for your brother—Clive, wasn't it? I'm afraid I call him "Chive" in my mind, as if your parents named all of you after obscure vegetables—I'm never opposed to having tea with anyone, as long as that person isn't dull or arrogant or boorish or overly interested in discussing the weather. But I do wish you'd save your romantic scheming for another victim. If I'm to be truly free to decide what to do with my life after Oxford, I can't be tied down to anyone, not even a dashing British Navy hero.

I'll admit that I have no way of sorting out that alphabet soup of gossip and no desire to attempt it. You know, if you cleared that clutter out of your brain, there would be more than enough room for all the chemical formulas in the world.

Mother made the enclosed mittens for you—she knits compulsively from November until April, as though she feels single-handedly responsible for the survival of Minnesota residents through another winter. (I left the seclusion of my bedroom to sew on the blue buttons, so you might say I contributed.)

Stay warm, and I hope to see you in a few months.

> Your friend,
> Johanna

From Peter to Johanna

March 17, 1944

Dear Jo,

Sounds like things are bustling along at the camp. Beyond the gawkers and newspaper editorial writers, no other signs of unrest? How was morale once the men went off to work?

Way to go with the baseball news. Tell your mother she made a lucky pick for her allegiance. The Cardinals are looking pretty good this year.

As for your spokesperson's story about learning Japanese and English for the Olympics . . . it seems too storybook quaint for a man who's fluent in the lingo of the main combatants during wartime. Much more likely that he completed training just like ours here at Camp Savage to be a spy and code breaker, or at least a diplomatic go-between. Does he know French too?

Be careful around him, Jo. If I've learned anything in this program, it's that people who can speak the language of the enemy are the most dangerous of all.

In Camp Savage news, I broke up a fight this week. I bet you never expected that out of our ramshackle university, but remember these boys are young and hotheaded (compared to my advanced twenty-six), and not all of them take well to nine hours of studying every day.

The commotion started in the gymnasium. I heard the shouting even outside, and inside, the noise was overwhelming, a general outcry mixed with names hurled out by the various sides: *Kotonks* for the mainlanders, *Buddaheads* for the more traditional islanders. There was a tight circle of onlookers around the scuffle, and I had to throw an elbow to break through, the head instructor alongside me. Once John Aiso and I separated the fighting duo, we recognized them as Terry Tanabe and Roy Sakakida. They were breathing hard, and Roy's nose dripped blood onto the shiny wood flooring.

When John demanded to know what had happened, Terry answered, "Defending my people." He is, unquestionably, the leader of the Hawaiian newcomers but is usually even-tempered, grinning his way through any difficulty.

Roy, realizing we were all staring at him and waiting, shrugged. "All I said was, how're they going to translate when they can barely speak English?"

Terry lunged at him again, John straining to hold him back. "We speak as well as you!" Which is true for Terry, from an upper-class family, but most of the Hawaiians use a pidgin English spoken by natives that sounds like uneducated drawl to mainlander ears.

Anyone could see Roy got the worst of the fight, not that he would admit it. Terry's father was a *kendo* instructor on Oahu, and his son must have been at the top of his class. No bamboo swords at Fort Savage, thank goodness . . . but none of the protective armor used in the martial art's sparring either.

Before John could launch into a long list of rules they'd broken and then mete out punishment, I saw my chance. "Are you going to be like the politicians you hate?"

Finally, someone asked, like I knew they would, "What do you mean, *sensei*?"

"Deciding who's in and who's out based on heritage. You're drawing your own exclusion-zone lines right through this school."

I've got to say it was a brilliant observation—sobered them up pretty good. Unfortunately, only the mainland students felt it sock them in the gut. Their families are the ones affected by the exclusion zone.

Besides restricting recreation privileges, John assigned both boys to a study hall. Together. And here's the best part: I'll be supervising. He didn't bother to ask me first, but I covered my surprise and agreed as if I knew exactly what I would do for a couple of hours each Sunday night alone with two students who would rather review chokeholds than grammar rules. I guess I have a few days to figure it out.

I know most Americans think that one citizen of Japanese descent must be the same as another, but it's not true. Besides the difference in the way they speak, the mainlanders are often more reserved and cynical because of the way America has treated them, which can be (and is) interpreted as surliness or snobbishness. The Hawaiians are generally more boisterous and bossy, used to different cultural norms, which can be (and is) interpreted as ignorance and hotheadedness. So it's a mess when we throw them together.

I want to prepare a lesson on the art of not taking offense, not just for Terry and Roy but for all the boys, because you and I both know these young men are going to face prejudice in whatever military unit they end up in. Their fellow American soldiers will bully and belittle them, call them "yellow Japs" and worse, and if there's a fight . . . the Japanese Americans will be the ones blamed and court-martialed. Every single time, no matter who started it. I can't let that happen.

Any advice for me?

Off to plan what might be the tensest study hall of all time. Wish me luck. Maybe I'll just make them do push-ups for two hours.

Your friend,
Peter

P.S. Tragic hero? Me? Ha. If you're determined to make a story out of it, nothing I will say can stop you, and I'll admit that my hapless teenage self wrote Aya a few poems while I was studying over in Japan. But like I said, she was scared of me. It's hard to fall hard for someone who looks at you like you're Al Capone. I'm happy for her. Who knows, maybe someday I'll find a love like hers.

From Johanna to Peter

March 21, 1944

> German Idiom of the Day: *klar wie Kloßbrühe.*
> Literally, "clear as dumpling broth," meaning
> transparently obvious, often used sarcastically.

> Context: A German officer's haughty response when
> a guard asked him if he understood that even he must
> stay far away from the gate so he wouldn't be shot. I
> translated it as, "Certainly, sir."

Dear Peter,

On one hand, it's kind of you to worry about me. On
the other, every single one of Ironside Lake's 1,900 citizens
is worrying about me, so you can leave that to them. I'll
be perfectly fine, and Stefan Werner is no troublemaker.
Yes, he's more outspoken about the Nazi party than many
of the men—most have stronger opinions about which
region makes the best bratwurst—but he knows his job,
like mine, is to keep the camp as peaceful as possible.
Most of our conversations are about items the men would
like added to the canteen or changes to the menu, for
goodness' sake. Hardly anything dangerous.

And now for some cheerful news for you: Today was
Thawing Day. If you haven't heard of it, that's because
Dad made it up. It's a different day each year, usually a
Saturday in late March or early April, but once the first
week of May, when we had a late blizzard. The qualifying
factor is that nearly all the snow must have melted.

Just after sunrise on Thawing Day, Dad gets out his
knee-high rubber waders and sloshes into the muck
of the town, fishing out stray hats, gloves, and mittens
accidentally abandoned and buried in the snow. He has a

near-magical gift for seeing a scrap of soggy yarn under slush, and by now he knows the places with the highest concentration of lost winterwear (school bus stop, diner parking lot, etc.). As girls, Annika and I went with him, digging through the geological strata of natural debris to extract the woolen artifacts. It was the best sort of treasure hunt.

Annika has long been too mature for such things, and now I join Mother in the task of cleaning the sodden outerwear. We haul the old metal washtub from the barn and toss everything in, pounding with a broomstick, then empty the murky water and start again. It's usually three rounds before Mother pulls out the best-looking specimens to throw into our wringer. The rest are subjected to a soaking in her potent brew of stain remover. I don't know all the ingredients, but it involves bleach, baking soda, and possibly arsenic. The barn smells like a chemical laboratory for a full week afterward.

Once everything is as clean and dry as can be managed, Dad strings a clothesline outside city hall, in full view of downtown. He used to hang a sign telling everyone to reclaim any lost items, but by now, people are used enough to the tradition that you can hear people talking about it in the streets. "Saw my first robin today; guess it's almost Thawing Day"—that sort of thing.

This year, owing to the early November snowfall, Dad gathered a record twenty-three mittens (only two matched pairs), fourteen gloves, eight hats, six scarves, three earmuffs, and two socks. "How does anyone lose a sock in the snow?" Mother always proclaims, but we get at least one every year.

As usual, Dad took several trips outside to greet the reclaimers at the laundry line, congratulating children at

the re-pairing of their Christmas-gift velveteen mittens,
shaking hands with the sheepish adults, and telling for the
hundredth time the story of when he discovered his very
own plaid muffler behind our abandoned chicken coop.
He likes to pretend it's a necessary civic duty as mayor, but
I've seen him mark his calendar weeks in advance with a
red star for a potential Thawing Day.

Cornelia Knutson showed up this year, helping me
pin the articles on the line and staying for several hours,
chatting with the women, arguing with several city council
members about what caused the end of the Depression,
and handing out licorice drops to children like she was
running for office herself.

All around a success, I think.

Only a few more weeks until the farm labor begins. The
men have been divided into units based on the number
of workers requested for each farm. They are anxious
to begin—you don't need me to tell you that long days
inside during a Minnesota winter begin to grate quite
quickly. I've heard the men jokingly refer to themselves
as *Kartoffelsoldaten*, or *potato soldiers*. I rather like the
name, and I certainly like the fact that their battles will be
against grubs and weeds instead of our flesh-and-blood
troops.

By this point, I finally feel like I'm in a routine:
paperwork and censorship in the morning, and then
Evelyn Davies usually drops by in the afternoon or invites
me to lunch, where I endure an hour of inane conversation
in exchange for better-quality food than what the mess
hall serves. Do you remember my roommate, Olive
Bradshaw? The one with the British accent who could
say more words in a minute than the two of us could in
an hour—combined? Evelyn reminds me of her, only less

good-natured. Olive only wants to know what's going on, whereas it feels like Evelyn wants to know what's going on so she can actively use it against you.

Afterward, I check in with the POW officers, who will remain within the stockade rather than going to worksites, and sometimes I send a report to the Algona office. Not especially dramatic, but not as terrible as I'd imagined.

Your language school seems to be having more conflict than our prison camp. How goes the study hall? Tip: If they begin shooting spitballs filled with actual artillery, call in reinforcements.

I'm afraid I can't think of a single other piece of advice to give you. If people were simple and diagrammable like a sentence, I'd have an entire instruction manual for you, but they just aren't. It's a shame.

I look forward to hearing how you manage, though if all goes well, you'll only have to keep writing to me until the fall semester begins and I'm released to return to Minneapolis. I hope so, at least. Maybe I should go out to the woods on our property and find the playhouse we built there as children—Annika and her brother, Erik, and I. Erik created a little wishing well near the edge of the stream, and every summer we'd toss a few coins in. I haven't been back there for years.

But that's silly. I don't need wishing wells. Just hard work so Camp Ironside will stay perfectly at peace.

On Thursday we have a special visitor. A man from the YMCA—they work with POWs, both ours and the Axis ones—is inspecting the camp, and Major Davies, from the way he frets, seems to think he'll report us to the Red Cross and that Roosevelt himself will shut the camp down. The major doubled the cleaning brigades and even set some of the men to painting shutters and trim a jaunty navy—probably the brightest color the military allows.

Can I admit something to you? It's awful and deeply unpatriotic, but part of me hopes we will get closed down and I can go back to the Cities. Don't tell anyone. It's not like I plan to bribe any of the POWs to start a riot or even slip a worm into the YMCA inspector's salad, but I won't complain if he decides our men are better off back in Iowa.

But *audaces fortuna iuvat*, as they say. Fortune favors the bold. And while I am many things, a bold saboteur is not one of them.

Jo

P.S./Appendix: Love poems, you say? Is there anything I could do to convince you to part with one of those sappy teenage verses?

EVIDENCE FOR THE PROSECUTION

FROM DR. HOWARD HONG TO MAJOR DAVIES

March 23, 1944

Subject: Report on Branch Camp in Ironside Lake, Minnesota

Dear Major Davies,

I concluded my inspection of the camp while you were out addressing the Rotary Club about the progress of the men here, so I'm dictating this note with my conclusions to your secretary.

Let me first applaud you on a well-run camp. I've made

a personal visit to almost all fourteen of Minnesota's camps, and this is among the most secure, sanitary, and well-ordered I've seen.

For the men's use, I've left a phonograph and some records, an accordion and a trombone (at the request of Otto von Neindorff, your aspiring orchestra conductor), some woodworking tools, and a collection of books in German, as well as a secondhand Ping-Pong table and two chessboards in the recreation hall. These are all provided by private donations to the YMCA for this specific program.

One retired preacher donated his German theological library, which I'm sure the men will find uplifting. Of particular significance for me is Kierkegaard's *Works of Love*, the volume that inspired me to leave my job in academia and join the YMCA War Prisoners' Aid effort. In it, you'll find this passage: "Men think that it is impossible for a human being to love his enemies, for enemies are hardly able to endure the sight of one another. Well, then, shut your eyes—and your enemy looks just like your neighbor." Wise words for us in these difficult times.

I have only one area of concern: the twenty-odd officers who have elected to remain at the camp rather than go out with the enlisted men. Your camp spokesman in particular seemed a restless, intelligent sort who shouldn't be idle for long. Although I'm sure a good many of the officers would find getting their hands dirty to be of some benefit, I suggest providing them with some kind of constructive activity to occupy their time.

In my conversations with the officers, the most frequently mentioned area of interest was English lessons. We have found in other camps that these classes can be a powerful tool for reeducation. Readings are pulled from classic American rhetoric, and instruction can also be given in the benefits of a democracy. Who knows what fruit the seeds of this instruction might one day bloom into? In fact, in New Ulm, they've had students asking about the process to become a US citizen after the war.

I'm sure your designated translators are quite busy—I've heard you have only three guards with basic German fluency. But if you can spare one of them, the YMCA will supply readers, paper, and other supplies for a classroom.

Actually, come to think of it, what about that woman civilian translator who accompanied me today? I'm sorry, I can't recall her name. I was a university professor before taking up this job, and there's something about the way she looks you right in the eye and fires away answers that exudes authority. She might be a natural teacher with that sort of confidence, and I don't doubt that she could keep a room of privileged German officers in line.

The main thing is to make sure the curriculum is straight-down-the-line pro-American. It will lean toward indoctrination, I'll admit, but for a good cause. If your translator accepts the job and does a fair job representing our country, she may have the most significant position in the camp.

Don't hesitate to call the main office if any needs or concerns arise, and keep up the good work, Major.

Dr. Howard Hong
Field Secretary,
YMCA War Prisoners' Aid

CHAPTER FOUR

From Johanna to Peter

March 27, 1944

Dear Peter,

I know I just wrote you a few days ago and you haven't had time to reply, but this is an emergency. A crisis. No time even for a daily idiom; I'm too distressed.

By now you're probably afraid I've been kidnapped and held hostage at improvised knifepoint after a Nazi riot in the mess hall, but I'm fine. My family is fine. The men in the camp are fine. Everything is fine. Except for the one thing that is very much not fine.

They've ordered me to teach an English class. Starting in three days. Three!

I should have known better than to take a job with the army. This time, their particular brand of Faustian cruelty involves propping me up in front of the officers— the officers, Peter—to educate them about the American government. Can you believe it? Major Davies seems to think they'll all be waving flags and whistling "Let's Knock the Hit Out of Hitler" by the time they're through.

I've never taught anyone in my entire life. Well, no one but myself, and that doesn't seem like a transferable skill. When I tried to explain this to Major Davies, he wouldn't hear a thing about it. For such a jolly fellow, he knows how to railroad a person into doing exactly what he wants, this time by means of a long-winded anecdote about his work during the Great War on radio transmissions. Something about increasing the range of aircraft technologies, and how he was given some task that everyone said couldn't be done, and he did it anyway. "Miss Berglund," he said, "you simply need to reimagine what is possible."

What am I going to do?

Write me as soon as you can with the best teaching advice you have. If you don't receive a reply, it's because I've run away to Canada to roam free with a herd of moose. Don't bother looking for me if you're planning to bring me back, and promise on our friendship that you won't reveal my location. Until the war is over and I can return without being press-ganged into education, I will subsist mainly on maple sugar and any squirrels I catch in a homemade trap.

Please send help.

Jo

P.S./Appendix: Attached is the latest editorial from the *Broadside*. Needless to say, it hasn't been a good day. Maybe I should have gone to the wishing well in Turner's Woods after all. What am I doing here, Peter?

Editorial in the Ironside Broadside *on March 24, 1944*

Dear Editor,

I had every intention of holding my peace about the POW camp. Frankly, I was in no state to say anything, worried about my Jimmy, like every other mother with a son overseas.

But yesterday I finally heard from him, a form letter addressed from a prison camp in northern Japan. It was dated three months after his capture. Think of it—ninety days of not knowing whether my boy was dead or alive.

Even in the uncensored sentences of his letter, his handwriting was weak and shaky. They're starving him to death, I just know it. I've heard the news reports from our boys who have seen the brutality of Japanese soldiers. Until we win this war, my Jimmy will be beaten and forced to work until he collapses—and that's if he doesn't contract some sort of horrid tropical disease like malaria.

At the end, he says, "Please don't worry about me, Ma." That was the very worst. Because no matter what hellhole he was trapped in on the front, his letters were always so cheery, making jokes about his fellow soldiers and the long mess lines. He censored himself, my Jimmy—I know it. So what is he leaving out this time?

I could fret myself to distraction trying to picture the horrors he must be facing, while only a half mile away, we mollycoddle the Axis ringleader's own men, bringing them musical instruments and books, letting them write endless letters home filled with sensitive information, no doubt, and serving them Communion, as if there is anything Christian about this terrible war they caused.

Enough, I say. I can't get justice for my Jimmy, but I can spread the word about what he's going through. Those Japanese are using the Geneva Convention for toilet paper, and if Mayor Berglund can't put some sensible limits on the rights, entertainment, and luxuries allowed to the POWs, then I say he's siding with the enemy. I believe any sensible patriotic citizen would agree with me.

Mrs. Martha Yeats

Telegram from Peter to Johanna, picked up at the Ironside Lake Post Office on March 29, 1944

REMEMBER THEY'RE MILITARY. VOCABULARY DRILLS.
START INSTRUCTIONS IN GERMAN, SLOWLY PHASE OUT.
SPEAK WITH CONFIDENCE. YOU ARE THE MOST CAPABLE
PERSON I KNOW. LETTER TO FOLLOW. PETER

From Peter to Johanna

March 30, 1944

Dear Jo,

I should have said *package* instead of *letter*. I've enclosed the best book I have on pedagogy. Look for my notes in the margin. That will give you more help than anything I could say here, though it's geared toward training linguists rather than average men.

Please ignore the pictures. Roy nicked a few of my books during our first study hall when my back was turned; apparently he aspires to work for *Detective Comics* someday. (The session was mostly sullen silence between Roy and Terry, by the way. I'm hoping for some improvement this week.)

Don't forget—nothing you say can change anyone's mind. You can pack your curriculum to the brim with patriotism, like my elementary school did, and it might have no effect at all. It's not up to you to make the POWs advocates for democracy. Just do the best you can to help them learn the language.

I'm sorry about Mrs. Yeats's letter. Even if she's exaggerating about conditions in the Pacific, it's a well-known fact that Japan hasn't kept their end of the Geneva Convention. They see POWs as combatants, captured or not. Then again, when a country is starving, how can it spare rations for the enemy?

At this point, I'd do almost anything to make this war end as soon as possible. When I think of my family in Japan and my family in the internment camp . . . we're all trapped until it's over.

Sorry, that was depressing. It's been a long week. Hmm, something light and happy . . .

I know! I started ukulele lessons yesterday. How did this happen, you ask? Well, last night, stumbling bleary-eyed from the teachers' lounge after a crash course in radio transcription, I heard music coming from the students' barracks, and based on the sound quality, it wasn't a radio station, but a student giving an impromptu concert. Normally this wouldn't be an issue, but it was halfway through the mandatory two-hour study period.

Study period, according to John Aiso, is "no time for frivolity." Frivolity is scheduled during meals, on Saturday afternoons and evenings after exams, and sometimes Sundays, so long as the student's religion allows that kind of thing.

When I knocked on the barracks' door, the music stopped. One of our new Hawaiian recruits, Makoto, sat on the stool in the center of the room, surrounded by a knot of attentive listeners, including Terry Tanabe, all standing around him like he was a Wurlitzer jukebox at a soda shop.

Makoto didn't attempt to put his ukulele away, just gave me a watermelon-slice grin and asked, "What d'you think, sensei?" before bursting into song.

To my surprise, the song was our fifty-word kanji vocabulary drill from that day set to a melody that he explained was a love song about a waterfall. A mellow little tune to be paired with military vocabulary, sure, but if it helps, why not?

When Makoto offered to teach me how to play, I agreed, then almost immediately wondered if it was a good idea. (Maybe because Terry was glaring at me. Ever since the fight, I haven't been his favorite person.)

Remember how terrible you are at Ping-Pong, swatting the air in nearly the opposite direction from where the ball was hit? After my first lesson, I think I've finally found a skill where I'm just as bad as you. I'm probably dishonoring Hawaiian culture more than showing an interest in it.

That's the only funny story I can dish out this time, but I'm sure you'll have some tales about your first days of teaching. Vent all you like. I wish I'd had someone to do that with when I first started out, but I didn't meet you until eleven months after moving to Minnesota. I could never complain to the other teachers here. They're all a decade or two older than me, and sometimes I feel like they can sense weakness.

I meant what I said in the telegram, Jo. You can do anything you set your mind to. Let me know how it's going.

Your friend,
Peter

P.S. The poems were mostly *somonkas*: two stanzas forming a love letter and a reply, with a set number of syllables for each line. But no, I can't send you any. Just because you're not advanced enough in Japanese to understand them, of course. That's the only reason. Not because they were horrible and I'm embarrassed of them. (I never have been very good at writing love letters.)

From Johanna to Peter

April 3, 1944

German Idiom of the Day: *seinen Senf dazugeben.* Literally, "to add one's mustard," meaning to put in one's opinion.

Context: An opportunity to do so was given at the latest meeting of the camp's men with the major. Enough mustard was added to grace every hot dog in Fenway Park, on everything from not enough latrines to more German food on the menus to a ban on playing the accordion after a certain time of night.

Dear Peter,

My earlier letter was slightly dramatic—I'm embarrassed about it, actually. Now that I have a full week of teaching behind me and another several planned, I'm surviving. I've created a makeshift lesson planner, commandeered some secondhand readers from our elementary school, and feel significantly better now that some details are ordered and listed out. How much more straightforward life looks when one has a plan.

Thank you for the telegram and the book. Your notes

were very helpful, although I'll admit, I'm now privy to more secret information about your program and its methods than I ought to be from reading them.

I'm trying to apply what you said, but it's difficult to speak with confidence to men nearly twice your age, half of whom would rather be anywhere else. At least your students have motivation to learn and to respect you. Most of the officers think they're smarter than me—which isn't true by half—and some resent being required to attend even two hours of class each day. How they managed to rouse themselves from laziness to actually command a war, I can't imagine.

The one bright spot is Captain Werner. I can't tell you how helpful it is to have him there. He pretends to be learning too, but I know he's just there to help the others, and me, when necessary. It really is a shame the Nazis got to him so early. He's convinced Hitler Youth is the equivalent of our Boy Scouts. I wonder sometimes what sort of man he would have been without the propaganda. What do you think, Peter? How much of who we are is determined by where we were born and other factors entirely out of our control?

Outside of the stockade, there was quite a buzz about Mrs. Yeats's letter. Dad had to make a public statement, reminding the citizens of what the Geneva Convention requires and assuring them that the American government has no plans to break their agreement just because Axis powers may have done so. It was a convincing speech, I thought, but you'd have to be deaf to miss the grumbling in the crowd afterward.

That was when I reread your last letter, and there it was: the bit of advice I needed. I know I've said it before, but, Peter, you're brilliant. You've given me an excellent idea to put into action. I'd give more details, but I have another letter to compose.

Oh, and I demand a personal ukulele concert when I'm back in Minneapolis. I confess I can't picture what the instrument looks like. Mother tells me one was played in the Gracie Allen picture *Honolulu*, which inspired Mother's desire to visit Hawaii someday. She's started a fund in a Dole pineapple can and is up to $15.68. Your story prompted her to flip through all the Matson Lines brochures she requested before the war from an agency in Duluth, whereupon imaginary travel occupied the rest of our evening. It was a surprisingly stress-reducing activity, so I suppose I should thank you for that too.

It's a good thing you don't keep a running tab, or I'd be so deeply in debt, I'd need a personal Second New Deal to bail me out.

Aloha,
Jo

P.S./Appendix: You may have given me more motivation to study Japanese by wagering your teenage somonkas on my abilities. Unfortunately, but not surprisingly, the Ironside Lake Public Library has not a single book on Japanese, so I am stranded in my mediocrity for the time being.

From Johanna to Brady McHenry

April 3, 1944

Dear Mr. McHenry,

You seem to be a man who appreciates directness, so I'll get straight to the point: I'm writing to propose an idea.

All my attempts to win people over to the possibility that the men in the prison camp are just that—men, and ones as worthy of dignity and good treatment as their own sons—have failed.

So I thought, Why don't we let someone else have a turn? And who better than the prisoners themselves?

If the *Ironside Broadside* will agree to print it, I'm proposing a column written by a different German soldier each week.

I will handpick the prisoners and translate their writing. There will be a diverse list of acceptable topics for them to choose from, including their life here, their family back home, or their hopes for the future.

Given this angle, I don't think people will be tramping to your press with buckets of tar and pillowcases of feathers, but I can't promise there won't be resistance. However, I believe this is worth taking a stand for.

Thank you for considering my proposal.

Miss Johanna Berglund
Translator, US Army

From Brady McHenry to Johanna Berglund

April 5, 1944

Dear Miss Berglund,

Yes, I accept unconditionally.

Miss Berglund, you brilliant girl! Do you know I've had an uptick in subscriptions at a rate of 32% over the past several months . . . and climbing? Everyone wants to hear about the POW camp, not because they like it or agree with it, oh no. Because it's interesting.

I happen to admire interesting. Daring too. And this

stunt of yours has both in spades. If we play our cards right on this one, we'll trump every last naysayer in this town, and I'll pull this paper out of red and into black.

But don't settle for writers who will churn out something blandly sentimental. Human interest is all well and good, but I want controversy, suspense, pathos! If you wanted something to give people warm feelings, you should have suggested a weekly homemaker tip, not a first-person column from our enemies. It's never been done, probably, in the whole country. And we're going to do it. Yes, by golly, we are.

Seems like you've got a flair for drama, so play it like a Dickensian author writing a serial on spec and add whatever your little heart desires. I'll do the rest.

Since these are prisoners, I'll send payment in copies for them to keep. There's nothing like the thrill of seeing one's name in print. If all our reporters were *pro bono*, I'd be one happy man.

Good doing business with you. I'll get the news out midmonth. Send me that first column by the twenty-first. You can have up to a thousand words, if you like—I'll bump the stock market to the back page if I have to. Bulls and bears can't compete with news like this!

Brady McHenry
Owner and Editor in Chief,
Ironside Broadside

April 5, 1944

Dear Pastor Sorenson,

Thank you for the use of your book. I'll admit, even after your warning, it was discouraging to read how much Martin Luther hated the Jews, wanting to burn their synagogues and expel them from Germany. It's no wonder the German citizens made no protest of the ghettos—their hero, the founder of their church, would have supported them.

And here we are in Ironside Lake, naming our building, our entire denomination, after this man. Why was he never held accountable for those terrible words?

One particular prisoner, Captain Stefan Werner, quite smugly informed me that Luther himself was cited in Hitler's propaganda, which I vehemently denied. Today I will have to go to him and admit that he had his facts correct after all. He'll smile at me with a look that implies a knowing, "See? We were right all along about the Jews and their influence, about our *Lebensraum* and racial hierarchy." And I will have nothing to say to him.

I always have something to say.

If this is what I find in the writings of the Church, perhaps I ought to stick with Greek tragedies. They might be more uplifting.

Johanna

April 7, 1944

Dear Johanna,

I do have an answer to your question, but I don't think you'll like it.

The one who will hold Luther accountable is God himself, who knows our hearts and can judge rightly. It is not idly that the apostle James warns that not many should be teachers of Scripture, "knowing that we shall receive the greater condemnation." There but for the grace of God go I.

And yet, I must remember: God is gracious, much more than I deserve. That is a comfort.

Even so, if we struck from the annals of sainthood every man or woman who spoke or wrote amiss, there wouldn't be a shrine or stained-glass window standing in all of Europe. Though, with all the bombings and shellings in the past several years, perhaps there won't be anyway.

I'm sorry. You didn't write to me to hear the mutterings of a grim and grieving man during wartime. I shouldn't have written on Good Friday, when all my thoughts turn to darkness. You are young and shouldn't be troubled with such things.

Speaking of which, I feel I should ask: Why do you write to me instead of speaking in person? I know I haven't been around when you stop to call, but I keep such regular hours that you could certainly modify your visits accordingly, and the parsonage is only a short walk from your home. I would be happy to speak to you about these things. When Erik was alive, you were at our home almost

as frequently as your own. I wish for those days again.
Often.

I hope this will not spoil Easter Sunday for you. To
me, it is the most blessed of all days, the light after the
darkness. And God knows we could use some light this
year, more than ever.

Peace be with you.

And with me, and with all of us.

Pastor A. Sorenson

A draft of a letter from Johanna to Pastor Sorenson, never sent

April 9, 1944

Dear Pastor Sorenson,

~~You're right that I didn't find~~ your answer ~~entirely
satisfactory, but at least it~~ gave me something to say to
Captain Werner. The exchange went much as I pictured
it: I had to admit what Luther had written but maintained
that he was wrong, that the Jews are just as much the
neighbors we are commanded to love as our own family
members.

He looked at me steadily, ~~emanating his usual calm~~,
then said something odd. "You speak of love. Well, I
love the human race. I love justice for past wrongs. I love
my country. And therefore, I must hate the Jews, not
personally, but for the sake of protecting all that I love.
Just as you Americans hate us Germans to protect what
you love."

I'm still thinking about it. Could it be true that love
requires hate? It's infuriating to me that, lacking a
coherent reply, I was forced to change the subject, asking

him to find a writer for an experimental newspaper column I'm attempting to start.

As for your last question, since I don't have your gift for tact, I'll just say it. Yes, our families have been friends for a long time, but I hurt your son and your daughter ignores me, and if that doesn't affect your view of me, you'd be a poor father indeed.

That's why I prefer to write to you, instead of meeting you in that office where Annika and I used to hide under the massive oak desk, trying not to giggle when your polished Oxfords got close enough for us to touch, smelling your pipe smoke as you paced, muttering fragments of Scriptures and sermons.

Those days are gone, I'm afraid. As a member of your church, I feel confident enough to borrow from your library, but as your daughter's former friend and your deceased son's former . . . whatever I was to him, I don't feel confident enough to meet your eyes.

I am a coward, Pastor Sorenson. It's that simple.

I hope you're right about God being gracious. ~~I think I sometimes test the limits of that. Does he listen to me anymore, do you think?~~

From Johanna to Pastor Sorenson, left in his office

April 10, 1944

Dear Pastor Sorenson,

Thank you for taking the time to reply. I will think about what you've said and will let you know if I need additional resources.

I'm sorry if I've offended you by writing, but my hours

at the camp are sometimes so irregular that I can't spare the time for a long visit.

By the way, Evelyn Davies, the camp commander's wife, had me over for tea earlier today and said the Easter Sunday sermon was "almost as compelling as the ones from my church in New York," which from her is like saying that you are the next great revivalist and ought to have your own radio preaching program. I would certainly tune in.

Thank you again for the book.

Johanna

From Peter to Johanna

April 10, 1944

Dear Jo,

I can hear birds out my window as I write this morning. Isn't it great how winters never last? Even if spring does make the grounds of Camp Savage into a swampy bog of mud.

A group of us always goes into Savage for church, and we added a few extra for Easter yesterday. (Even some who consider themselves, at least culturally, Buddhists. They heard there was going to be a potluck dinner afterward and made a temporary conversion. I'm telling you, missionaries should go out armed with homemade rolls and deviled eggs.) I'll admit to startling when I saw a blond woman in a blue Easter dress a few pews ahead of me, but of course it wasn't you.

What you said about what Captain Werner would be like if he'd been born on this side of the Atlantic . . . that's a question that's bothered me for a long time. How much of us is deliberate choice, and how much is society and conditioning and circumstances?

For example, my parents converted to Christianity before I was born, mostly to be accepted by American society. Both consider religious faith private, so I don't know how sincerely they practice. Sometimes I see the Shinto shrine and garden our students built on the grounds and I wonder: How much of what I believe and who I am is based on something fake? Or, put another way: Who would I be without the propaganda of America?

I guess that's why I wanted to go to high school in Japan, not for adventure or to meet my extended family, but to find out who I was by learning where I came from. I can't say I've sorted it all out yet.

But tell me: What did I suggest that was so brilliant?

Precommencement exams are in less than four months, the first graduation we've had with the accelerated curriculum. We're under pressure to make sure each student passes with flying colors. Fort Snelling is always looming, asking for progress reports and sending us news of the battles with Japan as if we've forgotten we're at war.

I've enclosed a short note from Terry, my Hawaiian troublemaker, to you and your mother. He and Roy are progressing in study hall, meaning that sometimes they even talk to each other without being forced to, but barely. On the positive side, their rivalry means that the enemy-soldier roleplay dialogues I have them act out in front of the beginners' class are worthy of Broadway.

Terry had a few suggestions if your mother ever manages to wrestle enough money from your thrifty father to make the trip. (I'm sorry about the postscript, but he refused to rewrite it, and you're the only one censoring letters, so I let it stand.)

Your friend,
Peter

From Terry to Johanna

April 10, 1944

Aloha, Johanna!

Finally, I have an excuse to write to the woman I've heard so much about. Not that Sensei Ito blabs your letters to everyone, but school takes up so much of our lives that there's not much else to talk about outside of it, you know? Especially stuck in study hall with that Kotonk they've paired me with.

He told me you were interested in Hawai'i, my home. You can't go now, obviously, since Uncle Sam isn't keen on boats full of Kodak-clutching *haoles* getting torpedoed in the Pacific. But don't worry; once the other boys and I get out there into the field, we'll end the war before you know it, and then tourists will be welcome again.

Here are my tips, better than any travel agent would give you.

- If you have a chance to go ashore and explore the lava caves, wait for a guide so you're not surprised by incoming tides.
- There have been rumors for years of building an airport in Honolulu. The war stopped all that, but if you can fly and avoid the steamers, do it. Mainlanders are sometimes seasick, and you won't see much if you're heaving inside your cabin for ten days.

- Be sure to peek in the Royal Hawaiian's lobby even if you can't afford to stay there. Or even their parking lot. I've never seen so many Rolls-Royces in one place. Someday, that'll be me, just you wait.
- Don't run around so much that you can't enjoy the ocean. These lakes you try to pass off as water in Minnesota are nothing. And don't get me started on the snow. Give me the sand and salt and coral of my home any day.

If you make it to Oahu, I'll show you the sights free of charge!

Terry Tanabe

P.S. Try to lie out on the beach awhile too. I saw that picture of you and Ito propped up on his desk, and both of you could use some island sunshine. (You might as well bring him along . . . Hawai'i's a better place for romance than family vacationing, if you catch my drift.)

From Johanna to Peter

April 13, 1944

German Idiom of the Day: *mit den Wölfen heulen.* Literally, "to howl along with the wolves," meaning do as those around you are doing.

Context: Captain Werner's answer for why so many Germans joined the Nazi party.

Dear Peter,
I feel like every new development here is the last straw, but this one just sets me fuming every time I think about

it. Do you know the latest thing my beloved hometown is upset about? The army commissary allowed the POWs ham for Easter dinner, and everyone just about went crazy when they heard about it. Yes, it's a rationed food and many of us did without this year, but I think it's rude to spend a religious holiday pointing fingers and raising a riot over one narrow slice of quick-cured meat per man.

The *Broadside* proceeded to publish the camp's monthly menu, which our staff of civilian cooks breaks down into minute detail. The guards receive butter allotments, while the prisoners only get oleo. Still, the outrage continued until our head cook cut out three chicken dinners and three meatloaf ones from the monthly schedule, replacing them with frankfurters and beans. Can you imagine? It's utterly childish.

Which is why I'm quite sure now is the time to put my plan into action. Your stroke of genius was your reminder that nothing I say will change anyone's mind. You see, I decided to let the POWs speak for themselves in a weekly newspaper column I've requested. As camp spokesman, Stefan will solicit and guide the writers, I will translate and accept the wrath of the town anytime someone says something objectionable, and Mr. McHenry will publish them so his sales will boom.

That's the least appealing part of this: being forced to work alongside Brady McHenry. His father was a reasonable man, if overly meticulous—when you saw a red slash on a notice reading "Ladie's Tea" or "Scrap Drive, Will Except Any Metal," you knew you'd spotted the terrible, swift sword of the Mighty McHenry Senior. Unfortunately, with his younger son off in the air force when the older McHenry passed away from a heart attack, it landed on Brady to keep the *Ironside Broadside* going. He seems to prefer sensationalism to reporting. We have a Zeus-Poseidon relationship, existing in uneasy teamwork to get things done despite our mutual dislike. (I suppose it would be more patriotic to say a Roosevelt-Stalin relationship. I think you can guess which of us is Russia.)

Too busy to write a long letter—must get our latest collective brilliance off the ground. The newspaper will announce the column on Monday. I don't know if I've been so excited and terrified since I held my letter from the University of Minnesota, not knowing whether there was an acceptance or form rejection inside the envelope. I'll certainly be the talk of the town (again).

Jo

P.S./Appendix: Thank Terry for the advice on Hawaii, although I certainly won't be taking the tips on sunning, since I burn in the back seat of our truck on the way to the lake if the windows are open. I wish he wouldn't tease you about me, though. Poor Peter.

Notice at the bottom of the front page of the Ironside Broadside *on April 17, 1944*

Dear Readers,

You may have noticed—my typesetters certainly have—that we've been overrun with opinions about the prisoners of war recently relocated to our humble town. While we at the *Broadside* understand the camp is breaking news and desire all of our citizens to make their voices heard, we also must hold unswervingly to our mission of covering a wide range of subjects.

Therefore, to better serve our reading public, from now on, all editorials related to the prisoner of war camp will be restricted to the weekend edition of the paper. If you're only subscribed to our weekly package, sign up today at the *Broadside* office, and we'd be happy to add this to your subscription. Don't miss a single opinion from your fellow citizens!

In addition, the *Broadside* is pleased to announce a new regular column, also in the weekend edition, called "The POW Potato Brigade," written by prisoners in Camp Ironside and translated by our own Ironside Lake native Miss Johanna Berglund. We at the *Broadside* are sure you'll find their unique perspectives on life at home and abroad fascinating.

It's always a joy to share the news with all of you, especially in such trying times.

Yours in the freedom of the press,
Brady McHenry
Owner and Editor in Chief,
Ironside Broadside

From Johanna to Brady McHenry

April 17, 1944

Mr. McHenry,

First of all, I have to say: That was shameless, using the column as a publicity ploy for your Saturday edition. Don't deny it—you don't care a thing about the prisoners, just your profits.

Besides that, you didn't say a word about the purpose of the column, which explains why I've already had a half dozen people accuse me of broadcasting Nazi propaganda. One particularly irate citizen called me at home in the middle of my favorite roast beef dinner and swore a blue streak at my father when he wouldn't hand the receiver to me. You could have spared us that by clarifying, or better yet, letting me make the announcement in my own words.

I've enclosed the first article, and I wanted to let you know that I'm keeping a carbon copy locked in my desk drawer to compare with the final. If you or your editors change anything other than grammatical errors, I'll charge right down there straightaway. I want people to hear these men as they really are, not use them as some sort of window display to sell more headlines.

I'm working with you because I have to, not because I like or trust you. Bear that in mind, please.

Johanna Berglund
Spokeswoman for the POW
Potato Brigade

From Brady McHenry to Johanna

April 19, 1944

Dear Miss Berglund,

Such suspicion! Tsk, tsk. Calm down, sweetheart. Somebody's been watching too many Hollywood pictures about disreputable newspapermen. I promise, I'm much more *His Girl Friday* than *Citizen Kane*. Good intentions and all that. Golly, have a little faith in your fellow man. (Then again, I guess you're no man. Gentler sex, my eye!)

Of course I'm using this little column of yours to encourage more subscriptions. I'd never dream of denying it. Humility is for people who don't have any brilliant ideas.

I can't see why you're upset. You want everyone to read the prisoners' column. I want to sell papers. This makes us both happy. Chin up, my dear. You've just been raised in the bland flour gravy of Scandinavian miserliness for so long that your instinct is to be suspicious of any attempt at making a profit. (I've written enough articles on your old man to know that much—he collects and washes the paper coffee cups after city council meetings to reuse them.)

About the content of the announcement: I gave people just enough information to keep them interested. Let them fill in the details with their own imagination, the suspense building as they wait for the first installment. I can practically feel the tension crackling in the air today, can't you?

Rest easy, little translator. I won't edit a thing beyond commas and apostrophes. You deliver the columns; I'll print them. We'll go to bat for those Jerries together, you and I. And Ironside Lake will never forget it.

Yours in the freedom of the press,
Brady McHenry
Spokesman for Common Sense—
and Cents

Note from Stefan Werner to Johanna, left on her desk after English class

April 18, 1944

I will have the first article to you by the end of the day today for you to translate. It should be quite entertaining. No quotes from Luther, so no need to worry.

I have not said it before, but I admire your courage in associating yourself with us. Careful, or you will find yourself the most popular figure in our humble camp. There is already talk of the orchestra dedicating its performance of "Lili Marlene" to you. Are you familiar with the song?

There is a request I wish to discuss with you. May I take a minute to speak to you after class tomorrow, in private?

—S

EVIDENCE FOR THE PROSECUTION

EXCERPT FROM THE TESTIMONY OF HELMUT ARNOLD, PRISONER OF WAR AT CAMP IRONSIDE TRANSLATED FROM GERMAN

We all knew our mail was being read by the Americans. They told us that along with the other rules about the camp life, and we were only allowed to write on the stationery they gave us at first. I think this was to control the length, as Miss Berglund—the nice woman who started the newspaper column—would have to read and censor them. After a few months, Captain Werner told us that they had relaxed the rules and we would be approved to send mail in other forms, but only on special occasions.

In May, I sent a birthday card to my mother this way, which the foreman of the farm I worked on bought for me. Others sent a postcard or anniversary card. Those were all approved.

Captain Werner sent letters of his own, I think. He always seemed protective of those. One time, I was on cleaning detail of the German officers' quarters and saw him hunched over a writing desk. Whenever I swept the broom past him, he'd shield what he was writing. Once, I teased him about having a secret sweetheart, and he grumbled about Germany being his only love.

Then he changed the subject to what kind of movie I'd want to see if the commander allowed an outing to the theaters. After I said a Western, with outlaw train robbers, he said something odd, which is why I remember it. "Here's something to remember, Helmut: The ones who tell the best stories always win."

He was a private man, the captain. Always friendly, but the sort who is hard to get to know. My father was like that, God rest his soul. He had only a very few friends, but for them, he would do anything. A good man.

As to how we were allowed this change with the letters, I cannot help you. Captain Werner only said that it was something approved "by special arrangement." I never thought to question it.

I do not know if Miss Berglund was involved. Captain Werner talked with her and seemed to like her, but he liked everyone, and everyone liked him. That is all I can tell you.

CHAPTER FIVE

April 20, 1944

Dear Johanna,

Glad the stay in your hometown hasn't killed you, dear. Didn't I tell you you'd be just fine?

I laughed so hard when I got to your comment about Clive/Chive that I nearly tipped my chair. He would think it's funny too. You'd just adore his sense of humour. It set me to thinking of alternate names for my younger siblings. Here they are, in order of age.

Tom: Tomato, naturally.
Rachel: Radish
Aubrey: Aubergine (Or "eggplant" to you Yanks.)
Charlie: Celery, maybe?

As for university news, one of the fraternities hosted an ice-cream social last week, where I finally got to meet GB (you must remember him, after all I gabbed about him to you). We got off well enough. I told him what I was studying, and he smiled broadly. Just when I thought I might have stumbled upon the only chap in America who wasn't surprised that a woman might be interested in chemistry, he said, "Have you thought about studying the molecular structure of dish detergent?"

Dish detergent, Johanna. As if the only possible application of my field of study must be squarely within the realm of domesticity. I fumed silently, all the while thinking, If I were Johanna, I would tell him to his face just what I think of that. But of course, I only smiled. Then I spent the next half hour hearing him recount victories on the athletics field. So that was a failure on all fronts.

Speaking of men . . . Peter (your Peter—I can never remember his last name) asked me over dinner last week if you'd said anything to me about a Captain Stefan Werner. I quite honestly said no, but it makes me wonder. Should I be concerned? Is there some sort of forbidden romance I should know about? Do tell all.

All the best,
Olive

The POW Potato Brigade column in the Ironside Broadside on April 22, 1944

> *Translator's note: Throughout, the game Americans refer to as soccer will be called by its German name, "football." Helmut insisted on this, because "you kick the ball with the foot . . . what other name would it have?"*

From what we hear from the radio (there is one in the camp recreation hall now, near the record player), Americans love

118

their baseball, boxing, and basketball. We listen to descriptions of games, though we know only some of the English words. You can tell by the announcers' voices when someone has scored a point or landed an impressive hit, but that is all the excitement that happens.

Football is about more than scoring or beating another man senseless. It is the only bloodless war.

Before the war, the football club in my town had been run mainly by Jews, so when they were sent away, I was worried it would close down, but the Reich Committee for Physical Education took control. To join the new club, you had to have two recommendations to prove you weren't a Marxist. (Maybe Marx liked football? I'm not sure, but they were very worried about Communists.) To be honest, I don't know what it means to be a Marxist, but I don't think I am one. Back then, none of it mattered. I just wanted to play.

Here, we are permitted to practice all kinds of sports at the camp during our time off. Since many of us are from Hesse, my team calls ourselves the Hessian Foxes, a mascot that is fast and clever and light on its feet. Our main rivals are the Rhineland Stallions. Sometimes we jeer at them about slaughterhouses and how their animals are destined for glue.

It's a well-known fact that the Stallions cheat, and also that they stole the cigarettes I hand-rolled from tobacco I bought at the canteen, only none of them have admitted to it.

The guards often take bets on who will win games, each having their favorites, and they watch us on Saturday nights, cheering and booing. We Foxes started with long odds after tryouts but are now winning more often than we lose.

I play defense, unless our goalkeeper, Dieter Bormann, gets stolen away by his orchestra practices. Most of the time I am good at it. But whenever a man doesn't know the power of his kick and the ball sails out of the field, I freeze. Even if I'm the one nearest the ball, someone else has to go fetch it, because I remember the day a man in the camp I was at before this one ran to retrieve the ball that fell between the warning fence and the outer fence of the compound.

The guard shouted at him once, twice, and then shot him dead. I watched it happen.

They told us he had been warned before, several times, about going near the fence. There would be an investigation. But that didn't change the fact that a man had died for no reason.

You might think that would make it hard for me to love football again, but it hasn't. I never leave the bounds, though, not even one centimeter.

I've been distracted from my argument. Here are more reasons football is a superior sport:

Football encourages teamwork. In other sports, one player can outshine all the rest and win nearly single-handedly, but not in football. We must all win together, united.

It is also a good remedy for stress and boredom. There are not many amusements for men inside a barbed-wire enclosure. Before we got a football, Hans, the man in the bunk next to me, carved an entire chess set out of soap, he was so bored. (He got very angry when I washed my hands with one of the rooks.)

Also, football is much more interesting to watch than baseball. I apologize to your Joe DiMaggio, but it's true.

In conclusion, football is the best physical activity outside of dancing, but since they don't even like the camp secretary to speak to us socially, the chance of us getting permission for a dance is low. Although there are many pretty girls here in America.

Hessian Foxes forever!

Helmut Arnold

Note from Stefan Werner to Johanna, left on her desk after English class

April 24, 1944

Excellent lesson today, but your constitution has a number of blind spots, as I see them. Should we have a class debate sometime? There is nothing officers enjoy more than a spirited argument.

I heard the men talking about Saturday's article, all of it very positive. They could hardly believe it was in a real newspaper, not a mimeographed bulletin like the Des Moines men make just for those in the camp. Helmut is puffed with pride, but the stallions are plotting their revenge for the next football game.

—S

From Johanna to Olive

April 24, 1944

Dear Olive,

No, you shouldn't be concerned about Captain Werner. Forbidden romance? I hope that's just your embellishment to get a reaction from me and not what Peter actually told you. Either way, it's nothing but pulp-novel nonsense. The captain is very intellectual, and we sometimes have good-natured debates during and after English class about the freedom of the press during wartime, or whether America was right to send athletes to the 1936 Berlin Olympics. That is all.

Sometimes I can hardly tell he's German at all, other than a faint trace of an accent; his English is that good. He attributes it to the dozens of American movies he's seen—apparently the Nazi government prefers German-made films but allows approved Hollywood pictures as well. For example, *All Quiet on the Western Front* was banned (strong antiwar message), while Laurel and Hardy films are acceptable (they're favorites of Hitler's, who is quite the movie buff). All very fascinating.

But most of our conversations relate to business around the camp. I can't very well ignore the camp's spokesman just because an overprotective friend in Minneapolis disapproves of him.

I'm surprised to hear you had supper with Peter—I didn't know he was thinking of taking you out. Of course, you met when we went to that movie together last fall, but he so rarely comes up to the Cities.

Anyway, don't let him encourage you to snoop on me from a distance, especially as you study for your exams. I hope they go well, and be sure to greet your Victory Garden–catalog family for me when you visit your uncle for the summer.

Sorry to write so briefly. It's been quite busy lately, partly because the POWs are headed out for the first week of farm labor today (soil preparation, mostly), but also because of a new scheme of mine to help public relations with the town. I'll write you a longer letter later.

Your friend,
Johanna

From Peter to Johanna

April 22, 1944

Dear Jo,

Good to hear from you, as always.

You might get annoyed at me saying so, but I think it was perfectly reasonable for people to object to the POWs' Easter ham dinner. I know the army isn't on the same ration rules as the rest of us, but thinking of enemy soldiers enjoying a treat you can't have yourself would make anyone annoyed. Maybe it doesn't do any good to complain about it, but be careful that you don't take the POWs' side right away without thinking things through.

I don't know how you thought of a column after reading my letter, but it's a swell idea. I only wish I could come up with something helpful myself, because morale is getting low around Camp Savage. Not a sudden drop, just a slow, limp weakening, like soba noodles in boiling water.

Military Intelligence Service's higher-ups have been asking why, and we keep trying to tell them it's a 9066 problem. That's Executive Order 9066, the relocation act that moved the coastal Japanese Americans to the camps. Most still haven't released our family members—something about "orderly process" or "administrative difficulties."

Instead of promising to exercise pressure on the relocation centers to move things along, the army decided to deal with flagging morale by sending us a guest speaker. Yesterday Staff Sergeant Dye Ogato stepped smartly at attention before an assembly of all our students. He graduated from our program back in 1942 and then served in the Pacific. As soon as he was introduced, I noticed the Purple Heart pinned to his lapel. A genuine decorated

Japanese American veteran, paraded in front of us like a zoo animal.

Ogato told us about transcribing captured diaries and reports on the island of Bougainville, writing propaganda to be scattered in enemy territory, and searching downed planes for any scraps of writing that might provide a clue to the Japanese army's plans. He sprinkled in everyday stuff too: the humidity that made your uniform cling to your back; the way he and his fellows tried to imitate the accents of the New Zealand troops sent in to reinforce them; how he'd sleep lightly in his jungle hammock, ready to roll out and into the nearest foxhole at the first sound of gunfire.

"The island was so quiet after sundown that you could hear the slightest sound," he said, and the room got quiet as death too, all of us listening to his every word. "I could actually hear the bombs released from the low-flying planes . . . including the one that nearly got me."

He managed to dive into the ditch air-raid shelter just as the bombs hit. Most destroyed the divisional headquarters, but one hit just in front of Ogato, and the ground caved in around him.

The only air he had was the tiny pocket he'd captured by putting his hands over his head before impact. So he started to dig frantically, clawing on all sides, until even that air was gone, filled in by falling dirt. "All I knew was the sky was up there somewhere, and I was going to do everything I could to see it again," he told us.

It took an hour before anyone came close enough to hear his cries for help and dug him out. They'd all assumed he'd died in the direct strike, like others had. That's what got him the Purple Heart . . . and a few bruises and broken bones. His commanding officer called him "the luckiest man on Bougainville."

After another year of service and a more serious wound, they discharged him from active duty to teach at a Japanese language school for Canadian troops, much like ours. That's where he was headed after speaking to us.

Don't get me wrong, Ogato told a great story, and it's always good to know our graduates are making a difference. Still . . . I don't know. Maybe I'm too sensitive (not getting much sleep these days with all the work they put on us), but it felt like we were being manipulated.

I'm telling you, Jo, the boys leaned forward like they were watching the final shootout in a John Wayne movie, picturing themselves in Ogato's place. Now all they can talk about is coming home with a medal pinned to their uniform.

Meanwhile, the *Hakujin* students (the non-Japanese Americans) clustered together in a group as they usually do. You could tell they knew it was all a ploy to convince the Japanese Americans that the United States would treat them fairly. They of all people know that's not true.

But it worked, and that's what matters, isn't it? The day after the speaker, my students attacked their studies with new energy. Propaganda again. It's a powerful thing, whether used for good or evil . . . or something in between.

Speaking of good or evil, I'm keeping up with the ukulele lessons. Do you have a favorite song? Hopefully a slow, simple one. If you say "Boogie Woogie Bugle Boy," I think I'll cry. Makoto's been very patient in teaching me, maybe because he likes laughing at me, but still, that's something. Every time I get ready to junk the whole thing,

I make a little improvement, and then I can't give it up. I guess the only direction is forward!

> Your friend,
> Peter

P.S. Ogata told us there was an Associated Press article about him after his decoration, but it only said the Purple Heart had gone to "an army specialist whose name and work is unmentionable because his job is a military secret." It made me realize . . . I've shared more with you about the training school than I should have. Civilian mistake, I guess. I'll have to be more careful now, and you can forget all the things I've told you about our classes and the MIS and fieldwork.

From Johanna to Peter

April 26, 1944

Dear Peter,

The column's out! So far it seems like the gamble paid off. Oh, there are a few who are upset—Mr. McHenry forwards those letters on to me like a Hollywood diva's fan mail—but my first column writer was a baby-faced twenty-year-old named Helmut, as obsessed with sports as he is uninterested in politics.

My main interaction with Helmut has been explaining to him that he can't construct a beer garden because the camp store will not be selling alcohol. ("But, *Fräulein* Berglund, they let them drink at the camp in Texas. I have read it in letters!" To which I responded that there are a lot of things they do in Texas that are barely legal in the rest of the country.) He's stubborn but so cheerful and charming about it that you can't help but smile. I hope he had the same effect on those who read his column.

Dad has always been my barometer of the town's general mood, and he's cautiously optimistic that the days of protest are over. "The news of the hour only lasts sixty minutes" is a truism he's been repeating lately. I overhear the occasional disparaging remark while in line at the post office, but for the most part, Ironside Lake is back to discussing the weather, or when strawberry-picking season will start, or why mothers are protesting the Golden Palace Theater's showing of *Double Indemnity*. (Answer: adultery, murder, and a scene with Barbara Stanwyck wearing nothing but a towel and a terrible blond wig.)

Which means I can spend any free time I wrest away from Major Davies catching up on my reading—*Le Morte Darthur*, which I've always heard of but never actually read—instead of reassuring Mother or preparing statements for questions Dad will face at the next city council meeting.

Inside the fort, my work continues to go as planned. Yesterday one of the guards drove me around in an army-issue truck to meet the farm management at each location that requested labor from the camp, some with fewer than a dozen workers, the largest employing thirty-seven. Though I realize it's only been a few days, it was encouraging that morale seems to be steady, and only one of the farmers, Old Man Lundquist, had any complaints (accusing one man of "making eyes" at his granddaughter when she came to bring them water in the afternoon). The POWs, it seems, work at a slower pace than most Americans, but they follow orders and work together well.

The men have been clamoring to see the latest movies, and Captain Werner has tried to persuade Major Davies that it would be good for morale. Things have been so calm lately that I tend to agree. I might write to Dr. Hong at the YMCA to see whether he thinks it's a good idea. Major Davies certainly won't do it; he has an irritating habit of taking weeks of hemming and hawing to consider even the slightest change. Better to take matters into my own hands.

Back at the camp, it's comforting to see the prisoners building and filling bird feeders with seed, constructing picnic tables, and lining the barrack walls with family pictures—and the occasional pinup girl. It's starting to look slightly less barren here.

Have our roles reversed at last? It seems I'm feeling more optimistic, and you less so. I can see why morale might be flagging, but I'm glad the speaker was helpful, though I can't imagine your boys being excited by the reminder that they might be bombed and buried alive. What a horrible thought. I'm grateful you're a civilian instructor here in Minnesota instead of curling up in a South Pacific foxhole.

I don't recall you mentioning before that you had any Caucasian students. How many of them are there? Are they mostly university students? I can't imagine there's no tension between them and the rest of the students. Or is the mainland-Hawaiian divide so sharp that everything else fades into the background? Tell me all about it.

As for music, I heard more than my fair share of big band while running the dance hall. Sinatra's "I'll Be Seeing You" seems simple enough. Actually—you'll think it's silly—I bought the record to play when I went to Minneapolis, because the way it goes through all the "old familiar places" made me think of it as my good-bye song to Ironside Lake. Before moving in with Olive, I would play it almost every night, humming along before drifting off to sleep. That was when I thought I wouldn't be coming back, of course.

If you want a challenge, try "Lili Marlene," a favorite of all the men here. There's an English translation, but it was originally a German poem from the Great War. It's cloyingly sentimental, probably even more so than your teenage somonkas:

> Underneath the lantern
> By the barrack gate
> Darling I remember
> The way you used to wait
> 'Twas there that you whispered tenderly
> That you loved me.

And so on and so forth, love and loss and longing and everything that makes a song climb the charts. I'm told Radio Belgrade would play it every night to sign off its broadcast, and the troops in Africa, both Axis and Allied, would listen to it before they went to sleep. Maybe they still do.

I've got a stack of letters to censor tonight, so I'll leave it at that.

All the best,
Jo

P.S./Appendix: So you've been feeding me military secrets? No cause to worry on my account; I haven't broadcasted them far and wide. My parents have always known the vague outline of what you do. They're quite proud of you, particularly because they also know about your family in the camps. (Dad is always going on about how it's "unethical and unfounded.") And I've mentioned you a few times to Captain Werner, but he was only fascinated that the United States would trust Japanese immigrants, so it was a good opportunity to explain the citizenship process. No one else even knows I have a friend in MIS, and I'll be sure to keep it that way.

From Rose Schlitter to Dieter Bormann
Translated from German and censored by Johanna Berglund

March 17, 1944

Dear Dieter,

I have received your latest letter. Actually, I have received three of them this week, all from early winter. Please, why must you use such flowery language? You know Mama reads my letters before delivering them to me, and it's humiliating to answer her questions. I'm very fond of you, but as I recall, there was no understanding between us when you left other than my promise to write.

Not much news. The war goes on, and we try to go on with it. I was quite a sensation last week at the *Heldengedenktag* celebration in Mama's pearls and my green crepe dress that perfectly matches my eyes—not to mention the meat pie I made, decorated with a plaited pastry swastika. Everyone went on and on about it as if it was actual art. It was almost embarrassing, the attention I got all night, when Arland was the real hero. He secured us the beef—not even from a can. I didn't ask how. He's such a dear for giving it to us for the party. Meat has been so rare these days that I'd almost forgotten what it tasted like. My mouth waters just thinking of it: tender and full of flavorful juices.

Which reminds me: I won't stand for you mocking Arland like you do. Yes, he's older than I, but he's an industrious man and invaluable to the war effort—the Reichsbank is the largest financial institution in Germany, you know. On top of that, no less than Walther Funk himself visited Arland's office last week to commend them for working extra hours, melting gold rings into bullion. (Arland said there were thousands . . . I wonder where they got them?) Imagine, meeting the minister of finance, shaking his hand! Besides, he's quite distinguished and wealthy, and an excellent conversationalist. I quite enjoy his company.

I hope you're in good health and that you hear from your family often. Keep soldiering on.

Rose

From Otto von Neindorff to his wife
Translated from German and censored by Johanna Berglund

April 24, 1944

My love,

What joy it brings to hear news of home, however far away! I'm afraid my letter won't be so homey, but I'll do my best. This one is all right to read to Christa. I know some of my letters from the front were frightening for her, and I'm sorry. War is a hard thing for anyone, but children should never have to know its horrors.

In fact, let me write my latest news as one of the stories

I'd tell her each night before she fell asleep. We will call it "The Mystery of the Phantom Music."

Once upon a time, there was a locked, walled city with a little chapel in the center. The men who lived in the city could not leave, and they were so brokenhearted about losing their freedom that they abandoned all music.

But there was one man, a soldier, who stole away to the chapel on Sunday nights to play the battered piano. Sometimes it even pushed away the nightmares he had when he closed his eyes to sleep.

One night, as he stood at the chapel door, he heard music coming from the piano already, different than any he'd heard before, haunting in places, bright and sprightly in others. For a long moment, he stood in the doorway, listening. Then he stepped inside and called, "Who's there?"

The music stopped, and by the time the soldier found the light, the door in the back slammed shut. Puzzled, the soldier decided it must have been another prisoner, perhaps one who was timid about his ability. He practiced as usual, but the mystery kept him awake late into the night, until he arrived at an idea.

The next Sunday, the soldier came early to the chapel and hid inside the confessional in the back, watching, waiting. Soon, a stranger entered. His skin was very dark, and he was not wearing the uniform for the walled city. But he sat down at the piano like a king on his throne, and the music that followed was like a magician casting a spell, so real and fresh that it came alive.

When the soldier left the shadows of his hiding place to tell him so, the dark-skinned musician startled. "Don't go," the soldier said, even though he could tell they spoke different languages. The musician stopped and stared, trying to understand. "Keep playing," the soldier said, pointing to the piano.

And that was when the magic began. Because when they played the piano, each demonstrating their favorite songs, they found that they could both understand the music, which said all they needed to say. And that night, the soldier slept peacefully, his dreams filled not with gunfire and death, but with jazz and Mozart mingled together.

It is a good story, I think. The happiest I could find from my time here so far. The musician, Raymond Harrison, works in the kitchens here. I had seen him clearing away dishes to be washed, but I never guessed what a gift he had.

Now I am out of room, though I have tried to write as small as I'm able. I am glad to have a friend here, and music, though I miss your lovely soprano to sing along.

Give Christa all my love since I can't be there myself. This fairy tale might not have the ending we would choose, but you are both princesses to me.

Yours always,
Otto

From Olive to Johanna

April 27, 1944

Dear Johanna,

For your sake, I'll banish the torrid German-American romance I was about to send to a producer. (Only joking, dear—don't get upset. You're always far too serious.)

Though I have to say, it's not so baseless as you seemed to think. You may be prickly, but you look after the outcasts, Johanna. I expect that's why, out of all the people in Minneapolis, you became friends with Peter, the almost enemy, and with me, the lonely, unwilling expatriate. In this case, though, someone could easily misinterpret your softheartedness toward this Werner character. (Is he handsome? I bet he's handsome, and that's even more trouble.)

As to your worry that Peter and I were on a date (don't deny that's what you were after), there hasn't been a social gathering less like a date and more like the regional conference of a scientific journal. You know I can read intentions like a Piccadilly Circus billboard, and while Peter's a nice enough fellow, he clearly asked to meet me to talk about you.

Which, come to think of it, worries me. I know he's your friend and you like to talk about linguistics—thank heavens, as he has probably spared me from a half dozen conversations about gerunds—but remember: If he begins to want more than friendship, you will only hurt him. You're going to Oxford as soon as you graduate and can afford the steamer ticket. He's going back to his family in California once the war is over. That means in a few years, there will be 5,000 miles between you, not to mention the racial difference. (You should see how people stared at the two of us at the soda fountain. My word, I've never felt so much like a criminal.)

You were right about one thing, though: Exams loom, and I must get back to organic chemistry. It's in moments like these that I want to be back in the sunny breakfast nook with Mum, reading the *Times* out loud to each other and spreading a thick layer of butter and marmalade on toast (no need for rationing in a daydream). Somehow, I'll forge ahead.

Oh, and don't write to me again here—I'll be at the farm soon and will send you a letter from there so you'll have my new address.

All the best,
Olive

From Annika to Johanna

April 29, 1944

Jo,

The Lutheran Daughters of the Reformation asked if I'd extend an invitation to you to speak at next Tuesday's meeting. Or more specifically, Cornelia Knutson did. She thinks you're the Good Samaritan incarnate and that the rest of our charity projects are wastes of time compared to the opportunity "on our very doorsteps."

You probably don't care what I think, but I'm going to tell you anyway.

It made sense to me, you taking the translator job. I even hoped that once you came home we might . . . well, things might go back to where they were before. But I don't know what you're trying to do by making the Germans seem sympathetic and kind.

How can you do it, Jo, knowing what happened to Erik?

If he knew what you were doing here, it would break his heart. And you already did that once, when he was alive. Erik gave his life for his country. For you. Against those men in the camps.

That's probably not fair, but I won't take it back. I'm

tired—so very tired—of letting you be the outspoken one, the one who always gets the final word and speaks her mind and expects the rest of us to meekly agree.

I know you're only doing it because you want to be free to return to the university. But for once in your life, Jo, think about how this will affect someone other than yourself. Think about how it feels for me to read that column every week knowing it's making celebrities out of our enemies.

Please let me know what you think about speaking at the LDR meeting, but I'm sure you'll understand why I won't be in attendance.

Annika

From Johanna to Annika

April 30, 1944

Annika,

I would—maybe should—have this conversation with you in person, but this way I can be sure to keep my temper in check and say only what I mean.

I never wanted to hurt Erik. I certainly never wanted him to die so far from home. But don't think for a moment you can blame that on me or say that my current work with the prisoners of war is somehow insulting his memory.

These men are brothers too, Annika. Most of them are around Erik's age, and some of them write regularly to sisters and mothers and girlfriends back home. I want Ironside Lake to view them as human beings and to treat them accordingly.

Yes, I want to go back to the university. I've never pretended otherwise. But that's not the only reason I'm doing this, and if you can't read the column, no one's forcing you to. Use it to line Augustine's litter box or even out your crooked coffee table leg for all I care.

Please send Mrs. Knutson and the rest of the LDR my regrets. I don't wish to speak to them. If this is the kind of hostility I should expect from the people who are supposed to be on my side, then maybe I'm better off with the enemy.

Johanna

EVIDENCE FOR THE PROSECUTION

FROM PETER ITO TO HIS FATHER, THOMAS ITO,
ENEMY ALIEN INTERNED AT GILA RIVER
WAR RELOCATION CENTER

April 23, 1944

Dear Father,

All is well at Camp Savage. My students are improving, but I don't know if it's happening fast enough. Between the long runs and the hours of study needed to keep up, some fall asleep with an open textbook as their pillow. They can't stand the thought of shaming their family or their country.

Are you still headed home next month? I wish I could take leave to help you move, but it's unlikely. Fort Snelling is cracking the whip, adding to our coursework while cutting our time till graduation, and still expecting the assembly line to work as fast as ever—like the Bible story of the Israelites in Egypt making bricks without straw.

To help, they've recruited more Hakujin teachers as enrollment rises, professors from the University of Michigan and Harvard who have only a head knowledge of the language. I should be grateful for the new forces, but it's hard knowing the good ol' USA could do so much better if they'd just listen to us.

Roosevelt canceled the executive order to relocate. Why not let the elders from the internment camps teach? The ones who are native-Japanese speakers, not second-generation slack-offs like me who dozed through Japanese classes as kids. "Stuck in the past," we kids would mutter before running off to baseball practice with our "real American" friends. Well, now the past has become the present, but Issei still aren't allowed to teach at our MIS school. No exceptions. The army refuses to trust someone born in Japan. Most of the time, they don't even trust us.

And maybe they have good reason not to. With all of the favoritism and red tape, it's enough to make us question our loyalties. I've talked about this with Jo too, the one person I know will understand and even sympathize, even though her situation is different from mine. Writing to her is the main thing keeping me sane.

When you get back to San Francisco, if you find my old gum company baseball card collection, use it for a fire starter. All of that seems silly now. But keep your love letters to Mom, the ones you wrote during the year you and Baba Yone immigrated to America ahead of her. That's family history—and no one should ever throw away letters to someone they care about.

Give my love to Mother, Baba Yone, and Marion. (Is she still seeing that scrawny, pomade-greased kid from San

Diego? Remind her again that he'll be five hundred miles away once you all go your separate ways. And also that her big brother hasn't approved him yet.) Don't pass on all my worries and frustration. I'm sure they've got plenty of their own.

Your son,
Peter

CHAPTER SIX

Delivered to Major Davies by Captain Stefan Werner, camp spokesman

May 1, 1944

Dear Sir:

We, the undersigned, respectfully request that we be allowed to worship as we choose. Every day we see the war bond poster put up by our English teacher, Miss Berglund, with artwork of people of different backgrounds praying and the words, "Each according to the dictates of his conscience." When I asked her if America would honor this belief, even for prisoners of war, she instructed me to write this petition.

Currently, a retired Baptist army chaplain comes to the chapel once a month, but on other weeks, services are led by a Catholic priest. Many of us are not Catholic and wish that a Protestant service be made available to us each week, even if sermons are in English.

We know it is difficult in this remote countryside to find

pastors available on Sundays to preach a second sermon. However, many of us have friends in other camps who say that their guards transport prisoners to a church in town. If no pastor can be found to come to us, we ask your permission to go to them.

Thank you for your consideration.

Signed,
Captain Stefan Werner,
representing thirty-two men of
Camp Ironside

From Pastor Sorenson to Major Davies

May 3, 1944

Dear Major Davies,

I will tell you honestly: Had I known what you were coming to ask me yesterday when you arrived at my door, I might have slipped out the back. Instead, I have wrestled with your question and, finally, have arrived at a reply.

When I spoke of this with my daughter, Annika, she began with practical questions and concerns, then as I addressed each, ended with an impassioned, "But, Daddy, they don't deserve to be allowed here, after all they've done."

I must say, I'm inclined to agree with her.

Ah, but none of us get what we deserve, and that is a profound grace. There's the trouble.

My heart tells me not to permit German prisoners to sit as parishioners in my church. But "God is greater than our heart, and knoweth all things."

I don't know if you are a religious man, Major, but I'll share with you a secret that isn't often preached from

141

pulpits: Sometimes showing grace breaks us before it heals us. Forgiveness can feel like a betrayal of justice. We want others to *deserve* grace, or at least ask for it, even knowing full well that the greatest grace was extended to us "when we were enemies."

I'm rambling again. I do that, you know. None of my sermons end on time, except sometimes the baptisms, if the babies begin crying too loudly. But this time I will own my self-deprecation for what it is: stalling to avoid writing what I know I must, in order for you to understand.

Here it is, then:

Your request is more personal than you might have realized, unless perhaps you've heard. The grapevine, I'm afraid, is more like a thriving vineyard in Ironside Lake.

You see, my son, Erik, died in North Africa while serving as a chaplain. As this is the same region where the POWs were captured, the simple fact is that one of your prisoners might have killed my son.

I had hoped to be able to get through the next several months with general goodwill toward them from a safe distance. And then you knocked on my office door.

I feel broken tonight, because I know what God is calling me to do, and I do not want to do it. My reasons are perfectly just. It might cause a fracture in my congregation. It might endanger my flock, whom I am called to protect. It might lead to any number of fears and failures that leave me unable to sleep at this late hour.

And yet. We are called to obey and forgive and love, even when we can't see the outcome of our choices.

Therefore, you will have my full cooperation if Camp Ironside should choose to send prisoners to attend Immanuel Lutheran Church. Our services begin promptly at 10 a.m., and I will do my best to prepare my congregation in the next several days. It may be difficult for them to accept. My plans for this week's sermon will need to be altered significantly, I think.

We will have a section reserved for the prisoners near the back, and I will in this case allow an armed guard to bring his weapon into the sanctuary as you requested, though I wish this were not necessary. Please instruct the assigned guard to be as discreet as possible.

Pray for us, Major, if you think of it. Pray for me. And do not allow me to change my mind: What I have written, I have written.

Pastor Anders Sorenson

From Stefan Werner to Johanna
Left on her desk after English class

May 4, 1944

My men who attended the movie on Monday in town all tell me to thank "the YMCA man" for providing funds for them to see it, giving it rave reviews. (As for me, I thought the overreliance on backlighting the detective, not to mention the flashback fades, felt dated. But our theater was not full of highbrow critics.) I'm surprised the major contacted the YMCA to make it happen. When I spoke to him last, he seemed to dislike the idea.

The newsreels before the feature were more interesting to me, especially the item on Nazi collaborators within France turning against and turning in their neighbors. The voice-over expressed disdain that anyone would make such a choice, and yet, I wonder how long your American ideals would last if it were your country that was occupied. How many of those you work and shop and pray alongside would be willing to turn on you, for the right price?

I ask because I know you like philosophical questions such as these. It is very interesting to think about.

Our cinematic outing also inspired our next columnist, who I believe has become something of a friend of yours. It is attached here. I think you will enjoy it, if your paper is bold enough to print it.

—S

From Peter to Johanna

May 2, 1944

Dear Jo,

You're not the only one more interested in our white students than the Japanese American ones. I didn't mention them before because they're a small minority, although you can't miss them with their fair hair and surnames like Bowers and Meyer. I think we have thirty or so sprinkled through all levels.

Some are young missionaries or businessmen who spent a few years in Japan, and their skills are quite good. Most are horrendous. Those conned their way into the school by showing up in Washington and pretending their few phrases qualified them to become linguists, which immediately got them a commissioned officer position.

Not the Japanese Americans, though. They're all privates or privates first class at best. The army hasn't handed out gold bars to a single one of them, though there's talk they will soon, again because of morale. Tacking a title onto a Japanese American won't solve the real problem, though. The Hakujin literally stand apart, clumping together for meals, spending their free time together, speaking English after class even though the program is supposed to be full immersion. If you ask me, they're holding themselves open to resentment.

Anyway, some good news—in just a few weeks, my family will be leaving the Gila River camp for San Francisco. Finally, one question answered. There are others still open: Will any of the furniture or clothing in storage have mildewed? Will Father be able to make a go of it with his grocery with all the anti-Japanese sentiment? Is Marion still on track to graduate high school next year, or will she need to repeat a grade?

If you've guessed I'm worried about them, you're right. Father says I fuss too much, but he doesn't know how it feels to be so far away when they really need me.

Thanks for the song suggestions. I'll give them a try if I have a chance, but Makoto's been bleary-eyed from study lately, so we had to cancel the last two lessons.

How's *Le Morte Darthur*? That's King Arthur and Camelot, right? The baseball team I played on as a kid was the Knights, so I checked out my fair share of illustrated legends from the library. I tried to get the boys to call me Galahad, but it didn't stick. "Gal," though, did, which, looking back, I should have seen coming.

And with that bit of trivia, I'll have to call it a night. But first, some tea! Green tea, which your British friend

Olive said tasted "like tepid grass clippings." Don't worry;
I forgave her. Eventually.

> Your friend,
> Peter

From Johanna to Peter

May 8, 1944

German Idiom of the Day: *Wo sich Fuchs und Hase
gute Nacht sagen.* Literally, "where the fox and rabbit
say good-night," meaning the middle of nowhere, the
wilderness.

Context: Stefan Werner asking me why I left the city to
come back to this place. My answer needed no idiom:
"I don't know."

Dear Sir Gal,
(Come on, you knew I wouldn't be able to resist, which
is also why I will never tell you any of my childhood
nicknames. Most were mean-spirited—you won't be
surprised to hear I was a loner as a child.)
You'll never guess what's happened. The POWs were
allowed to go to church. My church, Immanuel Lutheran,
whose faded pews haven't seen anything more unexpected
than Cornelia Knutson's outlandish hats in decades.
It was printed in the Religion section of the *Broadside*,
which usually only runs dull announcements supplied
by the ministers. Even Brady McHenry, who before this
hadn't darkened the door of a church since his father's
funeral, couldn't deny that Immanuel Lutheran was real

news this Sunday. I've clipped the article out so you can read it.

According to Annika, the Lutheran Daughters of the Reformation, which forms a significant percentage of the women congregants, were loudly divided on her father's decision to allow the POWs to attend our service . . . until they read the article, which they almost unanimously agreed was moving. (The exception was Mrs. Lewis, who is furious that they used "damning" in an article about church—she's probably censored hell and damnation out of the pew Bibles as well. I might flip through Revelation next week to check.)

Imagine that. Brady McHenry did something good for once. I suppose that through his outsider's perspective, the LDR women saw how much their little church looked like Jesus, against their will or not. I'm still shocked myself. Pastor Sorenson is a good man, but he's always reminded me of a bowl of oatmeal: consistent, traditional, and slightly bland.

But enough about me. How wonderful that your family can return home! I only hope they find California a friendlier place than when they left. From what I recall in the news from 1942, it was pretty bad on the West Coast. Isn't that why the MIS Japanese language school moved to Minnesota?

Speaking of which, I'm sorry if I upset you by asking about the Hakujin, but it seems to me that you're showing prejudice too. When your mainland and Hawaiian students literally came to blows, all you wanted was a way to create peace among them, while it seems like you're treating your non-Japanese students as an annoyance to be rid of. It's not like you to give up on people so easily, especially without really knowing them.

But for goodness' sake, don't be angry with me. I have trouble enough with Annika giving me the cold shoulder. She had the audacity to bring her twin brother, Erik, into things, as if like the ghost of Hamlet's father, he might come back to haunt me. Which sometimes seems to be fairly accurate.

Le Morte Darthur was more of a slog than I'd anticipated—Middle English, you know—but it was good to be in the habit of reading something again. Arthur's tragic flaw isn't nearly as interesting as most, in my opinion, and Guinevere's is basically just Lancelot. (I really despise stories of doomed love; they're so impractical.) People in books are much less complicated than the ones in real life.

From where the fox and rabbit
say good-night,
Jo

Article in the Religion section of the Ironside Broadside *on May 8, 1944*

POWs ATTEND LOCAL CHURCH

This Sunday morning, in addition to its 148 members, Immanuel Lutheran Church boasted 32 guests: prisoners from Camp Ironside. Following a petition to be allowed to worship "according to the dictates of their conscience," army officials granted permission for a small group of German prisoners to attend services under the watch of Private First Class Christopher Wright.

Each prisoner must be personally approved for the Sunday leave. Any behavior incidents will permanently disqualify their attendance. "We care a great deal about the safety and security of our American citizens," said Major Jeffrey E. Davies, "but we would be remiss if we ignored this prime opportunity to educate German soldiers about our long tradition of religious tolerance." Davies cited other examples of POW camps across the country enacting a similar practice with no negative consequences.

The service began with readings from the Old Testament, Epistles, and Gospels, and these same readings were repeated in German. The sermon itself, on the text of Matthew 5:45, was entirely in English. Pastor Anders Sorenson extemporized on the meaning of Jesus' description of the justice of God, who gives both sun and rain to all, regardless of merit. "How, then, shall we do any less and call ourselves children of such a Father?" he asked the silent congregation. The previous verses' call to "love your enemies" was never directly addressed.

A view from the choir loft would show the damning strokes of *PW* marked on the prisoners' backs as they leaned forward to hear and understand the minister's words. A careful observer, one who kept his eyes open during the closing prayer, would have noticed tears on the faces of several of the men, wiped away before the final amen.

The organist, Hattie Knutson, forsook American standards for Luther's hymns: "A Mighty Fortress Is Our God" and "Dear Christians, One and All, Rejoice." Congregants could hear the words in their original German from the back rows, softly at first, then thundering through by the chorus.

Immediately following the service, the POWs were returned to the camp in a large truck driven by PFC Wright. When the guard was asked what he thought of the potential risk, especially given that most of the POWs aren't fluent in English, he said only, "They understood something more important than the sermon."

Just like Victor Hugo's bishop, Sorenson has welcomed the enemy in and brought out the treasures of his home for them, and all who witnessed it could not help but be deeply moved.

According to Sorenson, the POWs will be permitted to attend services indefinitely, unless a more satisfactory arrangement can be made. "Scriptures teach that, just as we are sojourners and strangers in this world, we ought to show kindness to the stranger within our borders," Sorenson said in an exclusive interview with the *Broadside*, when asked if his actions might be seen as unpatriotic. "It is our higher duty as Christians to welcome these men."

From Johanna to Brady McHenry

May 9, 1944

Dear Mr. McHenry,

Since most of my letters to your office have been somewhat hostile, I wanted to include this note with the next editorial. I'm glad to hear that you've read *Les Miserables*. It's my favorite book. I translated parts of it in high school when I was learning French and particularly enjoyed the early chapters with the bishop. You're right; Pastor Sorenson was just like that.

Besides that, the article was much more . . . conciliatory than what I'm used to from you. I appreciate the change.

Next Saturday's column is enclosed. It's becoming the highlight of the camp's weekend, with everyone crowding around and asking for a translation. The writers become temporary celebrities, and Captain Werner has a long list of applicants to sort through. Again, I'm grateful for the opportunity.

Johanna Berglund

From Brady McHenry to Johanna

May 11, 1944

Dear Miss Berglund,

You're not the only one in Ironside Lake to have read a classic novel, Miss Berglund. Don't expect me to start a book-a-month subscription for you or anything, though.

I didn't think the old reverend had it in him, but he sure proved me wrong. It was such a sentimental story, I was hoping it would get picked up by one of the bigger papers. Hardly anyone outside the county notices we exist, even now that we've got a crowd of Jerries in our town. Apparently, it'll take more than a sappy human-interest story to make the big time. My old man thought it would never happen. He was pleased as punch to run a mom-and-pop paper with a staff of four, placing want ads about tractor sales and cattle auctions. Never had any vision for what the *Broadside* could really be.

Thanks for the column—perfect for the town crowd, and a little controversy thrown in too. I like a man who doesn't pull his punches.

Say, try to get me a love story sometime, will you? Some sad little Friedrich who's pining over his Helga back home. People eat that stuff up like Spam from a can.

Brady McHenry
Owner and Editor in Chief,
Ironside Broadside

From Peter to Johanna

May 12, 1944

Dear Jo,

I couldn't be angry at you . . . at least, not for long. You know that. Sometimes it's just easier to ignore the Hakujin than to get upset at them and all they represent.

After I got your letter, my first instinct was to leave it there. But I took a walk—without full military gear—and tried to think. Have I ever had a personal conversation with a Hakujin student? Ever asked if they wanted to join a group of us going into the city? Ever learned anything about where they came from or what motivated them to enroll?

The answer was no. Worse, even knowing it, even after more pacing and praying, I didn't want to. I still don't.

By the time I came back and the setting sun had cooled the temperature to a brisk spring chill, I'd realized something else: If one of the Hakujin had been at the USO club that first day we met, you'd have probably challenged him to a game of Ping-Pong instead of me. Just because you, like all of us, are drawn to what's most familiar.

Maybe that's why the Hakujin become officers. The government is made up of people, and people are inclined to trust what they feel they know and understand most.

It's something I'll have to think more about.

And about your question, the language school moved to Minnesota because your governor invited us. There were only fifty Japanese in the entire state before we got here and exploded the population. Really. Fifty. Maybe Minnesotans had no prejudice because they hadn't had a chance.

That's not entirely fair. People here have been

welcoming. News coverage is universally positive, with no bucktooth, slanted-eyed caricatures like back in California. Even the senior hostess at the Nisei USO Clubs tries her best once a month to make food we recognize from our mothers' kitchens. If all I have to put up with are a few wary looks on a weekend leave, I can deal with it. It's nothing like San Francisco.

The day the news of the attack on Pearl Harbor hit, I took a streetcar from the university to send a message to my parents to see if their grocery was all right. I knew what people might do. There are plenty of loose bricks in the city ready to be thrown through windows when things get hot.

The moment I stepped on the streetcar, a woman with red-rimmed eyes gestured wildly at me. She began shouting, "Kill him! He's a dirty Jap—he'll spy on us all!" Over and over, shrill and loud.

No one raised a fist toward me, but I could feel them push away, looking at the ground, leaving me standing alone. Someone finally calmed the woman down, but the streetcar driver, Alvin Kennedy, who knew me and bought tomatoes at my father's store, asked if I could get off to avoid trouble.

Clearly, that woman was distraught. For all I knew, she might've had a son in the navy. Even if she didn't, no mother wants a war. I knew all of that . . . but I still hated her in that moment, wanted to tell the driver to ask her to leave, not me. She was the one causing trouble.

December 7 will live in infamy for me too, but maybe not the same way it does for the rest of the nation.

The next month, I endured a loyalty interrogation to prove I wasn't a turncoat or a plant for Japanese intelligence. In the frantic few days after the removal

order, I helped my family sell their furniture and find
storage for what couldn't be pawned off. I stayed behind
when they were forced into an Arizona internment camp.
I traveled with my students to Minnesota in a train with
blacked-out windows, then in a car with an armed white
officer to protect us from suspicion or attacks.

And I am still here. America can't ask much more of
me than that.

There. I've told you one of my secrets. Not that it has
to be a trade, but after your letter, I feel like I have to at
least ask: What happened between you and Erik Sorenson?
I don't know if you realize it, but you never mentioned his
name to me in person, so I have no idea who he was. But
I get the feeling that he's one of the reasons you don't feel
at home in Ironside Lake.

If you want to talk, I'm always only a stamp away.

> Your friend,
> Peter

P.S. If everyone has one . . . what's your tragic flaw?

The POW Potato Brigade column in the Ironside Broadside *on May
13, 1944*

I was born in Leipzig, Germany. My comrades have all said
not to begin with my birth, because it interests no one, but
you see, I have a reason for you to know about Leipzig: It's
the same birth city as composer Richard Wagner's.

As a boy, I heard "The Ride of the Valkyries," and the
celestial charge inspired me for tedious lessons on the trumpet. My first wavering notes sounded nothing like a mythic
opera, but I pressed onward, all stubbornness and dreams of

glory, a picture of Wagner taped to my mirror so I would see him as I brushed my teeth each night.

Here at the camp, I am the conductor for our orchestra. The YMCA has given us an accordion, piano, a trombone, and music stands, all used, and in Algona, we were able to persuade the camp to use proceeds from the canteen to purchase a clarinet, two violins, a battered flute, and a trumpet. This last is a new instrument to one of our members, Bernhard Hoffmann, who made the change on finding there is not a strong market for secondhand tubas in Minnesota.

Each Sunday night, we have rehearsals for two hours before bed check. We've had no official performances yet, but many men loiter near the recreation hall to hear us. Our strongest member is a man half my age, Dieter Bormann, who at nineteen can play Bach's violin sonatas with aching beauty—enough to make a grown man weep. Some have been playing all their lives, a few are novices, but all are improving with each practice.

I have only one complaint. We have a stack of donated sheet music, mostly pieces from the classical era, but the leadership of the camp has denied us anything by Wagner.

The reasoning behind the ban is that Wagner has a devotee far more famous than myself: Adolf Hitler. The *Führer* would often begin his rallies with the overture to the opera *Rienzi.*

Have you ever known a celebrity who you learn from some interview shares with you a favorite book or vacation spot or kind of pie? This was what I felt toward Chancellor Hitler. He was a radical, yes, but to many, it seemed the time for radicalism, and besides, if he loved Wagner, how bad a man could he be? That was what I wondered in those early days.

But Wagner's works are not Nazi ideology put to music. He died many years before the Great War. There is nothing in the lyrics and certainly not in the notes themselves that could be considered propaganda. Given Wagner's significance for the musical world, omitting his works is a great mistake. Every aspiring musician, especially German ones, must be familiar with his works, and I wish that the young men of our camp might learn them here.

As I attempted to persuade the commander through our spokesman, trying to convey what I meant, I hummed my favorite of Wagner's works, "The Ride of the Valkyries." The commander stopped me, searching his brain as to how he knew it. Then he asked, "Aren't you humming the song from *The Birth of a Nation*?" I said I did not know, but the commander was quite sure. It played during a sequence in that film where the hooded Klansmen of the South rescue a town from a mob of murderous, newly freed slaves. He described it to me. A very dramatic scene.

It was only later that I began to see the irony. Recently, several of us were permitted to go under guard to view a movie in town. It did not escape my notice that the few Negros had a separate marked balcony and entrance, while we were allowed to sit in the main gallery. One of our men asked about it and received the explanation of "separate but equal," a phrase that seems common among Americans.

And there is where I see hypocrisy. You ban Wagner from a camp of Nazi soldiers but use his works in your own Hollywood movies that support policies against race mixing that are similar to the Nazi regime's. Something to think about, perhaps.

Music is as close as we can get to freedom. It transports us to scenes far from this place and reminds us of home.

Please do not deny us the works of great masters like Wagner simply because of your own prejudices.

Otto von Neindorff

From Johanna to Peter

May 19, 1944

Dear Peter,

I'm not sure what to say after your story about all you went through back in San Francisco. You probably don't want my pity—is sympathy close enough? Anyway, I'm proud of you for persevering. Though a small (admittedly cynical) part of me wonders if you told the story just to soften me up to your question about Erik.

Regardless, it worked. Maybe now you'll see why Pastor Sorenson and Annika don't care much for me and won't think I'm exaggerating.

Erik and Annika Sorenson were a few years older than I, but all through my childhood, we were inseparable, like siblings. My actual sister, Irene, was a complete bore, or so she appeared to me, always reading *Silver Screen* magazines and sneaking lipstick to put on in the school bathroom. The Sorensons were nothing like that. They'd play in the woods with me for hours, acting out the latest stories I'd been reading.

Erik was the quiet one who wore solemnity like a tweed overcoat. Annika was sweetness and light, always baking treats or whistling cheerful tunes. And I was . . . well, exactly what I am now, only with knobby knees and two perfectly even braids. But differences and all, God or fate or the home ownership plans of our forefathers threw us together.

As we grew older, especially after Mrs. Sorenson died, we drifted apart. At least, we didn't spend every waking hour of the summer together anymore. Annika had a large group of friends, and Erik and I had nothing in common to talk about, though sometimes we'd read in companionable silence on the Sorensons' back porch.

Erik was taking courses via correspondence with Luther Seminary for years before the war, all set to be ordained. On weekends, he played lead trumpet in a band—The Swingin' Loons, they called themselves. I didn't even begrudge them the terrible name because they could do a decent imitation of the hits, and I needed a live band for the dance hall I started and ran from May 1941 to August 1942 in order to raise money for university.

You know what happened in between those two dates. With separations looming, dances became more frantic after Roosevelt declared war. There was already talk of enlistments and even the draft.

One night, when the high-school band was spelling The Swingin' Loons for a set, mangling "The Chattanooga Choo Choo," Erik made his way over to me, so nervous that I knew he was going to ask me to dance. I never danced.

Not wanting to hurt his pride, I shoved a flashlight into his hands and asked him to check the perimeter of the gymnasium. We had chaperones make the rounds periodically to shoo couples out of dark corners and back into the proper society of the transformed basketball court.

This was in January. A warm January for Minnesota, but still, I doubt anyone was necking behind the gym.

He accepted the flashlight, then added, "Will you come

with me, Jo? I have something serious I need to talk to you about."

I wanted to joke that everything he talked about was serious, but the look on his face stopped me. This time he meant it.

So I hurried into my coat and out the back door, all the time thinking, So Erik Sorenson is going to be the first man I know to join the army. I was ready with my reply, planning to tell him how proud his late mother would be of him, holding back any worried questions, promising to write occasionally.

Then he proposed.

Well, there was a short speech leading up to it, but since I was expecting him to tell me he'd enlisted, for me, it came out of the clear blue sky, much like the attack on Pearl Harbor.

I . . . well, I may have suggested that he was only proposing to avoid the draft. I wasn't meaning to insult him, I promise. It was genuinely the only reason I could think of for his getting down on one knee to propose to me, of all people.

He was angry. *Hurt* might be a better word, if I'm honest. As we walked back inside, the night was so quiet that you could hear the crunch of frosted grass under our feet.

A few weeks later, he'd decided to become an army chaplain the minute he received his ordination in September. Partly to serve the foxhole converts, partly to prove that he had no fear of joining the war, partly, I'm sure, to get away from me. We still treated each other cordially, but things were never the same between us.

I only know that I missed him, and soon it was too late to even say that.

A few months after his deployment, I finally worked up the courage to send Erik one solitary letter, with the best attempt I could make at an apology. I don't know if he ever received it, because he was killed soon after. That's the funeral I came back for last year, the one you remembered.

I stared into his grave, feeling regret about . . . something. I'm not sure what. Not for turning down his proposal. Maybe for allowing him to leave without settling things between us. I couldn't help but wonder what would have happened if things had been different.

When Reverend Sorenson gave the benediction over the grave, his voice cracking with emotion, I bowed my head, but I couldn't pray. To be honest, I haven't prayed much since.

Maybe Erik would have changed, in time. Maybe we could have found a compromise. I could have given up Oxford to settle in the Twin Cities, and he might have found a church there to lead, close enough to visit our families, far enough away for me to feel like I had moved on. I can't say for sure. All I know was that he never understood my dreams, and he proposed at a time when emotions were high. No one was thinking clearly.

Except me. I always think clearly. And my *no* was the right choice.

So there. Now you know.

I've got a terrible headache. Maybe telling you was a mistake, but you did want to know, remember that. Please don't think worse of me because of it. I couldn't stand it.

Jo

P.S./Appendix: Maybe my tragic flaw is refusing to admit that I have a tragic flaw. Or that I'm a character

160

in a tragedy, even when my life seems to confirm I might be. No *deus ex machina* so far. For you accountants out there, that's "god from a machine," as in a Greek play when Zeus or Athena or one of the other deities swooped onto the stage to wrap everything up by punishing the guilty and commending the good. Wouldn't that be handy? But it seems God doesn't rescue us very often these days.

From Peter to Johanna

May 23, 1944

Dear Jo,

I'm sorry. Both that Erik died and that you can't go back and change how you parted ways. I know that's not much help at all, especially when someone dies so young.

From what you've said, I think you made the right choice, saying no to Erik's proposal, though you're probably also right that you could have done it more graciously.

But here's something I know: If God had wanted anyone else to be in Erik's life, he could have made it happen. But he didn't. He chose you. Is that comforting? It has been for me, sometimes, to think that we make choices and learn and grow, but that we're put in the places and with the people we are for a reason.

Your story made me wonder what things I haven't said that I should. The Ito family was never much for speaking from the heart, I'm afraid. Sometimes Father would give us a nod of approval for a good report card or a day of hard work at the store, and that was the same as a long speech of praise. But none of us ever know how much time we're going to get.

Speaking of conversations, I started one the other day with Kenneth Meyer, one of our Hakujin students. (The name was probably a giveaway.) He and a friend practice pitching and catching behind the mess hall every Saturday afternoon, and I asked if I could join them.

Fine, maybe "conversation" is a stretch, because a few shouts of "Go back a few yards" and "Nice one" probably don't count for much. But I did get to practice my slider for the first time in months, and it was something, anyway. I can't tell you the people in your life are there for a reason and not say the same for mine.

But sorry, you can't trick me into some kind of story exchange like we're swapping hostages. What sort of an espionage instructor would I be if I gave you all of my secrets, and all at once?

Don't take that the wrong way. I do trust you. But some things take time before they can be spoken.

Your friend,
Peter

P.S. I'm also holding out hope that you're living in a comedy. Also, I don't think it's as bad as you might think that you haven't had your deus ex machina. Who would want a god stuck in a machine who arrives on our cue? Some god that would be.

From Johanna to Peter

May 26, 1944

German Idiom of the Day: *Der Fisch stinkt vom Kopf her.* Literally, "the fish begins to stink from the head," meaning the source of the trouble is often at the top.

Context: Spoken during a heated political argument between two men, one a Nazi devotee, the other a Social Democrat.

Dear Peter,

You always know just what to say to make me feel better. Is that something you teach in your lessons about diplomacy? Am I an especially difficult practice case?

I'm sorry. I should have just said thank you, or that was very kind of you, or I appreciate your advice. But that would be far too normal, and anyway, you know that's what I mean, don't you?

As for speaking from the heart, I don't know about that, but I always appreciate it when people speak their minds. That's what I like about you. I never have to wonder where I stand or whether you have some hidden agenda. We can be perfectly honest with each other. If only you weren't living so far away.

Then again, we've had some very good conversations via letter, even if Mother does complain that I spend too much time typing in my room. I've moved my typewriter to the living room to please her, but now she pretends to be dusting the fireplace mantel to read over my shoulder. Mother never dusts, so I know it's a ploy.

In fact, she's doing it right now. Maybe she'll read this part and know I'm on to her game.

(Update: She did, and I could tell because she turned red and slowly dusted in the opposite direction, then had to polish the brass fireplace frame to keep up the illusion that she was spring cleaning and not snooping.)

Our north guard tower is now the proud owner of a radio antenna. I wouldn't have known what it was if I hadn't asked Private Wilkes about it. To me, it looked like a thin copper wire strung from the top of the flagpole, sloping up to the roof of the tower. Nothing at all like the RKO Radio Pictures logo.

When questioned, Wilkes said, "That's a long wire antenna, all right. Screwed in the ceramic insulator last night and hooked it up to the ol' radio set. Major's orders. I think he's sentimental for his radio days. The glory years, y'know. All of us know a vet or two talking about the Great War like there isn't one going on right now."

If that seems like a flimsy reason to you, I thought the same thing, especially after Wilkes's more forthcoming friend "Tank" McFearson told me he'd heard Davies muttering to himself, "It must work. I know it will!"

When I asked the major about it, his response was "Hmm? Oh, that. Nothing—don't let it trouble you," followed by a forced change of subject.

After English class, Captain Werner mentioned that several of his fellow officers had noticed the radio antenna as well. That might have been his subtle way of warning me, since curious enemy officers are never welcome in a prison camp. Like Wilkes, I tried to pass it off as one of the major's eccentricities.

I'll need to warn Major Davies about guarding his secrets more closely. Though I suppose it would be difficult to subtly install a radio antenna. The very nature of its requirements means it can't be low or concealed. Perhaps he should have hung laundry on it and pretended it was a clothesline.

See? I would be a terrible spy. Clearly, you need to give me some pointers.

It does seem odd to send such a talented hero with a background in radio transmissions to the middle of nowhere in an even greater hour of need—although it might simply be that he's past fifty, too old to be placed in an active-duty assignment. I'll have to press Evelyn for information about it. She's always inviting me over for tea or lemonade or lunch, sometimes even ordering one of the off-duty guards to drive us into town in an army truck, as if they're her personal chauffeurs.

I'd write longer, but I've got a stack of letters to censor. I have to admit, I choose some out of the pile deliberately to read the ongoing drama. Sometimes I even copy out the most interesting ones, although that probably goes against a postal regulation. It's like my own personal radio show: Will Marie's mother finally find out she's hiding the last chicken, named and kept as a pet? Can Gerhard convince his grandfather that, at ninety, he's a bit past his prime to join the *Luftwaffe*? What will become of Dieter and Rose's ill-fated romance?

Sometimes the storyline is more overtly tragic. There are brothers gone missing in France and homes destroyed in the Nuremberg bombings, death and loss and longing. I understand why we're keeping the POWs here, but some days I wish they could all go back to the tattered remnants of home and family they have left. How long can this war go on?

That's no way to end a letter. So tell me, were your parents able to return to California?

Jo

From Dieter Bormann to Rose Schlitter
Translated and censored by Johanna Berglund

May 25, 1944

Rose, my love,

Your last letter has brought me nothing but misery. Five

times in the past week, I've started a reply, and each time, no words would come.

No understanding? You know I could barely afford a pack of cigarettes to put in my kit, much less an engagement ring worthy of a woman like you. Now I wish I'd not only gotten on one knee but that I'd taken you in my arms and swept you off to the nearest church to witness our vows.

You must be only teasing me, but it's cruel when I'm so far from home, sacrificing everything for Germany and for you. Have a heart, Rose. I can't lend one to you—mine has been yours for so long that I haven't a hope of getting it back.

And this man is Arland to you now, is he, even at twice your age? Yes, I'm sure you kissed the hand that shook the hand of the minister of finance. He can give you everything I can't: a home in town, luxuries, beef for your stupid Nazi pie, and a hand to hold while the rest of us make real sacrifices. You say he's cultured and refined, but remember, Rose, even bears can learn to dance.

Have you forgotten our long hours walking beneath the cherry trees, talking of dreams and hopes and everything that could be, then holding each other tight when we ran out of words, our souls joined together? Can your well-turned-out banker give you that?

You and I, we were always made for each other. Please, Rose. You must remember.

Haven't you heard the Führer's vision? [CENSORED] I can see it, can't you? In that new Germany, we are together, the two of us.

I cannot speak of ordinary things, not when your words

are like ashes in my mouth. Remember the fire of our love, dear Rose. The flame will never die, not if we don't let it.

> Yours until the mountains fall,
> Dieter

From Heinz Werner to Stefan Werner
Translated from German by Johanna Berglund

April 21, 1944

Stefan,

Surely you know why I haven't responded to you. I am ashamed to even receive your letters, marked as they are with your disgrace: *Prisoner of War.*

Do not try to tell me you are serving your country. Name one single, solitary thing you can do to aid Germany or hurt America from within this camp. You cannot; it is not possible. There are some Germans who would take their own life before falling into the hands of their captors, forced to work on their farms like a common servant. There are days when I wish I still had such a son. But you are nothing like your brother. Leon would be ashamed of you.

And this woman you speak of—this American woman—it seems you admire her. At least the last time you disobeyed me for the sake of a woman, running off to Berlin to work for Miss Riefenstahl, she was a true German. The way you speak fills me with disgust. I could scarcely believe it, and then I remembered that you, like your mother, are a creature of passions and emotions. I should have known, praising you for your youthful enthusiasm, that it could be turned. You have followed your heart into a great deception, and forsaken Germany and your father.

As for your other question, the Wolves have sustained some losses recently, some disheartening for fair-weather fans, but I will never turn aside from our team. Our friend who we called the Megaphone can always be seen publicly talking about how the game will turn around. There is a man who understands loyalty.

I tore your last letter into shreds and did not intend to reply, but I knew that unless I did, you would continue writing. By all means, stay in America after the war—you can claim no part of a German victory. If you have been bewitched by enemy propaganda, you are no son to me.

Heinz Werner

From Stefan Werner to Johanna, left on her desk after English class

June 2, 1944

Now that I've read Father's letter, I know why you didn't want to give it to me. Thank you for delivering it uncensored, and please do not worry on my account. There are many things my father doesn't understand. My work here is one of them. I should not have expected, or even hoped, for it to be otherwise.

I'm sure he will not write again, so you will not be troubled by him any further.

As for your comment that my single, solitary task to aid my country should be to return and rebuild after the *war, I must say, my days at the Olympics have taught me that I am more of a runner than a builder*

—S

From Johanna Berglund to Heinz Werner, in German. Reconstructed from memory.

June 2, 1944

Dear Mr. Werner,

My name is Johanna Berglund, civilian translator from Camp Ironside. I decided to write to you to assure you that your son is executing his duty with excellence. While most camps elect the officer of highest rank to be their spokesman, Stefan was chosen because he won the hearts of his men. They would follow him anywhere. I have seen it in their eyes when he speaks to them each morning before they go to work on the farms, or in the evenings when arbitrating disputes. In addition, the camp commander and many others have praised his leadership and organizational abilities.

You have no cause to be ashamed of him. If you must blame someone for his imprisonment here, then blame his commanding officers in North Africa who surrendered, forcing his unit to be sent to America.

Stefan is making the best of a bad situation, something I personally have learned a great deal from. There is nothing more any of us can do in these difficult times.

Sincerely,
Johanna Berglund

| From Peter to Johanna

June 4, 1944

Dear Johanna,
    As requested, here are some pointers on being a spy:

1. Don't.
2. If you have no other choice, then give your situation context. Is it likely that the military would put important radio-related secrets right under the nose of a few hundred enemy soldiers? Probably not.
3. Blend in. This might be difficult for you. No offense, but you can be as subtle as a power lawn mower. (Analogy inspired by my weekly work detail at the camp. Sometimes I wish the ground was still covered in snow.)
4. Knowledge is power. Not just knowledge of other languages but understanding of people and how they think, what will persuade them, and how they will respond. It's the only thing I can't really teach my students.
5. Along with 4, be careful whom you trust. To get information on the Japanese, a few of our students have gone deep undercover, by all appearances loyal citizens, for months or even years. I'm sure others do the same to us.
6. Never keep incriminating documents. Burn everything. If the Japanese did that, my students would be out of work, with no field diaries or letters to translate that hint at future movements.
7. Failing all that . . . almost anyone can be bribed with good chocolate. (Including me.)

Now that we've gotten that out of the way: Yes, my family is home. I got a letter from them yesterday, short because they've got a lot of work to do, moving back in. They've been gone almost three full years; can you believe it? If I know Father, they'll have Ito's Corner Grocery up and running again by fall, assuming sheer stubbornness is enough to get it done. I'm worried, though, that they won't make a profit. Roosevelt may have declared they're not a threat, but I can't say their fellow citizens have decided the same.

Sorry for the short letter. The MIS is sending representatives to check on our students' progress and to discuss moving the school to larger facilities in Fort Snelling. We're all on edge and working twice as hard.

Your friend,
Sir Gal

P.S. If you keep calling me Sir Gal, I'll write directly to your mother and demand all your childhood nicknames and any other embarrassing details she'd like to disclose. Maybe that should have been on my list— know who your allies can be. I really should be doing this spy business myself instead of just teaching it, shouldn't I?

Evidence for the Prosecution

INTERVIEW WITH PRIVATE DON CASEY
CONDUCTED JANUARY 12, 1945

Q: Tell us what happened at Camp Ironside on the evening of June 7, 1944, following the D-Day invasion.

Casey: Well, I wasn't there when it all started. Four of us off-duty guards were throwing poker chips, with a radio in the background set to the news about the invasion.

Wasn't long before we heard the shouting, probably close to 1800 hours, just before supper. The shack they call a "guards' lounge" has walls so thin, you could hear someone cough as they walk by, and this was sure as heck louder than that. We ran out to see what the fuss was.

Turns out, the POWs were running toward the fence. Some were shouting. Others just watched. At first, I thought we had a riot on our hands, or a mass escape, and I thought, Maybe I won't have to go overseas to kill a Jerry after all.

But then we saw what was causing all the fuss: a car driving around the camp outside the fence, headlights dipping in and out of potholes. Two kids were inside, one of them hanging out the passenger window, and his voice was loudest of all.

Q: What were they yelling?

Casey: Oh, you know. "We bombed you off the map, Jerries! We're going to smash you Nazi scum and take Paris back for good! Go on home so you can get what you deserve." Things like that. Cussing some too—nothing that awful.

Q: And how did the German prisoners react?

Casey: Most of them were just standing at attention, listening. Others shouted back, in German mostly, so I can't tell you what they said, but it was trouble, I'll tell you.

Q: Was the vehicle permitted to be on that road?

Casey: There's no barricade or anything, but maybe the exterior guard should've stopped them for disturbing the peace. Guess he just didn't care enough. Stupid of those boys to do it right after D-Day. Like poking a dog with a stick through the cage bars. But didn't we all do things like that as kids?

Q: When did Miss Berglund arrive?

Casey: She was there the whole time, right in with the men, at least by the time I got out there. Hands clenched white in fists. I remember that part. She was right under one of the big streetlights we have by the gate, so I could see her real clear: pale blond on top, drab gray all the way to her calves, as usual.

The second time the boys drove around, they started a taunt about the German sweethearts back home. One of the men lunged out and made a break for the fence, until Miss Berglund tackled him. Well, anyway, she wrapped her arms around him and tried to haul him back. He jerked away, stronger than her by half, and she fell but kept clinging to his legs. Got to give her that, at least—she's determined. He dragged her across the dirt a few steps until he fell, like he hadn't realized he had a woman attached to his ankles like a ball and chain.

I'm telling you, if that Jerry had given me a reason, and if she hadn't been there to block him, I'd have shot him. It's happened at other camps when the POWs are asking for trouble. No law against it.

Q: Who was the prisoner?

Casey: Dieter Bormann. I knew his name right off because he was one of the young hotheads, always glaring at us like he'd stick us in our sleep if only he could get his hands on a weapon.

Anyway, another guard, PFC Chris Wright—a do-gooder Boy Scout–type through and through—jogged over and helped Miss Berglund up, scolding the prisoner. That's all Bormann got, all any of them ever get. Lectures and a few days in solitary, because of that convention they're always harping about.

Q: Was the vehicle still circling the camp?

Casey: Oh, they made another few turns around the perimeter, sure. Miss Berglund's mother drove into the stockade to take her home before they'd left, so she didn't meddle any after that.

Q: How would you describe Miss Berglund's demeanor during the incident?

Casey: If she were a boiler, I'd have hit the ground and covered my face, if that's what you mean.

Q: And toward whom was her anger directed?

Casey: Why, those boys. Not the prisoners, not even the ones who were doing their stiff-arm salute and shouting back in German. I know enough words in Jerry-speak to know they were spewing more threats than the murderer in *Double Indemnity*. Have you watched it? Best movie I've seen in years.

Q: Were you aware of an army investigation into Miss Berglund's actions at the time?

Casey: Are you kidding? Davies didn't start wondering about her till later. Didn't like to think badly of anyone, that one. If you ask me, that's why he was better off in a room full of radios than in command of a camp.

I wasn't surprised one bit when things happened the way they did. I've seen enough films with a *femme fatale* to know: Never trust a dame, and especially not that one. Cold to the bone, she was. Cold as ice.

CHAPTER SEVEN

June 7, 1944

> German Idiom of the Day: *mit Pauken und Trompeten durchfallen*. Literally, "to fail with drums and trumpets," meaning to go down in a blaze of glory.
>
> Context: Overheard in a discussion (in low tones) of whether Germany is, in fact, losing the war. The men were divided in their opinions.

Dear Peter,

You'll never guess what's happened tonight. If you say "the invasion of France," I'll punch you; we all know that. Although it is related.

Like every other town in America, we were all tense as soon as Roosevelt's radio address announced a major campaign. Some took his call to prayer seriously. Others took a joyride around the stockade to taunt our prisoners.

Practically the entire camp turned up to hear what

175

was going on, and around and around those two boys went, shouting and swearing until I was ashamed to be an American.

That was when Mother drove up. Most days, since my house is only two miles away, I bring sensible shoes and walk home. Any time there is so much as a spit of rain, though, Mother insists on picking me up in Dad's old truck, afraid I'll catch a cold. (All precipitation is essentially germs in liquid form, you know.)

While I raged about the hooligans' shenanigans, Mother nodded along like there wasn't a thing wrong. Then, instead of taking the road back to town, she puttered around the service road outside of the fence, slower than a first-generation Model T. Once we'd reached the west side of the camp, just around a curve, she swerved, pulling the truck perpendicular to the road and putting it into park. And then waited, ignoring my questions.

It wasn't long until the green Oldsmobile swerved around the corner, and it was all the driver could do to squeal to a stop before hitting us. Mother got out of the car and minced over in her one-inch heels.

"Why, if it isn't Timothy Yeats," she said, all warmth and solicitude. (I think she knows the name of every soul in town, as well as their children and pets and shirt size.) "And is that Ricky Cunningham back there?"

"Richard," the young-man-formerly-known-as-Ricky corrected.

She went on like that, asking after Timothy's brother, a soldier taken prisoner in Japan—his mother was the one who wrote that letter to the paper—and talking about the Christmas packages the Rotary Club was planning to send to the troops. "We're including the guards at Camp

Ironside too, naturally. Johanna is always telling me how tense the atmosphere can be here. The detained German prisoners so far from home, wanting the war to be over so they can return to their families."

"I guess so, ma'am," Timothy said, coughing uncomfortably.

She tapped the faded green hood of their Oldsmobile like she was patting them on the head. "Well, I'll let you boys be on your way. There's a prayer meeting at the church tonight. We'd love to see you there."

They sped away so quickly you'd have thought she threatened them with a shotgun.

When she got back into our car, I almost applauded. "You really showed those hooligans."

"Johanna, no one is a hooligan," Mother said primly, pulling out of the middle of the road. "Or at least not just a hooligan. They are brothers and sons and probably some hapless women's future husbands. More important, they have reasons for all they do that we'll likely never know."

I thought of the letters I censored, how real they made the POWs seem, how I began to understand why they thought and acted the way they did, even when I disagreed with them. Maybe, I thought, if I were pen pals with everyone in the world, I would understand people better.

When I asked if there really was a prayer meeting at the church, Mother shrugged and said, "There will be."

At home, she called Pastor Sorenson, then rang up half the church for a vigil of thanksgiving for the Normandy invasion. I stopped in for a half hour or so. There's something lovely about listening to other people pray, almost like attending a poetry reading.

Timothy and Richard-not-Ricky did not attend, but

Timothy's mother did, wringing her handkerchief like a sponge. Before I left, I saw Mother move to sit beside her and take her hand.

I'm afraid that at times I've dismissed my mother, who married at nineteen, raised two daughters, and never seemed to want more out of life than a quiet existence knitting, supporting Dad, and perfecting her smothered pork chop recipe. It's in times like these that I realize she's a stronger woman than I'll ever be.

I'd left the camp tonight sure I would be writing a furious missive to you filled with all my anger at those two boys. Isn't it wonderful when stories have unexpected endings?

Jo

P.S./Appendix: Mother also happens to make the best truffles in Minnesota. I read her bits of your letters, and she seized on the chocolate mention (clever man) and saw to it that I mailed you this box as a thank-you for letting me blather on to you for pages and pages these past few months. I stole three before mailing the rest. That is not an apology; they were delicious. Don't eat all the remaining ones yourself, and certainly not all in one sitting. Not that I ever tried that as a child, but if I had, I would advise you that it might result in getting sick at church all over your father's best Sunday suit. Hypothetically.

From Peter to Johanna

June 10, 1944

Dear Johanna,

Now I know where you get it from. Maybe your mother's just learned some subtlety to go with her courage. Reading your letter gave me a much-needed reason to smile today. So did the truffles, which melted slightly but were amazing. I've enclosed a thank-you note for your mother if you don't mind passing it on.

I was supposed to be asleep an hour ago, but today's language lesson is hanging on me. I'm hoping writing to you about it will help.

Today we began teaching interrogation techniques and policy. It was good fun at first, especially the roleplay scenarios. Some of the younger ones—back-row rowdies, I call them—started tearing into me, getting right in my face, screaming, "Tell us the truth, or we'll beat you!" when I refused to answer. That sort of thing.

I took the chance to explain that graduates from past years have found gentle, even conspiratorial, examinations get better results than empty threats. Sympathize, listen, request help, show cooperation as a path to a better future. Those are the tactics that work, especially when the soldier sees that the interrogator looks like them and speaks their native language.

I noticed that Makoto, my ukulele tutor, listened intently to that part, so I wasn't surprised when he volunteered to go next.

He stood behind me as I sat in the metal chair. "Think of something," he said quietly, so the rest of the class couldn't hear, in his now-familiar pidgin English. "De secret you most want to hide."

It was a little unnerving, a student taking control of my roleplay scenario, but I gathered up a piece of information and locked it in my head.

The trouble was, it worked too well. It made everything feel real. I can't explain it to you, Jo, because I knew the young man firing questions at me was a twenty-year-old musician with a heart as big as the ocean. And yet suddenly, when I had something to hide, the questioning made me push back in my chair, my stomach knotted up in my chest.

After the standard questions about name, rank, any knowledge of radio codes or locations of nearby airstrips, Makoto pressed in, rapidly firing the Japanese phrases. "I need to know where your army intends to go next. What are your plans? Where are you located now?"

I should have reminded him to ask only one question at a time, but there was an intensity about the dialogue that knocked me out of instructor mode. "I can't tell you. I won't."

"I must insist." His Japanese was perfect, formal, and absolutely unmoving. "The sooner we are sure, the sooner we can bring peace and end this bloodshed."

I stared back at him. "Why should I tell you anything? You are a traitor to Japan. To your own people!"

I don't know why I said that. It just came out, and I saw Makoto flinch.

He recovered quickly. "I am no traitor. But what if, by keeping your information . . . you are?" He paused. "Think of someone you care about."

I did, and he nodded as if he could see the face I was picturing. "The more we know about your army, the more likely it is that she will stay safe and the violence will end.

That's all we want. All of us. We want to go home to the ones we love."

And I realized: If I was tied to my chair, sweating in an enemy jungle base, hungry and exhausted and far from home . . . I would have told him anything. Anything at all. My deepest secrets would have been his.

He knew it too, but instead of grinning in pride, he turned to the class, bowed, and sat down. Everyone was staring, waiting for me to do something, but my mind was still swimming. It felt like I'd really been interrogated, like a dream where you're in front of your high-school class in your underwear. Exposed.

Once I'd collected myself to move on to the rest of the lesson, reading from a classified memorandum about examination techniques, the class settled back into routine. But I can't get it out of my head, that feeling of fear in my gut as Makoto questioned me.

Let's all be glad that he's on our side and not Japan's.

One thing I learned from that exercise: I thought I was perfectly in control of my emotions. That's how my father raised me and why he guided me into finance for a career. Maybe I'm not as tough as I thought. Good thing I'm a civilian teacher and not actually going over to the Pacific.

As for D-Day, sure, we were all gathering up the news as it came in. Some of the boys were disappointed, thinking the war's going to end before they have a chance to graduate and enter the field themselves. Especially after today's lesson, I hope it'll be done tomorrow.

> Your friend,
> Peter

Editorial in the Ironside Broadside *on June 10, 1944*

Dear Editor,

It's gone too far, this prison camp labor. At first, I was open to the idea. There was justice in forcing those Krauts to bring in crops for our boys, like reaping what they'd sown.

But when it begins to endanger our children, well, that's another matter altogether.

One young man at my daughter's school was telling her all about working alongside the Germans at his father's farm. Eating lunch with them, taking cues from the army guards who played cards with the men they were supposed to watch. Not only did this student speak to the enemy soldiers, but he learned a few words of German from them!

Is that the sort of camaraderie we want to be encouraging, I ask you? Our boys fixing farm machinery and harvesting crops alongside Nazis?

Besides this, some of the girls are talking about how they want to be secretaries in the camp once they're old enough, like Miss Berglund. They read all of her prisoners' columns religiously, sighing like their authors are tragically misunderstood heroes from pulp magazines.

Miss Berglund is no role model for our children. Anyone who looks at her shocking new hairstyle would guess that. Given the number of letters she sends to a "Mr. Ito" at another prisoner of war camp, Camp Savage, well, it's no wonder she's gone and dyed her hair black. Who do you think she's trying to look like? And if that doesn't give you pause about that newspaper column of hers, I don't know what will.

An American Mother and Patriot

Editorial in the Ironside Broadside on June 12, 1944

On the Subject of Miss Berglund's Hair:

Anybody who knows me knows I don't speak much into anyone's affairs but my own. But yesterday's letter stirred me up enough that I had to say something.

Earlier this week, Miss Berglund came into my shop like someone what means business. I thought it was odd because the Berglund women never come in, though Mr. Berglund comes by regular. (35 cents for a trim and a shave.)

"Frank," says she, without even a hello, "have you got hair dye?"

I allowed that I had, only I kept it mostly for middle-aged women whose names I probably oughtn't to write here. Whoever thought of making old unfashionable had a head for business, and that's a fact.

Then she said, "I want you to dye my hair black."

I stared at her, kinda startled, and said something along the lines of, "Why does a girl like you want to ruin that nice corn-silk hair of yours?"

She didn't answer, only set herself down like her mind was made up. Now, I've had young women wanting some ridiculous bob that they saw in a Hollywood glossy, not realizing it'll make their head look like a pool cue. So I know to give 'em time to think things over.

"Look," says I, "I can't go and dye your hair that dark. Might not grow out for months, and it sure won't wash out anytime soon. It'd be a crime."

"It'll be a crime if you don't." And then if she didn't tell me the whole story, sitting there in my chair.

She was talking to the prison camp spokesman, see, and he got on about how the Germans classified folks before the war. They gave inspectors cards with different shades of eyes, light to dark, like paint strips at the hardware store, to judge eye colors. That plus little tassels of hair—not sure if it was real hair or just the doll sort—numbered from pale blond to black. That's part of how they decided who was a sturdy German of good stock and who was Jewish or gypsy or African.

And here's the point of it: That German fellow told her—smiling, if you can believe it—"I don't understand why you of all people would fight the theory of a superior race. You're more Aryan than I am." And he tugged her pale hair like it was evidence.

I'd say I'm not a fellow easily stirred, but I was mad too. Mad enough to snap my gloves on and color that young lady's hair the darkest shade I had, Glint #1, Charcoal Black. (For 15 cents, cheaper than you could buy a package at the drugstore.)

I don't know nothing about letters to a Japanese fellow. Maybe it's true, maybe not, and it's probably none of our business either way. But if you think Miss Berglund's going around ten shades darker because she's cheering for the men what bombed Pearl Harbor, you've got another thing coming. Anyone who says otherwise, well, you won't be welcome at Frank's Barber Shop, and that's a fact.

Frank Hood
Proprietor of Frank's Barber Shop
Shave Half Off This Tuesday Only

From Johanna to Peter

June 13, 1944

Dear Peter,

I've done it again. You'd think with all the fuss around me taking this translator job there's nothing I could do to upset people more than I already have. But oh no. My latest *Ironside Broadside* appearance is about my hair, of all things.

You see, I dyed it black. Black as the licorice Cornelia Knutson passes around on holidays. Never mind why; it was impulsive and I'm never impulsive and I don't know what to do with myself.

When I first read *Little Women* at age seven—that's also when I asked my family to call me Jo—I thought it was mean when one of the girls (I'm sure it was Awful Amy) cried in despair, "Oh, Jo! Your one beauty!" after she cut her hair. But now I realize she wasn't being cruel, just honest. I think much the same whenever I look in the mirror.

Dad says it looks "striking." Mother hasn't said much either way, but she's bought a smart little hat for me "to cover up the roots once they grow in." From this, I deduce she is against a monthly appointment to re-dye my hair.

To be honest, so am I. Besides the unnecessary expense, I've made myself into the image of every storybook evil queen—pale skin, bright blue eyes, and long hair as dark as night. Sometimes as I get ready in the morning, I expect my mirror to inform me that I'm the fairest of them all, except for Snow White. Once blond starts to appear with the black, I'll look like a disheveled skunk.

I wonder what you'll think of it? Of course, I'm assuming you'll visit me soon. Do you get a longer leave after graduation? Mother and Dad would love to meet you. Mother hasn't stopped talking about you since she received your thank-you note. (Good work mentioning Stan Musial; he's her favorite player.[1])

My English lessons continue—some of the officers are becoming quite conversant—but none of my sessions are as interesting as yours, I'm afraid. For obvious reasons, we're skipping the unit on interrogation and manipulation of the enemy in our language school and focusing more on the separation of powers and trial by jury.

You're not going to tell me the secret you thought of during the interrogation, are you? I'm still amazed that someone as clean-cut as you could even have a secret. Let me guess:

- You don't want to become an accountant to help your father with his store. Instead, you've decided to take up a more disreputable career like piracy or tabloid journalism or law.
- You have a long-buried dream of wandering the countryside with a ukulele as a traveling minstrel, strumming Hawaiian hits and "I'll Be Seeing You" to great acclaim.
- Aha! I've got it: Aya has an older sister, one who you're secretly in love with, only she's back in California and you're trapped in Minnesota.

Tell me if I've figured it out.

Yours with a hat on,
Jo

[1] After your letter, Mother began trying to figure out how to make *sukiyaki*. I tell you this so you can pretend to be impressed even though it will be absolutely terrible. She truly believes that *sandefjordsmor* (a sort of Norwegian butter sauce) can substitute for soy sauce. If you decide to visit, be as polite as you can. I'll set our potted fern nearby in case you need to spit anything out.

From Brady McHenry to Johanna

June 13, 1944

Miss Berglund,

Apparently, you gave Stanley a dressing down while I was out today. Golly, he was upset. His toupee was crooked, even. When I finally squeezed out of him what you were so all-fired mad about, I could hardly believe it.

Sure, I'll print a correction. Might add to the drama. But don't think you can just storm down here and snap your fingers to make this paper conform to your every whim.

Be careful what friends you make, sweetheart. That's not a threat; I've just seen enough rising and falling in the world to know how the story goes. If you make an enemy of the town's newspaperman and a friend of a Jap, whatever his job, it's not going to end well for you. Better pick sides carefully is all I'm saying.

Brady McHenry

Notice at the bottom of the last page of the Ironside Broadside on June 14, 1944

It has come to the attention of the editor of the *Ironside Broadside* that Camp Savage is not, in fact, a prisoner of war camp, but a US military training center for Nisei (second-generation Japanese Americans) enlisting in the armed forces. The *Broadside* apologizes for allowing an editorial to be published with this factual error.

Notice distributed to all farms using POW labor and printed in the
Ironside Broadside on June 16, 1944
Typed by Johanna Berglund, several exclamation points removed

In light of recent complaints about lax treatment of POWs while on work detail, the US Army would like to provide the following regulations.

1. POWs and their guard(s) will be picked up at the Camp Ironside branch camp, and under no conditions may they be kept away from the base for more than twelve (12) hours.

2. POWs may ride in the body of the trucks, but not in the cab or in a private vehicle.

3. While they may operate farm machinery as needed, POWs are not allowed to drive cars or trucks at any time.

4. Conversations with POWs will be limited to orders relating to their work.

5. Under no conditions will prisoners be allowed near women.

6. Fraternizing with POWs will not be tolerated. Nothing whatsoever is to be given to the prisoners for any reason whatsoever, including money, stamps, cigarettes, drinks, etc.

We offer these clarifications for the safety of all involved. Remember that the charming youth toiling in your fields may also have set a booby trap that blew a unit of American soldiers into bloody bits. They are still the enemy, and they are here for the sole purpose of providing labor until the end of the war, nothing more.

Thank you in advance for abiding by these regulations. Any violation will result in the revocation of contractor status.

Major J. E. Davies
Commander, Camp Ironside

From Peter to Johanna

June 17, 1944

Dear Jo,

On your hair change: That took an awful lot of courage, and I'm sure you look smashing. Doesn't Hedy Lamarr have dark hair and pale coloring?

All right, I'll admit I asked Roy for that one. He made a pencil sketch of her to illustrate, which I've enclosed. Pretty sure no one could have eyelashes that long, but other than that, I'll bet you look just like her.

I'd love to visit after graduation, if your family will have me. We have new classes of students cycling through all the time, but instructors can take a few extra days of leave if they give enough notice. Forget Chicago (where most of the sightseers go); Ironside Lake is the only place for me.

I can picture it now: canoeing on the lake, strolling down the charming main street, stopping by the diner for a Dr Pepper and a spin of "I'll Be Seeing You" on the jukebox. And best of all, no textbooks anywhere . . . until you trap me after dinner to teach you how to conjugate past tense in Japanese. (Maybe your mother will save me with talk of baseball? I'd even volunteer to wash the dishes.)

Meanwhile, at Camp Savage . . . I'm trying, Jo. That's all I can say about getting to know some of the Hakujin students. You can judge for yourself how successful I've been after you hear what happened yesterday.

I've never been in a conversation that felt more like a scene from a movie. Pop some popcorn, pretend the newsreels and cartoons are over, and here's the feature: a lanky Japanese American instructor in a neat civilian suit enters the recreation hall and scans the room, eyes stopping on a freckled, towheaded student bent over a stack of books, drumming his pencil against the table.

"This is supposed to be free time, Mr. Meyer," I said cheerfully in Japanese. "Want to try a game of chess?"

He pulled a face and responded in English, "I don't like chess. I know good army men aren't supposed to say that. My old man always said it was like war strategy. But I hate it."

I told him he didn't have to be sorry and tried to suggest a game of checkers instead, when he looked at me straight in the eyes. "Listen, I know what you're trying to do, sensei. I'm sure someone put you up to befriending me. I don't mind. But it's not going to work."

Once I got over the wind-knocked-out-of-you feeling of being caught red-handed, I shifted into interrogation mode, switching to English to match him. "What if I'm tired of the way things are and want to do something to fix it?"

"You think you're the first one who's tried?" Kenneth pushed his chair away in a scrape of metal on concrete to look at me. "The week I came, I tossed my bedroll down on a bunk next to a Nisei student. He stared at me until I mumbled something about not knowing he was saving it and moved. That Saturday, when I asked if anybody wanted to go to a movie in downtown Savage, the only men who volunteered were ones who looked like me. So we went together. We've been doing that ever since."

I kept trying to think of something to say, but he seemed to need to get something out.

"My parents own a dairy farm outside of Sacramento. Took out a full-page ad in the newspaper speaking out against relocation back in January 1942 because no one would print their editorial. Do you think anyone here knows that?" He shook his head. "No. Because they don't ask. They probably wouldn't care if they did."

I tried a different approach. "You keep talking about *us* and *them*. Doesn't that make things worse?"

He laughed and tweaked the second lieutenant insignia on his uniform. "The army did that already by pinning me with these." Obviously, my poker face needs work, because he laughed again and said, "Yeah, we know it's not fair, most of us having rank over the others. Grates like a pebble inside your boot. But there's nothing any of us can do about it, so we don't try. Maybe you shouldn't either."

I'm telling you, Jo, I half believed he was going to say, "Checkmate." He had me completely surrounded.

Maybe some of the Hakujin don't keep to themselves because they think they're better than us. Maybe they keep to themselves because they know the US government thinks they're better—and they're ashamed of it.

It's in times like this that I realize just how powerless I really am. Just one man, a little speck of a civilian with a mosquito-loud voice, and just about as easily swatted away. (Can you tell we've had an infestation of the bloodsuckers recently?)

I'd love to hear your thoughts, since I haven't sorted my own yet. You always have a frank way of looking at things.

Your friend,
Peter

June 25, 1944

Dear Peter,

I got a surprise for my last column. It was written not by the latest POW Stefan had selected—Ernst, who wrote quite passionately about his hobby of bird identification both here and in Germany—but by one of the American guards, Private First Class Christopher Wright, who has never exchanged more than three words with me since the time I began here.

That's not an exaggeration. The words were *Yes* and *Over there*.

The column was intended to be for the POWs, but even when I explained that, Christopher didn't budge. "I have something to say," he told me, like a man who's set his course and doesn't mean to be driven from it.

So our writer this week is not an official member of the POW Potato Brigade but a lumberjack of a guard with a slight limp whose playing cards, decorated with Alaskan totem poles, are fuzzy around the edges from dozens of games of solitaire. Before reading his column, that was the sum total of what I knew of him from watching him, sitting alone in a corner of the guards' mess.

In any case, he may startle when I speak to him, but Christopher Wright is a good man. "Appearances can be deceiving" seems to lean toward the true side of "truism."

Speaking of which, yes, you're right: Ironside Lake isn't all bad. I know I complain too much about it. It's small—a few restaurants with dingy tabletops, a drugstore, two competing filling stations, the Golden Palace Theater that will never live up to its grandiose name, etc.—and everyone knows your personal business.

But it's safe, the countryside is lovely, and the people are hardworking and friendly enough. On the whole, it was a good place to grow up.

But now, here I am, grown . . . and still trapped here.

It's nice, though, thinking about you visiting. I hadn't realized how much I've missed you until I pictured you washing Mother's amaryllis-print china, ribbing Dad for cutting out strips from the funnies page, protesting that you simply can't give another Japanese lesson . . . and then sitting down on the sofa anyway to point out everything that's wrong with my character practice. I'm right about that last part, aren't I?

When could you come? We'll be here all summer. We usually take a vacation to Duluth, but it's election year, so Dad is busy campaigning. His reelection is being contested by wealthy "townie" Ed Bartholomew, and therefore not nearly as certain a win as Roosevelt's.

I've thought about your question and what Kenneth Meyer said about giving up trying to unite the two groups. And it seems to me that you're right about being a mosquito . . . but you've noticed by now that even a tiny little insect can make itself heard—and felt.

That's a roundabout way of reassuring you that you can make a difference. You already are. There's not much hope of you single-handedly removing prejudice against Japanese Americans or making other systemic changes, but systems are made up of people, and if you can change a few people, that amounts to something.

That's what I tell myself, at least. I admit the quest to win the town's acceptance for the POW camp has become about more than leaving Ironside Lake and going back to university. I've genuinely enjoyed my time with them; some are almost like friends now.

Time to work on another English lesson for the officers. We're going over the American Revolution today, and I'm attempting to make it seem as different as possible from Hitler's war of aggression, as I know Captain Werner will pounce on that as an analogy if I don't. Wish me luck!

Jo

The *POW Potato Brigade* column in the Ironside Broadside on June 24, 1944

To anyone watching, I probably have the easiest, most boring assignment of the war. Wake up. Drive a truck filled with POWs to a potato farm. Supervise them while they work, marching back and forth.

After that, it's back to the barbed wire and the sleeping quarters, where the night-shift guards share dinner with the daytime fellows. On Sundays, I try to listen to the sermon at Immanuel Lutheran and stand watch over a pew of POWs at the same time. Sleep. Then at Monday's reveille, wake up and do it all over again.

Not the work I thought I'd be doing, but in basic training they told us that being a soldier isn't about heroics, it's about following orders. And orders sent me here.

Which makes me think: These German fellows were doing the same, only for a different country. It's right for us to keep them here, away from the fighting, but it's not right to treat them badly. I'm not only talking about laws and treaties either. The government takes care of that, but we Americans make our own choices. Dozens of little ones that no one in Geneva ever thought of making into rules.

The question is, Who are you when you don't have a law telling you what to do? How do you treat a man you hate when you know he can't fight back?

Think about it. Right now, even.

Fighting a war is one thing. Calling names is another. And I joined the army because I don't care much for bullies.

This spring, the YMCA brought in boxes of books, some in English and some in German, including a book of poems by Rudyard Kipling. It caught my eye because I read Kipling's jungle adventures growing up and thought of myself as an explorer to exotic lands, instead of a boy wearing a dishcloth turban whose "machete" was a butter knife tied to a stick. I hadn't known Kipling wrote poetry.

There was a section called "Epitaphs of the War," all of them about men who died in the Great War. Short, like they were carved on tombstones. Here's my second favorite:

From little towns in a far land we came,
To save our honour and a world aflame.
By little towns in a far land we sleep;
And trust that world we won for you to keep!

According to the title, it was about the Canadians, but it might as well have been about these prisoners in this war, who maybe played war with sticks and butter knives as boys, just like I did. All they wanted was to win Germany's honor back. So they fell into step behind supposedly greater men with greater plans. They want their children to be able to sing their national anthem proudly, safe in the world they won back.

I wonder: As they fall asleep in this little American town, do they still think they'll win? Anyone who doesn't believe the rumors that Germany is being pushed out of France for good will find out the truth soon enough. But what they think of America when they go back home is up to us.

Listen, I'll never make a recruitment poster or a newsreel like my cousin and brother serving over in France, but I'm one of your US soldiers too. We know we're the army's secondhand leavings, marked as physically or psychologically unfit for overseas placement. I'll tell you straight out: I've got a limp from stepping in a bear trap in the Wisconsin woods. Not a bad one, just enough to see me sent here, out of the way.

All of us are doing the best we can with the job we drew. We don't need thanks or a street parade or daily deliveries of warm frosted cinnamon rolls, but we do ask for your respect, and for decency toward the men we guard.

Private First Class Christopher Wright

From Peter to Johanna

June 29, 1944

Dear Jo,

I can't wait to hear what people think of Christopher's column. He makes some very good points. Besides the articles you send me, the only part of our newspaper I have time to read is the front page, or sometimes the "Maps for the Armchair Tactician" feature. Like everyone else, we've gotten caught up in news of troops in France, but even more, the offensive in Saipan. Some of our graduates are probably there—or used to be, if they were killed in action. I haven't had a student die yet. I'm not sure how I'll handle it.

Maybe you're right and I should keep trying with the Hakujin. It's just that these days, I'm so tired. It doesn't seem worth it, not with graduation so close.

Whenever I can, I like to take walks at night before

going to sleep, to help let go of the stress. That's one thing Minnesota's got going for it that Tokyo and San Francisco didn't: You can see more stars. When I look up, I try to remember those Greek legends you told me about: Andromeda and the sea monster, Hercules and his twelve impossible tasks, Pegasus and his . . . wings (I can't remember anything else about him, sorry). Sometimes I don't remember which stars are supposed to form what shape, but they always make me think of you.

In my years studying in Japan, I learned different names and stories about the stars. Next week, July 7, is the *Tanabata* festival, a celebration of two star-crossed lovers. Literally. The legend goes that Orihime (your star Vega), a talented weaver, became sad because her endless work kept her from falling in love. Then one day she met and fell in love with Hikoboshi (the star Altair), a lowly cowherd. After they married, they began to neglect their duties, so Orihime's angry father separated the two of them with the great river of the Milky Way and only allowed them to meet one summer night each year.

All over Japan, archways flutter with banners, illuminations light up the sky, merchants set up elaborate displays . . . and teenagers eat far, far too many bowls of cold *somen* noodles. You'd have been disgusted with me, Jo.

That was in 1933, when I was only fifteen. I'm sure they've canceled the festival the past several years. Poor Orihime and Hikoboshi will remain apart until peace comes again.

Each Japanese child is supposed to write a wish on a *tanzaku* streamer and attach it to a bamboo branch. As a teenager, I thought that was silly, but this year, here I am with a strip of typewriter paper curled around a stick, leaning against my desk where I can see it.

Didn't you say you had a wishing well out in the woods? July 7 might be a good day to visit it.

Your friend,
Peter

P.S. I can't lie. You're right. If it's a Japanese lesson you want, you'll get it. I'll even bring my textbooks. How about August 11–13? That's after graduation, when I'll be much more pleasant to be around.

From Johanna to Peter

July 3, 1944

German Idiom of the Day: *Wenn man ihm den kleinen Finger gibt, so nimmt er die ganze Hand*. Literally, "if you give him your little finger, he'll take the whole hand," meaning someone who takes advantage of kindness.

Context: Stefan Werner said it to one of the POWs, Dieter Bormann. Context unknown because he stopped speaking when I approached.

Dear Peter,

I'm glad you enjoyed Christopher's column. I can't say for sure how the town reacted to it, except I know that Mrs. Roberta Wyatt, president of the Lutheran Daughters of the Reformation and a very influential woman, called Major Davies to express her admiration for "that fine young man" and request he be given a promotion, which is not, apparently, army policy.

Also, Christopher reported, in as few words as possible, that the men all saluted him at bed check this week. And some civilian woman—he didn't say who—used probably a month's worth of sugar and butter rations to present him with the best-tasting cinnamon rolls he's ever eaten. A brilliant tactic, mentioning that in the article.

You've given me a new appreciation for the stars in Minnesota. I went out for a walk late last night (don't worry, just in Turner's Woods near our house). Though it was a few days early, in honor of your festival, I tossed a wish in the well that I made with Erik and Annika as a child.

I couldn't bring myself to go inside the woodshed we built—too many memories past that battered playhouse door. It was hard enough to see the initials carved into the wall under the window: *JB, ES, AS.*

But I looked up at the stars on the way back, and that's something.

In other news, today I returned from yet another luncheon with Evelyn Davies and Linda Harrigan, Major Davies's secretary—a sweet, timid sort whose sole goal seems to be making sure Evelyn approves of her—when I noticed a strange figure standing forlornly inside the gate beside a little red wagon: Annika Sorenson. She was, she explained, delivering to the guards donations of back-issue magazines—*Life, Look,* and the *Saturday Evening Post,* mostly, although I saw a few *Theological Studies*—collected by the Lutheran Daughters of the Reformation.

"Did you draw the short straw?" I asked, and then immediately felt bad.

But Annika just said, "I volunteered," and I pretended not to be surprised.

I picked up the *Life* magazine with Princess Elizabeth

on the cover. "Remember when you forced me to use your grandmother's wire rollers to curl your hair up to your ears like hers?"

I swear, Annika actually giggled like we were fourteen again. "How could I forget? When I took out the curlers, I looked like . . ."

"Shirley Temple zapped with a cattle prod."

She nodded, and the laughter stopped. "That's what Erik said. He teased me for weeks."

The mention of Erik's name didn't bring the usual tension, just a distant wistfulness in Annika's eyes. We talked for a while as I walked her to the guardhouse. Little things, the warm weather and the sermon on Sunday. By the time I left her, she was swarmed with three grateful, slightly tongue-tied guards, surprised to find a pretty girl walking among them. Christopher Wright was there and actually acknowledged my existence by nodding at me, so that's progress.

It was odd to be speaking cordially to Annika again but also . . . nice. I still want to return to the university as soon as possible, but it does make me wonder if maybe I can leave some things in better condition than when I arrived. Is that possible? Or are there some hurts that can't be healed?

Annika was always the hopeless romantic of our town, so different from me. I was surprised there wasn't another pair of initials carved into the woodshed next to hers by now. Most of the young men are gone, of course, but I haven't heard rumors of a sweetheart across the sea. Maybe the war put her dreams on hold as surely as it did mine.

Any Independence Day celebrations? Or is that something your serious students don't have time for?

Dad always splurges on July fourth and buys us what he considers "highly overpriced" root beer floats at the soda fountain. Irene and her family will join us until the baby gets fussy. I always have to survive the parade first because of my familial association, wearing something properly red, white, or blue, preferably all three. This year all I've got is a plain navy skirt and white blouse. Maybe I'll ask to borrow one of Cornelia Knutson's hats—she has one bedecked with an orchard full of plastic cherries. Since she always wears the same three black dresses out of mourning for her husband, she makes her hats as colorful as possible.

The Major and Mrs. Davies will be leading the parade this year. Evelyn has grand visions of brass bands and bathing beauties from her New York days, and I'm sure she'll be disappointed to find that our grandest float is Old Man Lundquist dispensing samples of homemade cheese from a wagon pulled by his ancient plow horse. I can't wait to hear her report.

Jo

From Mrs. Berglund to Cornelia Knutson

July 5, 1944

Dear Cornelia,

I'd be delighted to join you for supper next week. Thank you for the invitation. It's been far too long. However, I'm afraid Johanna has asked me to pass on her regrets. She's busy with work, staying at the camp into the evenings most days. Sometimes I hear her late at night, clattering away on that typewriter of hers—she never handwrites anything, since she inherited Carl's terrible penmanship. It can't be good for her health, sleeping so little, but she won't be convinced.

I'm worried about her, Cornelia. I only share that with you because I know you'll be discreet, but when Jo commits to something, she is dedicated to an extreme. One look at the dark circles under her eyes tells me she's exhausting herself.

Sometimes I hear her arguing with Carl about whether it's just to imprison the POWs here at all, so far from home. This morning when I came to wake her up, she muttered something in German, half asleep. She'd overslept, which I'm sure you can guess she rarely does.

In any case, thank you for thinking of her, and do keep inviting her.

I was so glad to see you at yesterday's parade. It was rather daring, the high-school marching band choosing to play "God Bless America" instead of the national anthem, wasn't it? And the baton-twirling routine was very nearly perfect. I do admit to cringing when Evelyn Davies stepped in a pile of horse droppings. The way she screeched about "backward country living" before her husband shushed her . . . ah well. I suppose it can't be helped.

I look forward to supper on Monday.

Elaine Berglund

From Peter to Johanna

July 8, 1944

Happy Fourth of July to you as well. I'm sure you looked patriotic enough, with or without Mrs. Knutson's hat. As for what I did on good ol' Independence Day, I spent it working on my next strategy to reach out to the Hakujin students. I'd thought and thought about what to do, and I came upon my last possible strategy: food.

You laugh, but it's true. We even teach it in interrogation class. A bribe of delicious food can look very promising to a captive used to rations of unseasoned rice, and a full stomach never hurts to get someone talking.

I've got a camp full of hardworking men in their late teens and early twenties. A cheap buffet in town might be the best weapon I have, and Herbie's gives a good (slightly greasy) bang for the buck.

When I invited Kenneth Meyer to go with a group of students on our rare day off from classes, I expected him to ask why and taunt me into another verbal chess game. Instead, he immediately said, "I'm in."

I sputtered, giving him time to add, "Listen, I made that speech last time because I needed to get it off my chest. I wanted you to know I'd tried. But that's the thing. They're always telling us during drills that in the army, the one who tries doesn't count for anything. It's the one who keeps trying and doesn't give up who makes it." He shrugged. "So whatever your plan is, I want in. Unless you say a chess team."

"What makes you think I have a plan beyond getting dinner at Herbie's?"

Kenneth drilled me with a look. "Sensei, you teach strategy."

It was a fair point, and anyway, he was right. "What do you think about a baseball team?"

He considered that. "Don't make me play shortstop, and we've got a deal." We shook on it and everything.

So that's how I got my first Hakujin ally. It's odd, figuring out how to integrate a minority group that holds all the power and privilege. Not something I ever thought I'd need to do, and with less than six weeks until graduation, we're running out of time.

We had our first practice Sunday night with Kenneth and two of his buddies on the team, along with Terry and Roy and others, and I realized maybe I didn't need to. Maybe I just needed to let the boys play. Give them something to do where they have to work together and talk to each other.

They've taken to calling me coach instead of sensei. I like it. I got the idea from Helmut's POW Potato Brigade article about football—you should tell him he's an inspiration.

I'm glad to hear you and Annika are getting along better. I'll pass on your own advice back to you: Don't give up on people.

Your friend,
Peter

P.S. I notice you didn't tell me what you wished for. Suspicious.

From Johanna to Peter

July 11, 1944

German Idiom of the Day: *Da kannst du Gift drauf nehmen.* Literally, "you can take poison on that," meaning you can be completely certain of it.

Context: When I asked Captain Werner if there were any unauthorized Nazi gatherings after curfew, as we've heard about in other camps, he assured me that he would certainly know about them if there were.

Dear Peter,

Well, you've gone and bullied me into being social.
When I got your letter about your baseball team, I
was shamed into accepting a dinner-party invitation
from Cornelia Knutson. The purpose was stated as
"socialization and diverting activities." I think I was
picturing something out of Jane Austen—whist and taking
a turn about the room while making snide comments
about someone's cravat.

But I went anyway, only to find out it was a Monopoly
tournament, with an afterthought of dinner on the
sideboard—salmon pasties, blueberries, and popcorn balls
so glazed with corn syrup that the counterfeit bills stuck
to our fingers.

Cornelia had two Monopoly boards set up, the one in
the parlor out-of-the-box new, card edges crisp as a knife's
edge, while the one in the dining room was faded and
bent. When she noticed me staring at it, Cornelia smiled.
"We played every night until he passed, Henry and I. I
even let him win now and then."

Based on her performance, I don't think she was
joking. Besides me, the lady of the house faced down her
daughter Hattie, Annika Sorenson, and Martha Yeats,
the one whose son is a POW in Japan. After acquiring
three out of four railroads, Cornelia risked her last dollar
buying the green properties on auction and ran the rest
of us into the ground with rent. Meanwhile, the table in
the parlor—we could hear them through the archway—
played on at a sedate, self-conscious pace, punctuated by
stories of Evelyn Davies's many vacations to Atlantic City,
where the actual Boardwalk, Park Place, and the rest of
the streets are found. (Yes, she was there too. It was a full
collection of Ironside Lake misfits.)

I was sure it would be dreadfully awkward, but by the time I landed on Cornelia's Pacific Avenue hotel for the third time, even Mrs. Yeats was clucking at me in pity, and Annika was in unusually good spirits, though I caught her daydreaming a few times. By the time we'd finished the game and the popcorn balls, we were all talking and even laughing.

When I helped Cornelia carry empty punch glasses to the kitchen, I asked her if there was any ulterior motive in her guest list. She shooed me to put the glasses in the sink. "We women need one another, especially during wartime, when we never know what news the radio or a telegram might bring."

"Isn't that basically 'Eat, drink, and be merry, for tomorrow we die'?" I asked.

Without the slightest hesitation, she fired back, "Of course not. It's 'Eat, drink, and be merry, for tomorrow we may die, but today we're still here and there must be a reason for that.'" She twisted the wedding ring on her bone-thin finger and repeated, "There must be."

I hope she's right. I hope there's a reason I'm still here, when so many young people better than me—like Erik—have died.

It was, in all, a good use of an evening.

In other news, PFC Christopher Wright paid me a visit today. He asked if it was true that the major said the camp might shut down if there's any serious trouble with the town. I said yes, and for the split second that he made eye contact with me, I saw deep concern. He continued, "If I can help . . . I will. Just tell me what to do." Then he nodded and fled—it was at least at a trot—leaving me staring after him in wonder.

Now, I know that you're going to say he's been

admiring me from afar all this time. If by *admiring* you mean *actively avoiding*, then you're correct. Even in offering his help, he looked like a blindfolded man before a firing squad.

Am I really that frightening? Be honest, Peter. Were you afraid of me when we first met?

Failing that explanation, I can't come up with another. His column made it clear that he'd be happy to be transferred to another duty. Yet, out of the clear blue sky, he's ready to charge to the defense of the camp. I wonder what changed?

Jo

P.S./Appendix: I didn't mention what I wished for because it's the same thing everyone wishes for: that the Allies would win the war soon. I suppose it was like a prayer, wasn't it? Maybe I thought I could get God's attention if I used a more unconventional method. I admitted that to Captain Werner after church this week when he asked why I never bowed my head for the closing prayer at the end of the service. I rambled on about the playhouse in the woods and the wishing well and feeling a remnant of my childlike faith when I was there. He said he'd pray for me, which I report to you as evidence that he's not a terrible person after all. So there.

From Peter to Johanna

July 17, 1944

Dear Jo,

Monopoly, is it? I've never played. Our recreation hall is only stocked with the usual classics (cards, dominoes, chess, checkers) and a few traditional Japanese games, like *Gomoku* and *Richi Mahjong*, the tiles hand-carved by one of our students. I'm glad it tempted you out of your house. We're both learning about dealing with other people, aren't we?

Will I get to meet Mrs. Knutson when I visit? She sounds like a real character.

You know, I've heard other men lamenting trick questions from women, but they're usually more along the lines of, "Do my hips look wide in this dress?" not "Do you think I'm frightening?" So all I can think to say is: You're like the Grand Canyon, Jo. Some people stand before it and see strength and beauty, but others can only feel small and shake in their boots. (Only partly joking.)

As to PFC Wright's motive, maybe his brush with fame from his column has made him see himself as the camp defender. You might be able to use his help. Don't try to charge into battle all on your own; it's a bad tactical move. I know this because I taught cooperative tactics today, both in class and on the baseball field, and maybe, just maybe, saw a little bit of progress.

Another letter from my family came in with yours. I can never tell if Father's stoic updates are honest or attempts to keep me from worrying, but according to him, everything is fine. Maybe even California has calmed down and figured out who their true enemies are. My sister will be starting school in a little over a month, and she's terrified she'll be behind. The internment schools were overcrowded and under-resourced, but she's a genius with numbers, so I know she'll catch up.

As usual, time to slave away on exam preparation. Only one month until graduation of our largest class to date. Even Terry, whose idea of studying involves putting his textbook under his pillow so he can "subconsciously absorb it," has been caught going through flashcards, so you know it's serious.

Your friend,
Peter

P.S. That was good of you, to wish for the war's end. I can't say I did the same. I was thinking of things smaller and closer to home. As for Captain Werner . . . I can still dislike someone who talks about prayer, especially if it's in the context of making small talk. The less he knows about your personal life, the better.

EVIDENCE FOR THE PROSECUTION

CONSTITUTION OF THE UNITED STATES, ARTICLE III, SECTION 3

Treason against the United States, shall consist only in levying War against them, or in adhering to their Enemies, giving them Aid and Comfort. No Person shall be convicted of Treason unless on the Testimony of two Witnesses to the same overt Act, or on Confession in open Court.

POSSIBLE PRECEDENT: PROSECUTION OF THE SHITARA SISTERS, 1944

Relevant aspects of US citizens charged with treason/POW camp escapes; request full trial transcript.

Summary: Sisters Tsuroko Wallace, Florence Otani, and Misao Tanigoshi (maiden name: Shitara) were accused of treason and conspiracy to commit treason. The three women had been detained at Amache Relocation Center and sent out on a regular work detail, where they met two German POWs, Heinrich Haider and Hermann Loescher.

Two of the sisters began an affair with the men, and when the Germans decided to escape, the Shitara sisters provided them with aid and drove them across the border to Mexico. Upon their capture, the Germans implicated the Shitara sisters, American citizens of Japanese descent, in the escape.

Tactic Taken by Defense: Rather than denying or defending the sisters' actions, the defense chose to frame them as weak willed and motivated by romantic feelings. This, then, would not be considered treason, since they must prove a desire to harm the United States as the primary motive. The women were described as seduced, emotional, and harmless. This is believed to have affected the ruling.

Key Evidence:

- The incriminating (i.e., amorous) photographs of the Shitara sisters with the German POWs found in Haider's and Loescher's possession.
- Haider's and Loescher's original testimony in pretrial interrogations (assistance of sisters in escape, incl. transportation, provision of money and maps, and other aid).
- Haider's and Loescher's changed testimony during the trial, explaining that they tricked the women into helping and had no intention of returning to Germany to fight, resulting in lowered charges.

- General distrust of Japanese Americans and fear of race mixing ("Japanazi romance" in newspaper headlines).

Verdict: Found "not guilty" of treason, found "guilty" of conspiracy to commit treason.

Other Notes: Before the trial, the negative and sensational press surrounding the accused made it difficult to find an unbiased jury. Possibly the same effect in play in this case?

Avoid delays where possible; push for February grand jury proceedings and March trial. In the months before the case went to trial, all momentum behind proving intent to commit treason was lost.

By definition, it should have been impossible to convict of conspiracy to commit treason if no treasonable intent was proven. Possibly a compromise for public opinion.

All three sisters declined to testify on their own behalf. (Highly unlikely with our accused.)

CHAPTER EIGHT

July 18, 1944

Dear Miss Berglund,

After all I did to secure this position for you, I am surprised that I have not heard a single word from you this spring and summer. However, Major Davies has jotted off an enthusiastic note or two on your behalf explaining how vital you've been to the camp. Army-trained translators are notoriously overconfident in their abilities despite the fact that their training is inadequate, so I'm pleased that you are representing the superiority of university-trained professionals.

If you would write a short report as to your work so far, the university trustees would like to deliver it to the administrator of the foreign-language scholarship.

I must ask that you take care to avoid the rather abrupt manner you often displayed in class. The point of communication is not, in fact, to alienate as many people as possible in as few words as possible. Bear this principle in mind as you write, please.

If you could deliver your letter to me by the end of the month, I would be most grateful.

Dr. Sheridan Smythe
Chair of the Modern
Languages Department,
University of Minnesota

From Johanna to Dr. Smythe

July 22, 1944

Dear Dr. Smythe,

Thank you for inquiring after my progress. Prior to this, I thought I'd let Major Davies write on my behalf and spare you my "abrupt manner."

I will send a letter to you within the next few weeks. You should recall that I've never turned in a single assignment late, no matter how trivial.

And don't worry, I will have proper respect for the donor and his financial contributions to my university studies, no matter how mysteriously anonymous.

Finally, in defense of the army-trained translators, while I have a much broader and literary knowledge of German, the guards here have more practical instruction and aren't nearly the dullards you imply. I've learned a great deal from them in the past few months. It's an entirely different matter to translate Kafka and Kant than it is to calm a mob of angry POWs when the mess hall runs out of coffee at breakfast.

I hope to be rejoining your classes in September. Save a desk for me in the front row.

Cordially,
Johanna Berglund

A draft of a letter from Johanna to the University of Minnesota trustees and scholarship donor, never sent

July 23, 1944

To my Mysterious Scholarship Donor,

Well, you got what you wanted. I'm serving my country during wartime, and in doing so, I gave up the studies I love. It feels unreasonable that all of my hopes and dreams for the future rest on the favor of some anonymous Daddy Warbucks who's probably smoking a Cuban cigar in a Summit Avenue mansion.

A draft of a letter from Johanna to the University of Minnesota trustees and scholarship donor, never sent

July 23, 1944

To Whom It May Concern,

Dr. Smythe, my ~~stuffy~~ academic advisor, has informed me that you are using the scholarship ~~to blackmail and bribe young people into public service~~ to recognize students working toward careers in politics and diplomacy. I hope the following will help you understand how my current work aligns with this goal.

~~Even I am forced to admit that~~ my time at Camp Ironside has been fascinating. My work requires skills such as a nuanced approach to interactions, an understanding of people, and the ability to adapt to new developments~~, none of which I possess in abundance.~~

My recent tasks have included teaching an English class to ~~spoiled~~ officers ~~who resent being indoctrinated~~, censoring mail, serving as a liaison to the YMCA, making rounds of the camp to assess the men's attitudes, settling disputes about ~~the quality and number of latrines~~ important matters of day-to-day life, and regularly ~~infuriating half of the town's population by~~ editing a column in the town newspaper designed to improve the camp's relationship with the citizens of Ironside Lake.

Currently, the camp is ~~relatively~~ entirely peaceful. The community has reached a place of ~~grudging~~ acceptance since there have been no disturbances since the men's arrival. Around two dozen men even attend a worship service in town. When I visit worksites to assess conditions, the farmers report that the prisoners' work ~~is adequate~~ exceeds expectations.

I feel I have a duty to help my fellow Americans recognize their essential shared humanity with the POWs. If only the rest of Ironside Lake, the rest of the nation, even, could sit down and speak with ~~Stefan Werner about childhood memories and women's rights and the US Constitution~~ these men, they would want the war to end even sooner to prevent the loss of life on both sides, and would pursue a policy of peaceful reconciliation rather than vindictive punishment. However, this is something I feel I can do even more effectively from Minneapolis than Ironside Lake, since it seems my services here might not be needed for the duration of the year.

I hope this essay is enough to satisfy your ~~unreasonable demands~~ keen interest in the next generation and their pursuit of noble goals.

From Johanna to the University of Minnesota trustees and scholarship donor

July 23, 1944

To Whom It May Concern,

First of all, please let me extend my heartfelt thanks for the scholarship that enabled my first two years of study at the University of Minnesota. I believe it is vital to have women represented in all fields, as there are roles we are uniquely qualified to fill. I am finding this to be true in my current position.

I have attached a detailed description of my responsibilities here at the camp and how they might prepare me for a possible future career in diplomacy and foreign aid.

Major Davies will confirm that the government is seriously considering dissolving my position within the next month if there are no setbacks in relations between the camp and the community. Therefore, I'm excited to report that I plan on reenrolling in courses beginning in September. I hope this essay satisfies you that I am qualified for the scholarship to which you have so generously donated.

If you would like more detail, either about my current work or my future aspirations, please feel free to write me at this address.

Yours truly,
Johanna Berglund

ALLEGED NAZI BREAKOUT
ON LOCAL'S PROPERTY

A local farmer believes he saw one of the prisoners from the POW camp on his property last night at around ten o'clock in the evening. Lifelong Ironside Lake resident Jacob Lindberg reports that he was sitting on the porch smoking when he saw someone moving at the edge of his property.

"At first, I thought it was one of the Johansson boys trying to steal a chicken," he said. "But there was just enough moon, I caught a glimpse of his back. I'm sure I saw *PW* marked there. Dead sure."

According to Lindberg, when he called out, "Who's there?", unsure if the man was armed, the stranger ran for the trees.

Camp Ironside's only statement was a repetition of the safety measures in place: Curfew and bed checks ensure everyone is in their barracks, except on Sunday evening, the camp's day of rest. During the week, prisoners are taken to their work assignments under armed guard and are fully visible at all times while laboring. Guards regularly patrol the fence and are stationed day and night in two sixteen-foot guard towers overlooking the camp.

Our research indicates there have been dozens of escapes from camps across the nation, including several reported in Minnesota. Most were classified as "incidents" because the prisoners returned of their own accord the next day, sneaking out for drink or other entertainment. The New Ulm newspaper has reported three such incidents in the past year alone, with exactly the same security measures as our own camp.

What's more, under the Geneva Convention, an escape is not classified as a crime. Unless it can be proven that a POW has committed theft, murder, or another violation of the laws of the land, he can only be disciplined with time in solitary confinement (maximum of thirty days), a bread and water diet, and the loss of some privileges.

Mayor Carl Berglund has announced that he will investigate the camp's security and provide a statement for any interested community members at next week's town hall meeting, including procedure for reporting any possible escapes.

From Stefan Werner to Johanna, left on her desk at headquarters
Recalled from memory—original was burned

July 24, 1944

I did not want to answer your question while there were others around. They might see my answer as a betrayal, but I will tell you the truth.

Yes, it is possible that some have gone outside the compound, though I have not heard of it. A man could bend the wires of the fence and dig underneath like a badger, if he meant to bolt.

Still, I am not concerned, and your army men should not be either. It might be that some men slip out every now and again to meet a woman or to go for a moonlit swim or to fulfill a challenge. They are bored, and escape is something to fill the time. But if they do go, they always come back. Never has morning roll call revealed one of my men missing.

You are always clever, Fräulein Berglund. Take my advice in this: Be clever enough to let it go.

And please destroy this note. If my men or the major found it, the worst of it would fall on me.

–S

From Johanna to Major Davies

July 24, 1944

Major Davies,

While Miss Harrigan was out to lunch, I took six calls from her desk regarding suspicions of sabotage caused by our POWs. Six. In an hour. It seems like everyone in town thinks the camp operates a revolving door for saboteurs and thieves. I'm going to be hearing the telephone in my sleep tonight.

The following is an exhaustive list of reported incidents. Some have also notified the local police and possibly rung up Fort Snelling and the FBI and General Eisenhower's aide-de-camp, for all I know.

- Don "Danger" Dahl's tractor malfunctioned this week. He is sure it was caused by our men—despite the fact that his farm hosts no POW workers—because he found a footprint by the fence that "seemed like a German-made boot." When I pointed out that we gave our POWs American clothing upon arrival, he asked what a woman could possibly know about farm machinery and to put you on the line.
- Clarence Jakes at the Golden Palace Theater thinks the POWs stole fifty cents' worth of Nickel Naks that went missing last month when they went to the movies. I told him that Nickel Naks are disgusting and not worth stealing, and besides, they make too much noise rattling

around in the box. A sensible thief would have taken
a fistful of Whiz or Butterfinger bars instead. He hung
up on me, probably to suggest me as a suspect for the
candy larceny.

- Cornelia Knutson confided that her next-door neighbor, Mrs. Harold Reynolds, will probably report her
rooster as stolen by the POWs. However, what really
happened was that, last week, Mrs. Knutson threw
a glass paperweight of the New York City stock exchange out the window at it in frustration, clubbing the
aforementioned rooster in the head. It died instantly
"without suffering," and Mrs. Knutson buried it in her
begonia bed. I counseled her to admit her crime to Mrs.
Reynolds, and she has reluctantly promised to do so.

- Martha Yeats heard that Betty Madison's brother
Henry couldn't find his pitchfork after milking one
day. "What if those German boys got ahold of it and
use it to stab the guards as they sleep?" she asks. "And
how can any of us rest when we know there's a security
breach of this magnitude?" How indeed.

- Dorothy Lewis from the Lutheran Daughters of the
Reformation believes that the graffiti on the church
last month was actually put there by the POWs in a
"midnight rampage." This, to her, would explain the
"atrocious spelling." I hadn't heard of any such graffiti
and will look into it right away, but it seems ludicrous
that our men would vandalize an establishment that
has shown them so warm a welcome, and I expressed as
much.

- Brady McHenry's wasn't strictly a sabotage report,
but he did pass along the delightful statistic that he's
already received a dozen letters at the *Broadside* office,
some of which might be considered threats, regarding

Camp Ironside's "gross negligence." He said he'd be happy to bundle them up and bring them over tomorrow. I told him he could keep them, and also to stop calling me "sweetheart" and trying to get a quote from me on the record.

I would like to request that I not be called on to act as substitute secretary in the future. I have important work to do and can't waste my time being stenographer to the collective paranoia of a town whipped into a frenzy by a specious article.

Johanna Berglund

From Pastor Sorenson to Johanna

July 25, 1944

Dear Johanna,

Your father mentioned you interrogated him about the vandalism of Immanuel Lutheran some weeks ago. I wish you'd come directly to me. I never intended to conceal anything, though I am surprised you heard about it. I'd thought Annika and I were the only ones who knew. I wouldn't even have told her—the phrases written were not ones a lady should ever be exposed to—but her bedroom, if you remember, faces the church, and in the summer, her windows are open, so she was the one to hear the vandals in the first place.

As to why I didn't tell anyone, what could we do? Search every house, barn, and hand for specks of red paint? Ask at the grocery who bought several cartons of eggs at once? In any case, I had no intention of pressing charges even if we could find the culprit.

A small part of me wanted to nail my own "95 Theses" on the church door in response, like Luther himself, but about the treatment that Scripture demands of the foreigner in our midst. "Here I stand, I can do no other," etc. But I'm better with a paintbrush than I am a hammer.

The way I see it, though, whoever scrawled those cruel and obscene words wanted to make their mark. They wanted to be heard. And if Annika and I could ruin their hopes by going out at 3:00 a.m. with a bucket of soapy water and a can of paint, well, we've done the best we could.

I knew what I was getting into, allowing your prisoners of war into our church. Still, it makes me weary, even angry, scrubbing away so much mistrust. I think the reason pastors are more apt to believe in depravity is because we see so very much of it—not only in others, but also in our own hearts.

I know you think the current uproar is unreasonable, and I'm sure much of it is. But we are to be "wise as serpents and harmless as doves," according to our Lord. I would urge you not to be too much of the dove toward our brothers in your camp, and I will exhort the others in town to set aside some of their snakelike vigor for casting blame.

Peace be with you,
Pastor A. Sorenson

Article in the Ironside Broadside *on July 30, 1944*

FIRE AT CAMP IRONSIDE

Members of the Ironside Lake Volunteer Fire Brigade were called out late last night to battle raging flames centered on one of the camp's storage facilities. The fire was extinguished around midnight, and no one was seriously injured. Damage to the building was significant, but the flames barely touched the roof of the adjacent structure—the camp's chapel—before it was contained.

A guard on one of the tower platforms reportedly saw the rising smoke and alerted camp leadership. By the time the fire brigade arrived, many of the prisoners had abandoned their barracks and added to the general chaos by running around "in a disorderly manner," according to our source.

Yet the warning sirens installed in the guard towers were never deployed, presumably because the camp commander wished to keep knowledge of this late-night emergency from the general public.

Cause of the fire is presently unknown, but an anonymous source close to the scene indicated that it may not have been an accident.

Once again, Major Davies was unable to be reached for comment, but it is assumed that proper safety and disciplinary action will be taken. Some have speculated that this hazardous incident might cause a Red Cross investigation into the camp, as it would be a danger to the men to remain in a damaged camp, and a danger to our own citizens if the men were allowed outside the fence in case of another such emergency.

This is the second in a string of troubling incidents at Camp Ironside in the space of one week, the first being the recent alleged sighting of an escaped prisoner.

Notice posted to the Camp Ironside canteen
Translated into German by Johanna Berglund (three exclamation
points removed from original)

July 30, 1944

Due to the incident last night, matches and tobacco will no longer be sold at the camp canteen during the month of August. If there are no further disturbances, sales will resume on a trial basis, with restrictions on designated smoking areas. This policy will be strictly enforced. Fire of any sort is a danger to all of us in a contained facility.

Tomorrow, we will hold an assembly to review emergency procedures for disasters of all kinds so that all will be prepared to face them with order and discipline.

Major J. E. Davies

From Johanna to Peter

July 30, 1944

> German Idiom of the Day: *Er verlangt immer eine Extrawurst.* Literally, "he always asks for extra sausage," meaning he expects special treatment or privileges.

> Context: Grumblings about Stefan using his position as camp spokesman to smoke cigars with the major in his office.

Dear Peter,

No sooner had I posted a letter to my university scholarship donor assuring him there would be no incidents when some fool decides to burn the camp down.

Well, to be fair, it might have been an accident, but that's certainly not what the major thinks. I know because today I was accused of arson.

If you're shocked by that, imagine how I felt.

Although I heard no sirens in the night, I witnessed the hard work of the volunteer fire department the moment I reported to work this morning. Our central storage unit—where we kept extra clothes, donations, and bins for the weekly laundry truck delivery—was a charred mass of rubble, and the corner of the chapel roof has minor damage as well. Thank God that was all.

From what I gathered from the gawkers, guards, and prisoners alike, they found two cigarette butts in the rubble and think the blaze might have been lit by a careless toss of the still-burning stubs.

PFC Wright was the one who summoned me away from the crowd to see the major. Naturally, I assumed it was to ask me to make inquiries alongside Captain Werner about who had started the fire. I had no way of suspecting the real purpose. Wright looked grim as a gargoyle, but he's always uncomfortable around me, so it was impossible to tell the difference.

At headquarters, I found a clean ashtray centered in the middle of my desk, and when I asked about it, Major Davies brusquely reiterated the policy about smoking out of doors. After I reminded him that I don't smoke, he stared at me hard, as if trying to bore into my brain.

It turns out the real issue is twofold. First, the cigarette stubs found at the scene had the clean-cut lines and rounded red logos of Lucky Strikes, not the clumsy, hand-rolled-in-newspaper cigarettes that the POWs smoke. Our canteen only sells tobacco, not finished cigarettes, so the major concluded that the cigarettes in the rubble must have been left by a guard or staff member able to go into town and purchase them.

Second, I had a . . . discussion, you might say, with Stefan Werner regarding cigarettes recently. It got a bit heated, pardon the pun, and the major must have heard all of it from his office. Stefan found out about my resolve not to smoke and called me "the perfect Nazi woman," since apparently Hitler hates the vile habit. I didn't find his teasing at all funny, but I had completely forgotten about it. "You don't think I'd take up smoking just because Captain Werner approved of my abstinence?" I demanded.

Instead of admitting it was absurd, Davies looked me square in the face and said, "There was the incident with the hair."

And then he had the gall to open up the Acme Tires matchbook in my top drawer, which he had clearly done before I arrived. Yes, there was one match missing, but not because I had gone out smoking, just because I'd wanted to burn something earlier. A scrap of trash, that's all.

By then, my face was Campbell's tomato soup red out of anger, but it must have looked like shame, because Major Davies retreated to his office, muttering under his breath.

So now the camp commander suspects not only that I would break camp rules to defy a POW's teasing, but also that I'd lie about it to keep myself from blame. Dyeing my hair in response to Stefan's taunts is one thing, breaking camp rules is entirely another.

Besides that, the timing is all wrong. Yes, I was at the camp later than usual last night—Mother had to reheat dinner for me—but the fire must have begun at something like eleven o'clock. No cigarette smolders for hours before igniting, does it? And for goodness' sake, everyone knows to make sure a cigarette is fully stamped out before leaving it. I am the most practical person within this barbed-wire perimeter; I would never forget something so basic, even if I hadn't much practice.

Major Davies is also quite upset that today's edition of the *Broadside* covered the fire. The volunteer firefighters were asked not to report the incident, so that means either they broke their word, or someone else within the camp leaked the information to the newspaper early this morning.

I suspect that's why he declared on the spot, weeks earlier than his planned reevaluation, that my position will not be dissolved. With tensions inside the camp and out, we need a go-between, he said, to keep things as peaceable as possible. I'm sure it was to punish me for not admitting to something I didn't do. He knows I want to go back to university.

I still could. I could quit this moment and storm back to school for my third year, getting a part-time job, perhaps, to make up the difference in tuition lost from the scholarship. With all my practice at the typewriter lately, I'd make an unparalleled clerk. But there's the question of Dr. Smythe letting me back in, and I know my parents would be humiliated if I stole away from town in the night. Dad would never hold it over me, but I'm fully aware of his reelection bid in November. And what would happen to the column and the men who look at me as their champion? Even if a replacement could be found, a new translator certainly wouldn't keep that going.

No, I'm afraid I'm here to stay for now. The men will leave at the end of November, so perhaps I can start afresh second semester and make up for lost time. Unless the farmers request POW labor for another year and I'm trapped until the war ends.

To make matters worse, Brady McHenry canceled this week's POW Potato Brigade column. Not because he's concerned about letting the hubbub about the fire and the alleged escape die down—oh no—but to give him more space to print additional letters of outrage. ("It's the citizens who buy the papers, my dear, not the POWs.") Poor Kurt's heartwarming description of the wood carving class he started will have to wait until another week, I suppose.

Give me some good news, Peter. Please. I need it.

Jo

From Johanna to Peter, a graduation card

July 31, 1944

Peter, I'm an idiot. No sooner had I posted my letter when I remembered your students' examinations and graduation are this coming weekend. I know you're not the one being tested, but of course you'll be nervous on their behalf. So let this card congratulate you (and them) in advance. You're an amazing teacher—and a good friend. I'm grateful to know you.

Best of luck to all!

Jo

From Peter to Johanna

August 4, 1944

A letter and a store-bought card from you announced at mail call in one week—the boys probably all think I'm a celebrity. I sure felt like one.

Part of me wants to pass along what I know I ought to say: I'm sorry about Major Davies forcing you to stay as translator, and so on.

The truth is, I'm not. I think you've been wonderful for that camp, and for Ironside Lake, and maybe even the United States in general. I think this country needs a voice willing to speak up and question blind patriotism, and that's what you're doing by humanizing those POWs. And I think you should keep doing it.

You have to know I mean it, because I miss having you here. Selfishly, I'd rather you told me Major Davies was sending you back to Minneapolis on the first train. But even if it's not in the place you wanted to be, you're doing work you're brilliant at for people you care about, and that's something to be proud of.

It's rotten that Davies would accuse you of starting the fire, though. Do you think someone suggested you to him? Someone you don't get along with, maybe? It seems like quite the leap otherwise. Then again, I'm sure he was exhausted and angry and terrified at the idea of his camp being put under Red Cross scrutiny. Sometimes when things are that bad, a fellow will grab at anyone around to take the fall.

I'm writing this to you late the night before exams. Yes, I'll admit to having trouble sleeping. I am worried about my students, but not that they'll fail their examinations. A few will be held back for remedial work, but most will pass

or, more accurately, be rammed through. They're desperate
now, Jo. The tone of MIS communication is getting more
urgent every day. Since the liberation of Paris seems likely,
with the German forces taking heavy losses, the Pacific
theater will become more and more critical. This country
will be depending on my boys, and the trouble is, I know
they're just that: boys, eager and brave but inexperienced.

What I'm most afraid of is that they'll get over there
and be shoved into a life-or-death moment . . . and I
won't have taught them what they need to know. I'm not
an army man, Jo. I spent hours painstakingly translating
Pettigrew's manual on the Japanese military structure
and strategy, trying to apply it to my lessons, but it was
like a foreign language of its own to me. What if I got
something wrong or left something out? What if we have a
report read to us at breakfast one day that one of my boys
died in the line of fire, and I could have prevented it?

At the end of our ukulele lesson tonight, Makoto
solemnly gave me his beloved instrument. "You take care
o' her for me, coach," he said. I promised I would. It's
sitting on my desk now, the strings tight and ready for my
still-inferior plucking, surface carefully polished with a
few dabs of Brylcreem (I'm guessing by the musky smell of
it) rubbed into the wood. But soon its owner will be gone,
thousands of miles away, huddled in a foxhole or hugging
his knees in a bomber. And I'll still be here.

Maybe I know what you mean now, the feeling of being
trapped.

It's the first time I've felt bad that they're going into
danger and I'm staying safely behind, maybe because
I know this graduating class so much better. Roy, who
dreams of sketching a Japanese American superhero
comic someday. Terry, who confessed that he tried to get

dismissed for all his pranks because he was sure he'd flunk out and bring shame to his family. Kenneth, who's my starting pitcher and eats meals with the rest of the team now. And Makoto, who can be a master interrogator one minute and an island dreamer the next.

Pray for them with me, will you, Jo? I know you aren't praying much anymore, but this is important.

The one good thing about exams and graduation is that I'll be seeing you soon. It's crept up on me, and now it's almost here, my visit to beautiful Ironside Lake. I'll start packing my bags on Sunday, once this is all over. That's the best news I can give you at the moment.

Time to try (again) to sleep.

Your friend,
Peter

From Olive to Johanna

August 5, 1944

Dear Johanna,

It's been so long since my last letter that you're free to disown me as a friend. I meant to write, honestly, but spending the summer trapped with four young siblings and my aging aunt and uncle means I've barely gotten two consecutive minutes alone since May.

Not that there's news to pass along. My aunt's gnat-ridden cow, Molly, has been thoroughly informed about Linus Pauling's work on covalent and ionic bonding. She hasn't given me much feedback.

Let me know how you're getting on with the POWs. It seems people always either love you or hate you. You know what camp I've been in ever since you found me sniffling

on the steps of Folwell Hall and invited me to have a cup
of tea. (They really shouldn't make American university
buildings look so very English, with gargoyles and
balustrades, if they don't want us Brits to get homesick.)

Speaking of, I got a letter from Clive/Chive today. He
says all is shipshape on the coast and that the war could
end any day. Also, potentially of interest: He doesn't have
a sweetheart yet. (I asked.)

Time to weed the garden. I'm so dreadfully freckled
and sunburned, I plan to wear a sack over my head the
first several weeks back at university.

I hope your life has been more interesting than mine.
And have you heard from Peter lately? As you know, I'd
love to hear your news. Do tell all.

> All the best,
> Olive

From Peter to Johanna

August 6, 1944

Dear Jo,

Well, wouldn't you know it, just about the time I find
I like teaching, they've moved me on to something else.
How's that for a blow?

Jo, don't be angry at me . . . but that "something else"
is active duty.

I'm young enough—the other instructors are mostly my
father's age—and they desperately need the translators.
Since they're moving the language school to Fort Snelling
next month, they have a few officers there able to take
over part of the training, making my job as instructor less
necessary.

Besides, they had me tested, and—let me brag a little, will you?—I got the highest score in the camp. When it came time for an oral examination, the colonel, who had spent a number of years in Japan, said, "Young man, I honestly believe you'd be able to convince the most hardened *Kamikaze* to surrender and then mail his wages stateside to buy US war bonds." Oddest compliment I've ever gotten, but I don't think I've stopped grinning since.

So I'm off to Camp Blanding in Florida next Tuesday, uniform and all. Before you go congratulating me on heading someplace warm . . . they've cut our basic training in half, from sixteen weeks to eight. I'll be over in the Pacific by the first of October.

It hasn't fully sunk in yet, but as soon as they asked me, I felt a sense of relief. This time, I won't be sending my boys out to risk their lives alone. I'll be going with them, taking on some of the sacrifice myself. Maybe that's what I've wanted all this time; I just never realized it.

And guess what else? I'm an officer, Jo. A second lieutenant, with a shiny gold bar on my brand-new uniform, one of the first Japanese American officers in the war.

I know it's not fair of me to tell you like this, without any warning, but they only just decided for sure, and with everything going on in Ironside Lake, I didn't want you to worry.

It looks like I won't be able to visit you next week after all. That's my biggest disappointment. Please tell your mother I'm sorry—and maybe I can get a rain check for after the war.

Write back soon.

Your friend,
Second Lieutenant Peter Ito

From Johanna to Peter

August 9, 1944

Worry? You didn't want me to . . . Peter, I could just about march all the way down to Savage and talk some sense into you—or wring your neck!

Of course you were first in your class. You taught the class! Can't they see you'd be a hundred times more valuable to them training others than going yourself? I know you could have persuaded them, and don't try to tell me you aren't necessary. Fort Snelling or no, you have more students than ever. How could eliminating instructors possibly be helpful?

There, I'm turning into Major Davies with his exclamation points and dramatics. But you told me yourself there were dozens of necessary noncombat placements, like the radio broadcasters feeding propaganda across the ocean, or the stateside translators of leaflets to be dropped from planes. Why couldn't you fill one of those roles?

Peter, I'm scared for you. What if American soldiers can't tell the difference between you and the enemy? You'll be shot at from both sides. And do you know what the Japanese would do to you if you were captured? They'd treat you as a traitor.

I know the same is true for any of your students, and I should be this upset about any of them going into combat. But . . . none of them are you.

I'll pray because I know I should. Every day. But I also remember the vigil of members filling Immanuel Lutheran Church when the Sorensons received the telegram telling them that their son was injured and doing badly, and Erik still died.

The truth is, I don't understand. The more bad news that comes in the mail, the more I feel like the faith I used to claim might be an elaborate myth, teaching moral lessons without providing real comfort.

See there. What a terrible friend I've been. First I go on and on about my own problems, asking for advice and complaining. And now, when you've received the recognition you've long deserved, I talk about how your enlisting affects me and how upset I am.

Have I always been this selfish? How on earth have you put up with me for this long?

I want to send this right away so you'll be sure to get it before you leave, but I'll write again when I've calmed down.

Jo

Telegram from Johanna to Peter on August 11, 1944

IGNORE LAST LETTER. TRAVELING TO CITY TOMORROW
MORNING TO SAY GOOD-BYE. MEET AT USO CLUB NEAR 2
PM IF AGREEABLE.

Telegram from Peter to Johanna on August 11, 1944

VERY AGREEABLE. DINNER AFTERWARD? BRINGING MY
UKULELE. I HAVE SOMETHING IMPORTANT TO TELL YOU.

Telegram from Johanna to Peter on August 11, 1944

RISKY. USO JR HOSTESSES NOT PERMITTED TO DINE WITH
SERVICEMEN.

Telegram from Peter to Johanna on August 11, 1944

LUCKY FOR ME YOU ARENT A REAL JR HOSTESS. SEE YOU
TOMORROW.

EVIDENCE FOR THE PROSECUTION

FROM EVELYN DAVIES TO HELEN PEALE

August 14, 1944

My dear sister,

It seems so long ago that I clung to you at Grand
Central, sobbing like a girl off to boarding school.
Honestly, to take us at our age and uproot us from our
home and deposit us in this godforsaken wilderness . . .
it's disrespectful. Don't they realize all that Jeffrey did for
this country? And all I sacrificed, waiting for him with
nothing but a dime-store ring and a promise those long
years while he fought in the Great War?

But of course Jeffrey doesn't see it that way. By coming
here, he was pleasing the entire US Army and only
disappointing me. So he placated me with a fur muff and
promised that I'd find the fresh air "rejuvenating." Well,
it's August. The air smells like fertilizer, I'm practically
assaulted by mosquitos every time I step outside, and I
want to go home.

The other night, when I was expressing these reasonable concerns, Jeffrey brought up the camp orchestra as evidence of culture around us. As any reasonable person would, I scoffed at the comparison. A ragtag collection of German soldiers playing at Bach can't compare to our plush seats at the Metropolitan Opera or Carnegie Hall. The only classical stations we can receive are those from Minneapolis and sometimes Des Moines (that's in Iowa, dear—I'm sure you've never heard of it), which I don't need to tell you are positively provincial in comparison to the New York Philharmonic.

And what did Jeffrey say to that? "Be patient. I'm trying, my love." Trying. What is that supposed to mean?

I've nothing at all to do but page through catalogs and attempt to find someone worth talking to. Goodness knows I never see Jeffrey; the camp steals away so much of his time. I'd thought the girl he has working in his office, translating German, showed potential. No-nonsense, smart, reliable—just the qualities I worked hard to develop in my own young womanhood. But it wasn't long before I realized that she's nothing but trouble.

You'll never believe it, Helen. She's head over heels for a Japanese man. To hear the postman tell it, she writes letters to him every week. When I called him her sweetheart, she denied it vehemently, but how many matches have I picked out from the very first soiree? Dozens, it must be by now. And Johanna Berglund is in love with this Japanese—I can't remember his name, Wong, probably. The way she speaks of him makes it clearer than a crystal wineglass.

Why, only a few days ago, she announced she wouldn't be arriving for work the next day. No asking for permission, no advance notice. Apparently this Wong fellow joined the army and she wanted to say good-bye. Jeffrey, softhearted as he is, allowed it.

When she came back—I saw her just hours ago—she looked like a different woman, testy and pale, her mind clearly somewhere other than my conversation. Then, in response to my simple question about how her visit had gone, she snapped that she had work to get to and would I please leave her to it.

Mark my words, Helen, she professed her love to this Wong fellow, and he jilted her. It serves her right. A young woman that arrogant needs to be taken down a peg.

Even Jeffrey is coming around to my opinion of her. She's written a few letters to the YMCA without his knowledge or approval, authorizing a trip to the movie theater and the delivery of sheet music—Wagner, of all things—for the men. Without even telling him! There aren't many things my husband hates, but insubordination is one of them, and this girl is all that and more. Defiant, even. I saw that almost right away and told him so, but he didn't listen.

Pity me, Helen. Even the gossip in this town is utterly unremarkable. No scandals of any interest. Give me some real news, and I will live through you until I'm able to join you again. If I survive the next several months, that is.

Much love,
Evelyn

CHAPTER NINE

From Johanna to Peter

August 15, 1944

Dear Peter,

Did you know the expression "out of sorts" comes from the newspaper business? Brady McHenry informed me of this when I was trying to drop off the latest column quickly and without comment. The metal dies printed with letters were called "sorts," and if the trays were accidentally upset or a lazy typesetter didn't "mind his p's and q's," it all became a jumbled mess.

That's what I feel like right now. I've forgotten to include the Idiom of the Day, but I'm afraid if I scrap this and start over, I just won't, and that's not fair to you.

It was good to see you last weekend. Honestly. Good to know that you hadn't decided to go easy on me and let me win even one game of Ping-Pong, good to find conversation in person came as easily as our letters, and even good to laugh with you through your attempt at

Sinatra on the ukulele. "I'll Be Seeing You" has had many better arrangements, but none so unique.

If only we had left things there, instead of going for a stroll by the Stone Arch Bridge that evening.

That was your secret, wasn't it? In the mock interrogation, the thing you imagined that you didn't want anyone else to know?

I feel odd carrying on like everything is just as it was, but I also don't want to bring up our disagreement again. So that's what I'll do, and if you want to stop writing to me, I understand, and I wish you all the best.

So, yes. Camp Ironside. Nothing else has been lit on fire, thankfully. We received several dozen reports from suspicious citizens certain that our prisoners have been up to mischief, but nothing has been substantiated, and even those reports have trickled off.

The only other happening of note was when I heard Stefan ask Major Davies about his radio career, hinting, I'm sure, about the purpose of the antenna by the gate that I told you about before. He and the major have become almost friends over the past several months, but Davies only chuckled and said, "We can't go giving away all our secrets, can we?"

I pretended to be busily engaged with my paperwork, since I've fallen out of favor with the major, but not knowing does bother me. The guards say they've seen Major Davies stumbling toward the guard tower connected to the wire at all hours of the night. One of them, Tank—I'm not sure of his real name—nearly shot him, thinking it was one of the men trying to duck under the fence. According to Tank, Davies was wearing house slippers and clutching a notebook to his chest. He always orders the guard on duty away from the tower, takes his place, and, after fifteen minutes or so of adjusting the radio, comes down again. Strange, don't you think?

I tried asking Christopher Wright about it after church last week—he's always assigned to Sunday duty—but he seemed even more distracted than normal, looking over my shoulder and providing no useful information. It seems it will remain a mystery.

Tell me about training, if you like. Is it what you expected? How is Camp Blanding treating you?

Jo

From Peter to Johanna

August 19, 1944

Dear Jo,

I'm sorry, Jo. I shouldn't have told you, knowing what a difficult position it would put you in, especially at a time like this. Now let's be done with it for good. That's all I'll ever say about it again.

Camp Blanding is about as different from Camp Savage as possible: brand-new buildings, paved roads, property the size of a small city, and large swaths of sand instead of withered grass. If you look to one side of the grounds, you can see the parachute towers for paratrooper practice drops. (Glad I'm not in those units.)

Remember how I complained about Minnesota in January? Florida in August is a thousand times worse. The humidity is so thick that even my sweat sweats. There's a lake on the base, but I can swim through the air just walking from the barracks to the mess hall.

Not that I'm doing much walking these days. Before, I was diagramming sentences on a board for students. Now I'm training with a 37mm anti-tank gun. I'm not a terrible shot, but it's clear I've spent the last three years with vocabulary drills, not artillery drills.

There's also lots of running, and you know how I feel about that. I'm regretting every second helping of dessert I took at the Camp Savage mess.

Here's the best part. It was a tiny detail in the tour, and I haven't gotten there yet, but there's a large POW camp (Italians and Germans both) on the other side of the fort, where they're harvesting cotton and peanuts. Knowing that made me feel a little closer to you, but then I woke up in the middle of the night—not in a cold sweat; it's impossible to be cold here—dreaming of tank fire and remembered that I've left Minnesota behind.

Not for good, though. I'll be back; I know I will. God and I have had plenty of conversations about that, and besides, your mother promised me sukiyaki with custom Norwegian butter sauce, and I mean to hold her to it.

As for the radio, it does seem strange. I mentioned it to "Mugs" Renfroe, one of our radio specialists here, and he agreed that Minnesota would be the least likely place for war-related transmissions. So I'm no help in solving the case.

Lights-out soon, and for once I'm the one bound by the rules instead of the one enforcing them.

> Your friend still,
> Peter

From the scholarship donor, care of the board of trustees,
to Johanna

August 20, 1944

Dear Miss Berglund,

I have to admit, I was disappointed in your letter,
mainly because I'd heard so much about you that I
expected more than the vague form response you sent
to me. Don't let them starch all of the spirit out of you.
Then again, I suppose professionalism is the tyrant of the
day, and I did find your rundown of your daily tasks to be
informative, so thank you for that.

I have been told that it's now unlikely you'll be able
to return to the university in the fall. Let me assure you
that the language scholarship funds are yours to be had
whenever you reenroll. I'm delighted to see what you've
managed to accomplish in only a few short months, and
even more, what you've learned. It would be an honor to
continue to support you as you study and then sail off to
those Oxford tomes—if that's still your plan.

Finally, a word of completely unsolicited advice. (I
don't imagine you encounter any other kind.) Always
be careful to choose the better dream. Not the bigger
dream. Just the better one—some of the most worthwhile
pursuits can seem quite small to the undiscerning eye.
That task is most difficult when it involves changing our
minds, because it means admitting we were wrong. I
should know. I made a choice like that once, one that led
me to where I am today.

I certainly can't prove I didn't give up something
wonderful by mistake. But I chose the option that
looked most like love, and I have never regretted it.

Maybe you'll know what I mean someday, if you live long enough. I hope so.

> Yours truly,
> To Whom It Does,
> In Fact, Concern

From Johanna to Olive

August 23, 1944

Dear Olive,

Now it's my turn to apologize for being late to reply. So much has changed in the few months since you heard from me, especially the week just after I received your letter, that I can hardly think of what you need to know most.

First of all, Peter is gone, and I didn't realize how difficult that would be for me. He's joined the army, like his students, and is soon to be translating and negotiating somewhere in the Pacific. I know it doesn't do any good to worry about him, but I can't help it. Do you feel the same way when thinking about Clive? How do you deal with it?

But some better news: Although I can't return to university in the fall because of some unexpected difficulties here at camp, my mysterious donor wrote to me, promising my scholarship will be reinstated when I'm freed from my servitude to the army . . . but also obliquely questioning whether I ought to go to Oxford as planned.

The trouble is, I'm not so sure anymore exactly what I want. My time here has shown me that there are more ways to use language than just in academic studies. And, Olive, I'm good at this. Quite good. My English class students, the one who attend Sunday services at church, are now able to report on Monday with a respectable summary of the sermon, and when I walk around the camp, all of the men and several of the guards grin and wave. I'm liked here. You're so genial and popular that you might not understand how new and strange that sensation is for me.

Of course, I haven't given up on Oxford. I'm sure once everything calms down and I'm able to think more level-headedly, I'll have a direction again. It does feel strange to be without it, even temporarily. It's something I'll have to think more about.

Your friend,
Johanna

From Johanna to Peter

August 23, 1944

Dear Peter,

Camp Blanding sounds like just the place to turn you from a linguist into a soldier. You won't often be going to the front lines, will you? Don't you dare lie to me like you would to your family. I want the full truth.

I told Mother about the heat in Florida, and she insists that I pass on to you that peppermint helps cool the skin, so take that for what it's worth.

Have you found any prejudice among the non-Nisei soldiers? I expect most of them aren't used to training alongside several-dozen Japanese Americans.

Today I found Annika skulking around the camp. I suppose that isn't the right word since she's much too feminine and graceful for such a term. But she was hurrying for the gate, looking over her shoulder like a prisoner attempting to bolt in broad daylight.

When I asked in a friendly tone what brought her to Camp Ironside, she jumped high enough that, if Stefan had been watching, he'd have recruited her for Germany's Olympic track-and-field team.

The oddest part was, she recovered and coolly said something about visiting in support of the camp. No delivery of supplies, no excuse, no authorized reason to enter as a civilian, though clearly a guard let her in. Then she hurried away before I could ask any more questions.

Peter, do you think she was the one to leak the stories to the *Broadside* about the fire and all the other details Brady McHenry shouldn't have known? Or that she's looking for reasons to shut the camp down? It seems very cloak-and-dagger for a minister's daughter, I know, but just a few months ago, she was upset about the camp because of Erik's death. I can't think of any better explanation for her sudden change of heart. It's been bothering me all day.

Captain Werner still comes by headquarters quite often. Sometimes when he sees me at my desk censoring prisoner mail, he'll ask wryly, "Anything for me?" I have to shake my head and see the little spark of hope in his eyes die out. But he always asks again the next week.

Yesterday, I did have a letter to give him, from his sister, Amalie. I'll admit to passing it to him without reading or censoring it, but I didn't want to wait, partly because of the sheer happiness on Stefan's face to hear that someone from home had written to him, but also because his sister is not even eighteen and very unlikely to be passing along propaganda.

His father has never written again after denouncing his son's work as camp spokesman. He seems a harsh fellow, like a stock German villain in those wartime propaganda films. It makes me grateful for my own father, who kissed me good-night every evening until I decided I was too old for such things, and still makes delicious Saturday morning flapjacks.

But I'll make you hungry again for things you can't have. Deepest apologies. When you come home and visit us, I'll make sure we have flapjacks with blueberries and maple syrup and anything else you'd like.

Meanwhile, it's harvest season for potatoes, though sugar beets come later, in early October. That means the men come in twice as dirty from digging, washing, and sorting the roots. According to the farmers, all is going well. They were worried about sabotage, since "accidental" gouges on a few potatoes would leave them all open to rot, but so far, production is at normal levels.

The only thing out of the ordinary happened yesterday: Overnight someone tossed a burlap sack of rotting potatoes into Major Davies's office. By the time we got there, the place smelled like a thousand blighted tubers were festering inside instead of just seven. Even with all the windows open, we had to abandon the building and work in the officers' mess for the day while it aired out. Major Davies gave a long speech of warning to the men that I had to translate with a straight face while most of the men openly laughed. By today, however, the smell was gone, and we're once again in residence.

Back to work—I wrote this on my lunch break, and Linda-the-secretary has brought another stack of letters for me to censor. What drama will I find today, I wonder?

Jo

From Gerda von Neindorff to her husband
Translated from German and censored by Johanna Berglund

June 2, 1944

Dear Otto,

It was so very kind of the woman at the camp to let you send a card for our anniversary instead of that horrible letterform marked with *Internee of War*. I must say, it touched my heart to hold a beautiful piece of mail, even if I couldn't read the inscription on the front. What did the English say?

Christa is getting taller each day. You won't be able to call her *Entlein* for much longer. She's much closer to a full-grown duck, and the down of her hair has darkened until it more closely resembles yours. I've enclosed a picture of her in her new summer dress. (Actually, an old one of her cousin's, hemmed to fit her.) Some days I believe she doesn't realize there's a war at all. I only wish I could say the same for myself.

I'm so glad to hear your first concert for the men of the camp was a rousing success. Have you considered opening up a performance to the Americans in the town? Surely more than just the two hundred of you at the camp ought to benefit from all your hard work.

In my mind, I am listening to the music we used to play together. Do you remember how we met? You complained loudly about the uselessness of Mozart's *Marriage of Figaro*, and I had the nerve to argue with you. An hour later, when we'd exhausted ourselves in debate, I was sure you were the man for me.

When you return, I want a full concert of my own, with

all of the American jazz you've learned. After I've gotten done kissing you, of course—and that may take a while.

Missing you always,
Your Gerda

From Dieter Bormann to Rose Schlitter
Translated from German and censored by Johanna Berglund

August 20, 1944

My beloved,

It has been months since your last letter. At first, I suspected the American translator was holding them back from me out of spite. When I confronted her, she denied it, and though I didn't at first believe her, she insisted it was against the Geneva Convention to destroy POW mail. If this is true, then the reason I've received no letters from you is because you haven't written, and as with any lover's heart, mine constantly fears the worst.

Oh, Rose, do you still live? Are you well?

We aren't supposed to listen to news on the radio, only music, but sometimes when there is no guard posted at the recreation hall, Captain Werner tunes it to a station and translates, so I have heard of the Allied bombings of Berlin. Each time, I worry about you. Not my friends or my family. Your name alone is on my lips in fervent prayer.

If you are gone, I will never return to Germany. I'll throw myself into the ocean on the way there. Better still, I'll drown myself in the reservoir where we swim here near the camp. Even a day back home apart from you would be far too long.

Somehow, though, I can feel in my soul that you are still alive. We are connected, you and I. So perhaps your parents have been reading your mail and refuse to allow you to write to me, the failed and imprisoned pauper they never welcomed. Now that the wealthy banker has entered the scene, they urge you to forget me.

But I know you. I know your faithfulness and the purity of your intentions, white like the first snow of winter. You will never forget.

If you are reading this, Mr. and Mrs. Schlitter, please know that your daughter is the jewel of my heart, the treasure of my eyes, the only reason I get up and toil each day in this miserable country. I must know that she's safe. Please allow her to tell me even that much.

I await news with the last fragments of my shattered hopes.

Dieter

From Peter to Johanna

August 28, 1944

Dear Johanna,

Training goes on. I might have actual muscles appearing on my arms, but it's too early to tell for sure.

On Sunday, in one of our few snatches of free time, I gave Makoto back his ukulele for an impromptu concert. It gathered quite a crowd of GIs. Some are curious and ask questions, but once they realize that we speak English as well as they do, they leave us pretty much alone. Others are relieved to have us, recognizing what we'll be able to do, embedded in their units. (One fellow, Joe, calls me Tal, short for Talisman, because he saw a good-luck trinket at a Japanese laundry once and thinks I'll keep him alive overseas. Sometimes he even rubs my head.)

There are a few, though, who don't trust us. At the firing range, one of them said out loud, not even under his breath, "I came here to shoot at Japs, not shoot with them." Maybe the commanding officer was too far away to hear, but either way, nothing was done. I'm learning to follow my own advice and grit my teeth against lines like that. We're all going to have to work together eventually.

Tell your mother I'll give peppermint a try the next time I get my hands on some. Don't tell her that the likelihood of my coming across some here at Camp Blanding is slim to none. I'll keep taking cold showers and downing canteens of water to stay cool.

I have to say: I'd never do it myself, but the prank with the rotten potatoes was funny. I can picture the look on Major Davies's face as he turned red starting with the ears, his nose wrinkled from the smell. Still, I hope it doesn't happen again for your sake. Does that Captain Werner fellow know anything about it? You'd think he'd have heard someone planning a stunt like that or bragging about it afterward.

As for your friend Annika . . . Jo, if something doesn't fit with everything you know about a person's character from their past actions, chances are it's not true. In fact, after looking over your previous letters, I can think of a better explanation.

I'd ask for a dramatic drumroll, but since you're not here in person . . .

Annika has a sweetheart at Camp Ironside, and I'll bet you my last buck that it's PFC Christopher Wright.

Think about it. You have the mysterious deliverer of cinnamon rolls following Christopher's editorial (didn't you say Annika was a baker?), Annika's sudden interest in helping the soldiers at the camp, and Christopher's uncharacteristic determination not to leave the town.

My conclusion? Romance is in the air.

Whether I'm right or wrong, there are holes in your informant theory. How would Annika have learned about a fire in the middle of the night? She clearly wasn't there. If anyone leaked information about that or anything else, it would need to be someone inside the camp.

Feel free to pass on your admiration for my detecting skills. I'm willing to consult on any future cases and will accept payment in baseball game tickets or your mother's truffles.

At Camp Savage, all the students had gotten used to how frequently my name was hollered at mail call, between your letters and ones from my family, but here you've helped to make quite a few jealous. Keep letting me know how all goes in Ironside Lake.

Your friend,
Peter

From Johanna to Peter

September 1, 1944

Dear Peter,

You were right. Again. How I wish I'd just taken your word for it and left the matter alone.

But no, instead I persuaded Private Wilkes to drive me into town after his shift ended and over my lunch break, saying the major had approved a visit to the Carlson farm.

Major Davies hadn't specifically approved it, but he had said I was free to inspect the workplaces whenever a need arose. Since Christopher Wright was on guard duty there, I at least had a need to confirm what was going on.

Wilkes gamely drove one of the army vehicles and regaled me with stories of his home in Kentucky, letting me get by the whole conversation with throwing in just a few "Is that so?"s and "mm-hmm"s while I reviewed the pertinent details of your argument. It seemed fairly airtight.

After arriving at the farm and seeing the men eating their lunches on the ground with no sign of Christopher, I approached the farmer's wife, who was meting out a pitcher of buttermilk to the POWs. As soon as she saw me with a guard in tow, her blush told me she knew she was in direct violation of the order not to share food with POWs—heaven knows, in the middle of war, illicit dairy is our chief concern.

"I'm looking for Christopher Wright," I said, not even glancing at the pitcher, which put her visibly at ease.

"Two women in one day?" Mrs. Carlson said, raising her eyebrow and tsking teasingly before pointing me in the right direction.

That should have told me enough, but foolishly, I kept going.

I found them sitting in the shade of a towering oak tree, looking for all the world like a sentimental advertisement to sell soda or greeting cards. Christopher had his strong arm around Annika's shoulders, an open picnic basket beside them as she looked into his eyes and smiled like she hadn't a care in the world.

I'm quite sure I was smiling smugly when they startled out of their small lover's world and saw me. I even said "Aha!" like a cliché detective in the dramatic reveal of a radio serial. What kind of person does that, Peter?

A very flustered Christopher stood, brushing off his uniform like he was trying to rid it of traces of perfume, and stuttered out that Annika only visits during his lunch break and it hasn't interrupted his work. That is, until Annika cut him off with a blistering, "You don't need to explain yourself, Chris. We have nothing to hide. Father knows already, and if she tries to tell the major . . . there's nothing to tell. We haven't done anything wrong."

I should have taken the hint and apologized, but at the moment, I was annoyed at Annika jumping to conclusions and speaking about me like I wasn't even there, so instead I said, "I take it this is why you've been sneaking into the compound."

We argued about what did or did not constitute "sneaking"—I maintained that since she bent the rules and avoided being seen, it most definitely was—until Annika snapped, "Don't lecture me, Jo. You're so selfish, you could never understand what it's like to be in love. You've never loved anyone but yourself—not even my brother, who worshiped the ground you walked on."

I wish I could say I kept calm and walked away, or said something gracious like, "I'm so glad you're happy, Annika, and I didn't mean to imply that you'd done anything wrong."

Instead, I said something closer to, "I was selfish? What about Erik? He didn't care about me. The only reason he proposed was so he wouldn't be drafted."

I had forgotten your rule: Never say the first thing that comes to mind.

That is a good rule.

In the quiet that followed, I noticed for the first time that Annika was crying. I'm not sure how long that had been going on.

Christopher, whose face was so red he looked ready
to die of heat stroke or sheer embarrassment, tried to
explain that I should speak kindly of the deceased, which
was a tactical error because Annika whirled on him and
exploded, "Why would she be kind to him? She's the one
who killed him."

You can probably fill in the rest. I accused her of being
overly emotional; she claimed I had no heart; Christopher
begged us to stop.

And we did. I can't remember who turned away first,
but I do remember storming toward a wide-eyed Wilkes,
waiting by the truck, and ordering him to take me back
to the camp, which he did with no questions asked. All
soldiers have a healthy fear of a fused and lit grenade.

When I got home that night, after a distinctly
unproductive workday, I found a letter on the hall table.
"Annika dropped it off," Mother explained, along with
her usual worry about why I don't go over there more
often. I brushed her off and feigned a headache, taking the
letter up to my room.

It would have been better, I think, if I'd gotten out my
Acme Tires matchbook and set the letter on fire.

Maybe Major Davies wasn't so far off with his
accusations, come to think of it. I didn't set fire to the
camp storeroom, but I've burned my share of bridges,
haven't I? Now Annika will never speak to me again, and
after I read the letter, I knew why.

It was from Erik, the last he ever wrote. Until I read the
contents, I was amazed, looking at the date, that Annika
would part with it. She hasn't kept it this whole year
for sentimental purposes. She's kept it out of bitterness,
blaming me and for all I know waiting for just the right
moment to reveal it when it would hurt the most.

I've copied it out here, hoping you can tell me what to do. Or tell me it wasn't my fault. Or . . . something. I'll be returning the original to Annika in the morning, hopefully without actually talking to her. I can't imagine what we'd say.

Peter, what if Annika was right? What if my rejection made Erik lose the will to live? If my photograph had been there, tattered from months in the pocket of his uniform, would he have survived? It sounds like romantic nonsense, but I've heard doctors swear by it in certain circumstances.

At the very least, it seems I was Erik's last regret. He gave me his love without even mentioning his love for his twin sister. No wonder she hates me.

Why are you friends with me, Peter? Why do you keep writing to me, when anyone can see what a heartless monster I am, treating people as props and tasks and causes? Are you hoping you can train a modicum of human sympathy into me with your warnings and advice?

I'm afraid it won't work.

Or maybe I'm just plain afraid.

Write back soon. Please. I think maybe I can feel loneliness after all.

Jo

From Erik to his family

January 18, 1943

Dear Father and Annika,

One of the nurses agreed to write this for me. My hands are both cut up pretty bad. They tell me we won, though, and Rommel's on the run. When you read the news about North Africa, you'll know your son and brother was there, saving the souls who are saving the nation.

I know I was supposed to be away from the front lines, but no one's safe in a combat zone. Besides a concussion, I've taken some shrapnel to my rib cage and higher under my arm. The simple truth is, it cut up some vital parts of me, and they didn't get all of it out in time. When the fever's dull enough that I can stay awake, the doctor keeps trying to give me medicine for the infection. Not much sense in it. Men around me are dying, and I'm not fool enough to think I can dodge the same fate.

Sometimes I think of what might have been and look around at what is . . . and the difference leaves me feeling exhausted and empty. War isn't for the faint of heart, and it turns out I'm not as strong as I thought. Maybe I never was.

I've worked hard out here and hope to have made you proud. I'd have liked to have seen the church again, though.

Give my love to Johanna, won't you? Even if she doesn't want to take it.

Your son,
Erik

From Peter to Johanna

September 5, 1944

Dear Jo,

Can't write long; we've been doing double drills today, and I'm falling asleep on my feet, but I knew I had to dash off a note as soon as I could.

I'm sorry about what happened with Annika, and

I hope by now you've worked through it. It was just a misunderstanding. Some angry words that both of you should have thought more about before exchanging.

As for Erik, I will tell you it's not your fault, because it isn't. Shouldn't I know? If a fellow gets turned down, it's up to him to take no for an answer and move on with his life. Besides, it doesn't seem like he was in a love-sick despair. Maybe his spirits were low, but that was probably from seeing far too much bloodshed. You should take his mention of you as regard, not accusation. I think, from what little I know of him, he'd hate for you to think of it any other way, no matter what Annika implied.

The past is never in the past, not for countries, and not for individuals. But we have to have the courage to move beyond it. You're learning that already. I'm trying to. Annika's going to have to someday too, or she'll be trapped under layers of resentment, like Ssg. Ogato buried alive after the bombing, barely able to dig out.

You aren't to blame for Erik's death, no matter how much you feel like you are. Our feelings can lie sometimes. It's up to us to shout truth back at them whenever we can. That's what I want you to do right now.

Got to go now. More hard work tomorrow—only a month till we ship out.

Maybe I shouldn't say it, but I'm going to anyway: I wish I could be there right now so you'd feel a little less lonely. I miss you, Jo.

Your friend,
Peter

From Johanna to Peter

September 7, 1944

Dear Peter,

It hasn't gotten better. After getting your letter, I went over to the parsonage, stood on the porch shifting from side to side with nerves, and knocked. No one came to the door.

And before you say Annika might have been running errands or something, I saw the curtains move, caught a glimpse of her hand as she peeked out to see who was there. She just didn't come out.

I've done all I can now. If she wants to clear things up between us, then let her come to me.

As for Christopher, I found the Rudyard Kipling poetry collection from the camp library on my desk this morning, with an Alaskan totem playing card (the joker, not used in solitaire) marking one of the pages. His first-favorite poem, I assume, the one I've been needling him to reveal ever since his column. I suppose it was a peace offering, as if Christopher had anything at all to apologize for. Here it is:

The Obedient

Daily, though no ears attended,
Did my prayers arise.
Daily, though no fire descended,
Did I sacrifice.
Though my darkness did not lift,
Though I faced no lighter odds,
Though the Gods bestowed no gift,
None the less,
None the less, I served the Gods!

And a note at the bottom, scrawled in the handwriting I recognized from the draft of Christopher's column: "Job 13:15?"

I looked it up. "Though he slay me, yet will I trust in him."

He and Pastor Sorenson will get along just fine.

Ironically, Christopher's peace offering brought back all my old fears. What if Kipling is right, and the unnamed soldier was praying to no one at all? Or at least no one who was listening. That's what I wonder sometimes. I prayed for Erik every day, Peter. So did my parents—every dinnertime blessing mentioned him by name. Pastor Sorenson and Annika probably prayed more than that.

And yet he still died. A chaplain, neutral and good-hearted and just trying to follow his calling.

I don't think I'll ever understand. And now I'm realizing I haven't entirely forgiven God for it.

But that's more than enough about me. I'm sick to death of analyzing my relationships—it's making me long for my quiet apartment back in Minneapolis, with no one to bother me but Plato and Homer, since Olive was always out at some social event or another.

How are you feeling about deployment? I know you're supposed to say you're excited, ready to ship out, etc., but it can't feel like you've had enough training in only eight weeks. Just think, you'll soon be on the other side of the world.

Clearly, that's my cue to explore travel brochures with Mother again. She'll be delighted. She's noticed my dark mood lately but attributed it to a fever and attacked me with mustard plasters and pleas to stay home from work, which of course I haven't done. This ought to pacify her for a while, at least.

Jo

From Olive to Johanna

September 8, 1944

Dear Johanna,

I have to say, I was surprised to read your last letter, and I have to wonder if part of your hesitation about your future is because of Peter. You've always been so sure of yourself, never one to bob about waiting for a man to complete you. That's what I admired about you. I'm not saying a thing against women who want to have a family—my mother ought to be decorated with a dozen honours and medals for her dedication in raising the six of us whilst keeping up her hospital work—but it's not who you are, Johanna, or what you want for your life. I think in your heart, you know that. You want Oxford. It's what you've always wanted.

Even though you didn't ask about it, all's well here. I'm desperately glad to be away from the farm and back in classes. Good news: I've found someone to let out the flat with me since you're not coming back this semester. Penny Westcott, from the school of botany. Our sterile little windowsill is now abloom with plants, mainly geraniums and various herbs. (She also informed me that an olive is a fruit, so there goes your vegetable garden theory.)

I still miss you, but it's good to have someone about to talk with, and who can help me with some of my coursework. You always were hopeless with equations.

All the best,
Olive

From Johanna to Olive

September 13, 1944

Dear Olive,

I'm sorry for not asking after you and your windowsill geraniums, but since you only wrote once over the entire summer, there was a lot for me to fill you in about. Apparently, I don't know how to be a good friend to anyone these days.

Now about Oxford. You keep telling me over and over again about the kind of person I am—prickly, trapped in my books, more interested in goals than people. But what if that's only the person I have been?

Maybe you don't really know me anymore. Some days, I think I barely know myself.

I don't mean to say I plan to stay in Ironside Lake, but my time here might have been a catalyst, the part between my past and future that brought about change.

There, I've used a chemistry term, hopefully correctly. I don't know what else there is to say.

I hope you're doing well as the semester begins.

Johanna

From Peter to Johanna

September 16, 1944

Dear Jo,

Probably nothing I say will change your mind, but here's my advice for what it's worth: Apologize to Annika. That's all you have to do. Love keeps a short ledger.

(Though I never completed my accounting degree, so I'm not a certified authority on the subject.)

I don't understand you sometimes, Jo. You're always telling me how terrible you are with people—why calling your professor "pretentious" to his face is probably improper, how you shouldn't brutally critique the plot flaws of someone's favorite book, what you could do to make friends instead of holing up in your room, typing letters to me. But it never seems to change you.

I'm not saying you should stay in Ironside Lake and turn into a cutout cookie of a woman just like everyone else. Never do that. But I wish I knew why you push everyone away, even God.

Erik died when God could have spared him. It's a hard thing, I know. But you can't hold God accountable for promises he didn't make. He never promised us the easy path, never said we'd never feel loss or loneliness or heartbreak. But he did say he'd be with us through it all.

I guess a man thinks more seriously about his relationship with the Almighty when preparing for war. Only two weeks until we ship out. Am I ready? Of course not. I've gotten to the point where I don't feel on the brink of death every time we do PT drills, but I sure don't have the physique of the ideal GI. But I have to remember: I'm a quick thinker; I'm good with words; I'm well prepared. I'm ready for this.

One thing about army life, it doesn't have much variation. Food is still questionable. Florida is still unbearably hot. Running is still . . . every awful thing you can think of. I've nodded off twice while writing this, and I still have a letter to send to Father.

Business at their grocery isn't booming, but they're managing. Father keeps asking when I'll be back to help him. I haven't got an answer. Sometimes I'm sure he's upset at me, even though he's never said it directly, thinking I put the army above family.

It's harder than I thought it would be, the thought of leaving them—and you—behind without knowing what will happen.

That's how I feel, at least right now, about shipping out. I'd never lie to you; you know that.

Your friend,
Peter

From Olive to Johanna

September 20, 1944

Dear Johanna,

Clearly, I've offended you, though I have no idea how. You used to like it when I reminded you about Oxford and your dream of studying there.

Mum says I might be able to bring my siblings home early next year. There are still occasional bombings in London, but even Tom is eleven years old now, quite able to care for himself, and she misses us desperately. We've been gone far too long.

One of the freshers has taken up your corner of the library. He seemed an earnest chap, so I didn't have the heart to run him off, especially not being sure when, if ever, you'd come back to claim it.

Very busy these days. Third year promises to be just as difficult as everyone says. I probably won't have much time to write.

All the best,
Olive

A draft of a letter from Johanna to Olive, never sent

September 23, 1944

Dear Olive,

I understand that you're busy, and I don't expect you to write often, ~~but I wanted to make sure everything was all right between us.~~

Peter is important to me . . . but so are you. Ever since the first night we met, when you told me those lovely stories about your home in England and I could practically hear the sounds of the city and smell the countryside clover, I knew we'd be friends. Sometimes letters aren't the same. Especially ones written in haste.

~~I wish I hadn't said things quite like that~~
~~I wish I could take back~~
~~I wish~~

This is nonsense. We're in the middle of the war. This is no time for wishing.

Just keep calm and carry on.

From Johanna to Peter

September 25, 1944

Dear Peter,

Sometime today, I caught myself glaring at the dingy stockade silverware, complaining about the sudden chill in the air, and even demanding that someone turn off the radio when "Swinging on a Star" played again. Even perky Linda Harrigan noticed I was "awfully down" and tried to pry the reason out of me. I blamed indigestion because it seemed easier to implicate a poor stomach than to explain that, after work, I had a letter to write.

And we've come to it, haven't we? My last letter to you while stateside. I don't want you to leave remembering me as the griping girl who ignored your advice about her petty squabbles, so I won't talk about Annika or Erik right now.

If you were here in Ironside Lake, we'd give you a proper send-off. Earlier in the war, when young men were enlisting left and right, there was always some farmer willing to slaughter a chicken to make the usual ration-coupon fare into a feast for the brave serviceman's last meal in town. A notice was put up in the *Broadside* with the names of the boys shipping out, and the same roll was read in Pastor Sorenson's lengthy prayers concluding each sermon.

That's one thing, I suppose, to this place. Yes, everyone swaps gossip like schoolboys trading the same old marbles; yes, even the slightest change is met with horror; but everything that happens to one of us happens to all of us. Whereas I'm sure a big city like Minneapolis doesn't even realize you're gone.

Well, I do. And I'm proud of you, don't mistake me—but it's still harder than I expected.

Without saying a word about it, Father tacked up a map of the Pacific in the living room and set a box of pins on my desk. It's just like him, knowing I'll keep up with the news much more studiously now. Mother is already collecting items for a care package to send to you. Would you mind measuring your feet? I've tried to assure her that socks are one-size-fits all, but she remains dubious. Also, what is your favorite color?

I'm ashamed I don't know the answer to that one. It seems like something a friend should know, so I'll do my best to guess. Is it a spring green like the grass after a long winter? Maybe a sensible brown like Mother's truffles? Checkered black-and-white like a chessboard?

All right, enough stalling. Win the war singlehandedly. Isn't that what all you boys think you're going to do?

But then come back, and soon, if you can manage it. Not just to California, although I'm sure your family will be eager to see you. They're not the only ones who will miss you. I need someone around who's not afraid to tell me what he really thinks. Who I can always count on, no matter what.

Promise?

Jo

From Peter to Johanna

October 1, 1944

Dear Jo,

Thanks for the letter. Although I know it won't be my last from you, I'm keeping it with me today, not in my footlocker with your other letters, but right in the pocket of my sharply pressed uniform.

Sure, put those pins in the map as you read the papers, but know I won't be able to say much about where I'm stationed. The army's stricter on things like that than the language school . . . all my mail will be censored now, and I've got a new sympathy for your poor German boys. How's a fellow supposed to say what he wants to, knowing some stuffy official with a scalpel will be standing over it first, pecking for possible security breaches like a robin searching for worms? As someone fluent in Japanese, if I wanted to hurt the United States, it sure wouldn't be by leaking information in a letter to you, I'll tell you that much.

We're shipping out from San Francisco after a long train ride, and I got permission for a visit with my family, just for a day—what a reunion that will be! I saw them on a recruiting trip to Gila River in my first year of teaching, but it's been almost two years since then.

I wish I could promise I'll be back to you in a few months' time, or at least that I'll stay safe. But I know enough about war to know that's not fair.

Here's your cultural lesson of the day: In Japan, it's customary to send soldiers into war not with a chicken dinner but with a *senninbari*, a thousand-stitch belt. Traditionally, each stitch was made by a different woman—relatives, friends, acquaintances, even complete strangers. In Tokyo, mothers would stand by a street corner or train station and request that passersby stitch and tie a new knot. Others would pass the cloth through an assembly line to gather several dozen at once. They're meant for good luck in battle, or, if you're the poetic type, a thousand reminders of the reason you are fighting: to protect the women of home.

A few of the soldiers from Hawaii came to the language school with a senninbari displayed proudly around their waists at graduation. As a teacher, I was never meant to see combat, so no one thought to make a senninbari for me. In a way, I've created one for myself. Not with stitches—it takes me a full five minutes to thread a needle when reattaching a button—but with promises from the once strictly ornamental Bible that Baba Yone kept on the shelf to impress our American neighbors. She gave it to me when I left home to go to the language school.

I have 306 promises so far copied in my journal from the past two years, so there's still work to do to get to a thousand. Strung together, they're why I'm not afraid to go to war.

Jo, I can't tell you what religion I would have followed if my family had remained in Japan, or whether you would have married Erik if he'd come back from the war, or what Stefan Werner would have been like if he hadn't been born in Nazi Germany, for the simple reason that my family didn't remain in Japan and Erik didn't come back from the war and Captain Werner was born German and not American. God has chosen this story for us, and not another one, and I mean to live this story as best I can with the time I'm given. And you will too; I know it.

And now I'm off to the station, to be crammed in a troop train with dozens of other men equally as tired and sweaty as me. What a ride that will be.

Keep writing, and I'll reply whenever I can steal the time and paper.

Your friend,
Peter

P.S. I wear a size 10 shoe. My favorite color is pale blue, the color of your eyes, but since I don't think there's yarn in any shop in the country that could compare, you can tell your mother any shade will do.

EVIDENCE FOR THE PROSECUTION

FROM LT. COL. ARTHUR LOBDELL
TO THE MINNESOTA AND SOUTH DAKOTA
POW CAMP COMMANDERS

October 2, 1944

To my fellow camp commanders,

The POWs here at the Algona base camp have divided into two groups: those who refuse to believe reports that Germany is losing the war, and those who welcome the end of the war in any form. You, like I, might have noticed a rise in fistfights among the men in recent months. We believe this to be the cause.

In addition to the general tension, last week we caught one of our prisoners in the act of sneaking into the mechanical apparatus of the cannery where he was employed, intending to shut down the machine, causing thousands of dollars' worth of damage and more in lost productivity. He was immediately sentenced to solitary confinement, but this might not be the last incident among our camps.

Our saboteur was in the group who believes all is lost for Germany, and, out of spite, he sought to do damage wherever he might to America. But others might see themselves as enemy combatants still and, provoked by what they see as American lies about their victories, might choose this moment to strike.

Vigilance, men. That is what I suggest. Though we are on American soil, each time we enter our compounds, we step into enemy territory.

In response to these new developments, the War Office

270

urges that the following measures be taken in the Midwest camps under your control:

- Limit the access the men have to news reports regarding the war, including radio reports and newsreels before films. Provide topical magazines like *Farm Journal* or reading materials in German to keep them occupied with other subjects.
- Try to build morale in as many ways as possible. Schedule regular meetings with your camp spokesman and grant what requests you are able as far as quality of food and entertainment. "Bread and circuses" worked for the Romans; that will work for us as well.
- Be on the lookout for secret gatherings. Some prisoners are holding subversive rallies to garner support for the Nazi cause, calling our attempts at education "indoctrination."
- Instruct your censors to be especially vigilant in finding and reporting political content in incoming or outgoing mail.
- All translators must be instructed to listen for evidence of sabotage or escape. Desperate men may take desperate measures. So far, at our camps, no man has been free for more than a day or two, with no harm to the citizens and no media attention outside of the local papers. This has helped contain any embarrassment to our camps and the army at large.

We thank you for your dedicated service. Please direct any questions to the Algona base.

Lt. Col. Arthur Lobdell

CHAPTER TEN

October 4, 1944

Dear Peter,

I'm so glad to hear you're going to visit your family. I'd say tell me all about it, but by the time you get this letter, I imagine you'll already have written me. How odd. For several weeks, at least, our letters will pass each other. I'll have to adjust, I suppose.

Did you see any dolphins on the voyage? I've grown up around so many lakes that if you added them all up, the sum total might be an ocean, but I've wanted to see the real thing my whole life. Maybe that's one reason why Oxford held so much appeal, though I'll admit it seems like a distant dream now after so much has changed. I tried to get the old feelings back by rereading *Beowulf*, but it just wasn't the same.

That frightens me. I can't let this war steal my dream. It's taken enough from me already.

Here's a happier story for you. This evening, Evelyn Davies invited me to dinner (vegetable stew with tomatoes and carrots from Camp Ironside's own garden), and I felt I couldn't say no, even though I was about as much use to the "conversation" as one of her velvet throw pillows. Between her shrill rants, she kept trying to get information about you—I'd mentioned you joining the army—and I was looking for some way to escape.

It must have been half past eight, not so late that my parents would start to worry, when Major Davies burst in the room, shouting and gesturing wildly. My first thought was that there'd been some disaster: another fire, an escape attempt, or the death of a foolish athlete chasing after a soccer ball that strayed too close to the fence.

So it took me a few moments to register that Major Davies was shouting out of excitement, not fear. "I've got it, I've got it! Come and hear!"

As it turns out, Major Davies has been spending months trying to pick up the station that broadcasts the New York Philharmonic Orchestra, installing and turning the radio antenna and recording the weather until he found the perfect combination. Clear skies, no wind, no interference from the Des Moines station that shares the same frequency, and a number of technical factors that I didn't entirely understand, like tuning by adjusting the wire's length.

Major Davies's chest must have expanded ten inches from pride as he ushered us up the guard tower ladder to the radio inside, which broadcasted a crisp concerto like the orchestra pit was only two rows away instead of a thousand miles.

Evelyn started to cry, clutching her throat like she was choking. "It's perfect," she kept saying.

Then Major Davies held out his hand, and while I watched, they slow danced to the music, a four-step pattern in the confines of the tower's interior. By the third movement, I made my excuses to leave. I doubt they even heard me.

Even I thought it was sweet. The constant reminiscing that made me want to brain Evelyn with a curtain rod inspired Major Davies to spend late nights adjusting the tower, noting wind speeds in his notebook. Though I have to admit, it was disappointing to learn my wild theories about espionage and codes were all wrong.

This morning, Stefan came in for his usual visit with the major, having apparently been awakened by the noise—the radio tower is close to the officers' quarters. It's the first time I've ever seen him act in a less-than-pleasant manner. After the major explained, instead of being mollified by the story, Stefan seemed even more irritated. I suppose it reminded him of his family at home. What a hard thing, to be so far from the ones you love and without a sense of purpose.

In any case, I hope you're doing well. Are the K-rations as bad as they say, or haven't you had to break those out yet? I hope you found some California USO canteen to stockpile an assortment of sweets. In my brief term as junior hostess at the USO in Minneapolis, we were warned not to let a GI go through the doughnut line three times to stuff his pockets. The senior hostess thought that all of you Japanese American soldiers looked identical, which is nonsense.

Is there anything you need that I can send? Besides more letters, of course.

Jo

From Johanna to Peter
Returned to Sender on November 20, 1944, enclosed with the
message "Unable to Be Delivered"

October 14, 1944

Dear Peter,

Writing to you is comforting on difficult days. Have I told you that? No matter what emotional turmoil may be going on around me, you're always as steady and reliable as Dad's ancient Ford truck.

Mother says I ought to be using the V-mail forms to speed things along, but I can't bring myself to do it. Partly because of the length restrictions, partly because thinking of someone scanning my letter onto microfilm and delivering it in an airplane to be printed out again feels so . . . mechanical. This, I realize, is ironic coming from the woman who writes her letters on a typewriter, but at least my hands touched and sometimes smeared this sheet of paper.

Because the camp is closing for the winter at the end of November, I'm concluding English classes next week. Major Davies has decided to give me paperwork tallying up the financial contribution of POW labor by adding the profits coming in from each farm as they sell their crops. Important documentation, I'm sure, but— and I never thought I'd say this—I prefer teaching the officers. I've even assigned them a composition, a short essay describing what they learned about America and its government. That, I felt, was as patriotic of a final examination as I could concoct.

Stefan Werner turned his in early—in the form of a Potato Brigade column, which was published last Saturday. He dropped out of classes a few weeks ago when the harvesting started in earnest, claiming it was better for the camp spokesman to go out among the men during the longest workdays. His fellow officers look down on him for it, I know—I hear them mutter, accusing him of communist leanings—but I think it's admirable. More of the officers could benefit from rolling up their shirtsleeves and going into the fields with the privates.

I'll admit, Captain Werner has been a bit of a puzzle lately. I've attached his original draft of his editorial here, because for the first time, I made an edit to a prisoner's column, cutting out the paragraph near the end about me.

Before the past few weeks, I don't recall him ever implying he was considering remaining in America. The change seemed to happen right around the time the letter from his sister arrived, the one I didn't read, so I'm wondering if it was perhaps her idea. Major Davies has informed me that the POWs are responding in vastly different ways to the news that Germany will likely surrender soon, so I imagine more surprises and challenges will be in store as our men face a new reality that is difficult for them to accept.

He even left red flowers on my desk last week, along with a notecard bearing the Preamble to the Constitution in neat script—unsigned, but certainly from him. I suspect he intends to ask me or my father to be his American sponsor, something required in the naturalization process. I don't know what I'll say if he asks. I would hate to lose him again to the lies of Nazi propaganda, but neither am I convinced he's fully dedicated to democracy. If I had to guess, his father has refused to welcome him home, and Stefan wants to remain here and avoid the conflict and bad memories. Always running. What do you think?

I don't know what I'm allowed to ask you, other than

to inquire after your health and your spirits. So . . . are you healthy? Are your spirits up? Write back soon.

Jo

Draft of the column for the October 7, 1944, issue of the Ironside Broadside

I knew very little about America before coming here, and what I did know was because of the 1936 Olympics. I was a runner with the German relay team and still remember how proud I felt, with my father, sister, and younger brother, Leon, in the stands, their voices joining the roar of the crowd.

For all their talk of trade restrictions and boycotts because they did not approve of our chancellor's new government, America still sent their athletes to compete. In our facilities and food and competitors, it was our chance to show the world the best of our country.

I cannot fully describe to you the majesty of those few weeks, the sights that amazed travelers from all over the world. If you want to imagine it, watch the documentary *Olympia*, which shows a few of the wonders of the competition—the beauty of athleticism and grace and national pride.

During the event, Germany won 33 gold medals.

America, our nearest competition, won 24.

That is what I knew about America before the start of the war.

After learning more in our English class, taught by Miss Berglund, I can now understand the branches of government and balance of power that you have here. And for the time and place where they began in America, this system has worked. Allow me to say that it is a good country you have built, and you have prospered.

But when your country has been unjustly penalized after a war they did not seek, stripped of centuries of glory, crippled economically, it is not the time for leaders who would continue in passivity. America was ready for George Washington. Germany was ready for Adolf Hitler. Viewed through this lens, focused on at this angle, war was inevitable.

Can you understand? Or do you condemn us for trying to save ourselves from ruin and shame?

When I was young, I pretended to scoff at the dark tales of the Brothers Grimm that I read in storybooks, but deep down they taught me what I was already coming to know: The world is a cold and uncaring place, full of dangers, and I must be ready to face them. When I was told in *Hitlerjugend* that some of these monsters were called Jews, I believed them, and I grew up strong, first to beat them at races, then to fight them.

Here, I have met a clever woman with Prussian-blue eyes who tells me there is another way, and I find I want to believe her. That maybe, perhaps, there are loyalties that can go beyond the flags we salute and the anthems we sing.

It is the hope of a dreamer, of a boy who has heard too many fairy tales and dared believe that if the monsters were real, perhaps the promise of victory against all odds might be as well.

But in a time of war, all we have left are stories and hopes.

Someday, I hope to live in America and make this my home too. There is nothing left for me in the country that I once loved. It has been destroyed to rubble and ruin. I do not know if I will stay here or come back someday, but

I want to know what America is like as someone who is truly free. It will not be long, that much I am sure of.

Soon, this terrible war will be over, and once again, our countries will fight only on the field of competition rather than the field of battle. I look forward to seeing that day arrive.

From Peter to Johanna

October 5, 1944

Dear Jo,

I've stolen a moment alone on the ship to write. It's harder these days to find a space to myself, all of us crammed on the steamer like sardines in a tin, but I'm making do.

My visit home was wonderful, the whole family running out onto the sidewalk when they saw me coming in uniform, like something you'd draw on a war-bond poster (if they showed Japanese Americans on those). Father insists business at the store is "fine," but instead of breaking out the books to talk finance like he usually did, he insisted we keep the focus on family time.

Our conversation stuck mainly to cheerful things: the cake the Ariyoshi family brought over when they heard I was visiting, a stray cat Marion has adopted and named Kitty Grable, Baba Yone's newfound interest in growing herbs from her time tending the Gila River gardens. And best of all, Mother's famous miso soup, smelling like seaweed and the fish market and home. Even thinking about it makes my mouth water.

For a few hours, it felt like everything had gone back to the way it was before the war. But then the next day, after

I'd stayed up late talking with Marion and hadn't gotten much sleep—no new intelligence on the boy from San Diego—Mother cried seeing me off and my father was so solemn he might as well have been humming "Taps" under his breath. I'll admit I was feeling a little low boarding the ship bound for the Pacific.

The only one of my Camp Savage students on the ship with me is Terry. He's decided to be a war correspondent via pencil sketch—if the *New Yorker* knew what they were doing, they'd hire him on the spot. His latest was a send-up of seasick troops hurling their rations into the ocean, captioned, "Ain't no ocean in God's country of Tennessee," a direct quote from an especially green-around-the-gills sergeant who can't wait to get back on dry land.

I was on a steamer before when I made the journey to and from Japan in my teenage years. I can't help being a little smug that I can stroll along the deck with ease (although you can see my handwriting's none the better for it).

All of the soldiers have started calling me "Tal" now after Joe passed it along. Nicknames stick like burrs around here.

We'll be landing in another week in "the Pacific." That's as specific as I'm allowed to get, because [CENSORED].

Tell me what you've been up to lately. I can't say when the letters will reach me, but until then, thinking of you.

Your friend,
Peter

From Johanna to Peter
Returned to Sender on November 26, 1944, enclosed with the
message "Unable to be Delivered"

October 27, 1944

Dear Peter,

Finally, a letter from you! Never mind that it spoke of things that happened weeks ago. It was good to know you're doing well and not even seasick.

If I'd been your mother, I would have made a deserter out of you by locking you in the closet so you'd miss your ship, so it seems your family took your leaving rather well. As for Marion's boyfriend, maybe ask her about him again in a letter. Sometimes it's easier for people to write things than to say them in person.

I'd love to see one of Terry's drawings if he has time to sketch in the margins of your next letter. In exchange, Mother has completed your socks with great pride, as you can see. She's anxious to hear how they fit and whether you like them—there was a moment of panic in which she realized she'd selected navy blue and you're in the army, but I assured her it wouldn't matter.

On my end, here's the latest news: Annika Sorenson is organizing a costume ball in the very school gymnasium where I ran a dance hall for over a year . . . and she didn't even ask me for help. I had to hear about it from Evelyn Davies, who is absolutely thrilled. She's already been over to the administration building five times in the past two days to pepper me with ideas of "how I've seen things done in New York" while I'm supposed to be working. I was polite, I promise, but her shrill voice makes me feel like I'm trapped in an aspirin advertisement.

The purpose is to raise money to support the guards at the camp. Although I suspect, given Annika's involvement, that the real purpose has something to do with wanting to dance with a certain stoic, khaki-clad guard.

Mother has already informed me that I must attend. Her refrain has been, "What sort of a message do you want to send? You can't advocate for the camp and refuse to attend the first community event supporting it." The trouble is, she's probably right.

The only reason I'm looking forward to it at all is that the band will be—after much negotiation with Major Davies—the Camp Ironside Orchestra! Peter, you should have seen Otto von Neindorff's beaming face when I told him. I thought the glow in his eyes would cause a power surge in the dim recreation-hall light bulbs. They've doubled practices to prepare, and I listen in whenever I can. Even though I have virtually no knowledge of music, I've been quite impressed.

Looking forward to the next time-capsule letter from you.

Jo

The POW Potato Brigade column in the Ironside Broadside *on October 28, 1944*

If you don't know me from around town, I work in the Camp Ironside kitchen, one of a few civilians among all the uniforms. Every day we get a KP squad of 3–5 of the POWs to help out peeling potatoes and scrubbing plates and dishing out grub. There's some that're nasty to me, on account of my being colored, some who treat me same as anyone else. No different than any other men. That's what I've learned more than anything, just how normal these Germans are.

One of them started collecting food scraps for a compost for his garden, laid out neat as you could imagine. Could've been one of the pictures in a farmer-supply catalog. Spent all his canteen scrip on seeds and tools, attacking those weeds like they were an enemy invasion.

Another one was a baker back in Germany, and soon as we got a barrel of bruised windfall leavings, he went and asked if he could make *Apfelstrudel*. That's German for "sweetest thing you ever tasted." Soon as I smelled that cinnamon-sugar goodness filling up my kitchen, I marched right up to the German mess sergeant and got that man assigned to KP duty for as long as we got donated apples. Never knew something other folks rejected could taste half so good. If you want the recipe, you just go to the gates and ask for Kurt Freisler. Tell 'em Ray Harrison sent you.

There might be a few outside the compound who still grumble and complain on the principle of the thing. But anyone who's been inside the camp doesn't have a bad thing to say about these men, and that's the truth. Ask the farmer who delivers twenty dozen eggs every other day if the POWs are good for business or not. Ask the fellow who carts their laundry away in his truck twice a week if the men work up a sweat and dirty their clothes. Heck, ask the movie theater attendant if he heard so much as a single *boo* the whole run time of the movie we let the boys out to see.

The point of it is, I'm up close to these men every day, working alongside them, and I say they're good for Ironside Lake.

And maybe we're a little bit good for them too.

Man like me's got a dog-eared copy of *The Negro Motorist Green Book*, with safe hotels, filling stations, and eateries marked for when my family goes traveling. Inside there's a motto from Mark Twain, "Travel is fatal to prejudice."

The men at the camp sure did travel all right, whether they wanted to or not. Now here they are, a long way from Germany and all those Nazi slogans. So long as we've got them here, we've got a chance to tell them something different.

I know as well as anybody else—better, maybe—that it pays to be careful. I felt a little dangerous myself, the first day coming through the barbed wire, thinking I knew what these Germans were going to be like from newsreels and such. Should've known they'd be men just like me.

You'll be hearing soon about a chance to hear the POW orchestra come late November, before all the boys head back to Iowa. I'm joining in for a number or two. You should come on out and see for yourself. Take a good, long look at them. Talk to the conductor, Otto von Neindorff, a great musician and a great man besides. Listen a little.

You can tell 'em Ray Harrison sent you there too.

Raymond Harrison

From Peter to Johanna

October 11, 1944

Dear Jo,

I've arrived in the Pacific. Some of my fellow soldiers, the hams, made a show of kissing the ground. Spirits are high all around among the newcomers. To hear the men in my unit talk, they were worried the war would be over before we arrived.

I haven't gotten a letter from you yet, which is why I'm not responding to any of your news or questions. They tell me that's pretty common, especially if the sender isn't writing on the V-mail forms that can be delivered via air. You are using those, aren't you? Supposedly they can fit hundreds of thousands on one plane that way. I know it means you'll have to write in your actual handwriting, but don't worry, deciphering illegible characters on battle-smeared fragments is literally what I've trained for. Someone has to give me a challenge to practice on.

I'm getting along better with the other fellows now that they've gotten over the initial shock of having a Japanese American embedded in their unit. The only one who still dislikes me is a Pennsylvania man who heard me mocking the Phillies our first week on the ship (to be fair, they had a terrible season).

Speaking of which, tell your mother congratulations on her Cardinals winning the World Series. That's the Big Baseball Game, in case you didn't know. Everyone over here was waiting for that piece of news, like it was some kind of decisive battle. You could tell who the fans were by the scattered pockets of cheering.

Now that we've arrived, I'm starting to use the training I received. That's all I can say about it, but it's a real thrill, Jo, to get out of my books for once and do things. I never realized how different it would be on the front lines, like moving from paging through travel books to actually exploring a new country for the first time.

Have you ever thought, Jo, about using your skill with language for some humanitarian organization? I know your dream has always been Oxford and translating the classics, but once the war's over, they're going to need thousands of translators to help with aid and rebuilding. I've considered it myself, actually. I'm doing what I have to, fighting Japan, but when this is all over . . . well, I'm not a soldier at heart, and while I haven't had the courage to tell my father, I'm not much of an accountant either. If I could help people whose lives were ruined by war and rebuild some of what we've torn down, that would be the best use of my skills I could think of.

How is old Ironside Lake? Has the major come around to trusting you again? What about Annika? Send a story of Cornelia Knutson's quirks or your father's campaigning, anything to give me a minute back in Minnesota.

Your friend,
Peter

Editorial in the Ironside Broadside *on October 30, 1944*

Dear Editor,

Last week, I was awakened rudely to the horribly off-key strains of some song—the lyrics I caught are unprintable here—belted out by a drunken man wobbling down the street. My husband went out to threaten to call the sheriff, only to find the man was employed by our own US Army, one of the guards at Camp Ironside.

I've since learned this has become a common occurrence: packs of guards frittering away their wages on liquor and disturbing the peace during their off hours. Worse, I'm told the army knew this would happen. Some soldiers with a known tendency toward alcoholism were assigned—yes, deliberately assigned—to POW camps, to avoid sending them to the front.

Well, I say anyone who acts like a common drunk ought to be treated like one and locked up in the county jail for the night.

That Berglund girl's column, the one written by the camp guard, tricked us into thinking all of them are squeaky-clean, gee-whiz Willie Gillises, smiling at us from the cover of the *Saturday Evening Post*. All lies, I tell you!

This is why I have no confidence, none at all, in the major's reassurances that Camp Ironside is secure. Secured by whom? A bunch of rowdies disqualified for overseas service who swig troughs of beer before stumbling to their barracks? I'd wager half the lot of them are hungover for guard duty. How secure is that, I ask you?

Drink is the way of the devil, and when we let the devil roam our streets, heaven knows what will follow.

An Advocate for Reason

From Johanna to Peter
Returned to Sender on December 8, 1944, enclosed with the
message "Unable to Be Delivered"

November 1, 1944

Dear Peter,

You're right: The Big Baseball Game was an event in our home. Mother was over the moon with the victory. Cornelia Knutson came over to listen to it on the radio, but she became restless by the fourth inning and ended up debating the city's budget with my father. Mother got so annoyed that she shoved them onto the front porch until they rang the doorbell five times in a row, complaining about the cold.

I'm glad to hear that your unit is accepting you, though they should do far more than that, given the fact that you're the most accomplished among them and could save all of their lives in a tight spot. I wish I could ask about the work you're doing, but as I know you can't respond to that, I'll restrain myself.

As for Oxford . . . I don't know, Peter. I've always felt since I was a little girl that I didn't belong here in Ironside Lake, but at the same time I'll admit to loving safety and quiet and a library within walking distance. Oxford has all of that. Foreign-aid work would not.

Erik always talked about a "calling" to be a minister. When I asked him if everyone got a calling, he thought about it for a long time, then said that he wasn't sure, but that perhaps some were called to other people or a general goal, rather than to a specific place or occupation. That never sat well with me, so I haven't dragged God into any discussions of my future. We'll see what happens, I suppose.

All's quiet on the Minnesota front, except for another sour anonymous letter in the newspaper. They're starting to blur together, with slight variations in subject but essentially the same tone. One seems to appear every time things have calmed down at the camp.

Actually, that suddenly strikes me as interesting. I seem to get my best ideas while writing to you. I might have to speak to Brady McHenry after this.

Election day approaches, so Dad is out making speeches and canvassing for votes. Mother often goes with him, enlisting her endless charm for his campaign. I, you might guess, don't have enough charm to spare and have to ration it for general interactions with humanity.

Also, I have—behind Annika's back and I'm sure to her great displeasure—volunteered to help the LDR women at the dance, taking tickets and refreshing the punch bowl. I've always hated dancing, but maybe that's because I never learned. Erik wanted to teach me and promised not to be upset if I tromped all over his toes. He really was a good friend, whatever our differences might have been.

I still haven't chosen my costume, but Mother is making a Martha Washington ensemble, mobcap included, for herself. Dad going as old George seems slightly over-the-top to me, but I'll enjoy watching him sneeze his way through the night from the talc powder he's planning to sprinkle in his hair.

I've reached the maximum these V-mail letterforms will hold. See how you pressured me into using one? Finally, you'll be spared from my epics!

Stay safe. Tell me as much as you can about what you're up to.

Jo

From Johanna to Brady McHenry

November 2, 1944

Dear Mr. McHenry,

I realize this is an unusual request, and you'll probably reply that a journalist has a responsibility to protect his sources, but I have to at least try.

I need to see the anonymous letters and envelopes submitted to your office in the past ten months. You see, I have a theory: I'm beginning to suspect all of them were written by the same person.

I came to this conclusion by means of textual analysis. In censoring letters from the POWs, I've realized that each has a distinct voice . . . and that the anonymous letters to your newspaper did not. Even though the persona of each of the letters varied, the basic linguistic features were exactly the same. Sentence structure and length, slang (particularly racial slurs), tendency for dramatic last lines, etc.

I have a detailed analysis, with footnotes, if you'd like me to come to the office to explain, but the short of it is that I think I know who's been writing to the paper: Mrs. Evelyn Davies. She's wanted her husband to move back to New York City since the day she arrived and has hardly spoken of anything else. She must have decided that if the sentiment in the community turned against the camp, it might be closed down.

If you can give any corroborating evidence to my theory, I plan to confront her tomorrow. I have no wish to press charges, if such a thing can even be done, but I do want these letters to stop because I, for one, am tired.

I was going to finish that statement with exactly what I'm tired of, but the list is so long that I became exhausted just thinking about it. I'll leave it to your imagination.

As we're colleagues, I'm confident I won't have to resort to threats. I'm sure you didn't have the slightest suspicion that the letters might have come from the same person until I suggested it.

Be a person instead of a newspaperman, Mr. McHenry, and do the right thing.

Johanna Berglund

From Brady McHenry to Johanna

November 3, 1944

Dear Miss Berglund,

Textual analysis, is it? My, my, I'm afraid university training has spoiled your otherwise quite functional brain with fancy techniques. I went back to my files—I keep all correspondence to the paper—and each letter was written in a different handwriting. I assure you, all is on the up-and-up, no matter what you thought you saw in your sentence diagrams. Almost like finding shapes in clouds or omens in tea leaves, isn't it? You can believe almost anything is there if you want to badly enough.

Thank you for your concern, Miss Berglund, but you need to face the fact that public opinion in Ironside Lake is simply more dramatic than in more peaceful times. And as a newsman, I'm honor bound to report it straight, whatever inconvenience it might cause.

Please take your slander against poor Mrs. Davies and drop it directly where it belongs: the trash. I've spoken with the major's wife many times, and while her gossip and complaints are a reporter's dream, never once did she indicate being clever enough to plan the sort of conspiracy you've suggested.

As for being a consummate newspaperman, that shows what you know. I'm not a newspaper man, not really. Do you know what I really did at the ad agency in Duluth? Does anyone in this godforsaken town? Of course not. Once you leave Ironside Lake, you're generically off in "the city," as if there's only one.

We understand each other, Johanna Berglund. We are more alike than anyone in this two-cow town, because while I'm sure there are others who don't want to be here, we're the ones with the guts to do something about it.

Once Freddy comes home from the war, hopefully with all his limbs and a desire to do right by old Dad by keeping up the family business, I'm out of here. No one to tie me down, no family legacy to keep up, no regrets. I suggest you do the same.

Might I make another suggestion? Stick to translation

work. That column of yours is a hit every weekend. Why ruin a good thing?

Brady McHenry
Owner and Editor in Chief,
Ironside Broadside

From Johanna to Brady McHenry

November 6, 1944

Mr. McHenry,

I can't be mistaken. Analysis doesn't lie . . . but people do. Which is why your latest letter immediately made me suspicious rather than assuaging my fears. The more I thought about it, the more I looked over your past letters to me and the vocabulary you used, the more I began to wonder.

It was you, wasn't it? Not Evelyn Davies. How could it be? She didn't arrive until after the first anonymous letter was published. You, on the other hand, have a much more transparent motive: stirring up interest in your ridiculous newspaper. Anything for a sensation, anything for sales. I can't believe I didn't see it until now.

Remember what I said about the exposé. If we can't come to some sort of agreement that these anonymous letters will cease—which I will want in writing—I'll make sure your paper closes for good.

The *Broadside* isn't some silly Hollywood rag that everyone expects to be filled with inane gossip. Your father intended it to be a respectable news publication. I'm giving you one chance to make it right, and only one.

Johanna Berglund

From Brady McHenry to Johanna

November 6, 1944

Dear Miss Berglund,

No need for anything rash. I'm sure I can explain to your satisfaction everything about transcribing public opinion in a concise, interesting form. Which I'm not saying I did, but if I had, it would make perfect sense. When I took over the paper, subscriptions were down by 20% and falling faster than a Spitfire gunned down by Jerries. The readership was bored. My old man had been too sick to do anything but maintain the status quo.

The way I see it, there's nothing wrong with taking actual public opinion—the word on the street, if you like—and writing it down.

You see, back in Duluth, I was a graphic artist. I drew the ads—the perfectly staged kitchen, the delighted husband opening a tie box, the youngster with an Irish setter lolling at the heels of his Buster Brown shoes. It wasn't high-class gallery art, but we've all got to grow out of our dreams and take a job that pays.

Done right, the newspaper business can be just like drawing ads. You paint a picture for people, make them feel things, stir them up.

You call it "gossip"? Well, I say Ironside Lake ought to take what it dishes out. You don't think I know how people talked about me behind my back when I returned to take over the paper? Saying it was a shame Fred was off at war instead of me, predicting how long it would be before the paper went bankrupt, coming up with all kinds of reasons I might be a bachelor at nearly forty. Oh yes. I'm a careful listener, and I have my sources. I know what they said.

If I funnel even a little of this town's spite back at them, it's no more than they deserve. And if I make a wad of cash in the process, well, irony is a beautiful thing.

I'm sure you're thinking, Why is he telling me all this? Why write it all down so I can expose him?

First of all, because I know you won't do it. Anyone whose favorite book is *Les Miserables* isn't the vengeful sort.

More importantly, as I said, when Evelyn Davies comes into town, I make sure to buy her lunch and listen to all of her news. Who else do you think told me about the fire, or the other times I quoted an anonymous source in an article about Camp Ironside? And wouldn't you know that she just shared something very, very interesting about you: According to her husband, your long-distance sweetheart is a Japanese spy.

How would you like Peter Ito's name all over the headlines? I could do it. I have the information. What a story that would be! And right before election day too.

Consider that a warning. If you don't leak your information . . . I won't leak mine.

And even if you do choose to speak out, martyr that you are, and take your politician father and Jap boyfriend down with you, people won't believe you. They don't even like you. It'll all be for nothing.

You've yet to learn something very important, something I learned while sketching a hundred fantasy scenes to sell products: People believe the stories they want to believe, and they also hate accepting they were taken for a ride. It's not worth the risk, trying to expose me for something that, in the end, doesn't matter.

One last word. Be careful, Miss Berglund. Those who threaten the venerable institution of the press rarely find it works out in their favor.

Brady McHenry

From Johanna to her parents
Note left on the Berglund kitchen table

November 7, 1944

Mother and Dad,

I know I'm supposed to be at Dad's rally at the old pole barn tonight, but I have an errand of urgency. I'm off to the broadside office, and if it's closed, I'll batter down the door of the room McHenry's renting in town. He will speak with me.

If I don't come back, it's either because I was murdered or I did the murdering and am now on the run.

For context, that rat McHenry called Peter a spy. A spy! And threatened to write that in the paper. Can you believe it? I'm sick to death of everyone assuming and judging and spreading vicious lies, so I'm going down to set the record straight . . . and to withdraw my support of the paper. No more Potato Brigade column. I won't do a thing to support a paper run by a man like that.

I'm quite possibly the worst politician's daughter of all time, abandoning you both on election day, but I know you're fond of Peter and will understand. (But I did vote; I promise.)

To war!

Jo

BERGLUND WINS REELECTION

Roosevelt wasn't the only incumbent to achieve victory in this month's election. Mayoral candidate Carl Berglund will commence his fifth term as mayor of Ironside Lake, winning by a slight majority over businessman Edward Bartholomew. Supporters cite his work ethic and "everyman" appeal, though others have vocally protested his support of Camp Ironside and the POWs interred there, an issue that has become the focal point of this year's campaign.

In a post-election speech, when asked whether he envisions the POWs returning next year, Berglund said, "Coming from a family with a legacy of farming, I'll do all I can to ensure that our agricultural workers have full support to bring in a harvest. That includes POW labor where needed. Their contribution to our local farming economy can't be underestimated, in addition to the business the camp brought to grocers, launderers, carpenters, and other tradesmen in town."

It should be noted that cheering from the gathered crowd of supporters, which at other times in the speech had been quite robust, died out at this part.

He then expressed his gratitude to the city for its vote of confidence, something he values and "will never take lightly."

Berglund's wife was present at the celebration, assisting the Women's League in selling celebratory war bonds, pictured above. Notably missing was Berglund's daughter, translator at the POW camp, which has been the source of much controversy in our town.

From Peter to Johanna

October 15, 1944

Dear Jo,

I've gotten your first letter! For a while there, I'd thought you'd abandoned me, even though I knew a few weeks' delay is normal. I tore the envelope open like a starving man attacking a steak. Mugs Renfroe calls letters "five-minute furloughs home." I like that . . . although with your letters, it's usually a twenty-minute furlough, and that's if I only read them through once.

When I have a hard time getting to sleep out here, I think of Ironside Lake, or at least how I imagine it to be. Probably smaller than it really is, like those quaint Christmas village displays in department store windows. I think about you, listening to the camp orchestra practices, putting pins on your map as you read the headlines, drinking tea with Cornelia Knutson and her ridiculous hats.

Now I know why the sentimental war songs are about gazebos and apple trees and streetlights back home. We all want the ones we love to be safe, to live normal lives, while we're in the middle of chaos. It gives us something to hold on to.

And let me tell you, your story about the major building the radio tower for his wife might've topped it all. I read it to some of the boys, and I swear some of them were misty-eyed by the end. That's what we all want, really, even the boasters who talk about women like they're conquests on a battlefield: someone who really knows us, who we can care for and grow old with, even on the tough days.

It looks like a different kind of picture postcard out

here. Palms swaying in the moonlight, that sort of thing. I wonder if it makes Terry and Makoto homesick for Hawaii. How's your mother's saving fund coming for that trip, by the way?

There was once a time I'd turn up my nose at the nickel White Castle hamburgers the boys would bring back from Minneapolis on weekend leave. I'd give anything for one of them now. Even a greasy slider beats canned bully beef, and the bun would be better than hardtack. But a nickel can't buy me that now. Even a hundred bucks wouldn't be enough. So goes the army, I guess. Add that to a list of things I miss: burgers and clean laundry and pillows and long, hot showers.

There are rumors we're getting a full steak-and-eggs breakfast tomorrow, so I shouldn't complain. And I guess I don't need to tell you tomorrow will be a big day for other reasons. They always feed us better before [CENSORED]. A whirlwind basic training didn't make me feel less of a fraud. A teacher with a gun. Who'd have guessed?

There's so much I'm not allowed to talk about—where I am, what I'm doing, where I'll be going. All I can tell you based on what I've been instructed about what happens next is it might be a while before I'm able to write again.

And pray for me. Please, Jo. Pray for all of us.

> Your friend,
> Peter

P.S. Almost forgot about the war stealing your dream of Oxford. I don't have any profound advice except this: Don't hold on so tightly to one idea of what you want that you don't let God push you in another direction. A few years ago, I was studying to be an accountant, remember? And yet here I am, sure I'm where I'm supposed to be, even if I'm scared. I couldn't ask for anything more for you than that.

From Johanna to Peter
Returned to Sender on December 8, 1944, enclosed with the
message "Unable to Be Delivered"

November 8, 1944

Dear Peter,

Let me start by saying I'd send you a whole crate of hamburgers if I could. As it is, this letter will have to do. You're right; you are imagining Ironside Lake as more ideal than it is, but I'm probably overglamorizing your adventures as well, so we'll call it a tie.

Dad was reelected as mayor yesterday. I missed the rally because of some trouble with Brady McHenry that I don't have space to detail on this silly V-mail stationery, but I'm very happy for Dad. There are some who disapprove of his politics, but the farmers love him and some of the townsfolk have reluctantly decided he isn't a bumpkin trying out politics on a whim. This morning, I made him flapjacks to celebrate. The fact that half were burned and the other half were partially raw does not detract from the effort.

Meanwhile, the dance looms, and I have a ticket and a costume, which means I've surrendered to pressure and will attempt to be social. It's likely to be sharply nostalgic, especially the smells of heady perfume and cologne with undertones (undersmells?) of lemon cleaner covering the sweat of basketball practices.

My "costume" will involve plunking a wreath of greenery on my head, borrowing Mother's scarf to give my white dress the appearance of a chiton, and calling myself Athena. No mask—I haven't had time to make one, and it's not as if there's a booming masquerade shop on Main Street. I suggested spattering myself with spaghetti sauce to represent Athena's birth out of Zeus's head, but my mother nearly fainted and positively forbade it, so it looks like I'm forced to excise the mythological details that would have given my costume authenticity.

I don't think I would mind going so much if you were here. My suggestion for your costume would be Hermes, messenger of the gods. While the others in the Olympus pantheon have flashier domains—the sea, the underworld, war, love, and so on—Hermes has always been my favorite because of the sheer variety of those who pray to him for protection as the god of trade, shepherds, travel, sleep, and—of course—language. Fitting, don't you think?

And for goodness' sake, Peter, none of that nonsense about your uniform being a costume. If you're a fraud, I'm Miss America. You are the most genuine person I've ever met. The only one, besides my family, whom I truly trust. What was it you said about emotions lying to us and shouting back truth? However you feel at the moment, you will make your country proud in all you attempt.

This part is difficult for me to say. I'll admit to drafting it six or seven times before finally writing. Your last letter, asking for prayer for your first real mission, made me afraid for you. So much so that I stayed home from work, panicking Mother, who offered me a cocktail of home remedies before I convinced her I needed to be left alone. There was nothing wrong with me that she could fix. All I could do was kneel on the rag rug beside my bed, reading your letters again and trying to pray.

Which led me to conclude I care more about you than

I realized. Maybe I haven't been fully honest with you, or with myself. When you said those things to me by the Stone Arch Bridge about having deeper feelings for me than just friendship . . . it felt like Erik all over again, and I didn't want that for us. Selfishly, I was afraid of losing you.

I still am.

But when you come back, and you promised you would, can we start over? The whole conversation, from the very beginning. I'll take back every hasty thing I said . . . and we'll see what replaces it. If you still feel the same way about me after going away to war, that is.

Even if you don't, just come back soon, Peter. Please.

Jo

From Major Davies to Johanna, left on her desk

November 9, 1944

Miss Berglund,

When you've returned from your rounds, please come find me. I have an urgent and highly sensitive matter to speak with you about. It's about your friend Peter

Davies

EVIDENCE FOR THE PROSECUTION

FROM MAJOR DAVIES TO DR. SMYTHE

November 9, 1944

CONFIDENTIAL

Subject: Report on civilian personnel Johanna Berglund

Dear Dr. Smythe,

Your letter requesting an update on Miss Berglund came at exactly the wrong time for me to be objective. Today she has shown absolutely no sense of order or discipline!

What has prompted this, you ask? Given some bad news and a few honest questions regarding a US military serviceman, she actually physically assaulted me! I sent her home with a stern warning to compose herself, and now I'm considering whether I should even keep her on in her position!

I can't go into detail—military secrets and all—but she might be covering for a turncoat among our very own army. And if there's anything I can't stand, I assure you, it's a traitor! If one's word can't be trusted, well, what the devil can be?

Even my own German spokesman warned me to be wary of her, after she clearly lied about her involvement in the fire in the camp. He's the one who pointed out she might have allowed the accident to happen in the first place. I let that infraction go, but clearly I should have listened to him and taken action.

Since it's only three weeks before the men will go back to Iowa for the season, I shall keep Miss Berglund on staff for that long, at least. But you can rest assured that this winter I will be making calls from New York to find someone new.

If you have any recommendations from among your students, I would welcome them! Preferably a man. Everyone said it was foolish of me to choose a woman as a translator. Too emotional, they said. Nonsense, I said, she'll do just fine! And see what's come of that!

I don't know if you ought to pass this along to that scholarship donor of hers, whoever he is, but I felt that someone at the university ought to know. Miss Berglund's temperament does not suit the military, and I find it difficult to continue trusting her.

Respectfully,
Major J. E. Davies
US Army, Fort Snelling

CHAPTER ELEVEN

November 9, 1944

Dear Major Davies,

It was Peter, you know, who told me to begin letters with a compliment, but after our meeting yesterday, I can't think of a single thing to say to you that is both positive and honest.

However, I am sorry about throwing the intelligence files at your head. I was upset and not thinking clearly. If you put yourself in my place, you'd realize how infuriating it would be to be patronized when your best friend was accused of treason.

After taking the rest of the day off to rest my "delicate nerves," as you suggested, I've written out answers to your questions. If these aren't detailed enough for you or whatever investigative agency will be looking over them, I'll add to them.

Question: Did Peter Ito ever reveal any classified information about the language-school program?

Answer: I wouldn't know if something was classified, but he only ever spoke in generalities, except for possibly a few notes inside the instructional book he sent to me, which he forgot were there. Otherwise, the most detailed descriptions I heard were of the first snowfall or the behavior of his students.

Question: How often did Peter Ito speak positively of Japan, its government, or his remaining family there?

Answer: Peter and I never spoke much of politics. He was shocked by the aggression of Pearl Harbor and firmly on the side of the Allies. Mostly, he spoke of his family here in America, which the government held in a "relocation" (concentration) camp despite absolutely no evidence of American-born Japanese sabotage or espionage before or after America entered the war.

Question: Did Peter Ito ever reveal his reasons for joining the army?

Answer: He was deeply proud of the fine work he did in his teaching and wanted to use those skills in service of the United States alongside his former students.

Question: Did Peter Ito ever express hesitation about fighting against his native country?

Answer: First of all, his "native country" is America. He was born and raised here, even if his parents were born in Japan, and only spent three years of high school in Tokyo. As to hesitations, he always talked about his desire to shorten the war with as few casualties as possible, which is the most noble motivation I can think of.

Question: Did you ever have any doubts about Peter Ito's loyalty to the United States of America?

Answer: I know I said this emphatically in our meeting yesterday, but I will repeat it here: Peter Ito is not a traitor to his country. I can unequivocally state that he is as loyal as I am, and I'm sure new information will arise to validate my assessment.

The facts, as you presented them to me, are conjecture, a narrative cooked up by anti-Nisei sentiment, playing on deep-seated and completely baseless fears. Let's consider those, shall we?

Peter disappeared during the invasion of the Philippines and hasn't been heard from since, along with two other members of his regiment listed as missing in action without thought to treachery. And why? Because their ancestors emigrated from Europe—enemy, ally, or neutral, it doesn't matter—a few generations farther back than Peter's emigrated from Japan.

Yes, I ~~was~~ am Peter's friend. Rather than disqualify me, that makes my witness even stronger. I ~~knew~~ know him like no one else, and I can't think of a single thing to say against him.

So go ahead. Requisition the letters he sent to his family. Run a background check. Talk to every student he ever encountered and mentored and helped to thrive. You'll find nothing but a sterling-silver portrait of an honorable American, I'm sure of it.

Johanna Berglund

From Johanna to Thomas Ito

November 10, 1944

Dear Mr. Ito,

The army has asked me to write to you as a good-faith gesture, to ask you to comply with their requests in investigating Peter. Their thought is that, since Peter must have told you about me (I'm flattered they think so), a reassurance from me would mean more than empty promises from stern-looking officers in uniform. I don't know if that's true. After all, we've never met. But I hope you know that your son was a dear friend to me in a time when I badly needed one. I didn't realize just how much until I stopped hearing from him.

But back to the point: The Military Intelligence Service does want to exonerate Peter. I can promise you that because I shouted at them a good deal before I got at their motives. The army would be humiliated if it was made known that one of their language school's teachers had collaborated with Japan, so they are asking you questions and requesting documents as evidence to try to prove Peter's loyalty. Whatever help you can give them will help Peter.

And on a personal note: Thank you for raising such an honorable son. I have never doubted his loyalty, not necessarily because he has reason to love America, but because I know he would never lie to his students, and especially not to me.

With regard,
Johanna Berglund

From Thomas Ito to Johanna

November 13, 1944

Dear Johanna,

Peter has more than mentioned you. Sometimes we heard more about your life than his in the letters he sent us. I'm sorry it has taken my son's disappearance for us to be introduced.

You should know that I did not approve of Peter's decision to join the army language school as a teacher, much less go to war. This bothered him for a long time. He would try to persuade me, arguing late at night when my wife and mother had gone to sleep. He said it was not so different from the Japanese class he went to in California as a boy, taught by the elders in the community.

Now we know. It is very different, and everything I feared has come true.

I will answer any questions they bring to me. I have learned, though, that honesty is no guarantee of understanding. When I refused to say yes to question 28 of the loyalty questionnaire, they threated to take me away from my family. What was I to do? If I said I would renounce loyalty to the Japanese emperor, it would imply that I had any in the first place. There was no way to win.

That is why I'm worried they will decide Peter is disloyal. No matter how much evidence they see, they begin with a bias. That is where you and I disagree—you still trust the American government to seek justice. I have seen too much to have that faith.

This is not what I would have chosen for Peter. You are not who I would have chosen for him. And yet, after my father's death, I came to America, a country he disdained. I married a poor grocer's daughter of my own race, taking

on a new faith, a new occupation, a new life. I gave my
son a name both American and Christian: Peter, the rock.

As we say in Japan, shikata ga nai. It can't be helped.

Still, I am proud of my son. And I am proud that he has
a woman such as yourself standing with him, even now,
wherever he is.

You might ask yourself how I can make such a
statement. Enclosed in this package are all of your letters
to my son. They were with his personal effects, abandoned
at the base when he disappeared, and mailed to us when
no news of him could be found. I will ask your forgiveness
for reading them, but I wanted to understand why Peter
made the choices he did.

That is why I ask that you do whatever you can to clear
my son's good name. He deserves at least that much.

Sincerely,
Tatsuo "Thomas" Ito

From Johanna to Dr. Howard Hong of the YMCA

November 14, 1944

Dear Dr. Hong,

I don't know if you'll remember me. I'm the woman
translator at the branch camp in Ironside Lake,
Minnesota, the one whom you conscripted to teach an
English class. I've forgiven you for that now, though
for a while—well, let's just say that in the future, I'd
recommend asking a person before volunteering her.

I know you work primarily with prisoners here in the
United States but that the YMCA is also involved with
care of our prisoners overseas, so I have a request to make
of you.

My friend Peter Ito is MIA after the invasion of Leyte. That's all the information I could get out of the army, but they've had the nerve to suggest that, instead of being taken prisoner, he deserted or betrayed his unit to the Japanese. The idea is absurd, and I've taken it on myself to find out as much as I can.

I tried to place a call to the Red Cross but couldn't seem to talk to anyone who could give me useful information. They assured me that POW camps in all countries are required to register prisoners by filling out a capture card, to be filed with the International Red Cross, at which point the War Department would inform the next of kin by telegram of their son's whereabouts. All neat and tidy, like a brown-paper parcel wrapped by a smiley attendant at Donaldson's department store.

When I asked what could be done if such a capture card was never sent, they made excuses: the hostilities in the Philippines are ongoing, a full account of the killed and missing in action might not occur until a cease-fire, some governments refuse to cooperate with the convention agreements, aid workers can't go in until the danger has passed, which might take months . . .

I'm ashamed to admit I hung up on them at that point, but I can't tell you how frustrating it was to hear that nothing can be done. I can always do something, say something, make something happen.

Somehow, I suspect that Peter's not getting a full tray of meatloaf, green beans, and soft rolls, or playing in a ten-piece orchestra while working on his correspondence courses like our men here. That's not to say I resent our POWs' treatment, like all of the angry letter writers who fill the pages of our local newspaper. But maybe now I understand some of their resentment.

Please, Dr. Hong. I don't know what else to do. Are

there inquiries that can be made? Aid packages that can be sent to the area where he disappeared? Do you have a friend in the Military Intelligence Service who might shake someone by the lapels until they realize that their best agent is not an informant?

I would be grateful for any assistance you can give me.

Johanna

P.S./Appendix:

P.S. I read the volume on Kierkegaard that you recommended. It was quite good, and I can see why it motivated you to join a charity organization. Do you ever wish you hadn't?

From Pastor Sorenson to Johanna

November 15, 1944

Dear Johanna,

Cornelia Knutson told me her daughter Hattie went to practice the accompaniment for Sunday's service last night and saw you seated alone in the back corner of the church, but that you left before she could speak to you.

Please don't interpret this as a subtle way of telling you to go elsewhere. I wish all of my congregation would find refuge in the sanctuary during these difficult days. No, I don't mind at all you praying in the church. I just wish you wouldn't pray alone.

Remember that even our Lord, praying in agonizing pain in the Garden of Gethsemane, brought three of his disciples with him in his time of need.

Then again, they fell asleep instead of keeping watch

with him. I suppose that's a sobering reminder that people will fail us, even people we love. Perhaps those most of all.

Please come to me if there's something you need to talk about, or to your parents, or perhaps even an older woman like Mrs. Knutson. She has her eccentricities, but beneath that high-collared black brocade is a heart as wide and deep as the sea. We would all be happy to help as we're able.

> Peace be with you,
> Pastor A. Sorenson

From Johanna to Pastor Sorenson, left in his mailbox

November 16, 1944

Dear Pastor Sorenson,

Thank you for your concern. There's been a good deal on my mind lately. I've felt a special burden to pray for our troops overseas this week, and I've resolved to keep praying until I get an answer, or at least a fragment of peace.

You know how I've always liked quiet places and time to think by myself.

So please don't worry about me. I am fine.

> Johanna

From Johanna to Peter, never sent

November 16, 1944

Dear Peter,

You aren't dead. You can't be.

This is the stage of grief known as denial. I've decided

I won't move past it until I have definitive proof that I need to. Therefore, I'll continue to write to you as usual (although Mother says I shouldn't waste a stamp, since wherever you are, I don't have the address).

By now, I've read the papers and have at least a vague idea of your mission, the invasion of the Philippines. Old General McArthur[1] said he would be back, and I hate him for keeping his word, or at least for dragging you along.

After Davies questioned me about you, I thought about resigning in protest, but it's only another two weeks, and these men need me. When I think that now you might be a prisoner of war, far out of my reach, it makes me feel all the more that I should do what I can for them. I've felt like a sleepwalker, however, going through the motions of my work.

The first snow was today, and it occurred to me that we won't get the chance to make bets on the last snowfall. Spring seems impossibly far away.

Dad and Mother are worried about me—and about you, of course. They're forever asking if I need to talk, but what am I supposed to say? There's nothing they can do.

When I looked over the tactical map of the Pacific, next to a pin for the battle of Leyte was, in Mother's tiny, neat handwriting, "Peter captured." Not killed, not deserted, not turned traitor. Captured.

I can only pray that's the truth.

My last few letters to you were returned, and I have all the others, sent to me by your father. As I look through them, I can't help but be furious with myself. Why did I wait so long to tell you what you mean to me? I could say that I didn't know, that it was this final separation that told me, but that's not true. I've known for a long time . . . and it frightened me.

I'm a coward, Peter. That's the honest truth. And now it's too late to be brave.

The dance is in a couple of days, and I no longer care. If I hadn't agreed to take tickets, I'd stay far away. Maybe I should find a mask after all, so I don't have to explain why I don't look at all cheerful and carefree.

For the moment, I plan to bury myself in my work, translating and censoring a stack of letters. Is it terrible to admit I'm searching through them for anyone who might be as miserable as I am?

I'll answer as you would have: Yes, Jo, it is. You should want others to be happy, even if you can barely sleep from pacing your bedroom floor at all hours of the night.

Well, that's probably right, but at least if I find another tragedy or two, I can have someone to commiserate with. On with the letters, then.

Jo

[1] General McArthur . . . like King Arthur. Perhaps I have *Le Morte Darthur* too much on my mind, but it seems that both have the fatal flaw of pride. And if I've learned anything at all from epics and mythology, it's that one's flaw always affects others.

From Rose Schlitter to Dieter Bormann

August 29, 1944

Dear Dieter,

I would say that your last letter was outrageous and offensive, insulting me with one sentence, flattering me at the next. But that always was how you were, changeable as the sea, and I can't bring myself to be angry at you. In a way, I pity you.

Unlike you, I can write as much as I like, provided I have the stationery. But I'm afraid I'm running out of things to say. I've had less and less as the months have turned into years. You going on about your battles and tactics that I care nothing about, and now so far away in America. While your life stays in one place, my life is going on.

Which leads me to the most important news: I've accepted Arland's proposal. Never mind how he asked; it was very sweet and practical. Mother was in tears at the announcement, and Father has promised me a full reception dinner after the war is over, since the wedding itself will be quite simple. It will take place just after the new year, with greenery and punch and a new dress with lace at the collar. I am quite happy.

Try to understand. If you love me, you'll let me go. This is the last letter I'll be sending to you, as it isn't proper for a married woman to correspond with a former suitor.

I will always remember you, Dieter. Please do come visit our home if you return.

With regard,
Rose

Article on the Society page of the Ironside Broadside on November 16, 1944

CHURCH GROUP HOLDS ARMY BENEFIT DANCE

All residents of Ironside Lake are invited to a formal costume gala at the high-school gymnasium this Saturday, November 18. The event will be hosted by the Lutheran Daughters of the

Reformation in cooperation with Camp Ironside. Besides the price of admission, dances with army guards will be auctioned off. All funds collected from the evening will be used for a long-distance phone call home on Thanksgiving for each of the soldiers stationed in Ironside Lake.

"Many of us eagerly volunteer to roll bandages and send care packages to our troops overseas," LDR secretary Annika Sorenson said. "How can we ignore the opportunity to serve soldiers who are completing a thankless assignment on our doorstep? Many only have the opportunity to hear the voices of their loved ones briefly once a year. This would be a deeply meaningful gift to them."

Music will be provided by the Camp Ironside orchestra, under the direction of Otto von Neindorff. Currently, the orchestra is comprised of ten musicians, including an accordion, a piano, various woodwinds and brass, and a violin. They intend to play favorite selections from Beethoven, as well as a movement from one of Wagner's operas. The camp's assistant cook, Raymond Harrison, will be performing on the piano alongside the POWs for the closing numbers, a trio of jazz tunes borrowed from Duke Ellington and his band.

These are the only POWs who will be in attendance, and they will be under heavy guard to and from the camp. When questioned, Major Davies said, "We believe the entire community deserves to hear the artistry of these men. They have been practicing for months, and we assure you that all possible precautions will be taken to prevent any incidents."

So far, ten of the twenty guards, all eligible bachelors, have agreed to give up their off-duty time to attend the dance. Major Davies and his wife will also make an appearance. Tickets are available for purchase at the post office.

From Christopher Wright to Johanna

November 17, 1944

Dear Miss Berglund,

I didn't want to speak with you in case any of the men would overhear, but I wanted to leave you this note. There's been a change among the POWs over the past week. I'm a farmer's boy myself, and usually, just after harvest, folks are full of energy, you know? All their hard work paid off. Or maybe they're just plain tired out.

Not at my assigned farm. I can hear them whispering sometimes, shooting us suspicious looks, that sort of thing.

They've closed ranks. I've tried to ask Werner what's going on, but either he doesn't know, or he's in the center of it. Plays dumb every time. And if there's one thing Stefan Werner is not, it's dumb.

The POWs don't trust the guards as far as they can throw us, that's for sure. I see their mouths shut any time I so much as glance their way. But you're different. You're the nice lady who brings them mail from their family and teaches English and asks them how they're doing. If anyone can get out any information about what's happening—or what's going to happen—it's you.

It might be nothing. I hope it's nothing. But any chance you have to find out what's going on . . . take it.

PFC Christopher Wright

P.S. It's none of my business, I know, but why don't you and Annika work things out? She misses you. I can tell.

From Johanna to Christopher Wright

November 17, 1944

PFC Wright,

Thank you for your concern, and for thinking that I might be of some help. Unfortunately, at the moment, Major Davies is reluctant to let me out of his sight. Besides, I have more pressing matters on my mind at the moment and can't spare the time. We have only two more weeks with the men here. I'm sure they're just restless pending another change of location.

As far as Annika and me, there's nothing to say. We've been growing apart for years, and this is the inevitable conclusion. I will always think fondly of her, as I hope she will of me, but I'm sure she doesn't need me as a friend when she has you. That sounds bitter, but I truly do wish you both the best.

I hope to see you at the ball, although I will be assisting in taking tickets and not dancing. It was your article that set all of this in motion, I'm sure of it. Thank you for that. It's been good to see that, every once in a while, Ironside Lake can change its mind.

Johanna Berglund

From Dr. Howard Hong to Johanna Berglund

November 15, 1944

Dear Miss Berglund,

Thank you for your letter. I'm sorry to hear about the predicament you find yourself in. Nothing would give me greater pleasure than to be able to help you. Unfortunately—

(I do hate that word; the number of letters I drafted to prospective students of the university at which I taught beginning "Unfortunately," or "We regret to inform you," was staggering.)

But unfortunately, I have faced this particular challenge before. The most I could do is contact the Red Cross to try to expedite a visit to the camp where your friend might be held, but as the fighting in the Philippines seems to be only beginning, I'm afraid it won't do any good.

Japan has repeatedly violated the Geneva Convention—it seems almost a point of pride. That said, noting the last name of your friend and assuming he has Japanese heritage, it is possible that will put him in an advantageous position. I have heard stories of Japanese-speaking troops able to negotiate for better conditions, or making threats to inform the Red Cross of violations.

However, when it comes to direct action, I'm quite as helpless as you. I am sorry.

As to your other question: Yes, there are times when I wish I'd never abandoned my cozy tenure at the university. Especially at moments like this one, in fact, when I know the good I would like to do but am unable to do it.

And yet, if I'd never left the safety of my library, think of the stories I would have missed, the places I would never have seen, the people who would have gone unaided in a time of need. It was sometime this summer that I realized that, at the bottom of it, I am still doing what I love, though in a very different way than I had once envisioned.

I have a plaque in my office that gives the mission of my work: *Redeem the time.* For me, it refers to helping the POWs make good use of their free hours, in constructive activities for the mind, body, and soul, but it is also a reminder of how short our time on earth might be. Your uncertainty over your friend is, I'm sure, an unwelcome reminder of this as well.

So perhaps the best counsel I can give is that: Redeem the time, Miss Berglund, as you wait for news of your friend. You will not regret doing so.

> Sincerely and with sympathy,
> Dr. Howard Hong
> Field Secretary,
> YMCA War Prisoners Aid

P.S. I am sorry to hear that the English class would not have been your first choice of employment. However, if it's any comfort, I've gotten reports from your camp spokesman that you did an excellent job.

From Stefan Werner to Johanna, left on her desk at headquarters
Translated from German

November 17, 1944

The major tells me you plan to help von Neindorff load the orchestra instruments and equipment into the truck tomorrow night for the concert. Please don't bother; I will gather additional men to assist. The guards will approve us being out after curfew for something like this. I don't know about you Americans, but where I am from, gentlemen do not ask a woman to do such things.

I am glad you will be attending the ball. You will be quite lovely. I confess, I wish we nonmusical Germans might be allowed to attend along with the performers. Perhaps I could take the place of young Private Bormann, *who is in the infirmary. Alas, I can't play a note on his violin. As it is, you'll have to tell me about the music when you return.*

—S

From Johanna to Stefan Werner

November 17, 1944

Captain Werner,
Thank you for your concern, but I need to be there for translation purposes, and I'm quite capable of hefting an accordion while I'm at it.
Aryan womanhood indeed.

Article in the Ironside Broadside *written for the November 20, 1944, Society page*

ARMY BENEFIT DEANCE A HIT

Talk to anyone who attended the Army Benefit Costume Ball last Saturday night, and you'll hear nothing but praise for its smashing success.

Major and Mrs. J. E. Davies started off the dancing to the strains of a classical waltz. Alongside her husband's uniform, Mrs. Davies was resplendent in a green gown as the Statue of Liberty. After this, a swing dance mixer, called by the vociferous Johnny Clark from the post office, added more couples to the floor while refreshments were served and the silent auction for dances with the army men began.

Miss Annika Sorenson oversaw the filling of dance cards from those who contributed to the auction, packing each guard's evening with waltzes and foxtrots with the women of the town, both young and available, and married but seeking to support our troops. According to her, the LDR raised more than enough for a half hour long-distance call for each soldier stationed at the camp. She herself made a handsome half of a couple while in the arms of one of the guards, Private First Class Christopher Wright, for four consecutive dances, drawing complaints of monopolization. But any who saw the young dancers couldn't object for long, so striking a figure did they cut on the dance floor.

Highlights of the evening included the rose-bedecked trellis archway transforming the doorway, lively classical and jazz performances by the Ironside Lake orchestra, and a short-lived jitterbug competition in the center of the dance floor between two energetic couples before a stern LDR chaperone intervened to outlaw this style of dance.

There was also the appearance of a reverse Cinderella late in the night: a gentleman dressed as a Charlie Chaplin hobo, complete with grease paint, paid his fee, swept Miss Johanna Berglund into her lone dance of the night, and then disappeared. Could this Depression-era drifter in disguise be the reason she's shown no interest in local social mixers? Only time will tell.

At the end of the evening, ribbons were distributed for the best costumes to Hank Dahl as Robin Hood, and Jenny Johansson as Marie Antoinette. Mrs. Cornelia Knutson presented the award, though this columnist, at least, was unable to determine the precise nature of her own costume.

According to the major, the soldiers, even those unable to attend because of their duties at the camp, were grateful for this show of support from the community.

From Johanna to Peter, never sent

November 19, 1944

Dear Peter,

It's the middle of the night, but I'm writing this now—by hand, not on my typewriter, or I'd wake my parents—because I haven't been able to fall asleep. I can't send it, of course. But when we hear from you, or when you come back to us . . . maybe if you read this, you'll understand my predicament.

You might expect this to be full of details of the costume ball, so I suppose I'll oblige.

Annika was a lovely, if low-budget, Glinda the Good Witch, with a dainty tiara and a length of tulle under her pink skirt substituting for the massive hoops Billie Burke wore in the movie, fortunately for anyone dancing with her. Which, I might add, was almost entirely Christopher Wright. If anyone in town didn't know about her army romance, they do now.

You'll appreciate this: Cornelia Knutson came dressed as Joan of Arc. But not Joan of Arc in a demure French-style gown, or even Joan of Arc in armor with a banner held high. Oh no. Joan of Arc on fire. Not literally, but that was the effect she was going for with tongues of red-and-orange plaid leaping up to the waist of her high-necked white dress. The crowning touch was a gold cross necklace and a homemade chainmail collar made of bottlecaps. She has apparently been canvassing soda fountains and lunch counters for weeks.

Otto and his orchestra were magnificent, even though Dieter Bormann, their lead violinist, was resting in the camp's infirmary—supposedly from the flu, but I suspect he's nursing a broken heart based on the latest letter I delivered to him. I'm no musical expert, but the way they played, perfectly in tune, perfectly in meter with each other, was beautiful. Otto and Raymond Harrison played a duet near the end, their fingers flying over the keys so quickly, you'd have thought there was an entire hall of dueling pianos. Hearing the guests' hushed admiration, I've rarely been so proud of my POWs.

For the first half of the night, I managed to follow my plan of remaining off the dance floor. I like to think that my neo-Greco imitation of "Athena with a clipboard" intimidated even the most stalwart.

Until he arrived.

Now it's time for the rest of the story. All of those things are true, but none are the most momentous bit of news from the costume ball.

You see, Stefan Werner came. And danced with me.

I didn't recognize him at first. When he first sauntered up to me, all I saw was a collection of inside-out rags with exaggerated patches and frayed edges. But there, underneath the Charlie Chaplin hobo grease paint, were those steady gray eyes. And, all nerve, he whispered, "*Darf ich bitten?*" May I have this dance?

What could I say, Peter? I couldn't expose him in front of everyone. I had no idea how he had gotten in, how he'd escaped from the camp after curfew, but how could I ask him unless I took his hand and let him lead me onto the floor?

The orchestra began to play "Bewitched, Bothered, and Bewildered"—the music set must have been clairvoyant, because those were the exact feelings I was experiencing at the moment.

It's quite a long song, slow and gentle, very easy to be

overheard. I tried to pitch my voice as low as possible, asking Captain Werner, "How did you get here?"

His eyes actually twinkled like this was all a game. "Fences can be crawled under."

"You'll be caught!"

His only response was "We can't talk now," paired with a spin that jerked me along with him. "Unless you'd prefer to speak in German."

I tromped on his toes to inform him I would not. He just laughed.

It wasn't fair. My hands were slick with sweat, sure that one of the twirling couples around us—the major and his wife were only a few yards away!—would shout, "Halt! It's one of the prisoners!" And yet there he was, gliding in time to the music like he hadn't a care in the world, holding me far too close.

"You are a fool," I told him. "Why did you do it?"

As the last melancholy strains of the song played, he stepped even closer, his mouth just by my ear. "Don't you know?" Then he had the nerve to press a kiss to my cheek. "I must get back before they notice I am gone." With that, he squeezed my hand . . . and left. Out of the crowd of dancers, out of the gymnasium, out into the dark, leaving me staring after him.

It was just like Stefan to do something as outrageous as this, I told myself, trying to work up the appropriate amount of fury. He was bored and almost certainly hadn't thought about the potential consequences of his actions. Always charming, always a showman.

Still, it nagged at me. How had he gotten away? Was it his first—and last—escape attempt? Or was he the one that various townspeople had reported seeing outside of the stockade all this time?

Across the dance floor, I could see Major Davies tilting his head back to laugh at some joke my father had just told. In that moment, before the next song began, I knew I should have stormed across the gymnasium floor like a goddess on the warpath and ordered the guards out of the gymnasium to arrest Stefan before he could slip back under the fence.

But I didn't. And now Saturday night has turned into Sunday night, and still I've said nothing. Now I'm wondering if that was a mistake.

I can't sort it out. Flirt though he is, Stefan is not in love with me; I'm sure of that. So he must be flattering me because he wants something. I imagine he'll come to camp headquarters tomorrow morning and beg for a letter of recommendation to begin his citizenship process. I've firmly decided today that I can't in good conscience give it to him, not with what I know about his Nazi convictions. If Stefan wants to remain in America, he'll have to charm someone else.

Here's the trouble: If I go to Major Davies now to tell him that Stefan was at the ball and danced with me, his already low opinion of me would sink to new depths. As humiliating as that would be personally . . . it also affects you, Peter. I've been the staunchest advocate of your loyalty to the United States, and here I have been dancing with and covering for an enemy solider. Will it make him doubt my word about you too, the one person I was trying to protect?

I didn't go to church this morning, telling Mother I hadn't slept well and felt sick, which was true. But also true was that I didn't want to see Stefan in his back pew with the other POWs, and I certainly didn't want to risk him winking at me after the closing hymn, or worse, trying to speak to me.

Every man who has ever showed interest in me had some ulterior motive. Erik wanted to marry so he wouldn't be drafted. Stefan is using me to obtain American citizenship. And you . . . you don't mean it, of course, Peter, but you want someone to hold on to while you fight overseas. I don't doubt that you care about me, and I care about you, but all those things you said . . . you can't mean them. Can you?

As much as I hate it, there's really nothing to do now but to talk to Major Davies. I'll tell him my concerns about Stefan and ask that he have him monitored more closely. Then I'll face the consequences for my bad judgment. No more keeping his secrets, no more deception.

It's what you would do, isn't it, Peter?

Well, let's not fool ourselves. You would have done it immediately. But we can't all be heroes. Some of us are only ordinary mortals, trying the best we can and hoping it's enough.

Jo

Letter on the bunk of escaped prisoner
Found on Monday morning, November 20, 1944
Translated from German by Johanna Berglund

By now you have discovered both of us missing. Please do not waste your resources on searching for us, as we will have two days' lead and may already be out of your country by now.

The Fatherland needs its sons. Perhaps you will hear

from us again someday when we have rejoined the victorious Reich.

Captain Stefan Werner

EVIDENCE FOR THE PROSECUTION

QUESTIONING OF WITNESS #12, PRIVATE FIRST CLASS
CHRISTOPHER WRIGHT
DECEMBER 3, 1944

Q: Did you ever observe interactions between Captain Werner and the accused that suggested an understanding of some kind?

Wright: If there was anything between Miss Berglund and Werner, it was one-sided.

Q: Why do you say that? Please elaborate, PFC Wright.

Wright: One afternoon in October, when I was patrolling the grounds on a daytime shift, Miss Berglund asked me to accompany herself and Werner on an errand.

Werner was in charge of finding costumes, he said, for the dramatic tableau that two of the men would act out during the orchestra performance at the dance. Some opera piece about Icarus. Miss Berglund told him about a storage room where donated clothing was kept. Some people gave old shirts and pants and such, along with the records and books, not realizing the prisoners had to keep to marked uniforms, even on Sunday. I went along with them to see if there was anything they could use.

Q: So she asked you along because she didn't have a key?

Wright: No, she had the key. It seemed to me she just didn't want to be alone in a small, dark, enclosed space with Werner. And from the way he glowered at me, I guess he didn't much like having me there. While they sorted through the bins of clothes, I kept an eye on him like he was a mouse and I was the hawk. Then we left, and that was that.

Q: Did you have any idea—

Wright: Wait. I wasn't finished. I wanted to say, Miss Berglund could've taken Werner right inside with no one the wiser, if she'd wanted to rendezvous in private, either to exchange secret information or . . . well, anything else. But she didn't. She didn't because she's not that type of woman. She asked me to accompany her several times after that when meeting with him.

Q: Private Wright, were you aware that the clothing Captain Werner and his compatriot were wearing upon their escape—unmarked clothes—were the ones he took from the storage room under the guise of looking for a costume?

Wright: I . . . no. I didn't know that. But that doesn't mean . . .

Q: You attended the prison camp orchestra's performance at the dance. Did you see a "dramatic tableau" accompanying any of the songs?

Wright: There wasn't, was there? I hadn't remembered until now.

Q: Doesn't this seem like something Miss Berglund ought to

have known, given that she regularly attended rehearsals of the camp orchestra?

Wright: That seems like a question you'd have to ask her.

Q: Isn't it possible that Miss Berglund asked you along simply to give legitimacy to the errand? She may have known all along that Werner was seeking a disguise for his escape.

Wright: I . . . I just don't think she'd do something like that.

Q: Another guard we interviewed said Miss Berglund was often seen deep in conversation with Werner. After her English class, during inspections, before she left after working late into the evening—

Wright: He was the camp spokesman. That was her job.

Q: And that there was talk around the guard tower that they had more than a professional relationship.

Wright: Of course there was talk. Some people don't do anything but talk. But I'll tell you what I told them: There's nothing to see. Werner was likable. We all trusted him, all enjoyed talking to him. When you're surrounded by German all day long, it's nice to have someone who understands you, you know?

Q: Yes. I'm sure Miss Berglund felt very . . . understood by Captain Werner.

CHAPTER TWELVE

Article in the Ironside Broadside *on November 21, 1944*

ESCAPE!

Two German prisoners of war have escaped from Camp Ironside, presumably late last Saturday night. According to authorities, Captain Stefan Werner and Private Dieter Bormann were present for Saturday evening's roll call in their barracks but were discovered missing on Monday morning when the men assembled for transport to worksites. The entire camp was searched before local police were called in. State authorities and the FBI also quickly became involved.

It is believed that the escapees are making a desperate flight to Canada, where they hope to be beyond the reach of American law. No prisoners were allowed access to maps of the area, or even of the country. Since Germany is approximately the size of North and South Dakota combined, it is likely that the prisoners underestimated the time it would take them to reach the border, and their knowledge of extradition laws between the two countries would be minimal.

Officers on the Canadian border have already been notified with a description of both men.

Stefan Werner, camp spokesman, is pictured below. He is in his early thirties, 6'2", blond hair, clean-shaven, and speaks fluent English with little to no accent. There are no known photos of Dieter Bormann, but he has been described as stocky, with light brown hair, blue eyes, and a scar on his chin from a shrapnel wound.

Camp Ironside is under a strict lockdown, with guard shifts doubled and no one admitted through the gate without military clearance, no matter their errand or excuse. The prisoners' transfer back to the Iowa camp has been delayed while the search continues.

State police and the various federal agencies conducting the manhunt could not be reached for comment due to the urgency of this emergency.

Though it is unlikely that these two men are armed, they are certainly dangerous. Citizens are instructed to report any suspicious happenings and to volunteer with search parties as they are able.

All developments will be reported in this paper.

From Johanna to Peter, never sent

November 20, 1944

Dear Peter,

Stefan is gone. Escaped, along with one of his men, over the weekend. He danced with me and never went back.

How did I not see it coming?

Stefan was always loyal to Germany and didn't pretend to be otherwise, but he was so . . . genial about it that it seemed he couldn't possibly be any harm. Whenever he dropped by my office on some errand, he always seemed distracted, asking me to repeat myself multiple times. He blamed his lacking English skills, but now I wonder if he was eavesdropping on the major's calls to Fort Snelling, easily audible in the adjoining office.

Once, I caught him looking through the stack of censored letters on my desk. He said that he was interested in how many of the men were making use of the YMCA's provision of stationery and stamps. The excuse seemed plausible at the time . . . but what if he slipped in an unauthorized letter? It would have gone out with the mail, and I'd never know a thing about it.

Also—and this one stings the most because I realize it betrayed your trust—he was always asking about the Japanese language school, including mission types and whether you would wear a standard uniform and how you'd gather information. It didn't seem suspicious at the time because it flowed naturally from the conversation, but now I can see that he was searching for anything of possible use to Germany's allies.

It's so easy to see things looking back, isn't it?

They won't get far. They can't. Everyone in the state knows about them by now, and besides the police and FBI, posses of civilians are going out, armed with guns but not with knowledge of the law.

Is it terrible that I'm worried about them, Peter? Dieter's just a boy who found out the love of his life is marrying a middle-aged banker. He's so hotheaded that I can almost believe he thinks he'll make it to Germany in time to stop the wedding. And Stefan, who should know better, must be trying to redeem himself, to prove to his father that he's been loyal to Germany all along.

They're the enemy: misguided and reckless and devoted

to a cause I consider wrong. But they don't deserve to be gunned down in the woods of northern Minnesota by a pack of angry farmers who have decided not to take prisoners.

If I pray for them, will God listen to me? Or is he only granting the requests of the Allies these days?

Tomorrow, if they haven't been found, all Camp Ironside employees will be questioned. I'll have to tell them that Stefan was at the masquerade, and I knew it and didn't say anything.

For the first time in my life, I feel really, genuinely guilty. I didn't know Stefan meant to escape in earnest, but who will believe me?

If I'm questioned, I could mention Stefan and Dieter's possible motivation, explain what they might know of Minnesota's geography, tell them that Stefan is an accomplished athlete and might be traveling via canoe. Wouldn't that be enough?

If you were here, I know you'd say it wasn't. Peter, Sir Galahad himself, without a deceptive bone in his body.

The question is, Can I be as brave as you?

Must try to get what sleep I can. I'll decide in the morning.

Jo

From Johanna to Lt. Col. Arthur Lobdell

November 21, 1944

Dear Sir,

As my last official act at my desk before clearing it out for good, Major Davies has asked me to write an account of what I just told him in his office. He's too furious to do so himself at the moment, and we've been given strict orders to keep the phone lines open for any news of the escaped men. None of this is his fault, so please don't judge his command here harshly because of this.

The truth is, I knew Captain Werner, at least, had escaped. On Saturday night, I helped load orchestra equipment into the army truck. Captain Werner was there at the beginning, but I don't recall seeing him leave after the orchestra players and their instruments and makeshift stage were assembled. It's possible he and Dieter stowed away on that very truck, driving through the gates rather than tunneling under or climbing over them. This might explain why no traces of an elaborate breakout could be found.

But this, you might say, is no proof of my complicity, just an example of a way I might have been more observant.

True. But I saw him outside of the compound later that night. He appeared at the costume ball—I don't know why—and urged me not to turn him in, playing it off as a grand joke.

I did not alert the commander, foolishly believing that Captain Werner would do as he said and return to the camp. After thinking it through, I had intended to report it to Major Davies on Monday, but by then the escape was discovered.

I don't know how to convince you that this is the truth. Major Davies certainly doesn't believe me. I can tell that much from the vein-bulging fury on his face when he realized I could have prevented this.

All I can say is that I'm deeply sorry for my negligence, and I will take full responsibility and any consequences that will follow, which includes the termination of my employment.

I should end here, but I have one more thing to say.

Captain Werner is an intelligent man, Lt. Col.; I promise you that. If my word doesn't count for much anymore, ask any of the guards. Which is why none of this makes any sense. If you don't understand what I mean, think through the facts:

- As we taught about it in English class, Captain Werner has at least a rudimentary understanding of American geography "from sea to shining sea." It seems to me he must understand just how far Minnesota is from Germany and the utter futility of attempting to travel there.
- He planned his escape for the end of November, the beginning of winter, presumably with minimal supplies of clothing, and after a light snow that would make them easy to track.
- He deliberately revealed himself in a public place to a woman who would easily recognize him.

Now ask yourself, why?

I want you to ask that question because I can find no answer myself, and Major Davies isn't willing to entertain what he sees as meaningless philosophical inquiries from a traitor. But there's more to this than we're seeing. I know it.

Again, I apologize for bringing danger to my community and scrutiny to the POW camp system by not revealing all that I knew. I should have known it would all come out eventually.

> With regret,
> Johanna Berglund

*Speech from Mayor Carl Berglund to the town of Ironside Lake
on November 22, 1944*

I know that tensions have been high, understandably so. But I want to let you know that I've made calls to authorities all over the state, and they assure me that, without access to transportation and with the circulation of descriptions and photographs around Minnesota, there is no way for the missing POWs to get out of the state without being apprehended.

Sheriff Coolidge has determined that no vehicles of any kind have been stolen from citizens of this town, and there have been no other reports of theft or damage, so it's likely the fugitives are either walking or traveling the Mississippi River by boat. Both of these options mean their progress will be limited.

Besides that, security around Camp Ironside has been increased, and Major Davies reports that, while many of the remaining POWs are supportive of Werner and Bormann's escape, it is in the way that you might casually cheer for a high-school baseball game. Some readily admitted to collecting food to donate to the two men for their journey, but hardly anyone believes they can actually make it. I'm told there is a betting pool on how many days Werner and Bormann will remain free in total. The current average is nine days.

For the record, I put ten dollars on six. That means I fully expect both prisoners to be back in custody by the end of the week, thanks to the efforts of our diligent law enforcers.

Whatever developments come next, I'm proud of this town. Anyone who knows me knows that. I've been with you through hard times before, and we'll weather this storm too, the same way we always have: together.

POLICE UNCOVER SECRET NAZI LOVE NEST

Last night, police investigated a possible lead in the escape of two German prisoners of war. An undisclosed citizen reported that an abandoned shed in Turner's Woods, to the northwest of the city and close to Camp Ironside, seemed to have seen recent use.

Inside were several documents and two sets of discarded *PW*-branded uniforms, presumably of the escaped prisoners. Officials connected with the investigation said only that the documents will "need to be analyzed further," but our sources say they contain highly compromising material written by a civilian woman, possibly connected with the escape.

By the time this reporter arrived at the scene, all documents had been confiscated, but inside the woodshed, past sheer lace curtains, the sole contents of the shack were revealed: a cheap Eveready flashlight on a shelf by the door, a crude swastika painted on the far wall, and, filling up most of the floor, a sagging mattress that had seen considerable use.

The structure, located on the property of Mayor Carl Berglund, is roughly a mile and a half from the barbed-wire fence of Camp Ironside. Far enough, it must be observed, to be out of range of patrolling guards, while close enough for a prisoner to make a round trip, with perhaps an amorous detour in between, after nightly bed checks and before reveille sounded.

Authorities have suspected that the prisoners would need an accomplice on the outside to remain undetected for so long. This new revelation appears to confirm this suspicion.

Both men, Captain Stefan Werner and Private Dieter Bormann, are still at large, with authorities from across the state joining in the search efforts.

338

From Annika to Johanna

November 22, 1944

Jo,

Father said I should speak to you as soon as possible, but I can't. I just can't look at you right now, not until I've had a chance to explain myself.

If you've realized I'm the one who led the police to our old playhouse, you probably hate me, thinking it was out of spite. But it wasn't. I promise, I had no idea the documents would point to you. Neither did Chris, who was with me.

One moment, we were sharing the most magical kiss in the moonlight . . . the next, I noticed that the door to the playhouse was open, banging against the frame in the wind. When I saw what someone had done to the place we'd built—the German pinups, the letters, that terrible symbol—I panicked. We called the police immediately. What else could we have done?

Chris has told me what they're saying: that the papers inside were letters between you and Stefan. They asked him to translate some of them, since he speaks basic German. I'm sure you've heard by now, but if not, I wanted to warn you. Your name was signed on them.

But I don't believe it. Not only because it's so unlike you, but because none of them were in your handwriting. I know they weren't. You wrote all the scripts we acted in as children, remember? How many times did I try to get you to straighten up your left-leaning smudgy scrawl? And you would say, "It's the words that matter, not what they look like. Stop being so prissy."

I couldn't read the German, but these were in perfect,

flowery cursive, signed with Xs and curlicues and
everything else you can't stand.

I'll make sure they know they have the wrong suspect.

But what if they won't listen?

I can't figure out how the escaped prisoners knew about
our special place. I certainly didn't tell them, and you
know Chris barely speaks a word to anyone. It seems like
too much of a coincidence to say they simply stumbled
upon it. I'm sure there's an explanation, but you've
got to put it on record quickly before the paper prints
another horrid story. "A sagging mattress that had seen
considerable use"—yes, we wrapped it in a tarp and used
it to sled down the hill because our parents were too cheap
to buy us a toboggan for Christmas. It's outrageous.

Oh, Jo, what's going to happen to you now?

Annika

EVIDENCE FOR THE PROSECUTION

TRANSLATED FROM GERMAN

November 16, 1944

My darling Stefan,

How thrilling it is to write those words! You'll destroy
this after reading it, as you promised, won't you? There is
no one in the entire world who would understand our love.
They look at you and see only an enemy. I see the man
underneath, the one I have always admired.

Once you escape to Canada, please use the money I've
given you to send word to me. Canada is an allied country,

but if you are careful, you might live there until the war's end, when we can be reunited at last.

Oh, how I dream of being in your arms again.

Sometimes, waking in the middle of the night, I wonder: What if you spoke those words of devotion to me without thinking? What if you made promises you won't be able to keep? Have I helped you leave me in vain, never to see you again?

But then I remember your heart, true and faithful as the rising sun, and I set aside my fear. There is room only for love, overflowing for you.

Hurry away, my love. Hurry so that you may come back to me once more!

> With all my heart, forever and always,
> Your Johanna

CHAPTER THIRTEEN

WARRANT FOR THE ARREST OF
JOHANNA BERGLUND
FILED: NOVEMBER 22, 1944

To the County Sheriff:

Defendant to Be Arrested: Johanna Berglund

Charge:
  I. Treason
  II. Conspiracy to Commit Treason

Sex: F
Race: W
Age: 22
Address: 1384 Turner Ln., Ironside Lake, Minnesota

Remarks: Defendant not to be released on bail until the return of two POW escapees.

From Johanna to Pastor Sorenson

November 23, 1944

Dear Pastor Sorenson,

To start a letter from jail with "Happy Thanksgiving"
is entirely too good of an irony to pass by. I hope the
holiday finds you considerably more grateful than I am.

I called Dad and Mother this morning, but I thought I'd
send a letter to you. There's no limit on those. Apparently
not many people in the county jail write them, but they
have paper on hand for—I don't know, confessions, I
suppose. Likely in this uneventful town, their supply has
been used more often for endless games of hangman by
bored deputies.

See? Gallows humor. Literally. I'm clearly still in fine
spirits despite a lack of sleep—it's terribly drafty in here—
and the general destruction of my life.

They're still fiddling with bail requirements and the
arraignment—I'm told it's complicated because of the
military aspect—but no one expects me to be here longer
than three or four days, as long as they recapture the
POWs. I am a "low flight risk," even though I'm being
accused of directly aiding two prisoners' escape. This
seems an example of literary irony, but that's much more
fun to analyze in *Hippolytus* than to encounter in one's
real life, I'm finding.

All that to say, lacking any proper reading materials, I
may die of boredom in the space of three days. The silence
is beginning to grate.

If you have any recommendations for books, I'd
appreciate you giving them to Dad or bringing them to
me directly. I imagine they'd let my spiritual advisor in as

a visitor, though they'll probably search your volumes of Luther and Kierkegaard for saws and files.

If you don't mind associating yourself with the most despised woman in America—and I will understand if you do—I'd welcome a visit. It's very lonely here. Even my prayers seem to be Returned to Sender, but I suppose that's nothing new.

Johanna

From Pastor Sorenson to Johanna
Left in the top of a stack of books delivered to her cell

November 24, 1944

Dear Johanna,

I remember your reading pace and know these two volumes will only last you eight hours, give or take. If you remain here for much longer than that, which I hope you do not, don't be afraid of silence. It's where God is most likely to be heard.

I should know—I can't count the number of sleepless nights after my wife died, and then again after the news of Erik's death. While our situations are not remotely the same, I thought you should know that. In its own way, it may help.

We are, all of us, alone, living in our own narrow worlds, isolated from each other like pioneers in a blizzard. The world can seem very cold at times.

But at the same time, we are not alone. Never, not even if we look around and see nothing but blinding white. If we reach out, we'll find we've always been tethered to something solid and strong.

I've lost a beloved wife and son. Believe me when I say

344

that, at times, God tests and trusts us with silence . . . but he also speaks. Have you been listening?

I know I won't be able to keep you from reading, thinking about your case, and writing letters, and there's a place for all of that. But please, take time to be still. And while you're at it, you might read psalms 42 and 43. I've always found them to be helpful.

Know that I'm praying for justice to be done, and quickly.

Peace be with you,
Pastor A. Sorenson

Written by Johanna Berglund

November 24, 1944

Dear God,

Pastor Sorenson said I should talk to you, and as I have no intention of making an insanity plea, I felt it would be better not to be seen pacing my cell and muttering to myself. Besides that, I've found over the past year that it's easier to compose one's thoughts on paper. So, a letter. I'll at least save money on the stamp.

I have a pressing question for you. Most of it is a simple, somewhat accusatory "Why?" but it needs proper context, back to January 1943.

Do you remember? I suppose you do, being omniscient. It's the last significant conversation we had, so I too remember every detail. Dad sent me a telegram while I was at school, an extravagant expenditure in his nickel-and-dime economy. I read it twice, three times, to make sure I hadn't made a mistake. Erik had been reported wounded. Not dead. There was still hope. There was still time.

I crumpled on the hideous brown linoleum of my tiny apartment and prayed so fervently, I half expected the curtains to blow, like on Pentecost. I took short breaks to shuffle to the teakettle and refill my mug but couldn't even bring myself to drink it. I just emptied out the cold Earl Grey and refilled it again to have something warm to hold on to.

In those prayers, I reminded you of everything Erik was—earnest and loyal, patient and full of a desire to serve others. I described what he was meant to do, painted the picture for you with my imagination so you could see him as something more than one more body on a field stretcher, bleeding and barely holding on. And not only what he was, but what he would be. Erik playing "Stardust" on his trumpet; Erik taking a young, towheaded son to fish in the creek; Erik with gray hair, preaching in his father's pulpit at Immanuel Lutheran, that beautiful light of unshakable faith in his eyes.

If that wasn't enough, I made a promise of my own to you. I even wrote it down like a contract, signed it, and placed it securely inside my linguistics textbook, since I realized I didn't have a Bible with me in Minneapolis. I wasn't sure at the time if that was orthodox or not, but if I was going to be a heretic, I wanted to be a thorough one.

It's still in my desk at home, but I have it memorized.

"I, Johanna Berglund, do solemnly swear that if the Almighty God spares Erik Martin Sorenson and returns him to life and ministry, then I will come back to Ironside Lake and remain there until such time as I have fulfilled my obligation to my family and the town, as indicated by some sign yet to be determined."

It was all I had. Some small part of me suspected
that this was your way of—not punishing me, exactly,
but warning me to come back home. To remind me of
what I'd turned my back on: my family, my childhood
sweetheart, and my quaint hometown. I knew from Pastor
Sorenson's sermons that you require sacrifice, and I could
think of nothing more valuable to promise you than my
greatest dream.

But it wasn't enough.

That's probably why I fought coming back for so long.
It wasn't the town or the job or even my classes. It was
that I didn't want to be forced to hold up my end of the
bargain when you didn't bother to follow through with
yours.

But I came, just the same. You got what you wanted
after all. I'm here.

So where are you?

From Major Davies, posted at City Hall and printed in the Ironside
Broadside

November 25, 1944

To the People of Ironside Lake,

As you have likely heard by now, the two POWs
missing from Camp Ironside were apprehended late last
night, having reached a point 52 miles to the northwest
of the city. A citizen like yourself, aware of the escape,
saw the smoke of their campfire in the woods and called
the sheriff, an example of the good we all can do when
working together.

Captain Stefan Werner and Private Dieter Bormann
are being kept in a secure location until they can be

questioned by authorities. They are in good health and came peaceably upon their arrest.

Whatever the circumstances that led to their escape, rest assured that we will uncover the truth! Until then, please support due process by keeping all rumors to yourselves. Remember, loose lips sink ships.

I am aware that national news agencies have already picked up this story, and I apologize for the additional scrutiny it means for the good people of this town. God knows I never would have wished it on you!

Deepest gratitude to those of you who volunteered for citizen search parties and community watch groups. It is because of your vigilance that we were able to apprehend the prisoners!

Onward, my fellow Americans! Justice will prevail in the end!

Major J. E. Davies
US Army, Fort Snelling

From Olive to Johanna

November 24, 1944

Johanna, you're in the newspaper. The *Tribune*. And for aiding and abetting the escape of German POWs. Have you gone and lost the plot, or have the reporters? Someone around there must be mad, or else I am.

I know we've both been busy and haven't spoken in a while, and maybe that's partly my fault, but please write back soon. I'm desperately worried about you.

Olive

Article in the Ironside Broadside *on November 27, 1944*

TREASON SUSPECT CORRESPONDED
WITH JAPANESE SPY

While police have not released new information regarding the alleged crimes of former Camp Ironside translator and accused conspirator Johanna Berglund, the *Broadside* staff investigated a tip that has led to a startling new development.

Previously reported in an editorial in this paper was Berglund's relationship with Peter Ito, a teacher-turned-war-translator in the US Army, who met Berglund when she was at the university in Minneapolis. Their friendship is now the subject of close scrutiny, as Ito, who spent the majority of his formative years in Japan and whose parents were Japanese citizens, has disappeared in enemy territory and is under investigation for collusion with the Axis powers.

Many theorize that this connection might be where Berglund first developed anti-American sentiments, which grew as she fraternized with German soldiers at the camp, particularly Captain Stefan Werner, the charismatic camp spokesman.

Miss Berglund is currently released on bail, living with her father, Mayor Carl Berglund, only a month after his reelection to public office. A petition has been started to demand his resignation. Neither could be reached for comment.

Werner and Bormann are being thoroughly interrogated, and a source close to the investigation believes they have already made a full confession.

From Johanna to Olive

November 28, 1944

Dear Olive,

At this point, I don't want to place blame on anyone for anything, so whyever we stopped writing, I'm ready to start again.

As to who's gone mad, it feels like the whole world. But this is what I can tell you.

I've been accused of helping two of the prisoners in my camp escape. I'm sure you've seen their names. Once the men were captured and questioned, Stefan's and Dieter's stories both aligned perfectly: I had fallen in love with Stefan and wanted to help him return to Germany. To that end, I gave the men unmarked clothing and a map of Minnesota, then distracted the guards by requesting help in loading the orchestra equipment, allowing them to slip into the truck and out the gate. Stefan risked meeting me at the dance because he couldn't resist my charms (honestly, that's what they're saying) and wanted to confirm our meeting spot. Later, I rendezvoused with them at the shed in Turner's Woods and gave them money and supplies for their journey.

They also added that I had let them send uncensored letters filled with intelligence to Germany and POWs in other camps, described top-secret military operations to them, started the fire in the storage room, and supported a resistance group in Camp Ironside to stir up public opinion against America. I suppose if my friend Annika hadn't already found several incriminating letters he planted in the woodshed on my family's property, Captain Werner would have directed the police there after being captured, to corroborate the story he spun.

Even one of these lies would have caused trouble. All of them together, along with dozens of bits of circumstantial evidence, might be enough to ruin me.

But here is the one thing: I did see Captain Werner the night he escaped, and I did nothing about it. He let himself be seen with me in order to seal the case against me. His gamble paid off, because I didn't have the moral strength to go to someone right then and there and ask for help.

I'm not a traitor. But I have made some very poor choices these past few weeks.

They say the grand jury and the trial won't take place until late winter or early spring, which will give time for the counsel to prepare and for the publicity around me to die down. I'm certainly regional, and probably national, news. So here I am, trapped in my room, bound less by the terms of my bail than by my own fear to step outside my door.

It's ironic, isn't it? All I ever wanted to do was get as far away as possible from this place, to travel and see the world and experience life outside of this small town. And now I'm trapped to a few square yards of it.

Dad has temporarily disconnected our telephone, and my sister and her husband are going out of town for an extended vacation until everything calms down. Irene is pregnant with her second child and can't take the strain of being shouted at in the streets. It isn't a good time to be associated with the Berglunds, me in particular.

Dad's also hired a lawyer. Not a relative or friend of the family or even a resident of Ironside Lake—he felt like we needed someone with more criminal law experience. So I'm meeting with Charles Donohue Jr. of Duluth, and he is just as citified and stiff as his name indicates, droning through lists of questions and protocol. He probably doesn't realize that I've done extensive research on his previous cases and already know most of what he's telling me. I nod along anyway. We're discussing the particulars of treason next week.

I'm not in the best state of mind at the moment, so I'm sorry if this is confusing or if there are details I've left out. Most days, all I want to do is sleep, then wake up and find out this was all a dream.

Please don't tell me what the newspapers are saying, Olive. I probably don't want to know. But you believe I'm innocent, don't you?

Johanna

P.S. If you kept them (and can find them—I remember the mess that was your bedroom), can you please mail me the letters I wrote to you from Ironside Lake? I know I spoke about Captain Werner to you, and Donohue is looking for anything at all that might help.

From Dr. Smythe to Johanna

November 29, 1944

Dear Miss Berglund,

I regret to inform you of what I assume, given your relative intelligence, you have already divined: Word has reached the university of the legal trouble in which you are currently embroiled. Regardless of whether there are enough loopholes for you to result in an acquittal in court, as some of the newspaper accounts are predicting, you will not be welcome to enroll at the university in the spring, or ever again in the future. I'm sure you understand that such publicity can be—and already is—damaging to the reputation of our institution.

The private donor, whose identity is still concealed from me, has been informed of this change, and will, I'm sure, award your scholarship to someone more deserving.

Please do not contact me in the future; all letters from this address will be discarded before opening.

Dr. Sheridan Smythe
Chair of the Modern
Languages Department,
University of Minnesota

From Brady McHenry to Johanna

December 1, 1944

Miss Berglund,

The mail's been pouring in after my latest article. Too many editorials to print, even if we added a special section. Thought I'd drop you a few of my favorites, though I'm sure you're getting plenty at your home too, and at your daddy's office in city hall. I bet he never guessed his greatest political liability would be his own daughter.

What did I say about threats, hmm?

Maybe I was an artist once, but now I'm a newspaperman. One with some juicy headlines to write. You've turned me straight after all. No need to print anything but exactly what the people have to say about this.

Brady McHenry
Owner and Editor in Chief,
Ironside Broadside

Dear Editor,

A recent article incorrectly labeled Johanna Berglund as a "member of the Lutheran Daughters of the Reformation" when, in fact, she declined our invitation to join. I have her letter of refusal as proof, and given the way things have turned out, I see her reluctance to associate herself with the LDR as a credit to our organization. It is important that such an error be corrected at once.

I will add that all efforts of the LDR related to Camp Ironside, such as the costume gala, were solely and exclusively focused on support of our own United States troops. We were not consulted in the decision to allow German soldiers into our town or our church, and we hope that a discerning reader would recognize the distinction.

Mrs. Dorothy Lewis

Dear Editor,

Didn't we say this would happen, putting a prison camp on our doorstep? I was at the city council meeting when some concerned citizens presented a case that the POWs were being treated too leniently, but Mayor Berglund didn't listen. Bet he wishes he had now, unless he was in on it with his daughter since the beginning.

I got five minutes of time to talk about how the major used YMCA money to buy out my theater on a Thursday night to let some of them watch a film. Probably they were taking notes during the newsreels to smuggle information back home. They stole candy on the way out too. I know it,

354

but who do you think tried to talk me out of reporting it to the police? Johanna Berglund. We should have known it would have been her.

My boy went off to the city too, when he was her age. Now he only writes to ask for money. Well, good riddance, I say. Good riddance to all of them. I've got high-school students taking tickets who need to see what comes of leaving behind your home and your values. Let this be a lesson to them.

As for the POWs, they'd better not try to pass that lot off on us again next year, labor shortage or no. I, for one, won't let a single German goose-step his way through the doorway of my establishment, that's for sure.

Clarence Jakes

Johanna's notes after meeting with Charles Donohue Jr. of Clark and Donohue Legal

December 7, 1944

Hardly anyone has been executed for treason since John Brown raided Harpers Ferry. This seems like good news.

The prosecution will argue before a grand jury (23 citizens) to indict me. They don't need to prove guilt, just that a crime has been committed and there is evidence I should be tried for it.

I am not permitted to attend the grand-jury proceedings, nor is Donohue (no cross-examination of evidence or witnesses by the defense). If they return an indictment, the case moves to trial.

The chances of that, according to Donohue's estimation, are roughly 70%. The argument against me is mainly circumstantial, but the prosecutor is competent and has issued dozens of subpoenas for witnesses/documents. The testimony of both Werner and Bormann together is very serious.

It doesn't, apparently, matter how ridiculous I find that. I should calm down and save my energy for the trial. (At this point, I discussed the damaging nature of condescension to a client relationship.)

The treason charge likely won't stick—too difficult to prove intent within its parameters. The counts of aiding and abetting enemies of the United States or conspiracy to commit treason (more minor) might.

Statistically, women aren't convicted as often. I brought up Mary Surratt, conspirator to assassinate Lincoln. Donohue and I debated her guilt or innocence for twenty-two minutes.

Modern treason cases have rarely resulted in conviction. Related: the case of Velvalee Dickinson, the doll shop spy, in August of this year. Asked Donohue to elaborate, spent another thirty-nine minutes discussing the case—she smuggled military information to Japan via seemingly harmless letters about dolls (a code). Fascinating. She was not convicted of treason but "violation of the censorship statutes" and sentenced to ten years in prison and a $10,000 fine.

Two-hour appointment concluded. I learned more

about Mary Surratt's and Velvalee Dickinson's
fates than my own.

Given all this, a few notes as I prepare my
statements for the trial:

If sentenced to prison, I'd be thirty-two when
released, assuming I couldn't get out early on
good behavior.

- Research whether the Minnesota prison
  system has access to correspondence
  courses through the U of M. (Don't ask
  Smythe.)

- Create a reading list. Put *The Count of
  Monte Cristo* at the top in original French
  so guards don't realize it's about a
  prison break.

I'm sure my family could raise $10,000 for a
fine, somehow.

- If I could get information about the
  scholarship donor, I could try to convince
  him to fund my new academic endeavors as
  an inmate.

- Maybe the Lutheran Daughters of the
  Reformation would hold a bake sale?

- And maybe I'd have a better chance of
  being invited to Roosevelt's inaugural
  ball and receiving a full pardon.

To Do: Work on collecting documents to present as evidence of my intentions/behavior over

the past year. To seek out possible motives,
request any information I can nd about Stefan
Werner and Dieter Bormann before they came to
the camp. Also, begin preparing statements on
the relevant details likely to be raised at the
trial. (Parameters: "Please don't say anything
too shocking, Miss Berglund.")

From Johanna to Peter, never sent

December 12, 1944

Dear Peter,

I haven't "written" to you in a while, mostly because
I've been afraid to add to a stack of evidence the
prosecution will probably subpoena any day now.

Our old friend Brady McHenry has been keeping the
newspaper filled with the latest drama. The letters written
directly to me are even less tactful than the ones he prints.
Even McHenry won't let profanities or death threats be
printed in his newspaper, but dozens of each have found
their way directly to our door, some from as far away
as Dallas and Boston. How they got an address for me,
I'll never know. I wouldn't be surprised if people start
scribbling, *The Traitor, Ironside Lake*, and assume the
postman will just know where to send it.

The common theme of the letters is that I should be
ashamed of myself. Which, of course, I already am, just
not for the reasons the writers think I ought to be.

I keep playing the past year over again in my mind,
like a movie-theater attendant forced to watch the same
film every night from the projection room, trying to see if
this time, I'll be able to see the twist coming, find another

detail I should have noticed, a conversation I shouldn't have had, some sign that this would happen.

I don't have your faith, Peter. I don't go to church anymore, not wanting to draw any more unwanted attention to my parents or the Sorensons. When I read my Bible in my room on Sunday mornings, I see those promises you talked about, but I don't see them when I look around.

I'm afraid. Really, truly afraid. I try not to show it when talking to Donohue, but every time I think about going to trial, or to prison, I'm up all night with a thousand prickling anxieties.

It seems like it's nearing the end of the story, and I keep hoping for Peter ex machina, some dramatic entrance where you arrive to save the day and set everything right, but it hasn't come yet. And I'm not sure how much longer I can do this alone.

Jo

From Olive to Johanna

December 11, 1944

Dear Johanna,

My word. After two years of complaining to me about how undergrads have entirely too much drama in their lives, you tangle yourself up in this!

Of course I believe you're innocent. I didn't doubt it for a second. The nerve of those Germans!

What is your solicitor saying about your chances? I don't know a thing about American law, but none of this could stand up in a serious court, could it? (Your letters are attached. It took me an hour of searching to find them, and I accidentally cleaned my room in the process.)

Also, I have to say it was stupid, stupid, stupid of me to get angry at you before, when you said you weren't sure if you still wanted to attend Oxford. I was only afraid of losing you. Several times, I meant to write to you and apologize, but I never knew quite what to say.

And here's the worst of it: Just when I've realized what a terrible friend I've been, I'm going away. I've finished out the semester (which really was brutal), and the children and I are going home to Mum in England. For good, and hopefully in time for Christmas. All except Charlie, who's resolved to stay here and work the farm. At seventeen, he's man enough to make his own decisions, but I will miss him. And you.

Will you visit me in England? Promise? Even if you've given up on Oxford, I would love to show you around London.

Do send a letter anyway, with all the details you can about the proceedings. I've put Mum's address at the bottom here. I promise to write back this time, although the postal service is criminally slow and it might be Easter before you get it.

Must pack. Chin up, dear; you'll get through this. I only wish I could be there to help.

> All the best,
> Olive

Dear Editor,

I'm writing to complain about recent coverage of the arrest and arraignment of Johanna Berglund. The case hasn't even gone before the grand jury, and you've all made up your mind on the verdict. Whatever happened to innocent until proven guilty? Those of you who are so proud of yourselves as loyal patriots should remember that American virtue.

I've done a lot of thinking the past few weeks. And I've realized that maybe there are certain people given to every community. They are the advocates, the idealists, the ones you can't shush and tell to go along with the way things have been. In movies like *Mr. Smith Goes to Washington*, we give their parts to actors like Jimmy Stewart because we know they're heroes. We understand it takes courage to speak up, especially to suggest that your town or your country might be wrong.

That's what Johanna did, and she's being punished for it now.

Right now, all we have are a few incriminating documents, which could easily have been planted by the escapees, and the fact that Johanna was one of a handful of people in this town who treated the POWs as individuals. When the court actually looks at the facts, I know they'll find that all the hubbub is a cluster of skewed facts and out-of-context conversations, distorted by a public hungry for the drama of wartime.

We're not England, hurried into air-raid shelters and rocked by bombs every night. We're not France, celebrating the liberation after a long occupation. We're not even Russia, forced to quarter troops during the freezing winter.

We're America, an ocean away from the fighting, safe in our own borders, the quietest home front of all. Very little has been asked of us here. But let's not invent a spy and traitor just for the thrill of a good headline. Let's not disown Johanna Berglund without first finding out the truth.

Annika Sorenson

Christmas card from Cornelia Knutson to the Berglunds

December 21, 1944

To the Berglunds, but especially Johanna,

I'd wish you a merry Christmas, but that seems rude given all you've been through.

It was the same the year after the Crash. So many families were full of doom and gloom that they practically shuffled into the church, singing "Joy to the World" like a dirge, myself among them—Henry and I lost our fair share to the stock market, you know.

Johanna, you would have been only a young girl at the time, so perhaps you don't remember. I do. Wrote it down in my Bible, right next to the Christmas story. We all watched as gaunt, mourning-clad Anders Sorenson got up to the pulpit, only months after losing his dear wife, and said, "If the only gift we receive this year is Jesus, it will be enough."

Well, he was right then, and he's right still.

That McHenry boy refused to print my letter in that worthless rag of his, so I'm sending part of it to you directly, along with this apricot-fig fruitcake (extra bourbon). There are some of us still behind you, the ones who know you and won't stand for gossip and deception.

You're one of us, Johanna Berglund. I've watched you grow up and feel I know you. You let us hear those boys' stories, and I don't know a soul who wasn't moved by them at one point or another. Maybe you didn't want to be back in town, one step farther away from Oxford, but I speak for many others when I say we're glad to have you, and we'll defend you to the last.

Apparently, people aren't allowed to apply to jury duty, though. I was turned away by all three government agencies I tried, and they had the nerve to imply that I was biased. Imagine. Me, biased.

Much love,
Cornelia Knutson

Letter from Mayor Carl Berglund to Ironside Lake
Read at the city council meeting and reprinted in the Ironside Broadside on January 2, 1945

To my fellow citizens:

Since protests have led to a nasty town hall meeting, in an effort to keep the peace, I would like to have a chance to speak to all of you without being hollered at.

In light of the recent allegations about my daughter, I have been asked to withdraw from this office. I refuse to do so, not because I have any higher priority than the well-being of my family, but because doing so would reflect doubt in Johanna's innocence, which I do not have.

If the petition going around town receives enough signatures, as I am told is likely, and the majority of the citizens of this town have no faith in my ability to lead, I will honor the due process of our democracy. But I will not bow to pressure and resign before that point.

My wife and I stand resolutely beside our daughter in the midst of these false accusations. She may have made mistakes—who among us hasn't?—but I will not here go

363

into a defense of her actions. That will be left for the court-room and our judicial system, should the case go to trial.

My platform has always been simple: Represent the people. That's why I supported the prisoners of war as a solution to the labor problem in our county. Last year, representatives from area farms petitioned my office nearly weekly to address the worker shortage, and after months of planning and strategizing, we decided this was the best possible short-term solution. The government funds coming into the city, combined with the recorded surge in productivity from the recent potato and beet harvest, show that this plan succeeded.

Besides the financial benefit, I ask you: Have we not grown richer as a community in other ways through the coming of these young men? I know it's difficult to remember in the chaos of the past few weeks, but let me remind you.

I have seen some of the most closed-minded and strong-willed individuals in our community come to give unselfishly to these prisoners, hoping that German and Japanese and Italian mothers might do the same for their sons overseas.

I have seen costumed citizens discuss race relations in America, in fragmented English, with the conductor of a prison-camp orchestra . . . and walk away with a burden for change.

I have seen a pew full of boys just like our own sing "A Mighty Fortress Is Our God" in its original German, along-side Immanuel Lutheran's choir in English, and it sounded like the praise of many tongues and languages we will hear together one day.

Most of all, I have seen my own daughter learn to stand up for what she believes in, advocating for justice and mercy, especially for our enemies, with a force of passion that I have not managed to equal in all my years of public office.

And just as I have never been prouder to be her father, I have never been prouder to serve as mayor of this fine city. Thank you for the honor you've given me to be in that position for the past twelve years.

Carl Berglund
Mayor of Ironside Lake

From Charles Donohue Jr. to Johanna

January 2, 1945

Dear Miss Berglund,

As you requested, here are the highlights from my office's investigation into the personal life and character of Captain Werner, though I'm not sure there's anything of use.

Date of Birth: March 19, 1912
Hometown: Frankfurt, Germany
City of Enlistment: Berlin, Germany
Date of Capture: May 13, 1943
Decorations: Iron Cross, Level 2

Your mention of Captain Werner's competition in the 1936 Olympics intrigued me. I called up a rowing friend from my university days, now a district lieutenant governor of the Amateur Athletic Union. He looked through the records, and no one named Stefan Werner ever participated in an event or was listed as an official German athlete in 1936. It seems he exaggerated his athletic prowess to impress his men, or perhaps you.

A bit of additional investigation, including a vague reference to "experience with film equipment" in the transcript from his processing interview directly after capture in Tunisia, revealed that Captain Werner was likely in attendance at the games as part of the film crew for a documentary, *Olympia*, directed by the renowned artist and personal friend of Hitler, Leni Riefenstahl. It won a good number of awards and acclaim before *Kristallnacht* soured the world to Nazi propaganda films. His name is listed in the credits for the cinematography.

Our Captain Werner has quite literally had a closeup view of the best propaganda creation in all of Germany. Frustratingly, he has applied that knowledge to carefully scripting and editing the current legal debacle in which we find ourselves embroiled, and for which we will likely win no awards at all. I will settle for an acquittal.

This, however, is the only moral lapse anyone on my staff can attribute to him, and it certainly doesn't have the defamatory power I was hoping for. In all military and prison camp documents, his records are spotless. Indeed, everyone with whom he interacted praised him as respectful, well-spoken, and even charming, with an excellent command of English. These are factors that make him the worst possible witness against you, as his manner is likely to play well to the jury.

If this information gives you an idea for where we might go or whom we might add to our list of witnesses to call into question Captain Werner's character, do let me know. I'm afraid there seems to be quite a dossier of those testifying against yours. You haven't made this easy for me, have you?

Best wishes for your new year; I hope it will be better than your last.

> Sincerely yours,
> Charles Donohue Jr.
> Clark and Donohue Legal

From Johanna to Olive

January 4, 1945

Dear Olive,

How strange to postmark a letter to England. I'm happy for you and your siblings, and sad for myself. Is this what you felt like when I left to come to Ironside Lake? It really is awful, being left behind. At the same time, I know how much you've missed your mother. She'll be overjoyed to see all of you again.

As for my life, for now it's just me and a large stack of books. On good days, I wander down to the kitchen and help Mother with dinner, but then inevitably something will remind me of the trouble I'm in—a heap of peeled potatoes, like in the title of my former newspaper column, for example—and I'll feel that stomach-clenching fear again, paralyzing me.

Even Dad hasn't been himself lately. He tells me, quite fiercely, that he doesn't think a thing of the people demanding his resignation. But after someone threw a brick through our window in the middle of the night, I found him in his bathrobe, hurriedly sweeping glass, as if I might not have heard.

"I'm sorry," I said over and over again. He put his arms around me and told me it wasn't my fault, but I know it is.

The waiting is wearing on us all.

They've set the date for the grand jury for February 27. The dead of winter.

The men of the camp are all back in Algona now until the town decides whether to bring them back next spring. To say it seems doubtful is like saying that the bobby-socks crowd has a slight affection for Frank Sinatra.

I've just learned that Captain Werner was a filmmaker

before he was a soldier. A propagandist, if my lawyer is to be believed. That would explain his knowledge of terminology that surprised me after the men visited the movies. I suppose it also means you were right all along not to trust him. You can feel free to say, "I told you so." Everyone else is.

All of this is a bit gloomy. Whenever you get this letter, feel free to reply with all the updates on friends you left behind, and how your dog Webster is doing (he's rather old now, isn't he?), and anything small and amusing so I can take my mind off my troubles.

Thank you for being a good friend. And say hello to Oxford for me, from a distance.

Your friend,
Johanna

Article in the Ironside Broadside *on January 15, 1944*

IRONSIDE LAKE NATIVE AWAITS
TREASON BY GRAND JURY

The entire nation has been captivated by the sensational news of an alleged home-front spy in our small town. Johanna Berglund's grand-jury hearing will take place on February 27 in Duluth. If the grand jury returns an indictment, the trial will proceed within a month.

Local officials have cooperated with the FBI and other government officials to gather information on the controversial case, including extensive interviews with army staff and civilian workers at Camp Ironside, currently closed for the winter season.

Miss Berglund's father, Carl Berglund, is facing a reversal of public opinion. Only weeks after being reelected as mayor, Berglund and the city council received a petition signed by over 60% of voters in last November's race. In the face of mounting pressure to resign, the city council has determined to meet early next month to discuss next steps, and promises to release a statement at that time. Should Berglund resign, a new election will be held within two months to fill the vacant position. There is currently no official recall process in the state of Minnesota to remove public officials accused of malfeasance, abuse of office, or other crimes, so citizens of Ironside Lake will have to wait to see how their government will respond to these serious accusations.

No press can be present at the grand jury; however, if the case goes to trial, be assured that the *Ironside Broadside* will report every detail to our reading public.

From Johanna to Charles Donohue, attorney-at-law

January 26, 1945

Dear Mr. Donohue,

Well, now you know all of it. Probably more than I do. If you can think of any additional documentation that would be helpful, let me know, and I'll beg, steal, or borrow it.

That was a joke, for the record. The stealing part, I mean. I suppose it's not wise to allude to illegal activity in a letter to a lawyer, is it?

While I'm writing to you, which provides a convenient shield from your probing expression that might weaken my resolve, I want to add that I will not say anything to distance myself from Peter Ito, although I realize why you think it would be helpful for my testimony.

Peter is my friend, the best one I've ever had, not a casual acquaintance who shared my interest in language. I realize there are some mildly incriminating passages in our letters that could raise suspicions about either of our loyalties or patriotism, but I know Peter isn't a spy, and the case against him is so flimsy that it would be foolish for anyone to bring it up as an argument against me and my character. However, given how the press has been prattling about my "Japanazi" love triangle, I'm prepared to admit it may come up, so I wanted you to be aware of how I will respond.

If this case goes to trial, I hope we can raise enough doubt in the minds of the jury that they realize it's all a smoke-and-mirrors circus act. Better, I'm praying that the lies will stop and this entire deception will fall apart in front of them.

The unanswered question that still bothers me is not knowing why Captain Werner would target me so directly. At our last meeting, you pointed out that I was the only American whose record of defending the POWs would make me open to suspicion. I became—or rather, made myself into—someone with motive, means, and opportunity to aid in a prisoner's escape. In short, the perfect target from an objective standpoint.

The logical part of me knows this, and yet the planted love letters and Captain Werner's appearance with me at the dance feel especially spiteful, more than a man grasping at any sensation that might create unrest in the country of his enemies. His malicious lies might well ruin my life, and I have no idea what prompted them.

I'll admit, one of the reasons I hope the case will not go

to trial is so I don't have to face him again. Watching him being sworn in to testify against me while I'm helpless to protest is a scene that haunts my dreams these days.

Regardless, I'm prepared to answer all of the charges. I will tell the truth, the whole truth, and nothing but the truth, no matter what it costs. So help me God.

Sincerely,
Johanna Berglund

EVIDENCE FOR THE PROSECUTION

FROM AMALIE WERNER TO STEFAN WERNER

Note: Found in the possession of Captain Werner upon his recapture after the escape. No indication of any censorship whatsoever. Prisoner claims that the defendant never censored his mail. If possible, subpoena original letter from the defendant to Heinz Werner, the prisoner's father, referred to in this letter.

July 25, 1944

Dear Stefan,

I'm scribbling this in a hurry—Father's told me not to write because he's angry with you, and these days Aunt Karin watches me like the old hawk she is.

He's done it. Father has joined the *Wehrmacht*, like he's been threatening for months now, ever since the factory was bombed and the assembly lines rendered useless. (Did he at least tell you that? I told him he ought to.)

It was the letter from the American woman, Miss Berglund, that pushed him over the edge. Did you know she wrote to Father? I managed to read the letter before Father threw it into the fire. It was a glowing report about how he ought to be proud of you and the work you're doing there.

I mean no offense to you, Stefan—but you know how that sounded to Father. To him, a letter of recommendation from the enemy is more terrible than a denunciation.

Worse, the letter was opened by the censors. Nothing was removed, but, Stefan, I think we are being watched. Three times, I've seen a black car parked just down the street, by the Attenbergers', and Father came home half drunk last Friday night, raging about some "visitor" who had come to the factory to question him. That's when he decided to enlist.

Can you imagine, Father, of all people, under suspicion of disloyalty to the Nazi party? Simply because an American woman wrote him a letter? They must be mad.

Aunt Karin is as nervous as my kitten during a shelling, always jumping at shadows. She's forbidden me to leave my room.

Isn't there anything that can be done? I've already pleaded with Father not to go. Besides his age, he's injured from the last war, and the man of the house. But no, he storms about quoting Goebbels, Hitler's Megaphone and your old employer back when you were making films, going on about "total war" and "final and complete devotion." He's left Aunt Karin with an allowance from the banks, but what if the value of the *Mark* plummets as it did at the end of the last war? And what if the police arrest us because they suspect us of corresponding with the Americans? What will we do?

Please, Stefan, when will they release you? Aunt Karin

and I are alone in the house, with no one to protect us. We hear the Americans may be coming, or the British, or even the savage Russians. Can't they let you come home under these circumstances if you solemnly swear not to take up arms?

I'm frightened, Stefan, and I have never felt so alone. Please write as soon as you can.

Love,
Amalie

Postscript

February 22, 1945

Dear Peter,

I seem to start every letter to you since your deployment reminding you that I miss you, so I'll skip all that and say I'm still worried about the upcoming grand jury . . . but I don't feel quite as alone as I used to. I know you'd want me to focus on that and not on the hate mail or headlines.

To begin with, Mother and Dad support me unconditionally. Sometimes I forget to be grateful for that. Even after today's announcement that he would resign as mayor (thanks in large part to pressure from the spineless city council), Dad resolutely spent most of last night popping corn over the stove and challenging me to a jigsaw puzzle, while Mother insisted she wouldn't want to represent the people of Ironside Lake if they would believe something so terrible about her daughter.

Last Sunday, I rallied enough courage to go to church. I'll confess, it was more to make a public statement than to receive spiritual encouragement. The looks on people's faces when I entered, flanked by my parents, and sat in our usual pew almost made me turn and flee, but I sat down and kept my gaze straight ahead.

Halfway through the opening hymn, I heard an unusual sound. Cornelia Knutson might as well have been wearing Norwegian clogs, the way she clumped down the aisle with the shiny new walking stick she doesn't really need. She stopped right in front of our pew. "Is there room for me?" she whispered—or she probably meant to, it came out much louder.

"There is always room," Mother replied, tugging me deeper into the pew, and Cornelia settled in beside me, smelling like rose water and mothballs.

The collection of a dozen half-decent singers we assemble into a choir almost missed a beat of "Crown Him with Many Crowns" at the disturbance, including Annika in the second row. I could feel her staring, and for the first time in months, I stared back . . . and caught the old, familiar look in her eyes. If we had been little girls again, she'd be mouthing, "I'm sorry," across the space between us, and after considering it for a while, I'd accept.

That was always how it used to be. We'd quarrel over something or other, and Annika typically apologized first. Sometimes last too, if I felt I wasn't really to blame.

This time, we apologized to each other at the same time, and that felt better somehow, even though we didn't actually speak the words.

After the choir filed out of their neat rows, instead of taking her traditional place in the first pew, to her father's direct right, Annika smoothed her skirt to sit next to Cornelia. They stayed there for Pastor Sorenson's entire sermon—on the perils of gossip, delivered without a single knowing look in my direction—and when we stood for the closing hymn, I realized how foolish I've been, complaining about being alone.

I thought of the stack of other families' dishes beside our sink the first few weeks after I came home from the county jail. I hadn't had much appetite, but I'd noticed furtive knocks on the door as visitors who "couldn't stay" nevertheless came bearing hot dishes and baked corn and even a tomato and olive aspic ring.

I remembered how Pastor Sorenson still came over to play dominoes with Dad, and how, the Monday evening I sat at the top of the stairs just to listen to their familiar voices below, he said, "Hold on, Carl. It's winter now, but Thawing Day is coming."

And I thought back on all those letters, from you, from my parents, from friends and enemies alike. Even Erik's last letter.

That's when I thought maybe I was starting to hear something in the silence.

It wasn't deus ex machina, god from the machine, scripted and rigged and ready to enter on my cue. It was deus ex potluck, deus ex encouraging smile, deus ex newspaper column, and especially deus ex letter. God was in all the ways I've seen others care and challenge and stand by me this past year.

But even when all of that was gone, and I was confined to my room while death threats came in the mail . . . it was just God himself. He's there, Peter, and I think you were right: He's been listening in the silence all along.

A thousand promises, all of them true. I wonder if you're still adding to your collection, wherever you are. You can add psalms 42 and 43 to them, if you haven't already.

Tomorrow, the grand jury hearing takes place in Duluth behind locked doors. Donohue and I won't be there as the prosecution holds up sensational documents and swears in witnesses who will lie about me. Even Captain Stefan Werner will be there, under heavy guard. There's nothing I can do or say. I can't even watch.

But I've finally realized I'm not alone, and that's what matters most.

Jo

Telegram from Charles Donohue Jr. to Johanna on February 27, 1945

```
GRAND JURY DID NOT RETURN INDICTMENT. EARLY
REPORTS SAY ONE OF THE POWS CHANGED HIS TESTIMONY.
CASE WILL NOT GO TO TRIAL.
```

Telegram from Johanna to Charles Donohue Jr. on February 27, 1945

```
SHOCKED. NEVER DREAMT WERNER WOULD ADMIT TO LYING.
IS THIS DECISION FINAL?
```

Telegram from Charles Donohue Jr. to Johanna on February 27, 1945

```
IT WASN'T WERNER.
SPOKEN TO PROSECUTION. THEY DO NOT PLAN TO APPEAL.
NO CASE AGAINST YOU ANYMORE.
WE'VE WON.
```

A WRITTEN STATEMENT BY DIETER BORMANN

PROVIDED WILLINGLY BY THE WITNESS, WITHOUT ANY
COMPULSION AND FULLY AWARE OF HIS RIGHTS UNDER THE
PROTECTION OF THE UNITED STATES OF AMERICA
TRANSLATED FROM GERMAN

February 26, 1944

I, Dieter Bormann, being duly sworn, state as follows:

That I make this statement of my own free will and accord, having been informed of my rights under the Geneva Convention and the laws of the United States of America.

I am writing this because of several reasons, but one is what happened the night after your invasion of France. Some of your boys drove around the camp, taunting us, and fire rushed up into my bones. I lunged forward, wanting to tear through the fence and defend the honor of my country.

She stopped me, Johanna Berglund, grabbing my legs like I did as a boy when wrestling pigs in the pen to haul to slaughter. I kicked like those sows did, but because of her, I stumbled and fell, and then others restrained me.

Afterward, Uncle Otto (that is what we call von Neindorff) told me he thought Miss Berglund had saved my life. The guards, he said, would have shot me if I had bolted for the fence. It has happened before, at other camps.

I always wondered why she did it. She barely knew me. Captain Werner said it was because she wanted to suppress my patriotism and unman me, but it never fully made sense.

Uncle Otto also warned me never to do anything so foolish again. He told me not to throw my life away for a foolish cause, and I pretended to agree.

But when Captain Werner spoke to me of escape, I thought of what it would be to return to Germany a hero. If we could arrive before the new year, I would see my love and she would know I would do anything to be at her side.

He promised we would succeed, and I believed him. For weeks, we planned in secret, after others had gone to sleep. Captain Werner's plans were so detailed you felt they could never fail. He is the sort of leader you might follow anywhere, into any difficulty.

Before leaving, we memorized a careful story about how Johanna Berglund helped us escape. He made me repeat it a dozen times, not trusting, I think, that I would get the details right. But it was just that: a story.

Johanna Berglund did not help us escape. Everything I said about this was untrue. We found the maps inside one of the army trucks, we stole the clothing from a storage room, and we made the plans alone. Miss Berglund had nothing to do with the fire this summer. Captain Werner set it in order to see if the camp might be evacuated, making for an easy escape later on. He also had me hide rotten potatoes in Major Davies's office so he could search the documents there and pass on information to Germany. I was the one who wrote the love letters we left in the woodshed.

Miss Berglund was aware of none of these plans.

The only thing that was true was that she saw Captain Werner at the ball and did not turn him in, just as he said she wouldn't. He was very sure of that, and when I asked him why, he said, "Because she has forgotten I am the enemy."

I didn't understand why we spent so much time planting evidence against Miss Berglund when we would be safe in Germany. When I asked him, Captain Werner talked about the power of propaganda and creating suspicions to turn the Americans against each other, and I believed that too.

I remember the night we were recaptured. We were exhausted from traveling at night, sleeping in small snatches in burrows in the woods like wild things, eating what food we had stored from our rations. We moved so slowly. Captain Werner said it was out of caution, but then on the seventh night, he said we should rest and cook a fish he'd caught. He lit our first fire. I wondered if it was wise, but I sat close to the flames and soaked up the heat greedily as I tore meat from the fish bones, burning my tongue.

Soon I heard rustling in the forest, but Captain Werner said it was only rabbits burrowing for the winter.

If rabbits had guns and uniforms and shouted loudly in English, he might have been right.

I stood, ready to run, but froze when I saw Captain Werner. He was so calm, standing and slowly raising his hands in the air. What came of all his speeches about not going quietly, of taking a few enemy lives with him and dying with honor for Germany? Watching him walk toward the American Gestapo like a sheep to shearing, all the fight left me as well. We surrendered quietly.

Maybe that was always the plan. Why else force me to memorize that false story? I repeated it to all the interrogators they brought to us, but now I think Captain Werner didn't ever mean for us to get to Germany. He only meant to use me to convict Miss Berglund of treason.

Perhaps he even lit the fire that night so we would get caught.

Yesterday, on the train to Duluth, when the guards were asleep, Captain Werner showed me a note from Miss Berglund that he was supposed to deliver to me on the day we escaped. He has probably destroyed it by now, but I remember exactly what it said. I have been thinking about it ever since.

Captain Werner meant for it to make me angry, saying it was one more proof that Miss Berglund meddled in my life, that she was taunting me. He was worried that I would grow nervous during the trial and change my statement, so he said Miss Berglund was encouraging me to forget Rose, my true love, and turn my back on my country.

He was lying about that too.

I do not feel that I am betraying my country by telling all of this. If I can't fight for Germany, I want to be able to return to her and say that I have acted honorably, to tell those I love that I have nothing to be ashamed of.

That is the truth, and it is all I have to say.

From Johanna to Dieter, recalled from memory by Dieter Bormann

November 18, 1944

Private Bormann,

I have heard from Captain Werner that you are ill and being treated in the infirmary. I can't help but wonder if it isn't physical sickness but sickness of the heart.

Hear me out. I know you resent me for reading your letters to Rose in Germany, so I hesitate to write this, but I wanted to say that I understand, in part, what you're going through. It's easy to regret the words you didn't have time to say or actions you thought could wait until later, especially when it comes to someone you love and you run out of time.

However, I can also speak from experience when saying, Don't let bitterness and resentment ruin your life. It is time for you to live the life in front of you, instead of wondering what might have been.

Many of us, myself and Otto von Neindorff included, would be glad of the chance to hear you perform at the costume ball tonight if you change your mind.

Johanna Berglund
Translator, Camp Ironside

Article in the **Ironside Broadside** *on March 1, 1945*

TREASON CASE DISMISSED

Eager news media from across the country were disappointed with today's announcement that the long-awaited treason trial for Johanna Berglund has been dismissed on a technicality.

The key piece of information was the changed testimony by Dieter Bormann, one of the prisoners of war, in which he confessed to fabricating charges against Miss Berglund. According to the US Constitution, the testimony of two witnesses is required to prove overt acts of treason. Since only one testimony remained, and with its authenticity called into question, the grand jury refused to allow the case to proceed to trial.

The district attorney stated, "The public can be confident that the grand jury, made up of citizens like themselves, gave a most diligent investigation of the evidence from the prosecution, which they found insufficient to show that any crime was committed, much less that the prosecution displayed the high burden of proof needed to demonstrate an act of treason."

Some have already begun protesting the court's move, stating that Miss Berglund's collusion with the prisoners might have motivated a change in testimony.

The two escaped prisoners cannot have further charges brought against them under the Geneva Convention, but Captain Stefan Werner has been transferred to the high-security camp in Oklahoma for high-ranking Nazi officers and radicals. Dieter Bormann remains in Iowa with the other POWs who worked in Ironside Lake. No announcement has been made about whether they will return to Camp Ironside next month.

From Cornelia Knutson to Johanna

March 1, 1945

Dear Johanna,

I can't remember any news, outside of the ratification of the Nineteenth Amendment securing us ladies the vote, that has excited me more than hearing about your case. How are you feeling?

While I'm sure there are other pressing matters on your mind after your triumphant acquittal ("refusal to return an indictment" is much less dramatic, so I'll stick with this), I'm sure eventually you'll get around to thinking about what to do in regard to your continued education. You might wonder if, with all the fuss and the false accusations and your prison time, your anonymous scholarship donor has decided to revoke the funds.

I'm happy to report that she has not.

You see, I am the anonymous scholarship donor.

I hope you spewed tea all over your desk in surprise, because it pained me to keep that secret for so long. No one here thinks of me as a finance maven, but before I came to Ironside Lake, I worked for a prominent brokerage across the Brooklyn Bridge from the small apartment where Henry and I started our married life. Just an entry-level position, but I tell you, I was prepared to become the most influential woman on Wall Street. But when Henry's mother became ill and could no longer live alone, we came here to care for her together. Then, as the years went by and our children were born, I just . . . stayed. That was the better dream I told you about. I traded the Financial District for family, and when I said I have no regrets, I mean it.

Now I've got a tidy sum to my name at First National and in two discreet hiding places around the house, since the fool banks could barely weather the '30s. After the Crash, I decided it would be more worthwhile to invest in young lives than in stock. Greater return on investment, you know.

Oh, what fun the reading of my will is going to be! I almost wish I could be there, in the style of Tom Sawyer. Do you think you could help me manage it? We should speak further about this.

If you will allow me the honor, I would be delighted to continue to fund your education—in full, wherever you should choose to take it. Ever since I saw your ambition as a young girl, I thought, "I must watch this one." And I have, and you have proven far more entertaining than I'd ever dreamed. Who needs one of those newfangled home television sets when they have a neighbor such as yourself?

But first, I should apologize. You must have thought it quite a coincidence, my changing the requirements for the scholarship at the very time you were offered the translator position. I'm afraid that was deliberate. Your mother told me you had turned down the initial job offer, and I couldn't think of a single person better qualified.

And wasn't I right? We've all had our old ways of thinking challenged, myself included. You were just what Ironside Lake needed, Johanna, treason charges and all.

I'm sure you've got a good deal of resting to do, along with hiding from Brady and his jackals at the *Broadside* seeking out an interview, but when you have a moment, do join me for a luncheon. I'm most curious to hear your future plans.

I'm not trying to bias you in any way, but it seems you might never escape suspicion from some of our worst elements if you remain here. So I want you to remember, the good Lord never told us to stay in one place—he was always telling the saints in the Old Testament just the opposite, to pick up and move. The difference between Abraham and Jonah is one was running toward something; the other was just running.

I look forward to hearing from you, my dear girl. Hearty congratulations once again.

Cornelia Knutson

From Johanna to Cornelia Knutson

March 4, 1945

Dear Mrs. Knutson,

Given your absolute fleecing of us poor financial neophytes at Monopoly, I shouldn't have been surprised to read your last letter, but I admit that I hadn't the slightest idea you were my mysterious donor. I can't express how much I appreciate your support—both these past few months and during my studies at the university.

I still can hardly believe the trial is off. My lawyer, Charles Donohue Jr., said it's the most baffling case he's seen in all his years of practicing, which I have tentatively decided to take as a compliment.

All this time I was so focused on Captain Werner—his motivation, the flaws in his story, what others might have made of our conversations—that I almost forgot Dieter was involved. Thank God he didn't forget about me.

It's liberating, knowing the truth has come out at last, whether anyone chooses to believe it or not. I'm innocent in the eyes of the law, and in the eyes of those I care most about. That should be enough.

And yet, a selfish, needy part of me would like to be able to go to the post office without fearing a lynch mob—an activity that, I must say, I haven't attempted since the news came out.

As for my next plans . . . I honestly don't know yet.

Peter once suggested I consider serving as an aid worker after the war. At the time, I dismissed the idea, but the more I thought about it, the more I realized: I'm fluent in German, Italian, French, and . . . well, not quite Japanese, but I hope to get to that point. And there is a great need. Does that matter more than my comfort, do you think? Lately, I've been asking myself that, and especially if Peter . . . if he never comes back, I want to do something that would make him proud.

That would mean moving away from Ironside Lake again. After all that's happened, I'd be grateful to leave the whispers and mistrust that follow me around, but I find that I'm not as bitter as I once was. I've seen the best and the worst of this little town, and I've realized it's made up of people with their own prejudices and priorities and hopes and fears—just like me. We're all just fallible people trying desperately to make sense of an incomprehensibly complex world. I don't want to forget that.

Still, nothing is as clear as I would like it to be. My (many) lists of pros and cons, which I began making shortly after the news of the case's dismissal, haven't yet led me to a plan of action.

Might I come over for tea tomorrow? I'll bring Mother's gingerbread. I could use some advice if you're willing to give it.

Johanna

Notice in the Ironside Broadside *on March 5, 1945*

A MESSAGE TO OUR READERS

This is to inform our valued reading public that we will no longer be printing anonymous editorials in the *Broadside*. The reputation of a paper is only as good as the reputation of the writers, and as editor, I admit full blame in allowing such infractions of journalistic standards to slip by in the past. I humbly request your forgiveness.

We hope this change will bring back some of our subscribers and the local advertisers who have withdrawn their support in the past several weeks. Remember, free and unbiased journalism can't survive without your dollars!

Yours in the freedom of the press,
Brady McHenry
Owner and Editor in Chief,
Ironside Broadside

From Annika to Johanna

March 5, 1945

Dear Johanna,

I stopped by this afternoon, but your mother told me
you were at Mrs. Knutson's, so I'm leaving this for you.
At first, I didn't want to tell you at all, since things have
been more or less resolved between us, but Chris told me I
should. He's a thousand times braver than I am, and when
I'm with him, I seem to borrow some of his courage.

It was because of you that I met him, you know. That
verse you put in your letter to the Lutheran Daughters of
the Reformation when you first arrived home—"I was a
stranger, and ye took me in; I was in prison, and ye came
unto me"—nagged at me for weeks. I couldn't bring
myself to do anything kind for the Germans, knowing
they fought the same battles where Erik was killed, but
after reading Christopher's column in the newspaper I
thought maybe I could at least do something for our own
men. It shook me out of my grief for a moment, just long
enough to meet Chris. So I want to thank you for that.

Here is the last secret of all: I never told you that Erik
got your final letter. They found it in his pocket when he
died, along with part of a reply. Erik always was like that,
considering and redrafting every word, as if even a simple
greeting was as weighty as a sermon.

For a long time, I didn't want you to see it, because I
wanted you to feel guilty, forever unforgiven. That's the
ugly truth.

Daddy's favorite passage to quote in sermons, as
I'm sure you've noticed, is "Be ye kind one to another,
tenderhearted, forgiving one another, even as God for
Christ's sake hath forgiven you." "It's a small town," he

always said when I asked him why he left a bookmark
in that text. "We can easily hurt others, and once we do,
there's no escaping each other. Forgiveness is all that keeps
us together, and withholding it keeps us apart." At the
time, I thought that was very nice and spiritual-sounding
and harmless.

Sometime this winter, I realized he was talking to me.
Or maybe to both of us.

So here are the letters. I'm sorry I kept them from you
for so long.

Annika

P.S. I've been spreading the word about how the
Broadside unjustly turned public opinion against you
with their biased news coverage. It's the least I could
do, and you'd be surprised at how many agreed it was
shameful. You have more supporters in Ironside Lake
than you might think.

From Johanna to Erik

November 16, 1942

Dear Erik,

I got your address from Mother. I hope you don't mind
my writing. I'm fully aware of how awkward this might be
for you, though I don't mean for it to be.

I should have known you'd end up an army chaplain.
Do you remember the games we used to play in the woods?
You'd always let me be Robin Hood and Perseus and
Amelia Earhart while you were Friar Tuck, the Minotaur,
and—well, you did accept Charles Lindbergh, so I guess
sometimes you got the starring role. Annika was too shy,

always cast as the damsel in distress so she didn't have to say much, and I thought of the best lines a few beats too late, but you always had the right words at the right time, which is why you were always assigned the prebattle motivational speeches. I hope you still use that skill, although perhaps with a little more Scripture and a little less *Ivanhoe*.

But I've written too much again without coming to my real point. I'm sorry for letting you go with the way things were between us. In the months before you left, I told myself you were hurrying to finish up your correspondence-course seminary work for ordination and I had to prepare for university and there just wasn't time. When really, it was easier to ignore you and try to forget how terrible I'd been to you.

I can't say I regret turning down your proposal, but I am very sorry for how I did it and for not giving you a proper good-bye.

I don't know what else to say. But I have been praying for you, though I'm still not sure of the theology of how that affects a sovereign God. That's always been your area to sort out.

Someday, when you come back, maybe you can explain how it works. I'd be happy to listen.

Your friend,
Johanna

A draft of a letter from Erik to Johanna, never sent

January 12, 1943

Dear Jo,

It was good to hear from you. I really mean that.

I find my work rewarding, though the sermons I deliver

are shorter than my father's and sometimes cut off by a burst of distant gunfire. Still, it's discouraging when most of the solemn faces praying before a campaign come back afterward to drink and swear and carouse like all the others. It makes a fellow wonder how many of the fervent prayers he witnesses are nothing more than foxhole insurance policies, a bargain with God to live, but with no serious interest in faith. I try to remember that some of them must be sincere, but it's easy to fall into cynicism.

Besides that, I'm well enough, traveling to places I never thought I'd see outside of the pages of *National Geographic*. Funny, isn't it? You were always the one who wanted to see the world and who knew all the exotic languages on top of it. All I ever wanted to do was stay home, and yet here I am. Sometimes I feel guilty to be living your dream.

But you'll get there someday, I'm sure of it. I'll admit that I'd thought Oxford was just a little girl's fancy, something you'd give up once you grew older. But it was silly to think that way. Ironside Lake was blessed to have you, and I was blessed to know you, but you weren't ever meant to stay there. I always knew that, deep down, even playacting those grand adventures with you as kids.

So yes, I'll forgive you . . . if you'll forgive me.

But when I come home, save me at least one dance, will you? For old times' sake.

From Johanna to Annika

March 7, 1945

Dear Annika,

I'll come over again when you're home, but I wanted to say thank you for delivering Erik's letter. Maybe you were just keeping them aside until just the right moment. Or at least, it worked out that way.

And for goodness' sake, don't waste your time on the *Broadside*. Brady McHenry will go bankrupt in his own good time without me around to cause scandals.

Not that I'm leaving right now . . . but I am thinking about it. Another reason we need to talk.

Oh, and Dad's got Thawing Day on the calendar for the first week of April. If the weather holds, would you like to join Mother and me in the washing and drying this year? We could always use the extra help.

Your friend,
Jo

From Peter to Johanna
Delivered via the Red Cross on March 12, 1945

Following the inspection, all hands are directed to write a letter to be placed on file for if inquiries are made through the Red Cross concerning you. If such inquiries are made, this letter will be cabled through the Red Cross that you were of (. . .) health, etc., on the date listed. Please address to anyone who might make an inquiry and include:

Prison No.
Name and Rank
Date
Past and Present Health
Impression of Daily Life and Work (if desired)
Signature
Limit: 400 words
Insert everything of importance placed in your previous letters, as they may not have been delivered.

Prison Center 23
Second Lieutenant Peter Ito
March 1, 1945

Dear Jo,

I am alive and in tolerable health, after narrowly living
through a bout of malaria with the help of my two hardier
buddies, Mugs Renfroe and Joe Batterson. They paid back
the debt they owed me, saving my life like I saved theirs.
That's how I got captured—trying to pull them out of a
cave-in after a shelling near Leyte, until a rock thumped
into my skull (insert jokes about my hard head here. Ha.).
When I woke, I was in Japanese custody with a pounding
headache.

I've been assigned to labor at a railway depot, more
demanding than desk work. I use my language skills to
negotiate with our captors, and I'm probably the one
most content with our diet, mostly *okayu*, a rice gruel.
Whenever I've got a free moment, I'm participating in the
endlessly fun activities of sleeping or doing laundry.

I know I promised not to get wounded, captured, or
killed. One out of three is a solid 33%, nearly halfway to
failure on my own grading scale. Points for trying?

Please write if you can. They may let us receive mail
now that they're under the Red Cross's magnifying
glass. I wrote to you and my family dozens of times,
but they burned the letters in front of me. One of many
ways they've shown they don't much care for a Japanese
American soldier fighting for the Allies.

Almost to my limit, and I can't start over because we
only get one letterform each, but I still have so much
left to say. At the top of the list, even though I swore I
wouldn't bring it up again: I still meant everything I said

that day in Minneapolis, Jo. I love you. I always have and probably always will, even if I've tried my best to let go.

Not an idealized version of who I think you are, not who I hope you'll be once you change your dreams for my sake. I love you as you are, honest and brave and Grand Canyon beautiful . . . and very far away right now.

I don't know when I'll get out, probably not until the war's end, like your Germans at Camp Ironside. And even now, what worries me most is wondering whether you'll be glad to see me. I hope and pray so.

Peter

From Johanna to Peter

March 12, 1945

Dear Peter,

I won't bore you with the tedious details of how I reacted when I got your letter. Here is the summary so you can picture it: a shocked stare at the envelope, then tears, followed by running down to Mother and dancing around the living room with her like I was a little girl, racing out to the barn to tell Dad, practically shouting the news in the street, etc. It was quite a scene.

I want to ask you a thousand questions about your living quarters and the number of prisoners captured with you, to tell you to stay hydrated and to contact the Red Cross directly with a list of concerns, but who can tell what you'll be allowed to write in your replies? It makes me want to smuggle myself onto the next east-bound steamer and wander around Japan with your name and photograph, demanding that someone take me to you.

That is probably a terrible idea. Still, I feel like I have to do something, anything, other than just write another letter.

But you're alive. Thank God for that. And I have thanked him. Repeatedly. He's probably tired of hearing the same sentiments from me on a loop, like one of those catchy cereal jingles.

Really, this letter is a disgrace already. I should have asked Annika (who is still starry-eyed over PFC Christopher Wright, now stationed in Iowa) for some appropriately impractical lines to write to you after you've nearly been brought back from the dead.

So much has happened here since the last letter you've received from me, but all of that can wait. Given my reading habits, I'm usually a proponent of long stories, but there are more important things for me to say first. Or at least one.

Of course I love you. If you'd stayed around long enough to give me time to think it all over after I rebuffed you, you'd have known that. And even if you didn't pick up on it, I'd have told you directly if you hadn't been captured on your very first mission.

Yes, I'm joking. I'm fully aware that your uncertainty is justified, and that it took a string of separations and disasters to make me realize what I should have known from the start. I changed my mind about you so long ago that it feels like another person gently cut you off by the Stone Arch Bridge when you first tried to tell me I'd become more than just a friend. Who was she, other than a jumble of fears and failures? What was she thinking?

I can't say, but I'm not that woman anymore. And if you really do want me, flaws and all—here I am. I've done a lot of running over the past few years, but given the chance, I will run toward you, wherever in the world we choose to go next. And that, I think, is the right dream to follow.

Come home soon, Peter. Until then, I'll be waiting.

Love always,
Jo

Author's Note

Though Ironside Lake and many of the pen pals in this book are fictional, *Things We Didn't Say* is based heavily on the real experiences of POW camps in the Midwest during World War II. The public outcry when a camp was announced, strict guidelines against Americans fraternizing with enemy Germans, and occasional escape attempts all have counterparts in this little-known aspect of home-front history. Occasionally, though, I had to substitute a "this *could* have happened" detail, such as having Jo censor letters at the camp itself rather than through the official censor station in Chicago, and later New York, or making overseas letters arrive without many delays.

For the timeline of the story, I also chose to move up the date of the 1944 summer graduation for the Military Intelligence Service Language School by a few weeks. However, the heroism and tireless hard work of the men there (and anecdotes like sneaking out to the privy after lights-out in order to study) are all true to history. Historic Fort Snelling in St. Paul, Minnesota, has great information about these brave men if you'd like to learn more.

Jo and Peter and most of their friends live only in my imagination, but a few of the actual historical people who make an appearance include John Aiso, the head instructor of the Japanese language program; Dr. Howard Hong, YMCA representative for the War Prisoners Aid; Staff Sergeant Dye Ogato, Japanese American war hero; and Lt. Col. Arthur Lobdell, commander at Camp Algona.

Many of the locations mentioned in the book are real as well, including Camp Savage (located in a Minnesota city named after Marion Willis Savage, the owner of famous racehorse Dan Patch).

If you're intrigued by POW camps in the Midwest, I'd highly recommend a visit to the Camp Algona POW Museum in Algona, Iowa. It's full of fascinating information and displays, and I teared up when I paged through binders of real letters written by POWs to their families in Germany, much like the ones in this story. Jerry Yocum, vice president of the museum committee, was instrumental to me in my research, giving me a tour of the artifacts, explaining typical American attitudes toward the POWs, and allowing me access to hundreds of maps, letters, newspaper articles, and other documents from every POW camp in Minnesota, for which I am very grateful.

I'd also like to thank Masako Kedrowski for lending her language skills to give feedback on my Japanese references, as well as Kirsten van Leeuwen for checking the many German words and phrases in this novel. Your help was invaluable, though of course, in language or historical accuracy, any errors are my own.

To my Bethany House publishing family: It's been an exciting ride. I have so much to thank all of you for, but especially Dave, for seeing something good in this story; Rochelle, for shaping and improving it; and Elizabeth, for seeking and destroying the many errors that once littered these pages. Jenny, the cover is beautiful beyond what I could have dreamed. And of course, my marketing pals—Steve, Paul, Noelle, Brooke, Rachael, Chris, and Serena—you may tease me relentlessly, but I've loved having you surrounding me and championing this book.

As someone who works in publishing, I know I can't possibly list everyone in rights, contracts, typesetting, sales, and retail who contributed to getting this book into the world. Just know that they are all amazing, and I will be sending them cookies.

Now, to friends. My real-life pen pals deserve credit here, especially Mark and Amy, for their delightful correspondence. For the members of my writing, plotting, and brainstorming crew—Ruthie, Kelly, and Stephanie—thanks so much for all your support and feedback. My fellow Bethany House authors also fall into this category—I've been absolutely floored at how excited for this newbie writer and eager to help all of you have been. Thanks especially to Bev, who knew about this novel before almost anyone else. Your encouragement means the world to me!

And finally, to my biggest fans: my family. This book is dedicated to my mom and dad, first because I might never have another heroine with two well-adjusted parents, so I'd better take the opportunity, but also, and more important, because your love and support have gotten me here. Erika, you've been cheering me on since the start (including my awful elementary school stories), and I love you so much. Jake, thanks for letting me quote you in Jo's voice, and for always being on and by my side.

And for you, reader—thank you for picking up this book, imagining characters who are barely ever described (if you know what Peter looks like, let me know—I just know I love him!), and going on this journey with me and my characters. Feel free to drop me a line via social media or my website . . . by now, you can probably guess that I love mail!

Reading Group Guide

What were some of the major differences between this epistolary novel and a story told in normal narrative style? What did you like and dislike about the format?

The prologue reveals that Jo is on trial for treason, and then it flashes back to the events of the year before. How did you feel about having a hint of where the plot was headed as the story progressed?

Citizens of actual towns located near POW camps had similar reactions to the use of POW labor on farms and factories as the ones recorded in the book. What concerns, if any, do you think you would have had if you had been in their place?

Jo repeatedly characterizes herself as "a disaster when it comes to relating to people." Do you think her self-perception is accurate? Why or why not?

Which of the POW Potato Brigade newspaper columns written by the POWs or the camp staff was most interesting to you, and why?

Pastor Sorenson writes, "Sometimes showing grace breaks us before it heals us. Forgiveness can feel like a betrayal of justice. We want others to *deserve* grace, or at least ask for it." Has there been a time when you've had a similar feeling when faced with a choice to forgive?

How did you feel about Stefan Werner throughout the book? Did you find anything about him sympathetic?

Peter and the Ito family, like many Japanese Americans, faced hard choices and prejudice during WWII. Do you agree with Peter's decision to first teach at a military intelligence school and then join the army? What would be the difficulties of such a decision?

Jo's scholarship donor advises her to "choose the better dream. Not the bigger dream. Just the better one—some of the most worthwhile pursuits can seem quite small to the undiscerning eye." How does that apply to the choices Jo makes? Have you chosen any "better dreams" in your own life?

As the events leading to the treason trial begin to be revealed, who were you most frustrated with?

How do you think Jo's history with Erik Sorenson affected her in the present? Do you feel that their story was resolved by the end of the book?

What qualities did you appreciate in Peter and Jo's relationship? Since you only see them interact through letters, how would you describe the way they helped each other in difficult times?

What were the biggest surprises you had as you reached the end of the book, including the postscript?

At the beginning of the story, Jo states, "I've found that every letter has two messages: the one written on the lines and the one written between them." What were some of the subtexts or hidden tensions that you noticed in the story?

Amy Lynn Green is a publicist by day and a writer on nights and weekends. She was the 2014 winner of the *Family Fiction* short story contest, and dozens of her nonfiction articles have been featured in faith-based publications over the past ten years. This is her first novel. She and her husband enjoy reading, playing board games with friends, and cooking tasty food at their home in Minneapolis, Minnesota. Like her fictional characters, Amy loves writing letters, so feel free to send her virtual mail through her website (www.amygreenbooks.com) or on social media.

Sign Up for Amy's Newsletter

Keep up to date with Amy's latest news on book releases and events by signing up for her email list at amygreenbooks.com.

You May Also Like . . .

When deaf teen Loyal Raines stumbles upon a dead body in the nearby river, his absentee father, Creed, is shocked the boy runs to him first. Pulled into the investigation, Creed discovers that it is the boy's courage, not his inability to hear, that sets him apart, and he will have to do more than solve a murder if he wants to win his family's hearts again.

The Right Kind of Fool by Sarah Loudin Thomas
sarahloudinthomas.com

More from Bethany House

Reeling from the loss of her parents, Lucy Claremont discovers an artifact under the floorboards of their London flat, leading her to an old seaside estate. Aided by her childhood friend Dashel, a renowned forensic astronomer, they start to unravel a history of heartbreak, sacrifice, and love begun 200 years prior—one that may offer the healing each seeks.

Set the Stars Alight by Amanda Dykes
amandadykes.com

Determined to uphold her father's legacy, newly graduated Nora Shipley joins an entomology research expedition to India to prove herself in the field. In this spellbinding new land, Nora is faced with impossible choices—between saving a young Indian girl and saving her career, and between what she's always thought she wanted and the man she's come to love.

A Mosaic of Wings by Kimberly Duffy
kimberlyduffy.com

In 1946, Millie Middleton left home to keep her heritage hidden, carrying the dream of owning a dress store. Decades later, when Harper Dupree's future in fashion falls apart, she visits her mentor Millie. When the revelation of a family secret leads them to Charleston and a rare opportunity, can they overcome doubts and failures for a chance at their dreams?

The Dress Shop on King Street by Ashley Clark
HEIRLOOM SECRETS
ashleyclarkbooks.com

BETHANYHOUSE

More Riveting Historical Fiction

Secretary to the first lady of the United States, Caroline Delacroix is at the pinnacle of high society—but is hiding a terrible secret. Immediately suspicious of Caroline, but also attracted to her, secret service agent Nathaniel Trask must battle his growing love for her as the threat to the president rises and they face adventure, heartbreak, and danger.

A Gilded Lady by Elizabeth Camden
HOPE AND GLORY #2
elizabethcamden.com

As Chicago's Great Fire destroys their bookshop, Meg and Sylvie Townsend make a harrowing escape from the flames with the help of reporter Nate Pierce. But the trouble doesn't end there—their father is committed to an asylum after being accused of murder, and they must prove his innocence before the asylum truly drives him mad.

Veiled in Smoke by Jocelyn Green
THE WINDY CITY SAGA #1
jocelyngreen.com